IMPOSTER

EILEEN ENWRIGHT HODGETTS

ISBN: **978-0-692-12708-7**

Eileen Enwright Hodgetts

CHAPTER ONE

May 1952
Brighton, England
Anthea Clark

Anthea Clark did not approve. In the absence of the venerable Edwin Champion, recovering from a bout of pneumonia, the law office was in the unreliable hands of Toby Whitby, and in Anthea's opinion, Mr. Whitby was too young, too flighty, and too impetuous for such responsibility.

She took the precaution of opening the windows in Mr. Champion's office, hoping that the cold air blowing in from the English Channel would discourage Toby from sitting at Mr. Champion's desk. The thought of him scattering papers willy-nilly, leaving law books unshelved, and actually putting his feet up on the desk was more than she could tolerate; especially on this brisk spring morning when she had already received a dreadful shock along with her morning tea.

She returned to her contemplation of the police notice that had arrived in the morning mail. The victim's facial features had been blurred by immersion in the ocean, but she had recognized the face immediately. Now she awaited Toby Whitby's arrival so that she could ask him to relieve her of her duties long enough to go down to Brighton Mortuary and tell them what she knew. She had telephoned the officer in charge of the investigation a half hour ago to let him know that she was coming, and now she would be late.

The door of the outer office opened, and Toby blew in along with a gust of sea air. His brown curly hair, always in need of barbering, stood out like a halo around his head, and his cheeks were reddened by the wind. He grinned at her as he shed his outer garments and removed his glasses to

1

polish them with a handkerchief. Toby was in love, and his moods were governed by the arrival or nonarrival of correspondence from his beloved. Today he seemed to be in a good mood. No doubt he had received a letter or even a phone call.

Anthea, who had long ago given up on the idea of finding her own romance, wished that Carol Elliot would make up her mind. Marry Toby or don't marry him, but put a stop to this eternal indecision and the breaking and repairing of Toby's heart.

"Morning, Miss Clark."

"Good morning, Mr. Whitby."

On one momentous occasion just a few months before, she had actually called him Toby, but that was in the height of excitement and relief on finding him alive after an especially hair-raising adventure. Now that he was running the office on behalf of Mr. Champion, he was, of course, to be addressed as Mr. Whitby, but in her own mind, he would always be Toby, and her feelings would always be a puzzling mixture of admiration and exasperation.

Toby looked at the morning mail spread across Anthea's desk. "Anything interesting?"

"A police notice sent to local solicitors and business owners about a body washed up on the beach." She took a deep breath. "The body is not in good condition; they did not wish to publish the picture in the newspaper for fear of upsetting people."

Toby laughed derisively. "As if we have not all seen more than our fair share of bodies."

"The children," Anthea said mildly. "We have a new generation born since the war. They have been spared the sights we have seen."

Toby replaced his glasses and picked up the paper. He studied the photograph. "If he served in the forces, his fingerprints will be on file. It's just a matter of time. Someone will know who he is."

"I know already," Anthea declared.

Toby raised his eyebrows. His gray eyes, magnified by the strong lenses of his glasses, were alight with curiosity.

"Really?" He stared down at the grainy photograph. "Not much to go on. Are you sure?"

"Quite sure. I never forget a face."

Toby tapped the illustration with a dubious finger. "Not much face left."

"I know who he is," Anthea insisted.

Toby moved around behind Anthea's desk and read the words printed beneath the picture. "Foul play suspected." He grinned in a mischievous way totally unsuited to the dignity of an employee of Champion and Company. "'Foul play suspected'; do they still speak like that? It sounds like something out of a crime novel."

"I don't read crime novels," Anthea replied, hoping that he would hear the rebuke in her voice.

"There must be something they're not telling us if they're talking about foul play," Toby said thoughtfully. "It has to be more than just the bad condition of the body. I've seen for myself what a body looks like after it's been dragged along the ocean floor. There's a lot of scrap metal down there. It's still not safe to go swimming."

Toby returned his attention to the picture. "Do you really know him?"

"I wouldn't say I know him, but I know who he is. It's a face I could never forget."

She returned Toby's speculative look with a discouraging glare. "You have a vivid imagination, Mr. Whitby, but this is not the time or place for that kind of speculation."

Toby grinned. "I would not dream of speculating. So tell me who he is."

"He is, or was, a lieutenant in the Royal East Kent Regiment, and he saved my life."

Toby's look invited her to offer more information, but Anthea was in too much of a hurry. She was late, and she hated to be late. She also hated to repeat herself. It would be enough to tell the story once to the officer in charge of the inquiry into the lieutenant's death.

Toby was blessedly silent for a moment. When he spoke, she sensed the sympathy in his voice. "Painful memory?" he asked.

Anthea thought back on her life, on two World Wars and a fiancé lost so long ago that his existence had become irrelevant. She had trouble thinking of any memory that was not painful.

"No, not really."

Toby folded the paper and put it in his pocket. "We have no appointments this morning. I'll come with you and we can take my car. It's blowing half a gale out there; no point in you getting your hair untidy."

Anthea patted her gray bun to reassure herself that no hairpins had been misplaced. She looked at Toby's rambunctious curls and smiled. Despite his youth and his complete indifference to protocol, she could not help liking him. In fact, if she had been forty years younger, she would not be hesitating at his proposal and keeping him waiting for an answer the way that Carol Elliot was keeping him waiting.

Brighton Mortuary
Detective Inspector Percy Slater

Percy Slater waited in the outer office of the mortuary, wrinkling his nose at the all-pervading odor of formalin and Dettol. In a strange way, he was looking forward to being reunited with Miss Anthea Clark from the offices of Champion and Company. She'd done really well in the Southwold case. She had managed to keep a cool head while Southwold Hall was being blown to smithereens and her boss was accusing the Lady of the Manor of murder.

He'd be pleased to see her again, and if she really had a good line on the identity of the body washed up on Brighton beach, he'd be glad to hear it.

The door opened, and he saw that Miss Clark was not alone. Toby Whitby hovered behind her, his eyes hidden by fogged spectacles. As the fog dissipated, Slater was greeted with Whitby's cheerful smile of recognition.

"Sergeant Slater."

"Inspector Slater."

"A promotion! Congratulations."

Toby extended his hand, and Slater felt the usual discomfort at only being able to offer his left hand in greeting; he had left his right arm in Normandy. He was unable to shake hands as any normal person would shake hands, but at least he was still working, still solving crimes, still reading the telltale signs that separated accidental death from cold premeditated murder. At least he was not dead.

Slater addressed his remarks to Miss Clark; she was the one who had made the appointment. "There was no need to bring your lawyer, Miss Clark. We don't suspect foul play on your part."

"Miss Clark is only here to assist in identification," Toby said, "nothing else."

"Then let's get on with it," Slater said, anxious to be back in the open air and away from the smell of death. "We've put him in the viewing room. No need to look at the entire body, Miss Clark, just the face."

Miss Clark nodded and unexpectedly reached for Toby's arm as if she needed his help to remain upright. Now Slater was truly curious. What was Miss Clark's relationship to the deceased?

Slater opened the door and entered the viewing room, where the odor of death, decay, and seaweed had easily overcome the smell of formalin. He closed the door behind him, isolating the viewers from the more unpleasant odors, and opened the curtains on the viewing window. He folded back the green sheet and revealed the victim's battered face.

Miss Clark's face, seen through the small window, revealed nothing but impatience. She shook her head, muttered something to Toby, and the next minute, the door had opened and Miss Clark, still grasping Toby's arm, was standing next to the body.

"Miss Clark, there's no need—" Slater protested.

"I can't see anything from there," Miss Clark replied. "I'm sure you mean well, Inspector, but I'm not afraid of death. I was in London in the

4

Blitz, and you know what that was like."

She fumbled in the pocket of her tweed skirt and produced a pair of glasses. With the spectacles perched on the tip of her aquiline nose, she stared down at the face for a long, silent moment. Her expression behind the magnifying lenses was unreadable. She didn't lean in, yearning toward the body as Slater had seen parents and lovers lean; neither did she draw back as some did when faced with horrific injuries. She stood silent and still as if in respectful remembrance.

At long last she returned her spectacles to her pocket and stepped away.

"I know who he is. His name is Michael Cheviot. He was a lieutenant in the Royal East Kent Regiment. Now you have a name, I assume you can check his fingerprints."

Slater hoped that his sharp intake of breath would not betray him. A member of the Cheviot family? Surely not! But Miss Clark seemed very sure of herself.

He saw Toby looking at him; wondering. Yes, the lawyer had heard his sudden gasp and had tucked it away for use at some future opportunity. He had let down his guard, and now he felt an unreasonable spike of annoyance as Toby offered a suggestion.

"I expect his regiment has his fingerprints on file."

Slater scowled. He did not need Toby to tell him how to do his job. "I'm afraid that's not going to help," he said through gritted teeth.

"But if you check the fingerprints—"

"I can't check his bloody fingerprints."

"Why not?"

Irritation took the place of common sense, and Slater grabbed the corner of the sheet. With a quick jerk, he pulled the covering away to reveal the victim's bloated body and the arms ending in neatly severed stumps.

"No fingers," he said.

Miss Clark gave a faint cry and crumpled toward the floor.

Anthea Clark

The detective was apologetic. She thought he would be impatient at her weakness, but he had made efficient use of his one remaining arm and caught her as she slid toward the floor. She'd been surprised by his strength. With his gray-streaked hair and dour expression, she had thought of him as middle-aged, but the arm that caught her had the strength of a much younger man. Perhaps the lines on his face and the hurt behind his eyes were the result of the sights he was forced to witness every day. Maybe he was not old; maybe he was simply tired.

Now the three of them sat together in the police canteen while Anthea drank strong, sweet tea, and Toby asked her over and over again if she was quite sure she had not banged her head.

"No, Mr. Whitby. My head is perfectly fine. Inspector Slater was kind enough to catch me before I came into contact with the floor." She turned her head to look at the police officer. "I am so sorry."

"My fault," the inspector replied.

Anthea shook her head. "You did what you had to so that Mr. Whitby would stop talking about fingerprints and understand the importance of my identifying the body. There is no need to apologize. I really don't know what came over me."

The policeman sighed. "Death is always disturbing."
He looked at Toby. He seemed to be making an attempt at friendliness. "He knows what I mean. We've seen things we can't forget."

Anthea refused to look at Toby. She knew he was sensitive about the fact that he had never been in combat. His poor eyesight had kept him out of uniform, but he had done sterling work as a fire watcher on the roof of the Ministry of Defence. As for Slater, quite obviously something catastrophic had happened to him, although he chose not to acknowledge it. It was, she thought, as though no one should be permitted to notice his missing right arm.

The thought of Slater's right arm brought her mind back to the severed stumps of Michael Cheviot's arms. It was the lack of blood that had upset her; the pale unreality of the fish-nibbled extremities and the clean-cut white bones buried in the swollen and putrefied flesh; and not a drop of blood in sight.

"Miss Clark, I have asked one of the WPCs to bring us the file on Michael Cheviot," Slater said.

Anthea sipped her tea and tried to ignore the look of sympathetic disbelief on the detective's face. "I don't know why you should doubt me, Inspector. I know it's him."

"Did you know him well?" Slater asked.

Anthea knew that the question was a reasonable one. She was insisting that she knew the identity of the battered corpse, and without the benefit of fingerprints, Slater had nothing else to go on. Of course she should tell him what she knew. She glanced at Toby. She could hardly ask him to leave. He leaned forward and listened intently to her story.

CHAPTER TWO

June 1942
Canterbury, Kent

The night was filled with terrors. Anthea, who had lived through the London Blitz, was better prepared than her great-uncle Archibald, the retired canon of the cathedral who had never experienced a bombing raid. Even Lucy, Martha, and Godfrey, the evacuated London children who shared her great-uncle's house in the cathedral close, were better prepared than their host. They knew enough to grab their gas masks and hide under their beds as the bombs rained down on the city and its great medieval cathedral.

Anthea, roused from a deep sleep, found the children, dragged them from under their beds, and hurried them down the stairs. Her uncle's house had no bomb shelter. This was Canterbury, the sleepy heart of the Church of England, of no possible strategic value to anyone. Up until now it had escaped Hitler's wrath, but now that wrath was being visited upon them, and the city was unprepared.

She led the children down to the cellar, where they huddled together in the dark. What she wanted to do was to run outside and shake her fists at the Luftwaffe as they roared overhead, dropping their incendiary bombs and burning the buildings that had been sacred to the British for more than a thousand years. She wanted to see them and she wanted them to see her outrage. She no longer cared about her own life. Too many loved ones had already been lost. She was alone. No, she thought. No, she was not alone; for some reason, she had been given three children to keep safe, and that was what she would do!

Lucy, Martha, and Godfrey remained blessedly quiet. They had been sent from London to the supposed safety of the countryside, but not before they had already experienced the Battle of Britain and the first full wrath of the German Luftwaffe intent on destroying London. These children had long ago run out of the ability to be afraid.

Godfrey, with the acute hearing of youth and practice, called out the size and types of bombs as they exploded, and judged their distance from the cathedral. He only ducked his head and covered his ears when the bombs fell close enough to shake the ancient dust from the ceiling.

In a brief lull between explosions, Anthea heard footsteps on the stairs and saw the flickering light of a candle. Great-Uncle Archibald, his white hair standing on end and his black cassock torn and smudged, descended the last of the steps and kneeled down beside her.

"We have fire watchers on the roof," he said. "I've never seen anything like it. They're not wearing uniforms, but they're heroes. They're not going to let the cathedral burn."

"What about the town?" Anthea asked. She appreciated her uncle's love of the cathedral and the legacy it represented, but Canterbury consisted of more than the cathedral. Surely the bombs were falling on houses, schools, hospitals, even the famed Kent hop fields.

She saw the flickering candlelight reflected in the tears that coursed slowly and unchecked down his weathered cheeks. He gestured for her to leave the children so that he could speak without them listening.

"We have all become evil," he whispered. "Hitler is only doing to us what we have done to him."

"But he started it," Anthea hissed, realizing that she sounded like a child making excuses for a playground fight. Her childhood had been long ago, but the sense of who had started what had remained strong. Hitler had started this war, just as Kaiser Wilhelm had started the previous war. There could be no possible excuse for the fire that rained down from the sky.

Great-Uncle Archibald shook his head. "We bombed Cologne, a city with no strategic value, and we destroyed their cathedral. Now he bombs Canterbury. He is intent on ripping out the hearts of the people and destroying our will to fight. If this goes on much longer, I fear he will succeed."

He tapped her shoulder. "Stay with the children and keep an eye on them. I don't know what we'll find at the end of this night, but it won't be a fit sight for children."

Morning brought the sound of rescuers pulling away the rubble that trapped them in the cellar. They climbed the stairs and stood among the ancient bricks and beams that had once been Great-Uncle Archibald's house.

Anthea stared up at the sky, grateful for the bright sun and the brisk wind that blew away the last of the smoke. She saw immediately that the cathedral itself had been spared. Its tall spires still rose to pierce the sky as they had done for more than a thousand years, but around the cathedral the city lay in ruins.

She found Great-Uncle Archibald almost immediately. He was a stooped, staggering figure, wringing his hands in despair at the destruction of the cathedral library. Beside him the archbishop, in pajamas and a tin hat, stared at the nave of the cathedral. The walls, with their mullioned windows, stood upright against the morning light, and the archbishop was voicing his joy in seeing the ancient spaces so gloriously lit without the filtering effect of stained glass.

Unable to join the archbishop in finding any kind of joy in the night's events, Anthea moved on into the streets of the devastated city. While rescue workers toiled among the heaps of bricks and smoldering fires, children laughed and ran through the ruins, scavenging for all things bright that caught their attention.

Anthea saw that Great-Uncle Archibald's evacuees had reverted to their London ways. Godfrey was dragging a sack behind him and picking up objects here and there.

In the absence of any attention or oversight from her great-uncle, she felt it her duty to corral them and perhaps find them something to eat. No sooner had she managed to catch hold of Godfrey's hand and attempt to reassert her authority than a dark-haired man in a dusty uniform swept down upon them.

"Does this boy belong to you?"

"Not exactly."

He was a soldier, not a civil defense worker. A quick glance showed her a khaki officer's uniform and regimental badges, but sometime during the night, he had discarded his hat, and a fine layer of dust coated his hair. He swept a grimy hand across his forehead to keep the hair from his eyes and grabbed hold of Godfrey's sack of treasures.

Godfrey was not pleased. "Hey, that's mine. I found it. Give it back."

The man's voice was cultured, with nothing of the burr of a Kentish man or the strained vowels of a Londoner. "I'll give it back when I find out what you have in there."

"Show the officer what you have," Anthea said. "Don't make me tell the canon that you've been stealing."

"Ain't stealing. I found it fair and square, and the old man don't care what we do."

Anthea was inclined to agree with the boy's assessment of the value of the canon's guardianship, but she noticed the caution with which the young officer was handling the sack.

"What does he have in there?" she asked.

"Unless I'm mistaken, he's picked up some unexploded ordinance."

"Unexploded ord ... You mean a bomb?"

"An incendiary, I would say."

A worried frown creased the officer's face as he waved her away. "Stand back. Let me look."

Godfrey was still truculent and unappeased. "It's mine."

Anthea grabbed his shoulder and pulled him away. "Not anymore."

"I want to go back to London," Godfrey wailed. "No one stopped us in London."

The officer set the sack down carefully and opened the drawstring.

"It's mine," Godfrey shouted again, and this time, he made a run at the soldier, obviously determined to reclaim his loot.

The soldier fell to the ground with Godfrey's arms locked around his knees. As they fell, the soldier lifted the sack and hurled it over and beyond a pile of rubble. The resulting explosion knocked Anthea off her feet, and she lay on her back for a few moments, gazing up at the brick dust suspended in the air above her. She was too stunned to move.

When she was finally able to focus her eyes, she saw the soldier's face just inches from her own. Blood ran down his nose from a cut just above his hairline. His mouth opened and closed, but she heard nothing. He held up a hand, indicating she should wait, and slowly her hearing returned. When it did, the first sound that came to her was the sound of Godfrey wailing in terror.

"He's all right." The soldier's voice was calm and confident. "He's not hurt, just frightened. He won't do that again."

Anthea looked at the blood streaming down the soldier's face. "You're hurt."

He swiped at the blood with a careless hand. "It's nothing. Are you all right?"

Anthea sat upright and took mental inventory of herself. "Yes, I think I'm fine. I believe we owe you our lives."

The soldier raised his eyebrows. "I saw him pick it up, and I noticed the big red A the Germans so thoughtfully stenciled on the side. I didn't want the lad hurting himself or anyone else."

He rose from crouching to standing. "I'd better be on my way. I should be back at my unit by now."

He held out his hand and pulled her to her feet. "You're sure you're not hurt?"

She shook her head. "I'm not hurt."

"Good. Well, you'd better keep an eye on those children. Some of them have to learn the hard way."

He turned to leave and she called after him. "What's your name?"

He stood to attention. "Michael Cheviot, First Lieutenant, Royal Kent Regiment. I would salute but I seem to have lost my hat."

May 1952

Anthea set her cup back on its saucer. The taste of the sweet tea was still strong in her mouth. She felt her strength returning, and with it her determination.

"I have to go back and look at him again."

Toby shook his head. "I don't think that's a good idea."

"Michael Cheviot had a cut on his head. I was there when it happened. If I could just look at his head …"

Slater looked at her with an expression that seemed to indicate he had reached the end of his patience.

"Miss Clark, the body we have in the mortuary has been dragged for some considerable distance along the ocean floor. We cleaned him up and made him as presentable as we could so that you could see his face. I don't want to show you the back of his head; it's just not a fit sight for you to see. Looking for one cut among so many would be pointless."

"So you don't believe that I know who he is?" Anthea asked.

Slater's expression gave nothing away. "I believe your story, Miss Clark. I believe that a Lieutenant Cheviot of the Royal East Kent saved your life, but I am quite certain that the man we have in the mortuary is not that Michael Cheviot."

Anthea felt Toby stirring impatiently beside her. He was going to interfere, she just knew it. Toby was not one to take a back seat or realize when his opinion was not needed.

"Miss Clark sounds very sure of herself," Toby said. "Why would you choose not to believe her?"

"Because I know things that you don't," Slater said between gritted teeth. "Michael Cheviot is not in the mortuary. He's still alive."

Anthea was embarrassed that she had fainted, and she was equally embarrassed that she had told her story of meeting the lieutenant in Canterbury. This was a story she should have kept to herself. She didn't mind that Inspector Slater now thought her a sentimental fool, but she was ashamed to think that she had revealed so much of herself to Toby and that Toby would think that he was required to defend here.

She rose with as much dignity as she could muster. "Mr. Whitby, would you please drive me back to the office."

Toby shook his head. "I think we should wait and see the proof of what Inspector Slater is saying. He owes us an explanation."

Anthea struggled to keep her voice steady. "No, Mr. Whitby, he owes us nothing. I made a mistake."

The hot, sweet tea had not helped. She still felt faint and dizzy. Perhaps it was just the sight of that putrefied body; she had never seen a drowning victim. Perhaps it was the thought that the man on the slab, the man who bore such a resemblance to Michael Cheviot, had met such a violent death. Someone had cut off his hands! Had he been alive when that had happened? The thought was too horrible to contemplate.

She fought against her tears. She knew that her fondness for romantic stories was inappropriate for a woman of her years, but it was an addiction she could not control. During the dark days of the war, she had refused to relinquish her collection of books and magazines for recycling, hoarding them in neat piles beside her bed. After the war, when magazines were again allowed to publish frivolous articles and romantic stories, she had recalled Michael's face and had placed that face on every hero in every romantic story she had read. Now she could not shake the certainty that the face she had just seen was the face she had imagined so many times. She knew who had been dragged from the ocean. She knew that Michael Cheviot was dead.

A female police officer came into the canteen, carrying a sheaf of papers. Slater stood to speak to her. As they whispered together, the young woman glanced at Anthea and then looked away. She produced a newspaper clipping to show to Slater. They turned away from Anthea, still whispering.

Anthea gained control of her emotions. She didn't want anyone to see her this way. She knew what the officious young woman was seeing; an old woman in lisle stockings and sensible shoes, gray hair in a bun, a bulky cardigan obviously hand knitted, and a wrinkled old face without even a trace of lipstick.

Old fool, she said to herself. They think I'm an old fool. She looked at Toby. "Please, Toby, take me back to the office."

She had his attention. He had been focused on the detective, but now he turned to her with a look of sympathy.

"Don't you want to see what he has?" He came closer and spoke in a whisper. "He could be wrong. I'd rather believe you."

He gave her a conspiratorial smile and tucked a firm hand under her elbow. "Let's see what he has."

Slater dismissed the young woman and turned back to Anthea. His movements were clumsy as he spread the papers on the table.

"We have Michael Cheviot's service record."

Anthea waited. Toby was right; she could not leave, not now.

"You were right about one thing, Miss Clark. Michael Cheviot did serve with the Buffs, the Royal East Kent. Joined in 1941, went through officer training, and served with distinction in Africa and Italy. He was demobilized in 1946."

"So it is him," Anthea said. "He didn't die in combat. He died right here."

Slater shook his head. "I'm afraid not. As I have already told you, Michael Cheviot is still alive."

"How do you know?"

Slater looked down at the newspaper clipping. "We have his photograph, taken several weeks ago after an incident on the Downs." Slater pushed the paper toward Anthea. "There's your friend Michael Cheviot."

Anthea looked down at the clipping and the photograph of a car in flames and a man who appeared to be fighting the flames to reach the car door. The picture was grainy, but she could see the resemblance to the man she remembered. A smaller photo showed a man sitting up in a hospital bed with his hands bandaged."

Toby was beside her, eager for details. "What does it say?"

She glanced at the heading. "Local hero."

Toby leaned forward, squinting as he scanned the small print. "Lieutenant Michael Cheviot, formerly of the Royal East Kent, suffered burns to his hands in rescuing a woman from a burning car." He took a step back. "Bandaged hands; what a coincidence."

Slater returned the clipping to the file. "This all happened three weeks ago," he said. "Lieutenant Cheviot is out of hospital and at home with his mother in Hove. One of our WPCs has already telephoned the house to make sure that nothing has happened to him."

"What about the woman he saved?" Toby asked. "It doesn't say who she is."

Slater's expression was inscrutable. "She fled the scene."

"You mean she didn't stop to thank him?" Toby asked.

"No."

Anthea saw that someone else had come to stand quietly behind Slater's shoulder. She studied the new arrival. He was a young man with an olive complexion and small brown eyes that focused on the newspaper clipping. She told herself that if he was a policeman, then she was the Queen of Sheba. From his overlong Brylcreemed hair to his wide striped tie and black satin-sheened shirt, the man was a spiv, a common criminal dressed in plumage that could only have come from the black market. Anthea disliked and distrusted him on sight.

"Better watch out for those Cheviots," the newcomer warned.

"I do," Slater replied coldly.

"So why are you looking at them now?"

"That's for me to know and you to wonder," Slater snapped. The air between the two men positively crackled with dislike.

The newcomer straightened up and jabbed a manicured finger at the picture. "Are you looking for the runaway woman? She's half a continent away by now. You'll get no joy from the Cheviots, and I hear they've brought in Cousin Billy to mind the store."

"You're not telling me anything I don't already know," Slater growled.

The newcomer assessed Anthea with a quick dismissive glance and let his eyes graze across Toby's features. "Who are these two?"

"Miss Clark is assisting in the identification of the body we found on the beach," Slater said stiffly.

"Oh yeah. Well, good luck. No fingerprints, or so I hear."

Slater said nothing, but Anthea could feel his desire for this brash stranger to be on his way.

The stranger jabbed the picture again. "Leave this one alone, Slater. We have bigger fish to fry." He looked down at the newspaper clipping, and his eyes darted back to Anthea suspiciously and then back again to the picture. He raised his eyebrows inquiringly.

"Does she know who he is, because he's not Michael Cheviot?" he asked. "Do you want me to talk to them, see if he has a long-lost brother?"

"If there's any talking to be done, I'll do it," Slater snapped. "This is my case, and I'll thank you to leave it alone. I don't need your help with the Cheviots. Billy Cheviot and me go way back."

"So I've been told," the stranger muttered. "Be careful, Slater. Don't muddy the waters for the big boys."

Slater looked the stranger up and down, his eyes lingering on the colorful tie and form-fitting shirt. "What's the matter, Frankie? Are you frightened Billy will get banged up and you'll lose your black market tailor?" he asked.

Frankie pulled a toothpick from his shirt pocket and stuck it in the corner of his mouth. "Nothing says copper like a raincoat and trilby," he replied. He nodded his head at Anthea and departed, chewing casually on his toothpick.

"Who was that?" Toby asked.

Slater's cautious calm seemed to have left him for a moment. "Frankie," he growled. "That's all I know, although I doubt that's his real name. He's undercover; sent down from the Met in London."

"Nothing very undercover about turning up in the police canteen," Toby remarked.

Anthea was in agreement with Toby, but she wished he hadn't spoken, because she saw immediately that Slater had recovered his usual tight-lipped equilibrium. He looked at her with tired, bloodshot eyes that gave nothing away. She wondered why a plain-clothes officer from London was down here in Brighton, and why he talked so disparagingly about the Cheviot family. The man she had met in Canterbury had been not only heroic but also charming and obviously well educated, and he had called himself Michael Cheviot. It had been no more than a chance meeting; why would he lie about his name?

Slater extended his left hand. "Thank you for coming in, Miss Clark, but I'm afraid we can't accept your identification. I agree that there is a resemblance, but you can see from these clippings that Michael Cheviot is alive and well. I don't know who we have on the slab, but it's not Michael Cheviot."

CHAPTER THREE

Toby Whitby

Toby heard the disapproval in Anthea's voice long before he saw the object of her disapproval.

"We really cannot help you. Champion and Company does not deal with such matters."

He leaned forward in his chair to take a better look at whoever had disturbed Anthea's afternoon by bringing much-needed legal business into the office.

Miss Clark had been ominously silent for two days. She would not speak of their visit to the mortuary and she dismissed his solicitous questions as to her health. "I am perfectly fine, Mr. Whitby, and I am very busy."

She had driven him away by pounding heavily on her typewriter, although Toby was at a loss to know what she was typing. So far as he was aware, they did not currently have any clients who would require legal documents, and Mr. Champion had not telephoned with any instructions for her.

Now the typewriter was blessedly silent as Anthea dealt with the unwelcome visitor. Toby studied the potential client, who stood just inside the doorway.

His appraisal of her was based not on her assets as an attractive young woman but on the possibility that she might bring the firm an easily won legal case and a new source of income. His initial assessment was disappointing. He knew little of women's fashions, but he did know that there was nothing fashionable about the faded floral pattern of her dress or the way it hung loosely on her small frame as though it had been made for a larger woman. Her shoes, surely they were remnants of the sensible footwear of World War II, were run down at the heels. Her appearance radiated poverty; a woman defeated by the austerity of postwar Britain.

Her fair hair was scraped back and held in place by a frayed ribbon, but a single lock had escaped from its bondage. The loose curl was the only indication of what she may once have been. Although nothing about her indicated that she was possessed of serious money, the one rebellious curl told him that he was wrong in thinking her defeated.

Miss Clark was holding open the outer door. "Thank you for coming in, Mrs. Findlay, but we don't handle such matters."

The rejected client surprised him with her sudden animation. "It's Miss Findlay."

The client's outspoken words tugged at Toby's curiosity. Obviously, Miss Findlay was involved in some domestic arrangements that would have been more appropriate for a married woman. Equally obviously, Miss Findlay, for all her run-down poverty, was not willing to call herself Mrs. Findlay just for the sake of appearances. He focused on Miss Findlay's left hand. No wedding ring. No engagement ring.

He made up his mind. Mr. Champion was not here to make a decision, and Toby could not attach importance to any of the papers scattered across his desk; not a single one of them would solve the firm's financial problems. Why not have a chat with Miss Findlay and see what was going on?

"Miss Clark!"

"Yes, Mr. Whitby?"

"Would you step into my office for a moment?"

Anthea turned a mistrustful eye on the prospective client as if afraid that the woman would steal the spoons as soon as her back was turned. Toby leaned out of his doorway and waved Miss Findlay to a seat.

"I'll be with you in a minute, Miss Findlay."

Miss Findlay sat and smoothed her skirt down over her knees. Miss Clark glanced back over her shoulder before entering Toby's office and leaving the door open a crack.

"Don't worry," Toby said, "she won't steal the petty cash."

"You can't be sure," Miss Clark whispered. "She's really not our type."

"If she's able to pay for our services, she's our type."

Although Miss Clark shook her head vigorously, her hair remained unruffled, secured firmly into its tight bun. "Mr. Champion would never—"

"Mr. Champion is unwell, and this is my responsibility now."

"But—"

"Times are changing, Miss Clark."

"All I can say is that before the war, we would never have let someone like her into our office."

Toby sighed. "The war's been over for six years," he said, "and we are all struggling to make ends meet. What does she want?"

"Child support," Anthea whispered. "She's an unmarried mother."

Toby looked at Anthea's pursed lips and unsympathetic blue eyes. "I can see that you disapprove," he said, "but perhaps there are extenuating circumstances. The war was hard on all of us. Promises were made that could not be kept."

"He's not dead," Anthea hissed.

"Who is not dead?"

"The man who she said promised to marry her. She didn't tell me his name, but she says he's not dead and she has proof."

"All the more reason why he should pay child support."

"He denies being the father. She says that she tried to talk to his family and they wouldn't even let her in the door. If you ask me, she's the type who would—"

Toby considered that one playful curl of blond hair that had escaped to highlight Miss Findlay's face. Perhaps Anthea had a point; perhaps it would never be clear who the father of Miss Findlay's child was, but he could not rush to judgement on the strength of one unrestrained curl of hair.

"Miss Clark ..."

She was looking at him with a stricken expression on her face, and her hand, with its short, clipped nails, held to her lips.

"Oh, Mr. Whitby, Toby, I'm so sorry. I didn't mean to imply—"

He cut off her words before she could mention Carol Elliot, the woman he still hoped to make his wife, the woman who had given birth to the child of a German prisoner of war.

"Let's not talk about that," Toby said.

"But—"

He had Anthea at a disadvantage and could not resist the opportunity to tease her. "Not everything happens as neatly as it does in your romance stories," he said.

Anthea blushed and turned to leave. "I'll show her in."

"Yes, I think you should."

"Should I stay?"

He made a private comparison between Carol Elliot, with her bouncing red curls and infectious laughter, and the thin wisp of a woman perched on a chair in the outer office. Many formalities had fallen by the wayside in the aftermath of war, but Mr. Champion's prewar standards still held sway here. Propriety required that he should not be alone with a young female client. He was in no way tempted by her. She had already accused one man of fathering a child, and apparently, that man had denied her accusation, so who could know what she might say about her meeting with Toby?

"Yes," Toby said, "you should stay."

Toby remained on his feet as Anthea ushered in the client, who brought with her a faint odor of Dettol soap. The work-roughened hand she held out to Toby hinted of days spent in scrubbing floors or clothes, or something of that nature. He thought it unlikely that she would be able to pay any meaningful amount of money, but the father, if he was indeed the father, might possibly pay up, and the firm could still profit.

"Do you mind if I open the windows?" Anthea asked. "It's somewhat ... stuffy in here."

Toby felt relieved. He had smelt his fill of Dettol soap in the hospital when he was recovering from the battering that had resulted from the implosion of Southwold Hall.

Anthea cranked the window open, and a fresh breeze blew in from the English Channel, accompanied by the screeching of seagulls and the chatter of pedestrians on the promenade.

Toby realized that Miss Findlay was still extending her hand. He took it. The handshake was brief but her grip was firm.

"Toby Whitby," he said.

"Dorothy Findlay. Please just call me Dorothy. Your secretary seems upset that I am not calling myself Mrs. Findlay, but I don't believe in pretending."

Her voice carried the memory of a London childhood. She had made some attempt to smooth out the harshness of London's East End, but it was there just below the surface. Make her angry, Toby thought, and she'd be pure Cockney.

Anthea interrupted Toby's reverie by telling him what he already knew.

"Miss Findlay wishes to bring an action for child support."

"I see." Toby uncapped his fountain pen and turned to a fresh page in his notebook. "How old is the child?"

"He's ten."

A wartime fling! He knew the questions to ask, but it hardly seemed worth the trouble. He could already guess the answers.

"Were or are you now cohabiting with the father?"

Dorothy looked at Anthea.

"He's asking you if you lived with him, you know, out of wedlock?" Anthea sniffed.

Dorothy grinned. "You mean living in sin?"

Anthea looked down her nose, and Toby felt an urge to lean across and pinch some sense into her. She had always been stiff and unapproachable, but he had never seen her so judgmental.

He tried to keep judgement from his own voice. Anthea was displaying sufficient judgement for both of them.

"Were you and the father ever representing yourself as man and wife even though circumstances made actual marriage impossible? As your child is ten years old, and as ten years of cohabitation can sometimes constitute a common-law marriage—"

"No," Dorothy said. "Nothing like that! It was just the once. We told the people at the hotel, well, he told the people at the hotel that we were man and wife; just married. I kept my left hand hidden but they didn't even look. It was just the once. It's only ever been the once. Just with him. Not with anyone else. He's the father."

Anthea cleared her throat. "Does he know?"

"I couldn't tell him," Dorothy said. "He went overseas."

It was an old story, Toby thought, one that had played out over and over again in the desperation of war, where a momentary need to forget the world could be mistaken for undying love.

Anthea's voice was sharp and cold; obviously, she had no sympathy for a woman caught up in a moment of passion. "Perhaps he was killed."

Dorothy's eyes, wide and cornflower blue, brightened in anger. "I wouldn't be here if I thought he was dead. I was managing on my own. It's not easy, but I'm doing it. He's not dead, and now that I know he's alive, I think he should have to pay up."

"How do you know he's alive?" Toby asked.

Dorothy delved into her handbag and produced a crumpled sheet of newspaper. She set it down on Toby's desk, where it gave off a faint odor of celery. She smoothed out the creases.

"This was in the newspaper the greengrocer used to wrap my order. When I got home, I read it just to see what the local news was, and I saw the pictures."

She noticed the shock on Toby's face as he looked at the pictures. She seemed to mistake it for something else. "I have money. I can pay you." She opened her battered bag. "How much do you need?"

Toby had trouble finding his voice. He passed the newspaper to Anthea and saw her face turn white.

"What's the matter?" Dorothy asked. "That's him. I swear that's him."

Seeing the photograph again jangled his nerves and brought back the face of the man on the slab, white and bloated, with unseeing eyes, but nonetheless a face that could still be identified. Here was the same face on a man who was not dead; a man sitting up in a hospital bed.

He had no need to read the small print. He knew what it said. "Local hero saves woman from burning car."

Anthea spoke first in a voice that struggled for calm. "Are you sure he's the one?"

Dorothy glared at her. "Yes, he's the one. I'd know that face anywhere."

"And yet you didn't know his name," Anthea remarked.

"I knew his name was Michael; I just didn't know the last name. I knew he was in the Buffs, the Royal East Kent." She hesitated. "It was a spur-of-the-moment thing. I met him in a restaurant. He shared my table and we started talking, you know how it was. We talked about the food, the powdered eggs, the margarine. He told me he knew where we could get sausages, ones with real meat in them. He said he knew people."

"And did he know people?" Toby asked.

Dorothy dropped her voice to a low whisper. "I don't know. We didn't get that far. We were together in his car and …"

Toby had no need to press her for the details. He knew what it was like to fall suddenly and precipitously in love, or lust. A vision of the first time he had seen Carol swam into his mind, and he forced it aside. Now was not the time to think of the way she was keeping him waiting.

"But not to know his name," Anthea said in a tone of stern rebuke. "To go with a man and not even know his name."

"It's just the way it happened. He would have told me if I'd asked. He signed the register as Lieutenant and Mrs. Michael Leonard, and he winked at me when he did it. He said it was a half-truth, and I took that to mean that his real name was Michael or maybe Leonard, but definitely not Michael Leonard."

Anthea looked away, her face unreadable. Toby hesitated. This was not the type of case that had made Champion and Company a trusted name throughout the county.

The silence stretched out far beyond the point where Toby should have spoken. It stretched until Dorothy rose abruptly to her feet.

"I didn't come in here to be judged. I came for justice. I went to his house, and they wouldn't give me the time of day, wouldn't let me past the doorstep, but I thought that here—"

"You went to his house and confronted him?" Toby asked with grudging admiration. If the story was a lie, surely she wouldn't have gone to Michael Cheviot's house.

"I didn't see him," Dorothy said. "His mother wouldn't let me. She said he was convalescent and couldn't be disturbed. I don't care about that; if he's well enough to come out of hospital, he's well enough to talk to me. I want justice."

She looked over Toby's head at the law books neatly arrayed behind him. "I thought that was what you stood for," she said, "with your shiny brass plaque and your fancy offices. But I was wrong. You're ashamed to take my money, aren't you? Well, let me tell you something. Even if Michel Cheviot doesn't want to be a dad to my Eric, even if he won't let me so

21

much as stand on his doorstep, he should still pay his fair share of the cost. It's not easy raising a child on your own when there's no work left for women to do."

She tucked her purse under her arm and glared at Toby. "It's all very well for you men, isn't it? We women had to run the whole country while you were gone. I had a job as a welder and I was good at it, but you men came home and wanted your jobs back, and we were all sent back to being housewives. Go back to making babies, that's what the government said. Go back home and make tea for your husbands. Well, I've already made a baby, and I don't have a husband bringing home a paycheck and asking me for tea."

Toby could sense that Dorothy had a good deal more to say on the subject of women's unemployment and her own unfortunate situation, but he had no need to hear more. He had already made up his mind.

"Miss Findlay, sit down, please. We'll take your case."

Dorothy did not appear to have heard him. "I left Eric at home on his own without even a shilling for the meter and nothing for his tea," she said, "because I thought you'd help me. I wait at the bus stop outside your office every day when I go to work, and I look in the window and I see you all working." She gestured with her head toward Anthea. "I see her typing away and looking ladylike. I've always thought that people like you and her, and the old gentleman, were trying to put the world right. That's why I came to you. But you're the same as everyone else."

"Miss Findlay," Toby said.

She ignored him. "I'll go back to that house again. I don't care what they do to me. I want justice."

Toby raised his voice. "Miss Findlay, we'll take your case." Dorothy stared at him, defiance fading from her face. Her voice was shaky. "You will?"

"We will."

She sank back into her chair, overcome either with relief or panic.

"How much?" she asked.

"We will do this pro bono."

It was Anthea's turn to gasp. "Pro bono?"

Toby clarified his decision. "We will not charge you, Miss Findlay. Consider it a gesture of gratitude for your previous contributions to the war effort."

He looked across at Anthea. "If you will go outside with Miss Clark, she will take down all the details. We will have to know about your ... tryst ... with Lieutenant Cheviot; where you went, what date, when your child was born, all that sort of thing." He hesitated. "We will have to know of any other men before or after that date. It will be up to you to prove that there is no possibility that anyone other than Michael Cheviot can be the father of your child."

"Why should it be up to me?" Dorothy asked. "Why do I have to prove anything? He should have to prove that he's not the father."

Anthea interrupted with a firm hand on Dorothy's arm. "If the law worked that way, we would have chaos. Women would be able to accuse any man they fancied. The law says that he's innocent until proven guilty. Come with me, Dorothy, and we'll take down the details and draw up the papers."

Dorothy pulled back. "I don't want to go to that house again and have them treat me like dirt."

"The only time you'll see him is in court," Toby said. "I'll handle everything else. I'll serve the papers myself as soon as they are ready."

Dorothy followed Anthea to the outer office. Toby imagined that the conversation would be embarrassing for both women. Anthea viewed life through the lens of happy-ever-after romantic fiction, and Dorothy looked through a different lens. Her lens showed her the harsh reality of women's unemployment in a male-dominated world and the lifelong consequences of making love to a stranger.

In the outer office, Anthea's typewriter clacked in urgent rhythm, with the sharp tone of the bell dinging at the end of every line and the whoosh of the carriage returning to take up the next line.

Toby shifted in his seat, impatient to have the paperwork in his hands and be ready to leave. The need to take care of her child had driven Dorothy into the office. Memory of a soldier who had saved her life drove Anthea to type with speed and energy. Toby had no such high sentiments. He was driven by simple curiosity. Who was Michael Cheviot, and how could he be in two places at the same time?

He heard Anthea's tight-lipped "Goodbye, Miss Findlay" and the clatter of Dorothy's unfashionable shoes on the wooden floor.

Anthea came into his office and kept the folder of papers pressed against her narrow chest. "There's something you should know," she said. "I didn't want to tell you in front of that girl, because I think she is not aware of it, but you need to be aware."

Toby held his hand out for the paper. "Miss Clark, I have said that we will take the case. What else do I need to know?"

Anthea placed the folder in his hand and then surprised him by pulling up a chair and sitting down in front of his desk.

"Mr. Whitby, did it strike you as odd that Inspector Slater already had a file on Michael Cheviot?"

"Not really. I mean, he had his name in the papers and ..." Toby stopped speaking. He remembered that the file had been unusually thick, containing considerably more than Cheviot's service record and the newspaper clipping. He thought about the tense interaction between Slater and the undercover operative.

"Yes, Miss Clark, now you come to mention it, I think it is quite strange."

"Well ..." Anthea leaned forward. "I don't know why I didn't put two and two together immediately; it must have been the shock of seeing the body."

"Yes," Toby agreed, "it was quite a shock."

"The newspaper report gave the name of Michael's mother as Enid Trewin Cheviot," Anthea said. "I should have realized."

"Realized what?"

"Enid Trewin was a film star, or at least a starlet, in the days between the wars."

Toby shrugged. "I've never heard of her."

"Her fame as a film star was fleeting," Anthea said. "She wasn't a very good actress, and she didn't make the transition from silent film to the talkies. She was better known as a socialite. I have quite an extensive collection of magazines from before the war, and I consulted them to see what I could find out about her. Most of the articles were not about her acting roles, they were about her social life. She created quite a scandal with her various lovers. She ran with what they liked to call the fast set, country house weekends, that sort of thing; rich, bored, immoral people."

"And you think that Slater knows this?" Toby asked. "Is that why the file is so fat?"

Anthea's eyes glittered in anticipation of dazzling him with information. "He wouldn't care about that," she said, "but I haven't told you everything. Enid wormed her way into the social circle that surrounded the Prince of Wales. It was thought that she and the Prince ... dallied ... at some of the country house weekends. That sort of thing went on all the time, and the Prince of Wales was no saint."

Toby frowned as he listened to Anthea's breathless recounting of the scandals that surrounded the man who was destined to become Edward VIII; the man who would abdicate his throne for the woman he loved. Of course, that woman was Wallis Simpson, not Enid Trewin. He thought about Michael Cheviot. What year was he born? Could he possibly be ...?

He broke into Anthea's recital of the sins of the Prince of Wales. "Miss Clark, if Michael was born in 1926, is it possible that the Prince of Wales, the Duke of Windsor, is his father?"

Anthea raised shocked eyebrows. "Oh my goodness, Mr. Whitby, what a suggestion! No, I don't think that could possibly be the case. Enid Trewin married Ronnie Cheviot in 1925. I believe the Prince was invited to the wedding, but he could not, of course, attend, because of Ronnie Cheviot's station in life."

"And what was that?"

"He was a gangster," Anthea said decisively. "The Cheviot family were all notorious criminals. They ran the East End of London between the wars. I have no up-to-date information, but I suspect that they still do, and that is why Inspector Slater has that thick file."

"So Michael Cheviot's father is a gangster?" Toby asked.

Anthea shook her head. "Michael's father is dead, or so we are led to believe. Ronnie Cheviot fell from a cross-Channel ferry shortly after Michael was born. His body was never recovered, but after the necessary seven years had passed, he was declared dead."

Anthea sighed as if relinquishing a lingering memory. "Of course, I didn't associate the Lieutenant Cheviot I met in Canterbury with the Cheviot crime family. Why should I? He was a perfect gentleman."

Toby thought about Slater's expression when he had talked about the woman who had fled the burning car. He thought of Michael Cheviot's bandaged hands, damaged as he sought to rescue a woman who immediately ran away. Now he understood why the file was so thick. Slater had much more than a dead body to investigate.

"I have not been able to find any recent scandal about Enid Cheviot," Anthea said. "She has lived a very quiet life since her son returned from the war. You must believe me, Mr. Whitby, that I was unaware that the man I met in Canterbury was the son of a common criminal."

Toby knew that he was putting two and two together and making five, or maybe even six, but he had to say it. "Maybe he wasn't."

CHAPTER FOUR

Toby was glad to be out of the office and away from the need to pretend that he was busy, but even the warm spring air could not compensate for the sight of the battered world that surrounded him. Six years, he thought, and the beach was still littered with rusting anti-tank traps, and ugly gaps still remained where grand hotels had once graced the promenade.

He turned inland, passing the high street, where women queued with their ration books in hand. Two ounces of butter per person, four ounces of meat per week, no sweets, no imported treats, nothing but the monotony of just enough food to sustain life.

A sign outside a newspaper shop announced that a date had been decided for the coronation of the new queen. June 2, 1953, just a little over a year away. Toby imagined that the preparations would provide a distraction for some, but the thought of pomp and pageantry did little to raise his spirits. Elizabeth was young, younger than he was, but she would be queen of a country that had won a war and lost its way. She would be queen of a crumbling empire and queen of ration books and ruined buildings.

He drove up onto the clifftop road and parked the car. He couldn't approach his assignment in such a sour mood. He needed fresh air and a moment to compose himself. He climbed out of the cramped seat and stood to stretch his long legs. The afternoon was mild and sunny. Birds were calling to each other. The hedgerow was alive with scurrying creatures. The mating season was upon them.

Mating brought him to thoughts of Carol, and those thoughts worked their magic and restored his mood.

He climbed back into the Morris and set out for the seaside town of Hove. He made his way through the usual confusion of bombed and collapsed houses, hastily built prefabs, and streets that had somehow survived almost intact to The Laurels, home of Michael Cheviot. Even on this street, some houses remained unoccupied, with their windows blown out, their hedges straggling and unkempt, and their victory gardens a mass of weeds.

The Laurels appeared to be intact, although the gates that guarded the driveway sagged open on rusted hinges.

He straightened his tie and ran a hand through his unruly hair as he considered the house. The Laurels was an ugly Victorian attempt at Tudor architecture, and the eponymous laurels did nothing to improve its appearance. Dark and overgrown, they shrouded the ground-floor windows and left nothing but a small uninviting approach to the front door.

Toby, who had faced down the grim housekeeper at Southwold Hall, had no qualms about ringing the doorbell for as long as it took for someone to answer; a long, long time.

"Go away!"

He had expected to be greeted by a man, perhaps someone sent from London to protect Michael, one of the infamous Cheviots, but it was a woman who answered the door. She stood squarely in his path, with no obvious intention of inviting him in. He could see little of her, as the laurel bushes cast their discouraging shadows in through the front door and shrouded her in gloom.

He took a determined step forward, and the woman was forced to step back into the light. He could see her now, and he remembered what Anthea had told him. This woman had been a movie star.

She wore a dress of some dark, rich material that clung to her thin frame and reached to her ankles. Chains and diaphanous scarves were wrapped around her painfully thin waist. With an embroidered and fringed shawl draped around her shoulders, she was all aflutter as she backed away from him. Her dark hair hung to her shoulders with two wide white stripes revealing that the youth suggested by her clothing was an illusion.

"What do you want?"

"I want to see Michael Cheviot. Is he here?"

"My son is busy. Tell me your business and be gone."

Her speech and manner were that of someone accustomed to commanding servants to carry out her every whim, but he thought that the house itself had gone a long time without the presence of a maid to dust or a gardener to tame the laurels. For all her exotic clothing and the jewels that sparkled on her fingers, she was not half as intimidating as Lady Sylvia Blanchard had been. Perhaps she had once been the lover of the Prince of Wales, but the Prince was nobody now, living in exile with the woman whose love had cost him the throne, and Enid Cheviot was merely the widow of a gangster.

He wondered how much power the Cheviot family retained on the postwar crime front, and how far would they go to protect Ronnie Cheviot's son. He bolstered his courage by reminding himself that in serving papers, he was acting as an officer of the court. He had the power of the throne behind him; the power of the young Queen Elizabeth.

"I need to see him in person."

Enid took another step back and put her hand to her ear in an exaggerated pantomime of listening.

"He's playing the piano. It soothes him."

Toby stood still for a moment and heard the distant sound of music, a cascade of notes, light and trilling, falling silent against an ominous crescendo of bass notes and then ... jangling dissonant chaos!

Enid stamped her foot like a child in a tantrum and glared at Toby. "Your careless use of the doorbell has disturbed him. How could you? Don't you understand his need for solace?"

Toby fought the temptation to laugh. Michael Cheviot's need for solace was not his concern. The music, what little he had heard, was quite lovely, but musical ability didn't excuse his treatment of Dorothy Findlay.

"It seems he's no longer busy," Toby said. "Will you fetch him, or shall I go and find him?"

Enid held out her hand. "Whatever it is, just give it to me and be gone."

Toby inclined his head slightly in an exaggeration of everyday politeness. "I'm sorry that I didn't make myself clear. Toby Whitby, solicitor. I am acting on behalf of Miss Dorothy Findlay."

"Who?" Enid's voice was a parrotlike squawk in its surprise.

"Miss Dorothy Findlay."

"Never heard of her."

"I think you have. I think you were complicit in having her removed from your house."

Enid's penciled eyebrows shot upward. "That floozy? You're representing that floozy?"

Toby considered Enid's choice of words and rejected her description. There was nothing of the floozy in Dorothy; quite the opposite. She had simply followed in the footsteps of so many other women and girls, and given in to the pressure of war and the thought that her lover might never return. The urge to comfort a soldier before he went into battle was as old as mankind.

"Well?" said Enid, her hand extended to take the papers.

"In person," Toby repeated.

"But—"

Enid's protest died on her thin lips, interrupted by the sound of another car pulling up by the front gate.

She turned away from Toby and took two angry steps toward the front door. Toby seized his moment to stride down the hallway. The music had emanated from a room at the rear of the house. As if to guide him, he heard the music again; a repeat of the cascade of light crystal notes. He opened the door.

Michael Cheviot wore a red silk robe. His hair, long and unkempt, fell forward across his face as he hunched over the grand piano. His entire concentration was given to the movement of his fingers, flying across the keys and creating an outpouring of liquid music.

Toby was momentarily paralyzed, overcome by the beauty of the sound, but his mere presence, his breathing in and out, was apparently enough to disturb the temperamental pianist. Michael spread his long fingers across the keys and created a series of inharmonious chords before slamming the piano lid and looking up at Toby.

Toby was disconcerted at seeing that face again. It was the same face that had reposed cold, bloodless, and fish-nibbled on the slab at the mortuary. This face, however, was not cold and bloodless. This face was flushed with anger.

"What do you want? Who let you in here? Can't you see I'm playing?"

Toby flourished the brown envelope containing the papers that would change the pianist's life and disturb more than his piano practice.

"Michael Cheviot?"

"Of course I'm Michael bloody Cheviot. What do you want?"

Toby dropped the envelope onto the piano. "I'm serving you with a demand for child support."

"What the hell?"

"Miss Dorothy Findlay has named you as the father of her son, Eric, and you are being sued for child support."

"Whitby, what are you doing here?"

The voice came from behind him, and Toby turned to discover Percy Slater standing there. Michael's mother fluttered in the doorway.

"It's the police, Michael. The police!"

Michael's face reddened, and his full lips dropped into a sullen pout. "I told you I'm not to be disturbed." He ignored the presence of both Toby and Slater as he glared at his mother. "I should never have come back. If you don't get rid of these people, I'll go back to Cornwall. Just do it, Mother."

Toby tapped the envelope to remind Michael of his position. "You have been served, Mr. Cheviot, and Inspector Slater is my witness. You will be told a date on which you are to appear in court and answer Miss Findlay's claim for child support."

Michael's mouth retained its sullen pout, but he remained silent. Toby recalled the threat that Cheviot had just made to his mother. He tapped the envelope again.

"Apparently, you have an address in Cornwall, Mr. Cheviot. I will require that information. Removing yourself to Cornwall will not affect this suit. You will still be required to appear here in Brighton."

Slater elbowed Toby aside. "Are you done here?"

"I am."

"Good."

Slater stared at Michael for a long moment. He responded by looking away, his eyes resting on the window, where laurel bushes obscured the view.

"Are you Michael Cheviot?" Slater asked.

"Of course I am."

"Lieutenant Michael Joseph Cheviot, previously of the Royal East Kent Regiment?"

"Yes."

"Do you have anything to prove your claim?"

Michael turned back. "Claim?" he said. "You want me to prove I am who I say I am?"

His voice was a contemptuous drawl, with the clear crystal vowels and consonants of a good private education.

Slater was in no way intimidated. "I would like to see your identity card, your ration book, and your demob papers."

"Ask my mother; she'll show them to you. She'll also tell you that she gave birth to me. Apparently, it was a long-drawn-out, painful affair. She reminds me quite often how difficult it was, and how much she suffered and how it ruined her career; such as it was." He waved a hand of dismissal at Toby and Slater. "Go away. I need to play."

Enid caught hold of Slater's sleeve. "Leave him alone. Can't you see how he is?"

"Seems fine to me," Slater said.

Enid shook her head, pulling Slater into the hallway. Toby followed out of curiosity.

"Shell shock," Enid whispered. "That's what they call it. It's only the music that keeps him going, and when he burned his fingers ... You do know about that, don't you?"

Slater's even tones gave very little away. "Yes. The incident was investigated."

"He was a hero," Enid declared, "but look at what it cost him. Three weeks without music. I thought I was going to lose him. He was in despair, and now that he's recovered, now that he can play again, this lawyer comes and—"

Slater looked at Toby. "You've served your papers; no need to stay any longer."

Toby seized his opportunity. "Well, Inspector, I heard you asking the gentleman to prove he is who he says he is. I want to be certain that my papers have been correctly served. I think I'll wait to see the evidence of his identity."

"Then you'll wait outside," Slater replied. He turned back to the mother. "You show me his papers and prove to me that he is who he says he is, and I'll be on my way."

Enid nodded. "You are a policeman and you represent the law, so I suppose I'll have to show them to you. I don't know what the world is coming to when a mother can't be trusted to identify her own son."

She looked at Toby. "As for you; you should be ashamed of yourself. My Michael would never ..." She shook her head. "That floozy will get what's coming to her."

Slater's voice was that of a man who was accustomed to threats. "I wouldn't talk like that if I were you, Mrs. Cheviot. We in the force don't like it when we hear that someone will get what's coming to them. It usually ends up in bloodshed."

Enid drew back. "No, no, I didn't mean anything like that, just the cheek of the girl, saying my Michael is the father of her misbegotten child."

"I'll need your address in Cornwall," Toby said.

"For goodness' sake, why would you need that?"

"In case your son decides to go there instead of appearing in court to answer Miss Findlay's charges."

"My father has a house on Bodmin Moor and some tenant cottages," Enid said. "Michael went there for peace and quiet. The war was very upsetting for him."

"Upsetting," Slater muttered under his breath. "Yes, I'm sure it was upsetting for all of us."

Enid flushed, and Toby followed her glance to the empty sleeve of Slater's jacket. He was glad to see that the woman still had a shred of decency left despite her devotion to her son.

A door opened, admitting an odor of baking bread that made Toby realize that he had gone without lunch. A woman in an apron bustled into the hallway.

"Does he want to eat his lunch?"

The voice contained no hint of subservience and carried with it the brash tones and accents of the London slums.

"Mr. Michael is too disturbed to eat," Enid said stiffly.

With a lift of her eyebrows, the woman indicated that she was speaking of someone else; someone who was upstairs.

"Not him, the other one. You know ... him."

Enid's reply was sharp and cut off any further conversation about the other person, who was possibly upstairs and might want to eat.

"Not now. We'll talk about it later." Her voice was accusatory as she looked at Toby and then back to the cook. "This man has been very upsetting. Go and get Billy to show him out."

Toby made a mental note that Billy must have been the person who had forcibly escorted Dorothy from the premises. He waved a dismissive hand. "I'll see myself out."

He left by the front door and lingered in the shadow of the laurels, waiting for Slater to reappear.

Minutes ticked by, and Toby's stomach rumbled enthusiastically as he recalled the smell of baking bread. With rationing still persisting, and with no knowledge of how to make his own bread, Toby thought he had become accustomed to eating the National Loaf, a gray, mushy abomination that was the only thing available through his ration book. Now the smell of real bread awakened old memories.

While he waited for Slater, he filled his mind with thoughts of all the foods he had known as a child; bananas, lemons, butter, sweets. He was mulling over his preference between gobstoppers and licorice allsorts when Slater exited the house.

Toby met him at the gate. "Do you need a lift back to Brighton?"

Slater shook his head. "I drove myself here."

"Oh."

"What does that mean?" Slater asked. "You think I can't drive a car with just one arm?"

"No, of course not."

"It's specially adapted."

"I just wanted to talk to you," Toby said, anxious to move on from any discussion of Slater's missing limb. "I wondered what you thought."

Slater shrugged his shoulders. "His mother showed me his papers. He appears to be who he says he is."

And you know more about him than you're telling me, Toby thought.

"What were you doing here?" Slater asked.

"A young woman came to my office and asked me to pursue a claim for child support from him."

Slater raised his eyebrows. "Well, that's a coincidence."

Toby shook his head. "No, not really. She came because she saw his picture in the paper, rescuing the woman from the burning car. Apparently, my client catches a bus every day from the stop outside our office, so when she needed a solicitor, she thought of us."

"Not your normal line of work," Slater sniffed.

Toby ignored the jibe. "She discovered his name from the newspaper article, and she asked us to take the case. Quite a coincidence that he should look so much like the man Miss Clark remembers. Miss Clark is rarely wrong."

"Well, she's wrong this time," Slater said. "The man you saw in there is most definitely Michael Cheviot. According to the papers his mother showed me, he was demobbed in 1946; no mention of shell shock, although she swears he's still suffering. We have no postwar record of him doing anything, not even an employment record. First time he left any kind of trace was when he pulled the woman out of the burning car and got his fingers burned."

"And the body on the beach had no hands," Toby said.

"I don't need you to tell me that," Slater growled. "I can work that out for myself."

"So what do you think?" Toby asked.

Slater frowned. "You don't need to know what I think. I don't want you mixing yourself up in this."

"What? Why not? Dorothy Findlay is my client."

"Well, so far as your case is concerned, it sounds like it's her word against his. You won't have much luck with that."

"I'm bringing him to court," Toby insisted.

Slater turned away. "You do what you have to do for your client, but stay out of police business."

"I don't see how I can. Miss Clark identified the body, and I'm not satisfied that he is who he says he is."

"It's not up to you to be satisfied. Just accept the fact that Miss Clark was mistaken, and leave this alone. This is police business."

"There's someone else in the house," Toby said. "Michael's mother didn't want to talk about it."

"No law against having visitors," Slater grunted. He opened the door of a big black Wolseley and slid inside. The engine purred into life and the car jerked forward. Slater leaned out of the window.

"Leave this alone, Whitby, and don't come here again. Do you understand?"

Toby watched the car, noting Slater's erratic driving, until it had turned the corner at the end of the road. He looked back at the gloomy house with its shroud of laurels and listened to the muted sounds of the piano. He would be back; he knew it.

CHAPTER FIVE

Anthea Clark

Anthea stayed late at the office. Toby's description of his visit to Michael Cheviot was deeply unsettling. He described Cheviot as a sullen, moody man relying on his mother to protect him from the world. She could not, would not, equate that description with the dashing Lieutenant Cheviot who had risked his life to save her from Godfrey's scavenged incendiary.

She could not deny that the man pictured in the newspaper bore a startling resemblance to the Lieutenant Cheviot she had met in Canterbury, but so did the poor dead man in the mortuary.

Toby left at six o'clock, muttering something about finding a real loaf of bread.

"Black market?" she asked.

"If necessary," he replied.

Anthea could not approve of the black market, but she, too, had moments of yearning for prewar food. She lowered her voice to a whisper.

"White van parked behind the fish shop in The Lanes; he's the one with the bread, and there's a Belgian man in a black car who brings in stuff from the Continent. He has sausages. Good ones."

"Should I say you sent me? Would they know you by name?"

Anthea nodded reluctantly. "Yes, they both know my name. Sometimes I pick up little treats for Mr. Champion. He doesn't have much appetite, and Mrs. Ellerby, his housekeeper, doesn't take good care of him. I worry about him." She paused. "I worry about all of us if we don't get better food. You'd think we were the ones who lost the war, not the Germans. It was never this bad after the First World War."

Toby nodded. "Thanks."

She watched him leave, and then she seated herself so that she could see the bus stop from her window, and waited. The days were lengthening into the long twilight evenings of summer, and it was not yet dark when Dorothy Findlay stepped down from the bus. Anthea picked up her handbag and hurried out of the office, pausing only to lock the door behind her.

She followed Dorothy up the hill and away from the seafront until they reached a row of shabby terraced houses with tiny neglected front gardens. Dorothy turned into a gate in the center of the terrace. She pulled a key from her purse and looked upward. A light came on in an upstairs window. Anthea assumed that Dorothy and her son lived upstairs, perhaps in only one or two rooms, perhaps with a shared bathroom. Not surprising, of course, with so many houses destroyed in the war. It was, Anthea thought, only by the grace of God that she herself had inherited a house and that house was still intact; full of memories but still standing.

"Dorothy!"

Dorothy turned her head anxiously.

"It's just me, Anthea Clark, from the solicitor's office."

Dorothy's face was alight with hope. "Already? I didn't think it would be so soon."

"Oh no, not yet."

Anthea stood next to Dorothy in the tiny front garden. "I wondered if I could talk to you."

Dorothy looked upward at the lit window. "What about?"

"Michael Cheviot."

"Why?"

"To be honest, I'm worried. I don't think the man in the newspaper is the same Michael Cheviot."

Dorothy shook her head. "How many Michael Cheviots are there?"

"Well, that's the question, isn't it? Where did you meet your Michael Cheviot?"

June 1942
Tunbridge Wells, Kent
Dorothy Findlay

The tablecloth was stained, and Dorothy wondered why anyone would *bother with using a cloth when soap and detergent were in short supply. She supposed that someone in the Ministry of Food had issued an edict. All nonessentials were rapidly disappearing from daily life, so the presence of a tablecloth, even a stained one, in an official British Restaurant must have been intended to raise spirits and convey that things were not as bad as they seemed.*

She sat at the small table, smiled at the woman in the green Women's

Volunteer Service uniform, and handed over her ration book.

"I'll have the daily special," she said.

The elderly woman grimaced. "Not much special about it, love; a pinch of meat, could be horse for all I know, and mashed turnips, but we have runner beans, so that's a treat."

"That'll be fine," Dorothy said.

The woman examined Dorothy's ration book. "So, you're working here?"

"Learning to be a welder," Dorothy said, and held out her scarred hands as evidence. "I hope I get the knack of it before I burn my fingers off."

The volunteer laid a gentle hand on Dorothy's shoulder. "God bless you, my dear. We need you if we're going to win this one."

Dorothy looked down at the stained tablecloth, not wishing to continue the conversation that would inevitably lead to a whispered discussion of what would happen if they didn't win. What would Hitler do? What would life be like under Nazi rule? And always, subtly but inevitably, the suggestion that perhaps Britain should just surrender before it was utterly destroyed.

Dorothy gripped her damaged hands together. If welding would bring victory, then she would weld.

The volunteer waitress bustled away, and Dorothy saw her stop in the doorway, where a slim, dark-haired man in civvies had just entered. She saw him hand over his paperwork, saw the woman nod her approval, and saw her point to where Dorothy was seated.

Dorothy squirmed in her seat. She knew she would have to share a table; the restaurant was crowded and privacy was not to be expected, but she had a suspicion that the WVS woman was trying to do her a favor. Here she was, a young girl, away from home in a strange place, and there he was, a soldier on leave.

Dorothy kept her eyes down as the man took a seat.

"Hello."

She nodded, hoping he would see that she was not interested. She already had a boyfriend, or so she thought. Of course, he could be dead for all she knew; no letters, nothing. She heard that POWs were allowed to write home, but she'd asked his mother and there had been no letter, so who could say where Danny was? She could only hope that he was a prisoner and not another casualty of war. She'd written to his mother before she'd left London, just to let her know that she was out in Kent, learning to work in a factory, and hoping that Danny would come and find her if he ever returned home.

She wanted to think about Danny and not about the man who was now seated opposite her. The man quietly rearranged his knife and fork.

36

"What's your name?"

It couldn't hurt to tell him her name. "Dorothy."

"And where are you from, Dorothy?"

"London."

"You've had a hard time of it, haven't you?" he said. "I expect you're glad to be out of it for a while. What are you doing down here?"

She displayed her hands. "I'm learning to weld."

He reached out. Her hands were so burned and so calloused she could hardly feel the touch of his fingers. She could see him, but she couldn't feel him. She thought it was better this way; as though she was not allowing a complete stranger to hold her hand and stroke her palm with a long, thin finger.

The food arrived; two plates of unappetizing food presented with an apology.

She asked his name.

"I'm Michael."

"Hello, Michael."

"I have a car and some petrol."

She could feel her heart pounding as the blood rushed to her cheeks. What was he offering?

"Will you be going back to your regiment?" she asked.

"Very soon. Hitler's pushing hard and our training has been accelerated. We can't wait any longer."

"No, of course not."

She pushed her plate to one side. His lean, dark face was filled with a mixture of fear and excitement. She wanted to drive the fear away; she wanted to share in the excitement. His name was Michael. She did not need to know anything else.

May 1952
Anthea Clark

Anthea found it hard to hide her disapproval. Dorothy hardly knew the man. Was this the same Michael that Anthea had met in Canterbury, the polite and careful Michael who had apologized for not saluting? Toby's description of the Michael he had met, a sullen, fierce-tempered pianist, did not match the Michael of her memory, but neither did this one. How many Michael Cheviots were there?

She looked at Dorothy's face, flushed with the memory of sudden passion. The brief liaison had resulted in the birth of a child, and Dorothy was not ashamed, not even regretful. Anthea wondered what that moment had been like. How had Dorothy known that this was something she must do? What primal urge had led her to leave the restaurant with a complete stranger, knowing that the next stop would be a bed in an anonymous hotel?

Well, Anthea thought, her Michael Cheviot—she was becoming very protective of her version of the man—had not looked at her that way. He had been nothing but respectful. She glanced at Dorothy, seeing that she was still a young woman, still slim and upright, with hair that had escaped from its pins and was a curling golden halo around her head.

Anthea chided herself for being a fool. Of course Michael Cheviot, or whoever he was, had not been interested in any kind of relationship with Anthea. He had looked at her and seen her for what she was, a woman on the wrong side of middle age, tall, angular, and possessing all the inhibitions that could possibly result from a childhood spent among clerics and bishops. She sighed, set judgement and regrets aside, and smiled at Dorothy.

"So you never heard from him again?"

Dorothy shook her head. "Like I told you, I didn't know how to reach him." She shrugged her shoulders. "I didn't even know his last name; I only knew his regiment, the Buffs. Sometimes we heard things, you know. We heard they were in North Africa, and then they were in Italy, but some of them were in the Far East ..." She sighed. "I didn't know. I just assumed he was dead, because if he wasn't dead, he would have come looking for me after the war."

Her face darkened as she looked at Anthea. "I almost wish I hadn't found out who he was. I was better off thinking that he was dead."

Anthea thought of the body in the mortuary and the face that had struck such a chord in her memory. Perhaps the Michael Cheviot who had swept Dorothy off her feet was not the one who was now refusing to see her; perhaps her Michael was dead.

CHAPTER SIX

Toby Whitby

The sun was well above the horizon, and the deckchairs along the promenade were already fully occupied by the time Toby arrived at the office the next day.

When he opened the heavy front door, his mind was not on the mystery of the man in the mortuary, or even on his client's run-in with the police the day before, his mind was still on Carol. He had slept poorly and risen early, determined to speak to his fiancée on the phone and insist that she give him her answer. She had already accepted his proposal. She said she loved him and couldn't imagine life without him, but still she was not willing to set a date for the wedding. The problem was the job he had been offered in Rhodesia. He couldn't understand her reluctance to leave Britain.

"We could make a new start," Toby had told her. "No one would need to know anything about your past."

"I don't have a past," Carol hissed, and Toby knew that he had said the wrong thing.

It didn't matter to him that Carol did, in fact, have a past; one that was widely known in the village of Rose Hill, where she had been the post mistress. Every gossip in the village knew that Carol had conducted an affair with a German prisoner of war and given birth to his child. Although Vera Chapman had claimed the child as her own and taken her to America, the truth had been revealed. The child had been returned, and Carol and her daughter had left the village to escape the gossip.

Toby only wanted to save Carol from any additional embarrassment and take her to a place where no one would know anything about the identity of Anita's father. She could say that she was a war widow, Toby could be Anita's stepfather, and they would live happily ever after.

"I'll come up to Wales," Toby said. "We'll marry by special license, and we can be gone from Britain in no time. They won't hold the job open forever. I have to start making arrangements."

Their telephone conversation had ended without Carol giving him an answer. She would think about it. That was all she would say. He drove to the office in a state of anxious frustration. What if she said no? Would that be the end of the engagement? Was he willing to go without her?

By the time he had arrived at the office, he was so lost in his own thoughts that he failed to notice how the atmosphere in the office had changed.

He had been at his desk in his cramped little office for several minutes before he realized that he could hear voices coming from the closed door of Mr. Champion's office. He looked at the hatstand and saw Mr. Champion's black homburg. He looked at his watch. Late again. He stood up, straightened his tie, and knocked on his employer's office door.

"Come."

Edwin Champion, the founder of Champion and Company, was a shrunken figure in the formal clothing of another era; a high starched collar and a gray bow tie. He was smiling. The smile seemed to be genuine, but it was not intended for Toby. The chair in front of the desk was occupied by a small boy in a school blazer and short gray pants. Mr. Champion was leaning across the desk, offering the child black market mint humbugs from a paper bag. Miss Clark stood to one side, wearing an uncertain smile that betrayed her unfamiliarity with children.

"Ah," said Mr. Champion, "there you are at last."

"I'm sorry, sir, I didn't know—"

"Of course not. We did try to reach you on the telephone, but your line was engaged."

"Yes, I was talking to—"

"No matter. You're here now, and you can take care of business. We will speak later about your failure to be on time, and the carelessness of your dress. Meantime, this young man's mother has been arrested, and he would like you to have her released."

The boy looked up at him. His face was distorted by the quantity of humbugs he had crammed into his mouth and cheeks, but Toby saw his parentage immediately. The mop of dark hair that had certainly not seen a brush or comb that morning came from his father, but the wide blue eyes were a gift from his mother.

"Eric," Toby asked, "what happened to your mother?"

Anthea supplied the answer. "Inspector Slater has her in custody."

Eric appeared to be using his tongue to rearrange the candy in his mouth. "She said she wouldn't be long," he mumbled.

Anthea eyed her boss and then looked back at Toby. "Before Mr. Champion so kindly gave him a quantity of mint humbugs and rendered him speechless, I was able to ascertain that his mother found a piece of paper that she had been looking for and left home immediately."

Toby looked at Eric. "Do you know where she was going?"

Eric swallowed so hastily that his attempt to answer Toby's question resulted in a fit of coughing so severe that his face turned blue. Toby slapped him on the back. A humbug flew out of his mouth and landed on Mr. Champion's desk, where it stuck to the pristine green blotter.

Eric drew in a deep breath. "She said that she was going to see my father and she was going to make him pay for us to have a nice place to live. She said he'd been getting away with not paying for too bloody long."

"Language," Anthea hissed.

"That's what she said. I was only saying what she said. She was really angry. She went out in the dark and left me. I was on my own all night, and not even a sixpence for the electric meter."

He shot out a quick hand and retrieved the humbug from the blotter. Undaunted by the mass of green fibers now clinging to its surface, he popped the sweet into his mouth.

Toby looked at Anthea.

"Miss Findlay phoned us from the police station," she said, "and asked for legal representation, and then she asked me to go and get Eric because he all alone. When I arrived, he was still in bed. I had quite a time persuading him to answer the doorbell, but we're here now and he's ready for school."

Mr. Champion cast an eye over the boy's appearance. "Comb your hair, boy," he wheezed. "Show some pride in your appearance." He waved a thin hand in Anthea's direction. "Miss Clark will walk to school with you."

"I'm ten," Eric protested. "I'm not a baby. I can walk to school on my own."

Mr. Champion winked, and Toby saw a hint of mischief behind the old man's gruff exterior. "Nonetheless, Miss Clark will walk with you just to make certain that you go in."

Eric made another attempt at protesting, but Mr. Champion stood his ground. "She'll go with you, boy, and that's the end of it. Off you go."

Anthea opened the door, and Eric left the office with Anthea trailing behind him, promising to find him a comb.

Mr. Champion watched them leave. "The world is full of temptations for small boys, and Miss Clark will make sure he resists them," he said. "You'd better go and get his mother out of the clutches of Inspector Slater, or one of us will be taking that boy home tonight. He can't stay another night on his own."

Faced with the probability that he would be the one who would be taking the boy home, Toby hurried to the police station. The sun, shining with true spring warmth, had tempted people from their homes, and the streets were crowded. As he passed the pier, he saw a thicket of fishing rods sprouting from either side. Once upon a time, fishing had been a hobby for old, retired men, but not now, he thought. Now, with meat rationing still in place, fishing was essential. He silently wished the fishermen good luck.

Dorothy Findlay was not in a jail cell. He found her in Percy Slater's cramped office, where she was drinking tea from a thick white cup. She wore the same faded floral dress that she had worn for her visit to Champion and Company, but now it was looking distinctly the worse for wear. The hem drooped, one of the sleeves was torn, and a button was missing from the bodice.

The absence of the button gave Toby an opportunity to admire Dorothy's surprisingly generous cleavage. With her bodice unbuttoned and her hair falling in waves to her shoulders, Dorothy seemed like a different person. Toby thought back to his previous assessment of her. One loose curl had caused him to wonder about her, and now he no longer needed to wonder. Dorothy Findlay was a passionate woman who had been holding her passion in check for the sake of her son. Now it seemed that Dorothy had thrown caution to the winds and revealed her true personality, and even Percy Slater had taken notice.

The detective sat at his desk, writing clumsily with his left hand. His face was flushed, and he seemed determined not to look directly at Dorothy.

Dorothy sprang to her feet as Toby approached. "Where's Eric. Is he all right? No one will tell me anything."

"He's fine," Toby said. "Miss Clark is taking him to school. Don't worry about a thing. Just tell me what's happened. Why have you been arrested?"

Slater set down the pen. "I haven't arrested her; not yet. I escorted her off the premises for her own safety."

Dorothy darted him a look of gratitude. "I think that gardener would have broken my arm."

"He's not a gardener."

Slater's voice was only a whisper, but Toby heard him and thought of Enid Trewin's threat to fetch someone named Billy, who would remove him from the premises. He remembered Slater's gasp of surprise when Undercover Frankie told him that the Cheviots had brought in Cousin Billy. The state of the garden at The Laurels attested to the fact that Billy was not a gardener.

"And there was another man standing in the background," Dorothy said. "He looked kind of familiar. I've seen him before, I know I have. I just don't remember where."

Slater raised his eyebrows as he continued. "I saw no signs of another man."

Yes, you did, Toby thought. You heard the cook asking if the man upstairs wanted his lunch. There is another man in that house.

Slater gave Toby no opportunity to voice his thoughts as he continued with ponderous deliberation. "Miss Findlay did not at first wish to be removed from danger, and I was forced to handcuff her." He looked at Dorothy with grudging admiration. "It wasn't easy."

She smiled at him. "You did well for a one-handed bloke."

Slater looked away, and Toby saw the color rise in Dorothy's cheeks. She thought she had given the detective a compliment, but Slater couldn't see it that way. Toby set Slater's personal problems aside. The man was as prickly as a hawthorn hedge, and nothing good ever came of tangling with a hawthorn hedge; better to stick to the business at hand.

"Why you?" Toby asked. "Why not the locals?"

"Mrs. Cheviot rang the local police station in the small hours of the morning to complain that a woman, known to them as Dorothy Findlay, was loitering on the premises. The locals called me because they know we have an ongoing investigation."

Toby took note of Slater's words; an ongoing investigation. What was being investigated? Dorothy? Enid? The mysterious visitor at The Laurels? He tucked the question away for later consideration and looked at Dorothy.

"Why?"

"Because I found a receipt," Dorothy waved a hand at Slater's desk. "Show it to him, Inspector. He's my lawyer." She looked up at Toby. "I can prove it was him."

Slater took a paper from his desk and handed it to Toby. "It proves nothing."

Toby took the folded sheet of paper. It was a receipt from the Cavendish Hotel in Canterbury for room and breakfast for Lieutenant and Mrs. Michael Leonard, June 10, 1942.

Toby looked up and saw Dorothy's fixed gaze. "I wanted Michael's mother to see it. I wanted her to know that I'm not lying."

Slater shook his head. "It proves nothing. It doesn't even have Mr. Cheviot's name on it."

Toby tucked the paper into his pocket and suppressed his own doubts. "I'll take care of this. It may come in useful."

Slater shrugged. "It's up to you. Miss Findlay is not under arrest, so you can keep the receipt. Mrs. Cheviot wants to press charges, but I'm willing to give your client one more chance. I can see that she believes what she's telling us, and perhaps there's some truth in it, or perhaps it's mistaken identity, but she can't take the law into her own hands."

He gave Dorothy a stern look. "Don't do it again, Miss Findlay, or I will be forced to arrest you. If you are patient, you'll have your day in court. I suggest you go home and let your lawyer handle this case. Now, if you will wait outside, I need to speak to Mr. Whitby alone."

Dorothy frowned. "Why?"

Toby was reaching the end of his patience with his barely controlled client. "Just go, please."

"But you'll tell me what he says?" Dorothy insisted.

"If it's relevant."

He waited until his client had traipsed reluctantly out of the office. "Well?"

"I'm concerned for your client's safety," Slater said. "She appears to be very headstrong. She'll get her day in court, but until then I am holding you responsible for keeping her away from Michael Cheviot."

"Now wait a minute," Toby protested. "I'm her lawyer, not her keeper. The safety of the public is your job, not mine."

"I'm doing my best," Slater said. "If you can't control her, I'll have to arrest her."

"For what?" Toby asked.

"I'll think of something," Slater said between gritted teeth.

Toby sat down in the chair that Dorothy had vacated. "Why are you so interested in my client?" he asked.

Slater's answer came in the form of a question. "Does she know anything about the dead man we found on the beach?"

Toby considered the question. "No, I don't think so. Why would she …?"

He stopped speaking and sat in silence, watching the play of emotions across Slater's face.

"Given his resemblance to Michael Cheviot," Slater said reluctantly, "I have to wonder if the dead man is, in fact, your client's long-lost lover."

"Well," Toby said, "perhaps you should ask my client to take a look at the body."

Slater shook his head. "No. He's deteriorating rapidly. I don't want to put her through that. She shouldn't have to remember him that way." He paused, his expression softening. "Sometimes memory is all we have."

Toby smiled to himself. Apparently, Dorothy had made quite an impression on Slater. Perhaps it was the missing dress button, or the rough and tumble of making an arrest, but Slater was definitely warming toward Dorothy.

Slater reddened as though he knew Toby had detected his weakness. "Bring her in," he said abruptly. "At least she can tell me if her man had any distinguishing marks; tattoos, scars, something like that."

Toby nodded. "Seems like a good idea." He paused for a moment, giving Slater time to realize that Toby was not about to leave.

"What do you want?"

"I'm sharing information with you, so perhaps you could share some with me."

"What do you suggest?"

"Well," Toby said, "you want to hold me responsible for my client's safety, but you've failed to inform me that Michael Cheviot is the son of a notorious crime boss."

"His father's dead, and he has nothing to do with the family," Slater snapped.

"So we're not going to talk about the East End woman working in the kitchen, or the threat to bring in a man named Billy? I saw how you reacted to that," Toby said. "Given their reputation, I'm surprised they called you instead of killing Dorothy Findlay and throwing her body into the ocean."

The door opened before Slater could formulate a reply, although Toby could see that his challenge had stunned the detective.

"I need to get home," Dorothy announced. Her eyes went straight to Slater. Toby thought that perhaps the attraction was mutual.

Slater cleared his throat and took some time to phrase his question. "Miss Findlay, you say you were … intimate … with someone who called himself Michael Cheviot."

"Yes, that's what I say and it's the truth."

Slater cleared his throat again. "In that … time … did you notice any marks, distinguishing marks, on his … body?"

"You want me to prove I was with him?" Dorothy asked. "Do you want me to describe his—"

"No, that won't be necessary; other distinguishing marks."

"Like what?"

"A tattoo or a scar or …"

Dorothy shook her head. "You don't understand. It was just the once and it was quick." She paused. "I didn't think it would be so quick," she said softly.

Toby drew in a sharp breath. Had Dorothy been a virgin? Had this been her first encounter and maybe her last? He felt an instinctive dislike of the man who had done this to her so quickly and carelessly in an anonymous hotel, under a false identity.

Slater rubbed his chin thoughtfully. "Think back, Miss Findlay. Anything?"

Dorothy was silent, and Toby wondered what she was remembering. She shook her head. "Only his hands. He had lovely hands, long and thin."

Hands, Toby thought. It all came down to hands, and the corpse had no hands.

Detective Inspector Percy Slater

The body had been kept in cold storage, but decay was still inevitable. Slater knew that he would not have many more opportunities to examine the dead man.

It all came down to the hands. Whoever had removed them had done so with precision and determination; a clean cut at the wrists.

Colin Patel, the mortuary attendant, had an eager expression on his face as he drew back the sheet that shrouded the body.

Slater sniffed the air. "Doesn't this bother you?" he asked.

Patel shook his head. "I was a medic with the First Punjab Regiment. I saw worse than this." He smiled at Slater, a bright, eager enthusiasm revealing itself in the midst of the decay. "What we have here is definitely postmortem. The hands were removed after death."

"You can tell?"

"Oh yes. See the slight crumbling at the edge of the bone; if our victim had been alive, the bone would be green, wouldn't crumble like that. No, this poor man was killed, kept for a while, and then subjected to these postmortem injuries."

Slater looked at the eager expression on Patel's face. "I've never heard details like this before."

Patel nodded. "We're learning from anthropologists; they've known this for years, but it's a new idea for people like us. If you take the time, the dead will talk to you."

Slater looked down at the body. "So what else is he saying?"

"His clothes did some talking."

"Oh yes? What did they say?"

"Labels didn't tell me anything. It was all utility, on ration, but I found fibers caught in the buttons on his cuffs. Sacking. I would say he'd been placed in a weighted sack. He was never meant to surface."

"So finding him is just our good luck," Slater said bitterly. "I'm assuming the sacking got caught on all that old metal on the seafloor and ripped away."

"And up he comes," said Patel cheerfully.

"And up he comes," Slater repeated, thinking how much easier it would have been for everyone concerned if the body had remained in its weighted sack a little longer. Just a few more days, and the face would have been obliterated beyond recognition, and no one would have expected an identification.

Patel moved around the table and picked up the left foot, ragged with cuts and tears. He examined it with enthusiasm. "Obviously, these cuts and tears are also postmortem. I imagine he was dragged along the seabed."

Slater waited.

The student retained his hold on the foot. "Look at the architecture of this foot."

Slater looked at the cold gray flesh. "I don't see."

"Not the flesh, the bones."

Patel turned the foot to an angle it would never have achieved in life. "Fallen arches."

"What?"

"Flat feet; both of them."

"How did that happen?"

"Most likely a birth defect. It wouldn't have stopped him from walking, but I doubt he did much marching."

"What do you mean?"

"He looks to be about the right age for conscription in the war, but he would have been rejected. Even at the height of the war, the military wouldn't accept conscripts with flat feet."

He dropped the foot onto the slab and wiped his hands on a towel. "Whatever else this man was, he wasn't a soldier."

Slater stared at the body, wishing it would talk to him as clearly as it talked to Patel. So, the victim wasn't a soldier, but the man Anthea Clark had met in Canterbury had been a lieutenant in the Buffs. The man who had fathered Dorothy Findlay's child had been a soldier on leave, or so he said, and Michael Cheviot had been an officer in the Royal East Kent.

Slater rubbed his hand across the stubble on his chin, recognizing that he had been up almost all night and he needed to go home and shave. He focused on the place where the hands should have been, and he felt his own phantom hand clench and unclench. The arm had been gone for almost seven years, but his brain would not release the memory of a hand that could hold a gun or a pen, an arm that could fill out a jacket, a man who was whole; a man who could hold his own in a fight.

Dorothy Findlay; that had been quite a tussle. She hadn't wanted to be handcuffed, but neither had she wanted to quieten down and leave Michael Cheviot alone. He was still unsure of quite how he had managed to get the cuffs on her. He wondered if, in the end, she had simply allowed it to happen. He had forgotten what it was like to have a woman in his arms, and she had stirred his memory. It was different, of course, because she was someone he was trying to arrest, and because he only had one arm, but his one remaining hand had touched her warm flesh, and he had breathed in the scent of her hair. It had been … unsettling.

He dragged his mind back to reality. He had to assume that the victim's hands had been removed to prevent fingerprinting in the unplanned-for event of the body rising to the surface.

Unlike the rest of his family, Michael Cheviot had never been involved in a crime, and his fingerprints were not on file, but they would be in the regimental records. Retrieving them for comparison would take time, but he could start the process immediately. Anything was better than his current inaction. There was nothing to stop him from driving out to The Laurels and fingerprinting Enid Cheviot's piano-playing son. He thought of the picture of the local hero, sitting up in bed with his hands bandaged. The bandages were off now, but what would be left of the fingerprints? Would his journey be another waste of time?

CHAPTER SEVEN

Bodmin Moor, Cornwall
Colonel Hugh Trewin

Hugh Trewin strode into the public bar of the Bird in Hand with his springer spaniel at his heels. He was greeted with a chorus of grunts and mumbled salutations from the tweed-coated locals seated by the open windows. One or two of them instinctively raised their hands to tug at gray or nonexistent forelocks before returning to their conversation.

"Colonel!" The voice came from a man seated in the snug, where the shadows of the ancient chimneypiece obscured his face.

Hugh stared for a moment and then took his cue from his dog. Daisy was an old dog; as old in dog years as Hugh was in human years, but she still had her sense of smell and enough memory to recognize an old friend who was likely to slip her a piece of sausage or a crust of bread.

Hugh allowed his eyes time to adjust from the bright twilight that bathed the moor outside to the dim, smoky interior of the pub. He ducked his head and followed Daisy's wagging tail into the snug, where he found Robert Penhelen QC with a pint of cider and a meat pie.

Hugh was surprised that the old barrister greeted him with a worried frown instead of his usual smile; the smile of a man born with a silver spoon in his mouth, who had never worried about money or status.

Daisy pushed her nose against the distinguished gentleman's hand, and Penhelen abstractedly broke off a corner of pie and dropped it onto the floor. While Daisy busied herself finding every last crumb that could possibly be lodged in the cracks of the old flagstones, Hugh signaled to the barman and gave his order.

"I'll have a pint of Bodmin Special."

"You might want something stronger," Penhelen said.

Hugh's attention, which had been concentrated on lowering his old bones onto the settee, snapped into immediate focus.

"Stronger?"

Penhelen raised his voice. The Cornish tones of his early childhood had been obliterated by higher education and years in the law courts of London. Now he spoke to the barman with the unthinking authority of an aristocrat.

"Bring the Colonel a brandy."

Brandy, is it? Hugh thought. What bad news could he have for me? He considered the options. His wife had been dead these many years, her own life taken in grief over the son they would never see again. Perhaps Enid had disgraced herself, or more likely Michael had done something to bring shame on them all. He shook his head. He had lived through two World Wars, fought in the first one, offered to fight in the second one, and now he was at peace.

He sat down carefully. Daisy gave up her hunt for crumbs and rested her head on his knee. It was some years since either of them had been able to bring down a bird or a rabbit, but she was the only one who now held his heart. Whatever Penhelen had to say, it could not be anything that would require the stimulus of brandy.

Penhelen was apparently biding his time and waiting for Tom, the barman, to go into the saloon bar and fetch the brandy; not much call for brandy in the public bar.

Hugh spoke his thoughts aloud as he smoothed Daisy's head. "They wanted me to shoot her, you know."

"What? Shoot who?"

"Daisy."

Penhelen cocked his head to one side. "Your dog! Who wants you to shoot your dog?"

Hugh shook his head. "Not now. In the war. Rationing, you know. Said there was no food for dogs and I should shoot her."

"Obviously, you didn't."

"Of course not. Bloody uncivilized! I told them, if we become a country where a man can be made to shoot his dog, Hitler will be welcome to take us and I won't lift a finger to stop him."

He patted the dog's head again. "I kept her and she kept me. Rabbit on the table every night. Old Daisy made sure we didn't go through what some of you London folks went through."

Tom reappeared and set a glass of brandy down in front of Hugh. Penhelen nodded and waved the barman away.

Hugh crooked his fingers around the glass and looked down at his arthritic knuckles. Old bones, he thought; been around too long. He was ready to go, but not until Daisy went first.

He took a sip of the brandy and felt it work its warm path down his throat. There had been brandy in a chateau in Picardy, and a girl ... Roses are blooming in Picardy ...

"Colonel."

"All right. Fire away. What is it?"

Penhelen reached into the pocket of his jacket and produced a folded paper.

Hugh frowned and fumbled in his pocket for his spectacles. He settled them on his nose and reached for the paper. He took another sip of brandy, wondering if it would really be necessary, and unfolded the paper.

He stared down, seeing the vague outlines of a face. "I can't see what the hell this is," he said impatiently. "Do you have a light, Penhelen?"

"Yes."

Penhelen's voice was tentative. What on earth was the matter with the man?

"You'll have to light the lamp," Hugh said. "I can't see a thing."

He stared at the picture while Penhelen pulled the oil lamp to the center of the table and adjusted the wick. At last Hugh heard the scrape of a match, and an orange glow flooded the interior of the snug.

He stared down at the face. Dead; a dead face. He squinted to bring the picture into focus. There was something familiar about the features. He ran his hand across the regimental moustache that was still his pride. "What is this? Why are you showing it to me?"

"It's a body that was washed up off the Sussex coast. The Brighton police have sent a notice to lawyers and police stations and council offices, trying to identify the fellow. No hands, you see."

"No hands, really?"

"Cut off, clean as a whistle."

"Someone doesn't want him identified."

"That's what I think. No hands, no fingerprints."

Hugh sat back. "But why are you showing it to me? You're the lawyer; you're the one who has consorted with the criminal classes. You are far more likely to know the kind of chap who gets his hands cut off and his body thrown into the ocean."

"Well ..." Penhelen hesitated again.

"What?"

"I thought he looked a lot like your grandson, Michael."

Hugh stared at the picture. Penhelen was right, of course. The dead man bore a striking resemblance to Michael and even a passing resemblance to Enid, Michael's mother. He still cursed Ronnie Cheviot's memory and still blamed him for leading Enid astray. He could only thank God, and he did so frequently, that Ronnie had died before he could drag Enid and her son into his own life of crime.

Hugh took off his glasses and tucked them back in his pocket. "I see what you mean, but it's not Michael. The way Enid hangs over that boy, I would know by now if he had a cold, or a broken finger. I'd certainly know if he was missing."

He returned the paper to Penhelen. "I don't know who this is."

Penhelen's smile lit up his face. "Well, I'm glad to hear it. I didn't want to think of anything happening to Enid's boy, not after the way he distinguished himself in Italy."

Hugh nodded. "Mentioned in dispatches more than once. I had hopes of a medal for him, but I don't know enough people these days; couldn't pull the right strings."

Of course, Penhelen could have pulled strings, but he had not offered, and Hugh would not ask. It was because he would not ask his wealthy friend for favors that Hugh had been able to maintain their friendship since boyhood. Penhelen knew everyone; Hugh knew almost no one, and that was how he liked it.

"So, what is Michael doing now?" Penhelen asked. "If he needs any help, you know, finding his way in the world, I have contacts. Might be a good idea to find him something overseas, keep him out of London and away from the Cheviot clan."

Hugh shook his head. He would not accept favors from Penhelen, and more importantly, he couldn't imagine Michael doing anything meaningful in the colonial service, or anywhere else.

He could not explain Michael's behavior since he'd returned from the war. He thought they would be able to talk together as old soldiers, but he had scarcely seen the boy. At first Michael had hidden himself away in one of the tenant cottages, and then he'd taken himself off to Hove, where his mother had purchased a house. Hugh had looked forward to sharing war stories, but Michael had nothing to say. He had campaigned in Africa and Italy, was mentioned twice in dispatches, but he wouldn't speak of it.

"I understand there was some … shell shock," Penhelen said.

The two old warriors looked at each other across the light of the oil lamp.

"Shell shock," Hugh repeated. "That's what they call it now. We called it cowardice."

"But nonetheless," Penhelen blustered, "he was mentioned in dispatches. He did a fine job, and it's over now, isn't it? I'm sure he's right as rain."

Hugh sipped his brandy and remembered.

September 1941
Hawks Nest Lodge
Bodmin Moor, Cornwall

Enid Cheviot sank down onto the floral sofa and pulled a handkerchief from somewhere within the flowing sleeves of her chiffon dress. She pressed the handkerchief to her lips and gazed up at her father imploringly.

"He can't go. He's not strong enough. I brought him here to keep him safe, and now they want to take him. I even wrote a letter to the Duke of Windsor, asking him to do something. He owes me."

Hugh poured a stiff brandy from his diminishing stock and drank it in one desperate gulp. He made no attempt to hide his disgust. "I don't suppose your letter even reached the Duke. He's been sent into exile, which is better than he deserves. The man's a disgrace, and I don't know why you think he would owe you any favors, Enid."

His daughter started to speak, but Hugh waved her into silence. "I don't want to hear it. Whatever it is you did in the past, I don't want to know about it."

He poured another brandy and thrust the glass into her hand. "Drink that and pull yourself together. There's no point in you carrying on like this. Your son is twenty-one; he's no longer a student, and he's passed the physical. There's nothing else to do. He has to go. It might do the boy some good."

Hugh could see that his daughter was affronted by his remark and the implication that her son was anything other than perfect, but he pressed on.

"England needs every man."

Enid flourished her handkerchief again. "Surely we can beat Hitler without Michael's help. What about the Americans? Won't they come?"

"No one knows," *Hugh said.* "Maybe they will, maybe they won't. They were late last time, and this time, they may not come at all. Right now we're on our own with our backs to the wall."

He turned away from his daughter and looked out of the drawing-room window at the vista of rolling moorland and clear blue sky. The serenity was short lived, as a flight of Spitfires split the horizon, heading for home at RAF St. Eval. He turned back to look at his daughter, draped in wan dismay across the sofa.

"Oh for goodness' sake, Enid, pull yourself together. There's a war on, and the Trewin family have always played their part. No reason for Michael to be any different."

"He's not a Trewin," *Enid hiccupped.* "He's a Cheviot."

Hugh tossed his head. "Do not mention that name to me. If I had my way,

I would have his name changed by deed poll. I will not allow him to be connected to that family."

Enid's pale cheeks flushed in defiance. "I loved Ronnie and I married him."

"Against my will. The Cheviots are a pack of thieves."

Enid sighed dramatically. "It doesn't matter now. Ronnie's dead and they've never asked to see Michael. All I have left is the name. It's my last memory of Ronnie."

"Sentimental nonsense," Hugh muttered. He saw that his daughter was about to sink into one of her dramatic declines. He lowered himself into an armchair and fixed her with a stern eye. "Pull yourself together, Enid. Michael is not the only one who is about to be called up. It will only be a matter of time before women are pressed into war work."

"What? No!"

"Just a matter of time," Hugh repeated. "It might be the best thing for you. It's not safe here."

Enid shook her head. "What do you mean? Of course it's safe. We're in the middle of the moor. No one's going to come here looking for us."

"You'd be surprised," Hugh said. "The Cornish coast is ripe for invasion. Those brave chaps in the Spitfires can't protect our entire coastline. Everyone is making plans for an invasion. I'm surprised you don't know about it."

"I've been too busy worrying about Michael."

"Too busy to notice that all the road signs have been removed?"   "Have they?"

"Yes, they have. When the Germans invade, we don't want them to know where they're going."

Enid roused herself from her cloud of self-pity long enough to give him the skeptical look she had inherited from her mother. "How is that going to help? Won't they have maps?"

Hugh rose to his feet. "I don't know, my dear. Maybe it's just a psychological benefit; keeps us thinking we're doing something. One thing I know, if Jerry comes knocking on my door, I'll have my gun ready."

He reached out his hand and rested it on the head of Daisy, his new gundog. He thought of how he would need to go out before long and bag something for dinner; rabbit, hare, grouse. The butcher in Bodmin had no meat, so it was up to him. He was impatient to be on his way.

"Where is Michael? What's he doing?"

"He's ..." Enid took a shuddering breath. "He's packing."

"Good. The taxi will be here at any minute. I must say that I don't understand why he didn't join my old regiment and fight with Cornishmen at his

side. *Royal East Kent! What does he know about Kentishmen?"*

"What does he know about fighting?" Enid wailed. *"I don't think he's ever fired a gun. He's never even punched anyone. He's delicate."*

Hugh tried to feel sympathy for his daughter. She had disgraced him in her youth, but she was his only remaining child, and he had always tried to do his best for her. She was more or less alone, her late husband having drowned shortly after Michael's birth; not that anyone had found the body. It had taken seven years and the skill of Robert Penhelen to have Ronald Cheviot declared dead and to locate at least one of his bank accounts.

A youthful and surprisingly cheerful voice interrupted his reverie. "Well, I'm off."

Hugh started in surprise as his grandson strode jauntily into the drawing room with a suitcase in one hand and a knapsack over his shoulder. His face, normally marred by an expression of petulant dissatisfaction, was set in a resolute grin. His dark hair was slicked back from his face, and his moustache was trimmed to narrow military proportions. He was not tall, but he was standing tall.

Hugh was at a loss to explain the change in the boy. From the moment his call-up papers had arrived, he had sulked and fretted and begged for a way out, but now he seemed more than ready to go.

"Oh, Michael." Enid rose and flung her arms around her son's neck.

Michael untangled himself. "Steady on, Mater. Nothing to worry about yet. Officer training for a few months, not much danger there. I'll let you know when to start worrying. Right now, I'm only going as far as Sandhurst. I expect the most dangerous thing I'll encounter is a sandwich on the train."

He patted the pocket of his blazer. "I have my travel warrant. First-class seat. There's something to be said for being an officer."

Hugh thought of his own war. Yes, some officers had found it easy, setting up their offices amid the elegance of a commandeered French chateau, but some officers had led their troops into hell and stayed in hell with them.

He knew what Enid wanted for Michael, a desk job somewhere safe, but he looked at the smile on Michael's face and wondered what the boy himself wanted.

Daisy barked. Hugh turned to the window and noted that a taxi had stopped on the roadway by the gate. He lifted his eyes and spotted another Spitfire trailing smoke and limping toward the airfield. He saw the taxi driver climb from his vehicle and shade his eyes as he stared up into the sky. The Spitfire emitted one last cloud of smoke and burst into flames. Hugh held his breath as the smoke cleared, and he saw a dark speck against the blue sky, a parachute opening like a flower. The pilot had escaped with his life. The taxi driver nodded his satisfaction and climbed back into his vehicle. Hugh thanked his own personal god, a fierce god of war, that the pilot had lived to fly another day.

Michael opened the front door. "Stay where you are, Mother. I don't want to see your crying face on the doorstep."

He offered his grandfather a jaunty salute and retrieved his suitcase and duffel bag. "Well, wish me luck. I'm off to win the war."

May 1952

Daisy had taken advantage of Hugh's moment of distraction and was giving the laborers in the window seat the benefit of her soulful brown eyes. Hugh allowed her a moment to eat a chunk of Cornish pasty and a couple of potato crisps before he called her back to his side.

"Are you off?" Penhelen asked.

Hugh nodded. "I'll go home and ring Enid."

"But I thought you said—"

"Oh, I'm not worried about Michael. I'm sure it's not his face on the poster. I just thought I should arrange to go up there. This business of being shell-shocked has gone on for far too long. I think he needs a few strong words from his grandfather."

Penhelen held up a delaying finger. "I just had a thought."

"Oh yes?"

"Yes. It's about your daughter's husband."

"I don't want to talk about him," Hugh said. "I never understood what Enid could see in him. I'm just glad that he's out of the picture and we've never heard another word from his wretched family."

"But the body was never found and—"

Hugh would not allow Penhelen to finish his thought. Penhelen was the one who had drawn up the paperwork to declare Ronald Cheviot dead; now what was he suggesting? He wanted to silence him, but he couldn't; not while the possibility was slowly taking shape.

"This body they've found," said Penhelen, "the one that looks so much like your Michael; I see that no one has put an age to the man. The body is probably in bad shape, might be quite difficult to tell without a postmortem ..."

"Are you suggesting that Ronnie's been alive all this time, that he didn't die until now?"

"Just something to think about," Penhelen said.

Hugh's pulse was racing and he was feeling dizzy. "You think it could be him?"

Penhelen shrugged. "I don't know, but we should at least ask."

"Is there a name on that paper? Is there someone we can ring to find out the man's age?"

Penhelen placed a finger on his lips. "Let's do this quietly and discreetly. I have a meeting to attend in London, and I was planning on taking the De Havilland. You can fly with me. We can kill two birds with one stone, and no one any the wiser."

Hugh dreaded the idea of taking to the skies with Penhelen at the controls. Just because Penhelen had a sudden impulse to learn how to fly, and enough money to buy his own airplane, that didn't mean that Hugh should risk his life by flying with him.

"I could take the train and meet you there," Hugh offered.

Penhelen clapped him on the back. "No need, old man. I'll be glad of the company. We'll leave tomorrow morning, and we'll have this settled in no time."

"I should probably call the Brighton police," Hugh said, "and make sure we can see the body."

"Leave it to me," Penhelen said. "I may be retired, but I still know people. I know a man in Brighton. He's a clever old chap. We served together in France and we stayed in touch. His name is Edwin Champion."

CHAPTER EIGHT

Dorothy Findlay

The dishwater had turned from warm and soothing to cold and greasy, and still Dorothy stood at the sink. She listened for sounds from Eric's bedroom, but he was, at long last, silent. For some months now, he had refused a bedtime story. He was ten and he didn't need to be read to like a baby. Tonight had been different, and she'd ploughed her way through three chapters of Biggles Learns to Fly before Eric had at last consented to close his eyes.

She should never have left him on his own and run off to The Laurels to confront the Cheviots. He'd been frightened by her absence, and who could blame him? She should have waited for morning and handed the receipt to her lawyer. What had she hoped to accomplish by going to The Laurels? Did she expect to see Michael face to face? Did she even want to see him?

She lifted a frying pan from the greasy water and wiped it down with a dishcloth. She considered the water heater above the sink. She would have to put another sixpence in the slot if she wanted to reheat the water. Well, that wasn't going to happen. It was past midnight and she wanted to go to bed. She was already in her nightdress and robe, and all she wanted was to crawl between the sheets.

As she set the pan aside and started to dry the knives and forks, her thoughts turned to the police inspector who had tried to handcuff her. She smiled at the memory. She could tell how embarrassed he was at having only one arm and being unable to subdue her. It had been easy for her to do him a small favor and surrender to the handcuffs. She'd noticed how his face reddened as she pressed against him. Now her own face flushed at the memory.

She fished around in the water and located the dinner plates. It was years since she'd had contact with a man, and perhaps that was why she was so warmed by the memory of Inspector Slater's hand on her body. She wondered if he was married. She hadn't seen a wedding ring, but not all men wore rings. He was older than she was, with a touch of gray hair, but he looked stable and sensible, and that was what she needed.

She pulled the plug from the sink and watched the greasy water sliding reluctantly down the plughole. The pipe was blocked again. She should do something about it, but she wanted to go to bed. She'd do it in the morning. She would scrub her own sink before she set off to scrub sinks and pots in the kitchens of the Regency Hotel. She had switched off the light above the sink and turned toward her bedroom when she heard a sound from the street. A car door slammed, and men's voices drifted up on the still night air. Footsteps crunched on the graveled front path.

It could be a neighbor but she knew it wasn't. Although she couldn't distinguish the words, she knew the tone of the voice, with its echoes of her London childhood. She risked a glance from the window and saw two figures. She had half expected to see the man who had ousted her from The Laurels, but these two men were taller and slimmer; two men to do the work that the other man could have done on his own.

The front door was locked, and that would buy her a few minutes. She hurried into Eric's bedroom and shook him awake.   "Get up!"

He didn't move. She grabbed his hands and pulled.   "Don't make a sound."

"Mum!"

"Not a sound. "

"But ..."

"Someone's coming and they mustn't see you. Whatever happens, they mustn't see you."

"Why?"

"Never mind why, just do it. Promise me you won't move and you won't make a sound."

She pulled him into the kitchen and opened the cupboard under the sink. Thank goodness the frying pan and the washing up bowl, both of which usually lived under the sink, were still on the draining board. Eric had to curl up small to fit into the dark, damp space, but her cold determination had its effect. He crawled into the space and hugged his knees to his chest.

"Not a sound," Dorothy said. "Whatever happens, don't make a sound."

By the time the front door crashed open, she was in her bedroom.

Toby Whitby

Toby knew what would happen if he lost track of Dorothy Findlay. She would return to The Laurels yet again, and this time, Slater would not be so lenient with her, or with Toby.

Slater was holding him responsible for Dorothy's actions. She had been released into his care. Short of sleeping on her front doorstep, he could think of only one way to monitor her activities. She didn't have money for a taxi. She would have to take a bus, and Toby had the perfect vantage point for watching the bus stop. The windows of Champion and Company overlooked the bus stop. All he had to do was spend the night in the office, where he could watch and wait in comfort.

He positioned a chair by the window, where he would see Dorothy if she came to the bus stop. The first bus would come at 5:40 a.m. That would be her first opportunity to escape him, and he was not going to let that happen. He set his mental alarm for five thirty and dozed fitfully, dreaming first of his nights on fire watch in London, and then of Carol, and finally of a pianist playing music that chattered and cheeped like a chorus of birds.

He opened his eyes. Birds! The dawn chorus was in full swing, and pale daylight was filtering in through the windows. He looked out and saw the street bathed in the golden light of the rising sun. Two people waited at the bus stop, working men in overalls. There was no sign of Dorothy. He checked his watch. Five thirty-five.

He straightened his clothing and hurried to the door. The bus wasn't here yet. If Dorothy was trying to escape, he could still catch her. He looked up the hill toward the terrace where she lived. He couldn't see her house from here, but he could see someone approaching. The woman's high heels clicked on the pavement as she hurried down the hill. The sunlight picked out the yellow flowers on her dress and struck golden light in her hair.

Toby stepped out onto the doorstep. The woman came closer, and the clicking of her heels was drowned out by the rumble of a diesel engine as the bus rounded the corner.

He dashed down the steps to confront her. "Oh no you don't!"

The woman screamed and the two workmen turned their heads. Toby stopped abruptly, face to face with a woman he had never met; a stranger.

"Sorry."

"Sorry?" she screamed. "You nearly gave me a heart attack. You ought to be arrested."

"I thought you were someone else."

"I don't care who you thought I was. You should be ashamed of yourself. I've a good mind to call the police."

She was an attractive woman, her face made up for a day at an office or maybe a department store, and her fear was turning to anger.

The bus pulled up with a squeal of brakes. The two workmen shuffled past. One of them stopped to scowl at Toby before he turned to the woman. "You all right, love? Is he bothering you?"

"I'm all right. I just need to get to work."

The conductor swung from the pole and leaned out into the street. "Are any of you getting on?"

The woman gave Toby a final warning scowl and hopped onto the bus with the workmen behind her. The conductor dinged the bell, and the bus pulled away, leaving Toby alone on the street.

He had committed the early morning bus schedule to memory, and he dug out the information he needed. Next bus, 6:15 a.m. It was going to be a long morning.

He went back into the office to make a cup of tea. As he poured hot water over the tea leaves into the teapot, he heard the clangor of someone ringing the front doorbell. The thought of police flashed through his mind. Had the woman in the yellow dress reported him? No. There hadn't been time.

The ringing continued. Whoever it was, they were not going away.

He opened the front door and was confronted by a small, disheveled figure in striped pajamas.

"She's gone!"

Toby pulled the boy inside. "What do you mean by gone?"

"Tooken," said Eric.

"You mean taken? Someone took her?"

The boy nodded his head. Toby could see that he was very close to tears and struggling to overcome terror.

"They didn't know I was there. Mummy told me to hide. I hid under the sink in the scullery. I'm all wet."

The boy's shoulders were shaking. Toby put a hand on his shoulder and felt the soaked pajama material. He looked around the office. Anthea kept a spare cardigan draped over the back of her chair. It was gray and heavy, and came down to Eric's knees, but the boy huddled into its warmth.

"How long ago did Mummy leave?" Toby asked.

"I don't know. It was dark. I stayed under the sink for a long time. I didn't want to come out when they were there. And then when I was sure it was all quiet, I came out and she was gone."

Toby poured the tea and stirred a week's worth of sugar into the cup. He held it out to the boy. "Perhaps she didn't go with them. Perhaps she escaped and ran away."

Eric shook his head. "She was screaming. I could hear her screaming and using bad words, and then it was all quiet. They took her, I know. She wouldn't just go away without me."

Oh yes, she would, Toby thought. She'd done it once; she'd do it again

61

if she thought she could challenge Michael Cheviot.

He poured a cup of tea for himself. This was different. This was not Dorothy running off in the middle of the night to find justice for her child. Something had happened in that apartment. Someone had taken Dorothy against her will.

He looked at Eric. The boy was wrapped in the warmth of Anthea's cardigan and cradling a cup of hot tea, but he was still shivering. He patted Eric's shoulder. It had taken courage to come out from under the sink, and even more courage to run down the road in his pajamas, not knowing if the people who had taken his mother were waiting to take him.

Toby, who was not always sure what he thought about God, decided to put his doubts aside and thank God for placing him here at the office so early in the morning. He shuddered at the thought of Eric running helplessly through the dawn light in his bare feet and wet pajamas, looking for someone to help him.

"Stay there, Eric. I'm going to call the police."

Eric nodded his head. "If you weren't here, I was going to look for a policeman."

"Good boy."

"Do you have anything to eat?" Eric asked. "Mummy was going to give me sausages for breakfast."

A warning bell rang at the back of Toby's mind; not loud, but persistent; something he should remember; something about sausages.

Detective Inspector Percy Slater

Toby Whitby looked like hell. His hair was standing on end, his glasses were smudged, and he needed a shave. The child was in worse shape, muffled in an old cardigan, with tracks of tears across his cheeks, and his eyes puffed up from crying.

Slater lifted the lid of the teapot and found nothing but cold, stewed tea leaves. He set about making another pot of tea. He could talk to Whitby now, but Whitby didn't know anything. It was the boy who had to talk, and right now he was too upset to be rational. He needed a few minutes. Slater could wish for Anthea Clark's steadying presence, but he reluctantly conceded that Whitby was doing well enough, keeping his voice calm and steady, not betraying his inevitable anxiety.

"I sent the constable to fetch the boy some food," Slater said. He looked at the kid. "Eric, isn't it?"

"Yes, sir."

"Well, Eric, let's have a nice cup of tea and talk about what happened last night."

Eric's glance slid sideways to Toby. "I have to go to school."

"I think you can have a day off," Toby said.

"Mummy doesn't like me to miss school." At the thought of his mother, Eric hiccupped and swallowed a sob. "Where is she? Why aren't you looking for her?"

"We're looking," Slater said. He lifted his eyes and looked at Toby. "I'll go out to The Laurels, just to see, but I don't think …"

Toby nodded, and Slater knew that the lawyer was thinking what he himself was thinking. It was at best a long shot to expect to find Dorothy at The Laurels. If Michael Cheviot and his mother were behind this, Dorothy would not be at The Laurels. He thought of the body in the mortuary. The dead man had been tied into a weighted sack; was that what awaited Dorothy?

He set the kettle on the hotplate as he considered his options. It was quite possible that Dorothy Findlay was involved in something else; nothing to do with Michael Cheviot and the Cheviot crime family. No need to look for criminals from London when there was no shortage of criminals in Brighton; black market goods, drugs, prostitution. No. He turned his mind away from prostitution. He considered himself a good judge of character, and Dorothy was not a prostitute.

Perhaps she was mixed up in something even more sinister. The station was awash with rumors of Soviet plots and counterplots. No-last-name Undercover Frankie was not in Brighton to investigate some low-level black market activity and an unidentified body. Something big was brewing. Perhaps Dorothy was involved.

Slater looked at the empty sugar bowl. He pulled out his ration book. When the constable returned with breakfast, purchased with police emergency coupons, he would have to send him to get sugar. Kids responded to sugar.

He continued his train of thought while he waited for the water to boil. Russians! Could Dorothy be involved with Russians? The chief constable was convinced that Russians were everywhere, masquerading as honest British citizens. Britain hadn't fallen to Hitler, but it could still fall to the Soviet Union.

Slater dismissed the idea that Dorothy was a communist. If she was a Russian spy working undercover, why would she draw attention to herself by taking out paternity papers against Michael Cheviot? Were the two things connected? Was Cheviot a Russian spy?

He looked back at the boy.

"Eric?"

"Yes, sir."

"Did you hear anything the men said?"

"Yes, I could hear them," Eric replied. "I didn't like the way they talked."

Russians! Were they really Russians?

Toby interrupted Slater's worried thoughts. "What was wrong with the way they talked? Did they sound foreign?"

Eric pursed his lips and suddenly assumed a superior expression. "They talked the way that Mummy doesn't like me to talk. She says that she tries to talk like a lady, and she wants me to talk like a gentleman. They weren't gentlemen."

Slater frowned "What the hell does that mean?"

"That's it," said Eric. "They talked like you do, not like gentlemen; not like Mr. Whitby."

Toby intervened before Slater could express his indignation. "I think he means that they were Londoners."

"And what's wrong with being a Londoner?" Slater asked. He glared at the little boy making him responsible for his mother's attempts at social climbing.

The kettle whistled, and Slater turned away to pour hot water over the tea leaves. Eric had confirmed his worst fears. Dorothy Findlay had been taken by Londoners. The connection was only too obvious. Enid Cheviot and her son were still entangled with the Cheviot family. He shook his head. If the Cheviots had done this, Dorothy Findlay would be hard to find. She was young and blond, and the Cheviots could make money out of someone like her. Blondes fetched a high price in the white slave trade.

He heard the scrape of a key in the front door lock and saw the boy's eyes open wide with alarm. Before he had time to think, he reacted by trying to draw the kid toward him with his right arm. Frustration welled up as painfully as ever. It was hard for him to believe that he could still make that same futile gesture. Seven years, and still he tried to use his missing arm.

Eric saw the anger in his face and crept past him to stand close to Toby. He heard Toby speak with nonchalant reassurance.

"Nothing to worry about, old son, it'll be Miss Clark arriving bright and early."

"Is she the old lady?"

"She wouldn't like to hear you say that, but yes, she is."

"And what about the old man with the sweets?"

Slater thought that if Toby had been a Catholic, he would have crossed himself as he replied in a voice of desperate hope.

"He won't be in today."

Anthea Clark bustled in through the front door with her umbrella held at a defensive angle. She paused when she saw the welcoming committee.

"What is this?"

"My mum's gone. She's been tooken."

"Taken," Toby explained. "His mother has been taken."

Anthea looked from Toby to Slater and then back to Toby. "I see you've called the police."

"I thought it best."

Anthea set her handbag down on her desk and patted her hair. She took the lid off the teapot, looked inside, and gave Slater a nod of approval before she poured herself a cup. She patted Eric's shoulder. The smile she offered the boy seemed genuine, but it became tight lipped when she looked at Toby.

"I see he's wearing my cardigan."

"He came in his pajamas."

Anthea nodded. "My hand-knitted mohair," she said.

"I didn't think you'd mind."

"Mind?" Her smile relaxed again as she looked at the boy. "No, of course not. I'm sure your jacket would be too big for him."

"I thought the cardigan would be comforting," Toby replied.

Anthea shrugged, and Slater had the feeling that the shrug was more than just a shrug. The secretary was letting go of something that she had been holding for a long time. It was as though a layer of hard-won defensiveness was cracking. He envied her. He knew how that layer felt. He wished he knew how to make it crack.

"You'll be questioning the people at The Laurels?" Anthea asked.

"I'll go as soon as the boy is settled," Slater replied.

"What do you mean by settled?"

"Social services. They'll be sending someone to pick him up and take him to—"

"Take him?" Anthea shook her head. "No, Inspector, we will keep young Master Eric here with us, won't we, Mr. Whitby?"

Slater could see that Toby had his mind on other things. He knew that there was a quick intelligence behind Toby's disheveled exterior, and he imagined that Toby was mulling over the fact that Dorothy's abductors had London accents.

"Meantime," said Anthea, as though Toby's agreement was a given, "I will go with the inspector to The Laurels."

Slater looked at Anthea's stubborn face. There had been an aunt in his family with a face like that. She was gone, of course, killed in the Blitz, but her memory lingered on. No one argued with Aunt Prudence, but Anthea Clark was not Aunt Prudence, and this was a police matter.

"That won't be necessary, Miss Clark. I can contact his regiment and find people who were under his command. There's no need for you to trouble yourself."

She dismissed his suggestion with one word. "Nonsense!"

Slater thought he saw a knowing grin flash across Toby's face and realized that he was in a battle he could not win.

"I don't know why I didn't think of it before," Anthea declared. "Now that Miss Findlay has disappeared, I am the only one here who can claim to have met the dead man. It's fortunate for you that I'm here and available."

"She's quite right," Toby said. "You should take her."

Slater could do nothing but raise his eyebrows in astonishment. Since when had this become a subject for debate? This was a police matter.

"We all know that Michael Cheviot has deliberately burned off his fingerprints," Toby said.

Slater frowned and wondered why Toby had to put everything into words. Couldn't the man just keep quiet for once?

"So," said Toby, "you can go to The Laurels on the pretext of checking Michael's fingerprints, but the important thing is to take Miss Clark with you. If she identifies the living Michael Cheviot as the man she met in Canterbury, then you will know for sure that the man in the mortuary is not him, and you won't have to go looking for people from his regiment to aid in your identification."

"Are you ready?" Anthea was clasping her handbag and standing by the door. "We should go now."

His heart pounded impatiently. If she was still alive, the odds were against Dorothy Findlay still being in England, but it was too soon to give up hope. With young Eric's description of the London accents he had heard, he couldn't dismiss a connection to Billy Cheviot and his wife. With every hour that passed, the hope that Dorothy could still be recovered faded. An identification by Anthea Clark would certainly save time.

He ushered Anthea into the back seat of the Wolseley and placed himself next to the driver. The car had adaptations that could help him drive, but it was a difficult business, and he was glad he had a police driver. He didn't like the idea of Anthea watching him struggle with the controls.

The thought of his missing right arm brought the usual resurrection of anger. He could not accept the loss as an inevitable result of war. This loss had been personal. This had not just happened to him. It had been a deliberate act of one man.

"Inspector."

Slater tamped down his anger and turned to look at Miss Clark. She was leaning forward in her seat.

"How are you going to explain my presence? We don't want to make him suspicious."

"I'll tell them you're an observer."

"What am I supposed to be observing?"

The car pulled up at the sagging front gate of The Laurels, and Slater still had no answer.

"I know," said Anthea triumphantly. "I'll tell them I'm here on behalf of the war-wounded. I'm making sure that you have no difficulty fulfilling all your tasks as a police officer despite only having one arm."

"You will not."

"Do you have a better idea?"

Slater sighed as he opened the car door for his unwanted companion. "You only speak if you're spoken to, and you only tell that cock and bull story if you really have to."

Anthea nodded. "I understand. I'm sure it's a very sensitive subject."

"Just keep quiet."

"Yes, of course."

Slater rang the doorbell and saw a face he expected to see; the man with the broken nose, Billy Cheviot.

September 1939
London

Slater had selected his wardrobe carefully for his first day in plain clothes, determined to fit in with the other member of the CID. He was still only a constable, but one day, he planned to be an inspector, maybe even a superintendent. He would dress for his planned position, not his current one. He wore a gray suit, a dark blue tie, a shirt that his mother had stayed up late to iron, and, of course, a raincoat.

As he stood outside the gates of Wormwood Scrubs, he found himself wondering if joining the CID had been a good idea. He would feel safer in uniform, with a helmet and a baton and his fellow officers to help him maintain the thin blue line.

Uniform's task was a simple one. They were here to make sure that the prisoners being released were either met by relatives or put on buses and sent back to their homes. CID had another task; keep an eye on the big fish, look to see who was waiting to meet them, and commit all those faces to memory because, without a doubt, they would be seeing them again.

Slater reread the typed notice that had been sent to all law enforcement officers. Despite the official notepaper with the crown emblazoned at its head, he still found it hard to believe that his government would do something so obviously dangerous. Hitler had marched into Poland, and war had been declared. Blackout regulations were in place, with wardens to ensure that people took them seriously. London had been plunged into darkness, and now the government intended to fill that darkness with criminals.

The notice was unambiguous. Any inmate with less than three months left to serve and all Borstal boys who had completed six months would be released.

"Madness!"

Slater looked at his new governor, Inspector Charlie Neville.

"Sir?"

"Releasing them," Neville explained, "is an act of utter madness. We're going to be far too busy fighting our own crime wave to defend ourselves against Hitler. It's started already. Enough people are taking advantage of the blackout without our government releasing the professionals. My daughter came home in tears last night; someone had made a grab at her in the dark.

"Right now it's just lads copping a feel, bumping into women in the blackout and having a quick grope, but letting this lot loose on the streets will change everything. No one will be safe, and how in the hell are we supposed to put a stop to it? Break a shop window, grab what you can, and make a run for it, and we can't even shine a light to see what's going on. Kill someone, bury them in the ruins of a blitzed house, and who's to say they didn't die in the air raid?"

"At least they're not releasing the murderers," Slater offered. "The hangman's going to be very busy in the next few weeks; that's what I hear."

Neville was not to be mollified. "They'll hang the condemned men, but there are plenty more murderers out there. Any of the men about to be let loose on us could step up to murder." He consulted his watch. "Look sharp, they'll be opening the gates any minute now."

Slater looked at the tension on the faces of the uniformed officers as the hour drew near. The red-brick walls of the old prison towered above them, an impregnable fortress to hold the worst of London's criminals, and any minute now the gates would open and the prison would no longer hold them. They would all come pouring out; men who had been serving sentences for assault and battery, armed robbery, smash and grab, fraud, theft, drug dealing, prostitution. Britain couldn't spare the men to guard them, and so they were to be let loose on society.

As excitement mounted, the uniformed officers drew their batons and linked arms to hold back the families and friends who milled around the high wooden doors, waiting to welcome the unexpected release of their loved ones.

"Why didn't they release them straight into the army?" Slater asked.

"The army doesn't want them," Neville replied, "and we don't have conscription ... not yet."

"You think it will come to that?"

"Sure to."

Neville looked Slater up and down. "They'll probably want you. I'll be left with all the old crocks."

The gates creaked open, and the first of the prisoners sauntered out into the open air. They came out in twos and threes, lifting their heads to the open skies and taking in deep breaths of the crisp autumn air before turning their attention to their waiting families.

A hulking broad-shouldered man emerged with his jacket slung over his *shoulder. His hair was cropped short, his eyes were small and set close to his nose, and his nose had been broken and healed in a misshapen lump.*

"That one," said Neville. "Keep an eye on that one. Billy Cheviot, the worst of a bad bunch."

Slater nodded. "I know him already, sir. I put him in there."

May 1952
Anthea Clark

"Perhaps there's no one home," Anthea said.

Slater banged on the door again.

"They're home."

"Why are they taking so long to answer?"

He frowned as he looked at her. "Half of police work is patience."

"What's the other half?" Anthea asked.

"Impatience," Slater replied, and he began a thunderous knocking at the door.

Anthea felt a new tension in the air as the door opened abruptly, and they were confronted by a giant of a man breathing heavily and scowling. She saw how Slater straightened his shoulders and pulled himself upright, but she could still hear contempt in the big man's voice as he looked at Slater's empty sleeve.

"Hello, Percy. I see you lost a wing."

"Hello, Billy. I see you broke your nose again," Slater retorted.

With the pleasantries completed, Slater pushed his way in through the front door. Billy stood back, making no effort to impede their progress.

He turned his head and grunted over his shoulder. "Police again."

A woman's voice responded, husky and querulous. "Why did you let them in?"

"Old friend," Billy replied.

"Old friend? We don't want any of your old friends in here. I've told you already, I won't be involved."

The woman pushed Billy aside, and Anthea had her first view of Enid Cheviot. She thought her a ridiculous creature; a middle-aged woman still yearning for a place in movie history.

Anthea's mind whirled with comparisons. She supposed that Sarah Bernhardt, pale and ethereal, swooning on a chaise longue, and Theda Bara, her eyes heavy with kohl, dazzling her admirers as Cleopatra, were still Enid Cheviot's role models. She was all aflutter with scarves and shawls, but beneath the wispy wrapping was a woman so ridiculously thin that it was a wonder she was still able to walk.

However, although she seemed no more than a vapor, Michael Cheviot's mother had a formidable will. Even now she was standing firmly in Slater's way. The man with the broken nose turned away, moving quickly as though he had some urgent task to perform.

Anthea was not accustomed to being aligned with people of power, and she found pleasure in watching Slater assert his authority. It helped that he was backed up by a burly uniformed constable who had been their driver and who produced a pair of handcuffs when Slater threatened to arrest Mrs. Cheviot.

"Where is he?" Slater asked.

"He's in bed."

"Well, get him out of bed."

"He needs his rest."

"He can rest when I'm done with him."

Enid fluttered up the stairs, trailing scarves, disdain, and a cloud of expensive perfume.

As she disappeared from sight, Slater turned to the constable. "Take a look around outside, Pierce, and see if there's a locked shed or garage. Find me some reason to get a search warrant, and keep an eye on Billy Cheviot."

The constable went out through the front door, and Anthea waited in anxious anticipation. She could remember every detail of the man she had met in Canterbury. She knew the color of his eyes and the way his hair flopped forward across his forehead. His face and hair had been smudged with dust, but she knew that his skin had been pale in contrast to his dark hair, and his eyes had been a warm brown, his jaw square and determined.

His voice floated down the stairs, irritated and petulant. "What the hell do you want this time?"

He appeared at the top of the stairs, illuminated by a ray of light from the window on the landing. She saw his dark hair and pale skin. She waited for his eyes to turn toward her, but his attention was on Inspector Slater.

"My mother is making a complaint to the chief constable. This is police harassment. I have better things to do than answer your questions."

"This will only take a moment," Slater said stoically. "I just want to take your fingerprints."

"Why?"

"To be quite certain that you are who you say you are."

Michael, trailing a red silk dressing gown in a way that was reminiscent of his mother's trailing scarves, arrived at the foot of the stairs. He smiled and held out his hands.

"I suppose you are going to compare them with my army record."

"I am."

Michael shrugged. "It's a good idea, Inspector, but I'm afraid it won't help."

He pushed past Anthea and she waited for him to notice her. He didn't so much as pause as he led the way into a drawing room where a little sunlight made its way through the laurel bushes and shone patches of light on a pale Chinese carpet.

He turned on a light, a standard lamp with a fringed shade, and held his hands out, palms up beneath the light.

"Burns," he said.

Anthea watched as Slater examined the hands. Michael was wasting their time. She knew it and Slater knew it. Michael's heroic escapade with the burning car had taken care of any possibility that his fingerprints could be matched.

Slater continued to look at Michael's hands. "I understand you were in Canterbury during the bombing," he said casually.

"Yes, I was. What of it?"

Anthea knew she had to speak. "I was there," she said. "My uncle is an archdeacon."

She held her breath. Surely now he would turn and look at her. He turned his head. He examined her from the top of her head to her feet. He looked away again.

"Why were you in Canterbury?" Slater asked.

"I was finishing officer training at Sandhurst," Michael said, "and I had a spot of leave."

Anthea's heart was pounding. He had been in uniform. Why would he have worn his uniform when he was on leave?

"Is this about that woman, the one who claims I fathered her child?" Michael asked. "I can assure you that I don't know her. Yes, I was in Canterbury, but I am not the father of her brat."

He pulled his hands away and tucked them in the pockets of his dressing gown. "That's enough. I've done nothing criminal. Now get out of my house and take her with you."

He looked at Anthea again. "She's too old to be a policewoman; who is she?"

Anthea waited for Slater to explain and tell him the lie she had invented. He shook his head.

"No one."

She felt the pressure of Slater's hand against her elbow, urging her toward the front door. She knew he wanted her to keep silent. She kept her lips pressed together so that words would not burst out of her mouth.

She sank into the back seat of the car, overwhelmed by sudden grief. The man she had met in Canterbury, her Michael Cheviot, was truly dead. She found a crumb of comfort in her certainty of that fact. At least her Michael Cheviot was not a sullen, contemptuous mother's boy. She could restore her version of Michael to his place in her memory and replace his face on the heroes of her romance stories. Her Michael could continue to be perfect, and time would not change him.

Slater turned his head. "He didn't seem to recognize you."

She waited until she was sure she could command her voice not to tremble.

"Well?" Slater asked.

"No, Inspector, he did not recognize me. He is not the same man."

Saying it aloud brought relief.

"So," said Slater, "we're back at square one, aren't we? If he's Michael Cheviot, then who is the man in the mortuary, and why was he in Canterbury wearing Cheviot's uniform?"

Slater's driver appeared from around the side of the house and settled himself into the driver's seat.

"Well?" Slater snapped. "Did you find anything?"

"A light on upstairs, but the window was open, and it's an easy climb down to the ground. It wouldn't be a good place to hold a prisoner. I looked around the back garden. Two garden sheds and a garage all locked up tight. I had a go at looking through the windows, nothing to see."

Slater shook his head. "No grounds for a warrant?"

"Well ..." The driver squirmed in his seat as he produced something from the inside pocket of his jacket. "I found this snagged on a bush."

Anthea leaned forward and caught a glimpse of what the policeman had found. Slater squirreled it away into his coat pocket, but she had already committed its description to her memory. A long strip of fabric, not a scarf, but maybe a belt, cotton print with a pattern of blue flowers. If it belonged to Dorothy, her son would surely recognize it.

She hoped that finding the belt was a good sign. If Dorothy's abductors intended to kill her, they wouldn't bring her to The Laurels; they'd take her out onto the cliffs, where no one would see her.

She leaned forward and tapped Slater's shoulder. "She was here, wasn't she?"

He turned to look at her, and she saw that genuine anguish had overtaken his usual sour expression. "But where is she now?" he asked.

Dorothy Findlay

One way or another, she was going to get out of this situation. She had felt no surprise when the two men who abducted her had brought her to The Laurels. She knew the Cheviots were behind this. She had glimpsed the house and the dark foliage of the laurel bushes as the two men had dragged her from the car to a tumbledown shed in the rear of the property.

She wished that they had left her in the shed instead of moving her to the dank darkness of the coal cellar. In the shed, she had at least been able to see daylight through the filthy windows. She had been tied and gagged, but she could look around. She could see tools and gardening implements, and imagine how she could somehow use them to free herself. She would be free. She made that vow. She would be free and she would return to Eric. Poor little blighter must be scared out of his mind.

She had thought that some of the garden tools would be sharp enough to cut the ropes that tied her hands, if she could just reach them. Her hands were still strong from her war work as a welder, and she had been sure that it was just a matter of getting herself into the right position. She tried to roll across the floor and found herself tangled in the folds of her long nightdress and robe, but she was closer to the old wheelbarrow, where she could see the rusty blade of a sickle. She rolled again.

That was when Billy Cheviot had burst through the garage door and tripped over her. He had not expected her to be able to move. What was he going to do? Would he tie her to the wall?

No, he had not tied her to the wall. He had picked her up and slung her across his shoulders. He was in a hurry, cursing her for tripping him, and cursing the police.

So the police were here. They were looking for her. She squirmed against Billy's shoulder, sending him off-balance and crashing through a rosebush. She felt a sharp tug at her robe and saw that her belt was snagged on the thorns.

Billy clamped down on her with one hand, and with the other, he opened a door set in the side of the house. The choking scent of sulfurous coal told her where she was. This was the coal bunker, a place without windows and not a place where she would find a sharp object or a way to get free.

In the shed, she had at least been able to tell night from day, but here she had no way of telling time. She wondered if they would leave her here to die. Although death seemed to be a distinct possibility, she refused to give up hope.

She was perched precariously on top of an unstable pile of coal, and she sensed somehow that her head was only inches from the ceiling. Something crawled across her face; a spider? She willed it to be a small, harmless money spider and not something large and given to biting. She tried to calm her breathing and draw only shallow breaths through the coal dust that clogged her nose and the sulfurous gag that Billy had shoved into her mouth. If she panicked and allowed her breathing to become ragged, she would choke. If she moved too much and lost her balance, she would slide off the coal tip and break an arm, or maybe even her neck.

She was not ready to break her neck, not yet. Sitting in the dark, divorced from sound and light, she could think of only one thing. Her belt was snagged on a rosebush, and Billy had not noticed. It was a small thing, but it was hope, and while she had hope, she would not give in to despair.

CHAPTER NINE

Toby Whitby

Toby picked at the remains of Eric's breakfast.

"Hey!" The constable who had delivered the breakfast regarded him with disapproval. "That's for the boy."

"I don't want any of it," Eric said. "Where's my mother?"

The constable looked at Toby for guidance. Toby was silent. He couldn't imagine that anything good had happened to Dorothy Findlay, and the image of the bloated corpse in the mortuary was foremost in his mind; tied into a weighted sack and dumped in the ocean. Was that what had happened to Eric's mother? Why? What did she know?

He nibbled on Eric's leftover scrambled eggs, grimacing at the unique and unpleasant taste of powdered egg. He turned over everything he knew. Dorothy was suing Michael Cheviot for child support, and for some reason, Michael did not dare to go to court and dispute her claim. What reason did he have that was so compelling that he would take the risk of having Dorothy kidnapped or even killed?

With a grimace of dislike, he swallowed down the last of the egg mixture. He'd been up all night and he was hungry, and powdered eggs were better than no eggs. He wondered idly whether the sausages Dorothy had promised to her son were still in her kitchen. Probably not; they'd probably been picked up by the crime scene investigators. He thought of the risk that Dorothy had taken, going down into the Lanes, among the spivs and black marketeers, just to get some sausages for her son.

He dragged his mind away from sausages and his own illegal loaf of bread. He had to think this through. Dorothy had come to him for help because she recognized Michael Cheviot's picture from the newspaper. She knew nothing about the body in the mortuary, but Anthea Clark did know about the body. Anthea had identified the dead man as Michael Cheviot. Michael Cheviot could not be alive and dead at the same time; he couldn't be playing the piano at The Laurels and lying on a slab with his hands cut off. Michael Cheviot could not be in two places at once, but two people could claim to be Michael Cheviot. Why?

He picked a sliver of tomato from the plate and chewed thoughtfully, hardly bothering to register that it was canned and virtually tasteless. He had assumed that Dorothy's disappearance had something to do with her suit for child support, but perhaps that was the wrong way to think about the problem. Perhaps it had nothing to do with money, and everything to do with her ability to recognize the man who had fathered her child. Michael would have to face her in court, and she would know if he was an imposter.

What of Michael's mother? If this was all a hoax, why was she allowing it to continue? And who was the cook making lunch for? Who was the person upstairs who could not be spoken of?

He set the plate down on his desk and poured a cup of tea. His thoughts were going around in circles and taking him nowhere. He had no solution to the problem. He could only hope that Anthea would be able to tell him something when she returned from The Laurels. If the Michael Cheviot at The Laurels was the man she'd seen in Canterbury, then the problem would be solved. The dead man was no more than a stranger who bore a passing resemblance to Michael Cheviot. Everything else was pure coincidence. Of course, none of that would explain Dorothy's kidnapping.

The ringing of the telephone brought a welcome end to his whirling thoughts. His relief was short lived as he heard Mr. Champion's voice.

Edwin Champion placed little faith in telephones. He rarely resorted to placing his own phone calls, and he believed that telephone conversations should be brief and to the point.

"Whitby, why are you answering the phone? Where is Miss Clark?"

"She's out, sir."

"Out? I don't pay her to be out."

"No, sir, I—"

"Never mind about that now. I want you to take your motorcar to Shoreham Aerodrome and meet two gentlemen who will be flying in from Cornwall in a private plane."

Cornwall! Michael Cheviot had an address in Cornwall!

"Whitby, are you listening to me?"

"Yes, sir, you want me to go Shoreham Aerodrome. Who am I to meet?"

"Colonel Hugh Trewin and Robert Penhelen. Penhelen is a Queen's Counsel and younger son of a baronet, so treat him with respect. If you've ever thought of becoming a barrister, he's someone you should know."

"I've never thought of—"

"Never mind that now. Trewin is Enid Cheviot's father, Michael's grandfather, and they have an interesting theory. Go and meet them and ring up that detective chap and tell him they want to see the body."

"Detective Inspector Slater is out with Miss Clark at the moment."

Mr. Champion broke into a fit of coughing. Toby held the receiver to his ear and waited for the spasm to pass. The cough sounded deep and painful. The old man should have been in bed, not up and about and giving orders.

The coughing came to an end, and Mr. Champion was able to gasp out a few words. "You go to the aerodrome, meet them. Take the road across the Downs."

"It would be quicker to take the coast road," Toby argued.

"It would not," Mr. Champion said. "I am told that a repair crew is, at long last, repairing the bomb damage along the road. The road is impassable. Do as I say, Whitby. Take the road across the Downs. I will come to the office."

"Are you sure you should come in?"

"Of course I should come in. I can't have Miss Clark gallivanting around with the police. I don't know what the world is coming to, I really don't. As for you, don't argue with me; just do as I say."

With the dial tone in his ear, and his instructions very clearly understood, Toby looked at Eric.

"Do you want to come and look at aeroplanes?"

A hint of a smile lit the boy's face, followed by a desperate shoulder shrug. "I'm not dressed."

Toby considered the amount of time it would take to go to Dorothy's flat and find clothes for the boy. The flat was a crime scene. He probably wouldn't be allowed to enter. He should leave the boy behind, but he'd seen that hint of a smile, and the boy needed something to cheer him.

There was something else to consider. If the man coming by plane was Enid Cheviot's father, this boy could be his great-grandson. He didn't plan to say anything, but he needed to see the two of them together. Perhaps there would be a resemblance; perhaps even a recognition, blood calling to blood.

"You can't walk around the aerodrome in your pajamas, so you'll have to stay in the car, but you can look out of the window. Will that be all right?"

He wasn't accustomed to having passengers in his car. The Morris was quite small, nothing like a Wolseley or an Armstrong or any of the big prewar cars. He hoped the two men from Cornwall would fit in the back seat. Eric settled himself in the front passenger seat and pressed his nose to the window. He seemed lost in thought as they drove out of Brighton, diverting from the coastal road and climbing up onto the Downs.

They crested the last rise, and Toby saw the graceful white terminal building basking in the sunlight. A small plane, approaching from the west, hovered above the runway, making its final approach.

Toby looked at Eric, thinking that the boy had probably never been so close to an airplane. He was not even old enough to have a clear memory of the days when the skies were filled with Spitfires and Messerschmitts locked in combat above the rolling hills of Sussex and Surrey.

"Eric."

The boy's shoulders heaved.

Toby reached out a hand and touched the shaking shoulder. He wished he could give the boy the assurance he needed, but Eric was smart enough to know that he may never see his mother again. The best that Toby could do was to distract him and give him something else to think about.

"Eric."

Eric pulled his nose away from the window. His face was streaked with tears but he managed a reply. "Yes, sir."

"Let's have some fun."

Curiosity glinted in Eric's dark eyes. "What kind of fun?"

Toby studied the long downhill slope of the empty road ahead.

"Let's see if we can get all the way down to the aerodrome without using the engine."

Eric cocked his head sideways. "You can't."

"Bet I can."

Now he had the boy's attention. "What are we betting?"

Toby saw a hint of the real Eric Findlay beneath the worried exterior. Dorothy's child had a touch of her feistiness and courage. He hoped it would be enough to see the boy through whatever lay ahead.

"I'm betting my sweet ration," Toby said. "What about you?"

Eric did not hesitate. "All right."

"Are you sure?"

Eric studied the slope. "I'm sure."

Toby had already made his mind up that he would have to fail because he could not deprive the boy of his sweet ration. Yes, he would have to fail, but he would give the boy a good run for his money.

He switched off the ignition and silenced the engine. Now the only sound was the drumming of the tires on the paved road. The Morris careened down the hill, picking up speed and swaying alarmingly. Eric clung to the door handle. His face was flushed and he was fully absorbed in the contest. At the last possible moment, Toby let in the clutch, and the engine burst into life.

Eric let out a cry of triumph. "Told you."

"Yes, you did."

They drove sedately up to the terminal just in time to see the plane skitter to a halt on the grass taxiway.

Two men and a dog emerged and waited while the dog sniffed at the grass and relieved herself.

A dog, Toby thought. Where on earth was he going to put a dog?

"That's a springer spaniel," Eric said eagerly, his tears momentarily forgotten.

"How do you know?"

"I belong to the Dog Spotters Club. Mummy bought me a book from the newsagent, and you have to write down every dog you see." The sadness returned. "I don't know what's happened to my book. Will it still be there when Mummy comes home?"

"Of course it will," Toby replied. He could not imagine that Dorothy's kidnappers would be interested in Eric's little dog-spotting book. It would be there, and he would make sure that Eric retrieved it. He could not be so certain that he could retrieve Eric's mother.

He told Eric to wait in the car and walked out onto the runway to greet the new arrivals.

A big gray-haired man with a military bearing held the dog on a leash. His ownership of the animal was attested to by the scattering of white fur across his navy-blue blazer. Toby studied the blazer badge; a bugle, a crown, and the word "Cornwall."

The man extended a hand. "Colonel Hugh Trewin, Duke of Cornwall's Light Infantry."

"Toby Whitby."

"Yes, yes, Champion spoke highly of you," Trewin said. "He was quite sure you'd be able to get to the bottom of this nonsense."

"I'll certainly try."

The other man was slightly built and wore a gray suit of such impeccable cut and style that Toby was suddenly very aware of his disheveled appearance.

"Robert Penhelen."

He did not need to add his title. Toby was in no doubt that this was Mr. Champion's friend, the eminent and aristocratic barrister who could pave the way to undreamed-of career heights.

"Right," said Trewin. He gave the dog's leash a sharp tug. "Come along, Daisy. You've done your business, and there's no need to be looking for rabbits on the runway."

"Where is the car?" Penhelen asked, looking past Toby's Morris, apparently unable to believe that this was the vehicle sent by Champion and Company.

Just wait until they find that there's a small boy in pajamas in the front seat, Toby thought. He waved toward the Morris. "I'm afraid I had to bring my own vehicle."

"I see," said Penhelen. He turned to his companion. "You shouldn't have brought the dog. You'll have to put her in the boot."

"Never."

They were close to the car now, and Trewin spotted the boy in the front seat.

"Who is that? Did you bring your child?"

Toby shook his head. "Not my child. He's a client's child. His mother is ..."

His voice faded as Trewin opened the car door and looked at Eric. Was it really going to be this easy? Would Trewin recognize his great-grandson and short-circuit all legal proceedings?

"Out!" said Trewin. "Small boys do not ride in the front seat."

Eric scrambled out and stood in his pajamas and bare feet, his eyes cast down at the ground.

Trewin looked back at Toby. "What is this? Why isn't this boy dressed?"

"Something happened in the night," Toby said, "to his mother."

Trewin's face softened. "I see. Well, I've always found dogs to be a great comfort at times like this. Daisy can sit on his lap in the back seat. I'll sit with him. I don't mind a bit of dog hair."

Eric scrambled into the back seat, and Trewin pushed Daisy in behind him. He paused for a moment, his face close to Eric's as he persuaded the dog to climb onto Eric's lap.

"Do I know you, boy?"

"I don't know you, sir."

"What's your name?"

"Eric Findlay."

Trewin shook his head. "Findlay? Findlay? No, I don't know you." He looked at the boy again and then looked back at Toby. "Who is his mother?"

"Dorothy Findlay."

"You say she's a client?"

"Yes."

"And something happened ..." Trewin shook his gray head. "Well, we won't speak about that now. I am sure it will end well."

He clambered into the back seat and patted Eric's knee. "What an adventure you're having," he said heartily.

Penhelen wiped the front seat with his handkerchief and settled himself, making small, fussy adjustments of the seat.

"Very well," he said, "we shall go to the mortuary."

"The mortuary?" Toby repeated. "I planned to take you to the office."

"No, no. Time is of the essence. The body is decaying even as we speak. Take us to Brighton Mortuary."

Toby started the motor and glanced nervously at the fuel gauge. The needle hovered near the empty mark. Well, he would just have to trust to luck. He had no money on him, and there was no way that he could ask the two distinguished visitors for a loan.

He slipped the Morris into gear and pulled out onto the road.

Penhelen leaned forward and tapped the fuel gauge. "You're getting pretty low, young man."

Colonel Trewin spoke from the back seat. "Stop fussing, Robert. We've no time to waste."

Penhelen sat back, and they rode in silence broken only by the dog's excited breathing.

"Have you seen the body?" Penhelen asked, dragging Toby's attention away from the flickering fuel gauge and the dog's warm breath on his neck.

"Yes, I've seen it."

"What age is the man?"

Age? Toby had not thought about age. The battered skull retained only minimal traces of hair. Had any of the hairs been gray? He didn't know. He hadn't looked.

"We saw the picture the police sent around," Penhelen said, "but we couldn't put an age to that face. What's your opinion?"

Toby shook his head. "I don't know. I accompanied our office secretary to examine the body because she thought she might know the man. She said nothing about his age. I expect she saw only what she expected to see."

"Exactly," said Penhelen. "Smart answer. Champion told me you were smart."

"Thank you, sir."

Trewin leaned forward, thrusting his head between their shoulders, his voice becoming increasingly Cornish as he warmed to the story he was telling. "When my daughter took up with Ronnie Cheviot, I knew it would come to a bad end. It was all very well her wanting to be in the moving pictures, and I didn't discourage her. I knew she'd never be a star. I thought she'd realize it was hopeless and come back home, but instead, she met this fellow and he promised her the moon. He said he would use his own money to make films just for her."

He shook his head. "Of course, it wasn't films that interested him. Maybe he thought that Enid would be his ticket to respectability, country weekends, dinner with the Prince of Wales, that sort of thing. I'm afraid Penhelen would know more about that sort of thing than I would."

"I can assure you," Penhelen said coldly, "that the Prince of Wales, who is a personal friend of mine, would not have accepted the company of Ronnie Cheviot."

"Of course not," Trewin agreed. "All Ronnie did was to drag her down to his own level. When she told me she was pregnant, I got out my gun and I made sure he married her; dreadful fellow, but I couldn't let her give birth to a bastard."

He lowered his voice. "I can't say I'm sorry about what happened to him. No sooner was my grandson born than Ronnie up and disappeared. Fell off a Channel ferry on the way to France, that's what his chums said; fell off and drowned. Never knew whether to believe a word of it, but he was gone and that's all I cared. His body never turned up, so who can say?"

"How long ago was this?" Toby asked.

"Long time ago," Trewin said. "Michael was just a babe in arms."

"But the body wouldn't be …" Toby fell silent without finishing his protest.

"Ah!" said Trewin. "I think you understand."

"You think that he was never dead."

"Not until now," Penhelen said.

Toby drew in a deep breath as he unwillingly added yet another loose piece to the puzzle in his mind. Where did this one fit?

CHAPTER TEN

While they waited for the mortuary attendant to prepare the body for viewing, Toby put in a phone call to the office.

Anthea answered the phone. She sounded breathless and excited.

"Where are you, Mr. Whitby?"

"I'm at the mortuary with these two old gentlemen from Cornwall and—"

"Where is Eric?"

"He's with me."

"I need to see him. I have to ask him something."

"He's in the car with the dog."

"What dog?"

"Her name is Daisy."

"What?"

"The dog's name is Daisy."

"Really, Mr. Whitby, why does it matter what the dog is called?"

"She's Colonel Trewin's dog," Toby said, "and she came with them on the plane."

"A dog! On a plane! Whatever will they think of next?"

"Eric's taken to her. I think she's helping him. He's very worried about his mother."

Toby could hear Anthea breathing, but it was a moment or two before she spoke. "I think you should tell him that his mother is still alive."

Toby took note of her hesitation. "Are you sure?"

"No, not completely, but we found a clue."

"Who did?"

"Inspector Slater did, or rather, his driver did. They want to speak to Eric and show him what they found."

Toby shook his head as he looked at the two Cornishmen waiting impassively in the outer office.

"I can't bring him now; we're at the mortuary."

Anthea tutted impatiently. "Yes, yes, I understand where you are, but you must report to the police station as soon as you can. The inspector wanted to know your whereabouts, and I told him that I was not at liberty to divulge that information. I see no reason to be helpful to him when he is so hostile to us and our attempts to help him solve his case."

"Oh yes," Toby agreed. "He's hostile. I'm not sure what I've done to upset him, but he's quite determined to keep me out of the picture."

"Well," Anthea said firmly, "Miss Findlay is our client, and that makes it our business."

"Quite right," said Toby, suddenly decisive and quite certain of what needed to be done. "If Slater won't tell us what he knows, we'll have to find things out for ourselves. The first thing we need to know is the identity of the dead man."

He glanced over his shoulder at the two elderly Cornishmen; maybe they had the answer, and maybe they didn't, but time was wasting, and every moment that passed made it less likely that Dorothy Findlay would be found.

He lowered his voice. "Miss Clark, do you think you could do a spot of snooping for me?"

"Snooping! Mr. Whitby, really, I—"

Toby interrupted her protest. "I'd do it myself but I am tied up here, so I'm relying on you. I'm thinking about the woman who was in the burning car, the one who fled the scene. It was obviously a put-up job, and she must know something. We need to find her and get her to talk."

"But how could I do that?" Anthea asked.

"By all accounts, the car was on fire," Toby said, "and Michael pulled her out. Even if the whole thing was staged, the fire looked pretty real in the photographs, so I don't think the passenger escaped unscathed. She probably had some burns that needed treatment."

"Well," said Anthea dubiously. "I could phone the local hospitals, but surely the police have done that already."

"If they have," Toby said, "they haven't told us about it, and maybe they never will. I'm afraid we'll have to make our own inquiries. Start with hospitals that have burn units."

He waited for Anthea to respond. She was silent for a moment.

"Miss Clark?"

"I'm thinking, Mr. Whitby."

"I see. Well ..."

Anthea's voice was sharp and decisive. "Obviously, she is not in the same hospital where Michael Cheviot was treated. If this really is some kind of criminal conspiracy, she wouldn't be anywhere that would be easy to find."

"Private clinics?" Toby suggested.

"Yes," said Anthea. "I agree. I shall begin with private clinics."

Toby heard movement in the outer office. A tall, dark man in a white coat was shaking hands with the two men.

"Miss Clark, I have to go now. I'll report to Inspector Slater as soon as I am able. Meantime, start making phone calls. I'm relying on you."

The mortuary attendant introduced himself as Colin Patel, medic, First Punjab Regiment.

"Let's get on with it," said Trewin. "I'm sure he's not a pleasant sight, but needs must."

Patel looked over at Toby. "Last time you saw him, he was still quite fresh, but we don't have a deep freeze, just refrigeration. It slows down the decay, but—"

"We've all been in combat," Trewin said impatiently. "Penhelen and I were together at the Somme. We know what to expect."

All three men nodded their heads knowingly, united by a brotherhood that Toby had been unable to join.

"Follow me."

They followed Patel into the postmortem room, where the body lay under a green sheet.

The smell of decay was stronger than ever. Patel drew back the sheet and released a wave of foul air that caught in Toby's throat. He held his breath and fought down the urge to gag.

"What exactly do you want to know?" Patel asked. "So far, we have failed to make an identification. I have spoken to Inspector Slater several times about this, but I understand he's no closer to a solution."

Patel paused and looked up at Toby. "Does the inspector know you're here?"

Caught in the need to lie, Toby hesitated. Penhelen, with a linen handkerchief pressed against his nose, filled the uncomfortable silence. "Next of kin," he said firmly. "We understand that this may or may not be Colonel Trewin's grandson."

"Or son-in-law," Trewin muttered, peering closely at the obscene caricature of a face. He shook his head. "I can't tell."

"If it is of any help to you," Patel said, "I can tell you that this man had flat feet. He could not, or should not, have been in the army."

Trewin gave a bitter laugh. "If this is my daughter's husband, I can assure you he would have found a way to avoid being in the army. He could connive his way out of anything. Probably connived his way out of drowning."

He stared balefully at the corpse and then back at Penhelen. "What do you think, Robert?"

Penhelen shook his head. "Hard to say."

84

Trewin extended an arthritic hand and touched the mangled hair. "I don't see any gray hairs."

Patel cocked his head to one side. "You are looking for his age?"

"Yes, that's exactly what I'm looking for. Could this be a man of fifty or even older?"

Patel's response was firm and unequivocal. "No."

"You're sure?"

"Quite sure."

Trewin waved a dismissive hand at the body. "How can you tell from all this mess?"

Toby stepped forward. "I saw him a couple of days ago, while he was still ... fresh." He looked at Patel for confirmation. "I thought he looked younger than fifty."

Patel slipped a hand under the mangled head and lifted it slightly. He leaned down and studied the back of the skull. He looked up again. "This man was not yet fifty," he declared. "This is the skull of a young man."

"Pish and twaddle," Trewin muttered. "How can you be so certain?"

"Well," said Patel, "as you know, when a baby is born, the skull is not fully formed. It closes over time. Although we are mostly unaware of what is happening, our skulls are not fully joined until we are in our forties."

Toby instinctively lifted his hand and felt his own skull. It seemed to be all in one piece under its thatch of hair.

"On this skull," Patel continued, "I can see that the lambdoid suture is not fully joined, which means that this is the skull of a person in his late twenties, early thirties. This is not the skull of a middle-aged man."

"Then who the hell is it?" Trewin growled. "Michael passed the army physical; he doesn't have flat feet." He turned away from the corpse. "I was really hoping it was Ronnie."

Penhelen shook his head. "I think we have to accept that it's not."

"So for all we know, the bastard is still out there," Trewin growled.

Penhelen's voice was firm. "We had him declared dead. Enid's property is safe."

Patel lifted the sheet to cover the face, but Trewin stopped him. "Are there any distinguishing marks, tattoos, birthmarks, anything?"

Patel pulled the sheet back to expose the entire body. Toby held his breath as the odor of decay filled the room.

Patel's fingers passed across the dead man's limp genitals and pointed to a small mark on the thigh. "There is something that I don't understand," he remarked. "This man's flat feet would keep him out of the army, but I have made an extensive examination of the body, and I can say that he has been shot, several times. This is a bullet wound. Nothing serious, it did not penetrate the muscle."

The two old soldiers peered down at the faint mark on the bloated flesh. Trewin nodded. "Flesh wound."

"Yes," said Patel. He slipped his hand under the body. "The other is on the back of the calf. Do you want me to turn him over?"

Toby prayed silently that Patel would not submit the corpse to any additional turning or moving. His prayer failed, and Patel turned the body on its side to show another faint mark; another flesh wound, another gust of foul air.

Trewin grunted. "Are you saying he's been in combat?"

"I am saying that he has received bullet wounds. I cannot say where, but I can say that they were fully healed. The damage was inflicted some time ago. Ten or more years."

Toby turned his mind back ten years. 1942. He had been a civilian then, just as this man must have been a civilian. Toby's poor eyesight kept him away from the front lines; this man's flat feet would have kept him out of the uniformed service. The Blitz had brought about a number of ways for someone on the home front to be injured, collapsing buildings, fire, shrapnel, the V1 and V2 rockets, bombs. All these things were possible, but not a bullet wound, and definitely not two bullet wounds.

Up until that moment, the body in the mortuary had been just one piece in a pile of loose pieces; a jigsaw puzzle with no shape and no picture to follow. He stumbled from the room and out into the corridor, where he could breathe clean air. His thoughts were racing. He leaned back against the wall and stared down the long corridor while the pieces rearranged themselves and the picture took shape.

If this was the picture, everything else made sense. The dead man had been in combat. Somehow he had passed the physical exam, or had he? Had someone taken his place at the exam, or more to the point, had he taken someone else's place after the exam? Was this the man who had presented himself as Michael Cheviot? Was this the man who had served in the Royal East Kent in Africa and Italy? Was that where he received his wounds?

He heard the door open behind him and heard the heavy footsteps of the two Cornishmen. He didn't want to look Trewin in the eye. He couldn't tell him what he thought, not yet. He would need more proof. What proof? He needed to talk to someone who had been in the Royal East Kent alongside Michael Cheviot. He needed to know if Cheviot had been wounded.

"Whitby."

Penhelen was standing in front of him, peering at him with an intense intelligent gaze. He was a Queen's Counsel, the very peak of the legal profession; he would not be easy to fool.

He looked around for the colonel, but the old man was stomping toward the outer doors. Perhaps he was going to check on the dog, or even on Eric, who had been left in charge of Daisy; the dog bringing the boy some degree of comfort.

"Whitby." Penhelen was still looking at him.

"Sorry, sir; overcome by the smell," Toby said.

"Poppycock. You've had a thought, haven't you? Champion told me you were a smart one. Well, spit it out, man. Bullet wounds, what does that suggest to you?"

"Combat."

"A flat-footed soldier. How did he pass the physical?" "He couldn't."

Penhelen sighed regretfully. "I have no illusions about young Michael Trewin. Hugh's done his best, of course, but blood will out, as they used to say. His father was a nasty piece of work. Enid likes to think that Michael is sensitive and shell-shocked, but that's not what I think. Now that I've seen what we've just seen, I don't buy a word of it. He's not shell-shocked, he's a lily-livered coward who sent someone else to fight on his behalf."

He raised an inquiring gray eyebrow in a gesture that had probably swayed any number of judges and juries during his distinguished career. Toby said nothing.

"Well?" Penhelen asked.

Toby threw caution to the winds. "That's what it looks like."

Penhelen looked toward the closed outer doors. The colonel was nowhere in sight.

"Something's happened," Penhelen said. "It's been six years since the war ended and Michael came home. For the first few years, he hid himself away in Cornwall, but now he's trying to get back into the swing of things, and the man who took his place on the front lines has become a danger to him."

"Why?" Toby asked. He took a deep breath and tried to order his thoughts. "Michael doesn't want to sign up, so he finds someone who looks like him but has flat feet. Why didn't he just send that man to take the physical in his place? The flat feet would have made him fail and he'd be free and clear. People did it all the time, and I'm sure that his London relatives would know how to do it. He didn't have to go through all of this."

Penhelen nodded his head in agreement. "Good question."

"Well," Toby said, "I have a theory, but—"

Toby hesitated.

Penhelen looked toward the outer doors again. "Spit it out, man. I don't want to be saying any of this in front of Trewin."

"I don't think this is just about Michael Cheviot not wanting to fight, I think it's about the other man." He gestured with his head toward the mortuary door. "I think that man wanted to fight and he couldn't, because of his flat feet. We're assuming that this was all Michael's idea, but what if it wasn't? What if Michael just went along with someone else's plan, and now it's all going wrong. Our mystery man has spent the last six years hiding, and so has Michael. Now one of them wants it to be over."

"Hmm." Penhelen gave Toby a long thoughtful look. "I like the way you think. You've turned the whole problem on its head. You're suggesting that our mystery man back there is a grandstanding hero, and Michael is a victim."

"Not an innocent victim," Toby said. "Someone killed the imposter and removed his hands, and Michael took part in a staged car accident where a woman fled the scene and he burned off his fingerprints."

Penhelen scowled. "That has all the hallmarks of a Cheviot family crime. It's the kind of thing Ronnie Cheviot would have done in a heartbeat."

"There's something else," Toby said.

"What?"

"It's pretty clear that Michael signed up with the Royal East Kent, and when it came time to leave, he didn't go."

"It certainly looks that way."

Toby looked into Penhelen's troubled eyes, knowing that Penhelen had already come to the same conclusion. "That makes him a deserter."

"Desertion in wartime; death by firing squad," Penhelen whispered. "His grandfather will never live down the shame."

The outer doors opened with a sudden explosive crash. Toby turned toward them, feeling a flush of guilt rise on his face. He saw the same guilty expression on Penhelen's face. The idea that they both entertained, the conclusions they had both reached, could not yet be repeated to Colonel Trewin.

Guilt was replaced by alarm when Toby saw Trewin's white face.

"That boy," Trewin gasped. "Who is he?"

"He's my client's son."

Trewin shook his head. "When I first saw him, I thought I saw something, but I knew it couldn't be. I went out to look for the dog, and I saw him walking along the beach ... walking away from me just the same way ... I could have sworn ..."

Penhelen placed a tentative hand on his friend's shoulder. "He's just a boy."

"All these years of looking and I know it can't be him. He'd be a middle-aged man, but everything about him ..."

Penhelen met Toby's inquiring look with a shake of his head. Now was not the time to ask questions.

Trewin took a deep breath and seemed to pull himself together. "I'd better go and rescue my dog," he said, "before they both go swimming in the Channel."

CHAPTER ELEVEN

Detective Inspector Percy Slater

The interview room contained entirely too many people, and only the dog was silent. Everyone else seemed to have something to add to the confusion.

The boy clutched the belt of his mother's robe and cried, muffling his loud gulping sobs by burying his face in the dog's fur. The old colonel, with a bemused expression on his face, patted the boy's head and made gruff but comforting noises.

The distinguished gentleman in the excellent gray suit had already introduced himself as a Queen's Counsel. Slater tried to avoid his piercing gaze. This was a man who was at the peak of the legal profession, with a place at the Inns of Court, a silk robe, a white wig, and an ability to run circles around any police officer who was not quite sure of his testimony. He had made several requests to see the chief constable, but so far, Slater's superior officer had not put in an appearance.

Slater tried to keep the irritation out of his voice as he held out his hand to the crying boy. "Give me back the belt, sonny; it's evidence."

Toby glared at him. "He's not doing any harm. He's told you it belongs to his mother. Let him hold it for a minute if it makes him feel better."

Slater felt the irritation that so often accompanied any interaction with Toby Whitby. He didn't have time to analyze why the young lawyer annoyed him so easily. He didn't want to look at the possibility that he was envious of the fact that Toby had come through the war unscathed. He knew that was an unreasonable envy. Toby had wanted to fight, but his thick glasses were obvious proof of his poor eyesight. So Toby had escaped uninjured and Slater had returned without an arm. He shook his head. Now was not the time.

"Does your chief constable have any idea who would have taken her?" Penhelen asked.

Slater added Penhelen to his list of irritants. He forced himself to be calm despite the chaos. "The chief constable has a number of other important inquiries," he said. "This is my investigation."

"Are you aware of the family background?" Penhelen asked.

Slater restrained a contemptuous snort. Of course he was aware of the family background. "I was in London before the war," he said. "I know the Cheviots."

"Scum of the earth," Trewin snapped. "Why don't you get Enid in here and give her the third degree. Find out what she knows. She says she has nothing to do with them, but I don't believe her."

"No, neither do I," Slater said. "I saw Billy Cheviot at her house. Where's there's one Cheviot, there are usually a whole tribe of them."

Trewin frowned. "I should have known it. I knew they'd never leave her alone."

"What about the person upstairs?" Toby asked. "There was someone up there that Mrs. Cheviot didn't want to talk about."

Slater was annoyed with himself. The cook had referred to a person upstairs; someone who did not want to eat lunch. He should have followed up on that one.

Impatience clawed at his stomach. He shouldn't be in here waiting for the chief constable to come in and placate the Queen's Counsel. He should be on his way to The Laurels to squeeze whatever information he could from Enid Cheviot.

His mind was full of thoughts of Dorothy. He had a vivid memory of arresting her. He could still feel the warmth of her body as he struggled to control her and slip her hands into the handcuffs. He remembered having his arm around her, and the feel of his hand on her waist.

In her final struggle, she had turned to face him, and he felt the swell of her breasts pressed against his chest. She had smiled then and stopped struggling. He knew that he had not been the victor. She was the one in handcuffs, but he was the one who had lost the fight. Now he was in danger of losing the woman. His only consolation was the thought that if someone wanted Dorothy dead, they could have killed her that night. They had taken her alive. He could think of only one reason why, and that reason filled him with impatience.

He heard the door opening behind him, and the heavy tread of the chief constable. The chief shook hands all around, muttering reassuring phrases, and then he zeroed in on the dog. Slater groaned inwardly. He had forgotten about the chief's passion for gundogs. Now he and Trewin were deep in conversation about the dog's ancestry. Daisy! Ridiculous name for a dog.

Dorothy's son released his grip on the dog and retreated to a chair. Slater looked at the boy's tear-stained face and again regretted his impatience with the boy. He wondered how the chief and the old colonel could allow themselves to be distracted by a dog. The boy's silent anguish was the loudest voice in the room, but they were talking about the dog's ability to keep the pantry stocked.

"She's an old girl now, of course," Trewin said. "Her hunting days are over, but she was with me all through the war. There's many a family that wouldn't have had meat on their table if Daisy hadn't done her part. I had orders to shoot her, you know."

The chief patted the dog's head. "Glad she's still here." He turned his attention away from the dog and back to Penhelen. "We'll do our best," he repeated, "but ..."

Slater was suspicious of his boss's tone of voice, of the use of the word but, of the way the chief let his words trail away.

Penhelen nodded knowingly, picking up where the chief had left off. "But we are still in dangerous times."

"Yes, we are," the chief said, "and Miss Findlay is just one woman." He nodded to Slater. "Do your best."

The door closed behind the chief constable, and the room was momentarily quiet. Do your best, Slater thought. When had he ever done less than his best? He picked up his raincoat. He wore the same coat that he had worn on his first day as a detective. It was the coat he had worn to watch Billy Cheviot being released from Wormwood Scrubs. The coat was his uniform now; his badge of office. He shrugged the coat over his shoulders and inserted his arm into the sleeve. It was a maneuver he had practiced over and again until he could do it smoothly without looking clumsy or weak.

He looked around, noting that everyone was staring at him. They were waiting for him to make the next move, but he was not the first to speak.

Colonel Trewin's voice was firm and decided. "I'm going to The Laurels. Don't try to stop me. She's my daughter, and if I can't get the truth out of her, no one can."

Slater thought of the overwrought, fluttering creature who occupied The Laurels. Father or not, Trewin would not learn the truth from her. She knew nothing. Michael was the one who knew. The mother called herself an actress, but the son was the real actor. The son was the one who was living a lie, and the colonel would get nothing from him.

It seemed that Trewin could read Slater's thoughts. "I'll ask him some questions, you know, life in the trenches, that sort of thing, see what he says."

Penhelen placed a restraining hand on his friend's arm. "Wrong war, old chap. No trenches this time, thank God."

"You know what I mean," Trewin snorted. "Army life is army life. I'll know soon enough if he's lying."

Penhelen shook his head. "He's been home six years and never said a word about it. You'll get nothing out of him. He's smart enough to keep quiet. He'll blame everything on shell shock."

"Shell shock," Trewin muttered. "Damned cowardice if you ask me. He may have his mother fooled, but he doesn't fool me."

Slater contemplated the angry old man. "So you're convinced that your grandson was never in the war?" he asked.

Trewin's face crumpled, the anger draining away into a look of infinite sadness. "God help me," he muttered, "but I think it's all a lie. I saw him leave home with his travel papers and his kitbag, telling me he was off to Sandhurst for officer training. Enid was weeping and flinging herself about, but I wanted to be proud of him and I wanted to believe him. I should have known better, and now there's a dead man with Michael's face and a couple of war wounds. What other proof do you need?"

The color returned to Trewin's face. "If you won't get the truth out of him, Slater, I will, even if I have to choke it out of him."

Slater was aware of Toby standing at his side. "Don't let him go," Toby said softly. "He's no match for Billy Cheviot."

Neither am I, Slater thought, clenching a phantom muscle in his right arm. No, he was not going to permit the thought of Billy Cheviot to keep him from doing his duty. If he took the first step in that direction, he would soon find himself invalided out of the force. He summoned a confident smile.

"Thank you for your input, Colonel, but this is a police matter."

"She's my daughter. You can't keep me from her," Trewin insisted. "I'll be damned if I—"

Penhelen's smooth, urbane tones interrupted Trewin's bluster. "He can lock you up for interfering with a police inquiry," he said, "and it would take me some time to bail you out. In the meantime, what would we do with Daisy?"

The door opened, and a WPC poked her head in at the doorway. "Chief wants to see you, sir."

Slater grimaced. Now what? He followed the WPC from the room, hoping that Toby and Penhelen could prevent Trewin from making any rash moves while he was gone.

The chief constable's office was furnished with the remnants of an older, more formal lifestyle. Reginald Peacock, the chief constable, sat in state behind a massive oak desk. Behind him gold brocade drapes framed a view of the crowded promenade and the Palace Pier. The walls were lined with bookcases, and the carpet was a faded oriental. Slater stood uncertainly in the doorway, waiting for an invitation to sit in one of the leather chairs arrayed in front of the chief's desk.

"Come in, Slater."

As Slater stepped into the room, a figure turned from the window. The man he knew only as Frankie was wearing a short leather coat and a bright blue shirt. His brown hair, beyond regulation length and locked into place with Brylcreem, was swept into an exaggerated pompadour, leaving one curl to fall forward onto his forehead.

The undercover agent nodded a greeting. "Here we are again."

The chief settled back in his chair. "So you've already met," he said. "I won't introduce you again. We'll just call him Frankie."

Slater looked at the undercover agent and thought of the way he had disrupted the interview with Anthea Clark. "With all due respect, sir, I think I can be trusted with Frankie's real name."   Peacock gave a short bark of a laugh. "Settle down, Slater. Even I don't know his real name. Better that way. As you can see, he's undercover."

Of course he is, Slater thought. Someone like him can blend in, but someone like me … No, I'm just a raincoat and trilby hat. They'd spot someone like me a mile away.

"If he's undercover, why is he hanging around our station?" Slater grumbled. "Shouldn't he be lurking in dark corners?"

Frankie made himself comfortable in one of the leather chairs and waved an inviting hand to Slater. "I know what I'm doing; don't worry about me. I'm here to ask for your help; we need local knowledge and someone whose presence won't raise too many questions. I think you'll find this assignment is more interesting than dragging bodies from the ocean."

His voice was well modulated, the accent of an educated man, but Slater guessed that Frankie could cast that accent away anytime he wanted to. What accent would he choose? Welsh, Scottish, or just a mocking imitation of Slater's own London accent.

Slater remained standing, stiff with suspicion. "We have an unidentified body, possibly a deserter, and—"

Frankie interrupted him impatiently. "That war's over, mate. No one's interested in deserters."

Slater ignored the interruption. "And a missing woman," he said.

Frankie shrugged. He sat back in the chair and crossed his legs. Slater's eyes were drawn to Frankie's shoes, blue suede with a rawhide lacing. American? He wondered irrelevantly whether undercover had a budget for clothes such as leather jackets and suede shoes.

Frankie gave Slater a long considering look and shook his head. "Your case is one missing woman, Slater, old boy, and one dead body. We have bigger fish to fry. These are dangerous times. One war's ended but another one has started."

He cocked his head to one side. "How do you manage with just the one arm?"

"I manage just fine," Slater replied, "not that it's any of your business."

"It will be my business if things get physical," Frankie said. He shrugged. "You come highly recommended by your chief constable despite your disability. Well, it's your brains and your local know-how we want, not your brawn, so I suppose you'll have to do." He sprang to his feet and looked at Peacock. "We'll take him, sir. He can start tomorrow."

Slater stared from one man to the other. Start what?

Frankie zipped up his leather jacket and looked at Slater inquiringly.

"Can you shake hands?"

Slater reluctantly extended his left hand. "Of course I can." "Right." Frankie's grip was strong, and Slater returned as much strength as he could, but he knew his left hand would never be as strong as his right hand had once been.

Frankie released his grip. He took a step toward the door and halted. He turned back and stared at Slater for an uncomfortably long moment. His expression softened.

"What does she look like?" he asked.

"Who?"

"The missing woman. What does she look like?"

Slater struggled for professional calm. What did Dorothy Findlay look like? He had trained himself to be a keen observer, but his sudden rush of attraction for Dorothy, and the close quarters of her arrest, had blurred his vision.

"Well, she's blond ..."

"Natural or bottle?"

"I would say natural. Yes, definitely natural, not bleached. Her hair's long and it curls. She was taken from her house in the night. I think she'd be wearing a blue floral robe. I have the belt, if that will help."

Frankie shook his head. "Probably not. Doubt that's what she's wearing now. What else? How old?"

"Young."

"Teenager?"

"No, older than that, but still young. She's quite pretty."   "How do you know she's not dead?"

Slater's nascent resentment of Frankie reemerged, but he kept his voice steady. "I don't know, but I hope. She's young, she's blond, and I've heard there's a ... market ... for blondes ... in the Middle East."

Frankie pursed his lips. "There is. Middle East, Far East, anywhere that a natural blond is a rarity. Is she a virgin?"

The chief constable, still seated behind his desk, coughed irritably. "Must you?"

"It affects the market value," Frankie said.

Slater shook his head. "No, she's not."

"And you would know because ...?"

"Because she has a ten-year-old son who would very much like to have his mother returned to him," Slater snapped.

Frankie looked at the chief constable and then back at Slater. "I may be able to help you, Slater. In fact, this may not be too far removed from your new assignment. We've been looking into some comings and goings at Shoreham Harbour. At first glance, it seems like nothing more than an old sailing barge bringing in black market goods, sausages and the like. We know the locals haven't cracked down on it, because it's hardly worth the trouble; people need food."

He ran a hand across his smoothly styled hair and flicked a finger against his leather jacket. "We all buy from the black market from time to time, don't we?"

"I don't," Slater said stiffly.

"Some of your colleagues do," Frankie replied. "That's why this man has been running in and out of the harbor without a word being said."

Slater resented the Londoner's implication, although he knew it contained a kernel of truth. Black market goods could be found in every back street and in almost every home. Obviously, smuggling was alive and well all along the coast.

"Customs and Excise board every ship that comes into the harbor," Slater protested.

"Yes, they do," Frankie agreed. "They examine every vessel that ties up on the quay, but that's not every vessel that enters the harbor, and that's one of the reasons we want to bring you on board. You can investigate a local problem without raising any warning flags, but if the Met gets involved, things may go differently."

Slater shifted his weight impatiently. "What's your point?"

"The barge comes in on the tide," Frankie said, "and rides the current up the river, no sails, no motor, just ghosting up on the flood tide and running back on the ebb; takes a flat-bottom boat to do that, and some cooperation from the police farther up the river. If I had a woman I wanted to get out of the country, that's the way I'd do it."

He looked at the chief constable, and his dark eyes were suddenly very serious. "Or if I had someone to bring in; someone who could make a lot of trouble." He looked back at Slater. "Like I said, if Slater here went to investigate, there would be no alarm bells. Local bobby looking for a missing woman, nothing unusual about that."

He pushed back his sleeve and displayed a gaudy gold watch, the finishing touch to his undercover wardrobe. He frowned abstractedly. "I'm running late. Your chief constable will have to fill in the details." He reached inside his pocket and produced a tattered booklet. "Tide tables," he said. "Better check for the next high tide."

He twitched his leather jacket back in place and smoothed his hair. "You won't see me coming and going," he said, "but you'll find me here when you need me."

He opened the door, peered up and down the corridor, and departed silently.

Slater felt a rising desire to laugh. Frankie was too dramatic for his own good. He caught the chief's eye, hoping to see the same amusement.

"He's not exactly undercover, is he?" he asked. "He was lurking around the canteen. Nothing undercover about that."

"I suspect that he'll look very different the next time you see him," Peacock replied, "and I doubt he'll be called Frankie."

Peacock resumed his seat. "I'm giving you a temporary transfer to the Met. You'll be under Frankie's direct command." "For how long?"

"Until after the coronation."

Something in the chief's tone made Slater swallow his protests. "Why, sir?" he asked. "It's still a year away; why should we be so concerned about the coronation now?"

Peacock rose and walked to the window, standing with his back to the light so that Slater could not see his expression but could only hear his grim tone.

"Frankie was right when he said that one war is over and another is just beginning. It's not just idle talk to say that these are dangerous times. We may be facing sedition, treason, even civil war."

Slater went to stand beside Peacock. He needed to see the man's expression. Was he serious? Civil war! How? Why?

Peacock turned to acknowledge him. "The new queen is very young. Some would say too young."

"But she's queen," Slater protested. "Nothing they can do about that. I'm sure no one expected the King to die so suddenly, but she's the heir."

Peacock ran his hand across his chin. "Not necessarily."

"I don't understand you."

"There are some people, people with influence, I might add, who think that the Duke of Windsor would be a more suitable monarch."

Slater's mind was reeling. If he had faith in anything, he had faith in the British institution of monarchy and the peaceful transition from one monarch to the next. Surely no one could truly believe that young Elizabeth should be pushed from the throne by the exiled Duke of Windsor.

"Has the Duke agreed to this?" he asked.

Peacock shook his head. "We don't know. We only know that it has been suggested by some elements of the aristocracy. Not everyone was happy that we resisted Hitler."

Slater could hardly contain himself. "Resisted?" he hissed. "We did more than resist. We beat him into the ground."

"And destroyed our own economy," Peacock replied. "The Duke of Windsor was on good terms with Hitler, even admired him. The Duke and Duchess visited Hitler before the war, and it's possible that Hitler made him an offer. Keep Britain out of the war and I will make you king, and the American woman can be queen. We could be facing the same situation again now with the Soviets courting the Duke.

The propaganda is already out. Elizabeth is too young, her husband is a foreigner, half German, half Greek, and comes from a family with a history of mental illness. Wouldn't it be better to bring back Edward the Eighth? Isn't an American divorcée a better consort than a Greek-German prince?"

Slater was shocked into silence. Why had he never heard this before? He would not be surprised to hear that some lunatic was planning to disrupt the coronation or even blow up the royal coach; the world was full of lunatics, but this was something new. He had no idea that sedition was brewing in the House of Windsor itself.

Like everyone else, Slater had seen photographs of the King's funeral. The Duke of Windsor, returned briefly from exile, was just one of the dignitaries walking solemn-faced in the funeral procession. He had been in naval uniform, and Slater had wondered if a man who had given up his throne and abandoned his country should be allowed to wear that country's uniform and display its badges of rank.

Slater found his voice. "The Duke of Windsor had his chance," he grunted, "and he gave it up so he could marry that American woman. Are you saying that he wants to come back now and be king?"

"I don't know what the Duke wants," Peacock replied, "but I know that the talk is getting out of hand. The British government has a D-Notice in effect to cover the royal family; no British paper will print a word of this rumor, but the foreign press can print anything they like, and we can't stop them."

"And foreign newspapers come over on every ferry," Slater said. "What are they reporting?"

"They're saying that the Duke of Windsor has been making clandestine visits to Britain to talk to his supporters."

Slater stared out of the window at the people sunning themselves on the promenade. He told himself that it didn't matter which member of the House of Windsor sat on the throne. His life would be same whether the golden coach was occupied by the young woman with the foreign husband, or by the old uncle with the divorced wife. His mind was made up.

"I'm sorry, sir. I'm not the man for this job. I need to get back to my own investigations. I have a body to identify and a woman to find. All this talk about treason and goings-on in high places is not for me. I'm not interested in a transfer."

Peacock turned to look at him. "Sorry, Slater, this is not up to you, and you're knee-deep in this already."

"No, I have a missing person and an unidentified body. I don't see how—"

"Enid Cheviot," Peacock said.

"What about her?"

"Before she married Cheviot, she was Enid Trewin, a struggling actress trying to make her way up the social ladder."

"Yes, I know."

Peacock ignored the interruption. "Rumor had it that she and the Duke had a little something going on."

Slater took a deep breath. He could see where this might lead. "Do we have any proof?"

"We can't prove that she slept with the Duke," Peacock replied, "but we can prove that she stayed in touch with him after her marriage. We have a letter that she wrote to him during the war, asking him to use his influence to keep her son out of active duty."

"What was his reply?"

Peacock waved a dismissive hand. "He never saw the letter. It was intercepted by the censors."

And she found some other way to keep her son out of the army, Slater thought.

Peacock turned his eyes away from the activity on the promenade and looked inquiringly at Slater.

"So, we have an unidentified body, a woman who writes letters to the Duke, and another woman who disappeared after she claimed that Michael Cheviot was the father of her son, and we have a barge that slips in and out of one of our harbors. Need I say more?"

Slater reached out and took the tattered book of tide tables. "No, sir."

Dorothy Findlay

She thought she was going to die. Coughing no longer helped. Her throat was clogged with coal dust. She tried to remain calm and breath through her nose, but her nose was clogged. Her head was spinning. She scrabbled with her feet, trying to remain perched on top of the coal. She couldn't go on, not even for Eric.

The door opened, flooding the coal bunker with blinding light. A rough hand pulled her out into the open air and ripped off her gag.

"Cor struth, look at you. What the hell you been doing to yourself?"

Dorothy stared up into Billy Cheviot's face. She wanted to say so much, beginning with the fact that she had been doing nothing to herself;

he was the one who had been doing it. She couldn't speak; all she could do was cough up coal dust in between gasping breaths of clean air. She couldn't fight him. She had to breathe. She had to stay alive.

Billy held her at arm's length and looked at her as he might look at an unsatisfactory piece of fish. He wrinkled his nose.

"You stink, woman."

She didn't know how she could still feel shame, but she did. She'd gone all night and most of the day without a chance to go to a toilet. What did he expect?

"I won't get nothing for you, not like that." Billy glared at her as if she was responsible for her own condition. "I'll have to hose you down."

She coughed up the last mouthful of coal dust. She had no time to think about what he'd just said; not about hosing her down, not about getting nothing for her, or what any of that meant. She was finally in a position to do something. She couldn't run with her hands and feet tied, but she could scream. Her eyes flicked from the rear wall of The Laurels to the house next door, where the upstairs windows stood open. She thought she saw a woman looking out. This was it, her one chance. She screamed.

The woman leaned from the window, staring down at her. Dorothy had an impression of tightly curled blue hair, thin eyebrows, several chins.

She screamed again.

The woman closed the window abruptly.

Dorothy gathered her breath for another scream, but before she could make a sound, she heard another voice. Someone had come up behind her.

"Who is this sad creature?" the voice asked.

She turned her head and saw … No, not really. He could not be who she thought he was. This was the top of the slope that would lead to madness and defeat. She would not think of this person; she would think of Eric. And she would think of Slater. He would find her. She knew he would.

CHAPTER TWELVE

Anthea Clark

Anthea was surprised at the air of command her employer had assumed. Until Mr. Champion entered Percy Slater's office, she had been the one making plans. Inspector Slater had not returned, and so she had taken over. Toby would convey Mr. Penhelen to the train station to catch the express to London, and he would also take custody of Eric and the dog, Daisy. She, Anthea, would return to The Laurels with Michael's grandfather, and together they would get to the bottom of the whole affair.

She was glad to see Mr. Champion in such apparent good health, but she resented the way he was now demolishing everything she had planned. She had looked forward to confronting Michael. She was now fully convinced that he was not the man she had met in Canterbury, and she was equally convinced that the man in the mortuary had died so that Michael could stay alive. She wanted to know why.

While she had been making plans and putting them into practice, something else had happened; something so unexpected that she had no idea how to react. Perhaps she was just a foolish old woman imagining things, but she was quite certain that Hugh Trewin had winked at her. She told him that she would be willing to go with him to confront his daughter and grandson, and he had winked. She wouldn't mention it, of course. Perhaps he had a droopy eyelid, or a facial tic. No, she wouldn't mention it, but she found a place for the wink in a corner of her heart that had been a long time without warmth. It was tucked in there next to her memory of the young officer in Canterbury, along with her motherly affection for Toby Whitby, and along with the faded sepia of a man in uniform; a man who had not come back.

Mr. Champion's voice, usually somewhat breathy and tremulous, had become a voice of command as soon as he entered the office.

"Absolutely not," he declared upon hearing Anthea's plan. "I won't hear of it. Mr. Penhelen's meeting in London is not until tomorrow afternoon, and he can take the midday train. Until then I shall expect both of these gentlemen to stay at my house. Bring the dog and bring the boy. Plenty of room in the car."

Anthea looked at the eminent barrister and the warlike old colonel, and she saw their spines straighten and their eyes snap forward. Apparently, her feeble, pedantic old employer had once been a commanding presence in the trenches, and the old soldiers still recognized his worth. Nothing more was said about Anthea and the colonel going to The Laurels.

So now what was she to do? She could go home as she did every evening, but then what would she do? No, she was not going to be excluded. She had made the initial identification. She was not going to be left out now. Mr. Champion and his cohorts had been raised to act as gentlemen. They didn't know how to confront Enid Cheviot, but Anthea had no such scruples. She would be quite happy to choke Enid with her own fluttering scarf until she spoke the truth.

She made up her mind. She would ask Toby to drive her to The Laurels.

"Miss Clark. Miss Clark!"

She turned to find her employer fixing her with a puzzled gaze. "Are you coming?"

"Coming where?"

"My housekeeper is preparing dinner, and we would be glad of your company."

Anthea could not suppress a sour thought. Not only was he preventing her from going to The Laurels, he was assuming she would help to serve dinner. Her annoyance dissipated as she caught Colonel Trewin's eye and saw it droop again. A tic! Surely it was a tic, but ...

"I'm going to the office to make a phone call," Toby said.

"You're not coming for dinner?" Penhelen asked.

Anthea saw Toby's indecision. Penhelen's influence and contacts could be the key to a bright future for Toby, but she suspected that Carol was expecting a phone call, and she knew that Toby was waiting for a decision from her. Toby shook his head. He was going to make his phone call. She gave a silent cheer and followed Mr. Champion outside to the waiting Armstrong.

The hour was still early. Anthea knew that people of Mr. Champion's class rarely dined before eight, or even nine, and the cook and housekeeper would certainly need time to make a meal for so many unexpected guests. Where would they find sufficient food?

The housekeeper, red-faced and distracted, met them in the hall. This was not the first time Anthea had been in the house, but she had never gone beyond Mr. Champion's walnut-paneled study. Now she could see through the open door of the dining room, where a white linen cloth sat slightly askew on a long table, and beyond that, she could see a terrace and a garden where early spring flowers bloomed.

Mr. Champion took Daisy's leash from the colonel and offered it to the housekeeper. "Find her some food, Mrs. Ellerby, and a bowl of water."

Mrs. Ellerby hesitated, but Mr. Champion thrust the leash into her reluctant hand. "Too long since we had a dog in the house," he said jovially, "but Mrs. Ellerby will cope."

"Oh yes," the housekeeper muttered. "I'll cope."

With Daisy out of the way, Eric stood in the wide hallway, looking small and forlorn. Although it was now late afternoon, he was still wearing pajamas; no one had thought to fetch clothes for him. She should have taken care of that, Anthea thought. She should have gone to the flat and fetched his clothes.

It was Hugh Trewin who finally took notice of Eric's predicament. He put an arm around the boy's shoulders.

"Come on, old son; try not to worry. We'll find your mother. We're all very clever fellows here. Don't you worry about a thing. Why don't you go into the kitchen and keep Daisy company? You don't want to be out here with us old stiffs. Go on, there's a good chap."

He patted Eric's head and followed him with his eyes as he went through the green baize doors into the servant's hall. Anthea saw him lift a hand and swipe it across his eyelids.

A few moments later, the housekeeper appeared with a pair of scissors in her hands. Her approach to Anthea was hesitant, but nonetheless determined.

Anthea knew it would come to this. She had ridden in the car with the guests, she had entered by the front door, but now she would be relegated to her true position. She was Mr. Champion's employee and she was a woman. What would it be? Cooking? Serving? Finding clothes for the boy?

Mrs. Ellerby offered her the scissors. "Miss Clark, I wonder if you would be so kind as to go into the garden."

Into the garden? Was she to pick peas or dig potatoes?

Anthea had not intended to snap, but her voice was sharp and resentful. "What do you want?"

"I thought," said Mrs. Ellerby, "that you being a lady, you might not mind selecting a few flowers for the dinner table. The lilacs are coming into bloom, and perhaps some of the tulips."

Flowers! Mrs. Ellerby wanted her to pick flowers. Mrs. Ellerby had called her a lady. Anthea's mind wandered along long-forgotten pathways to a time when summer had meant light muslin dresses, tennis on the lawn, music lessons from an elderly Italian man, and flower-arranging classes from Mother. Anchor your arrangement with three tall, straight blooms. Work in threes, Anthea, and keep it natural. Don't be so rigid. You are always too rigid.

Anthea snatched up the scissors. "Yes, yes, of course. Do you have a cutting basket?"

"I set it down in the dining room," Mrs. Ellerby said. "I was going to do it myself, but we're all at sixes and sevens in the kitchen."

"I understand," Anthea said sympathetically as she followed the housekeeper into the dining room.

Mrs. Ellerby was red-faced with anxiety. "Now, where did I put it?"

Anthea found the willow basket on one of the dining chairs and held it up for Mrs. Ellerby to see. "I have it."

Mrs. Ellerby nodded in relief, but she made no attempt to return to the kitchen, where she was obviously needed. She sidled close to Anthea. "Miss Clark, I'm sure you hear things that I don't hear."

Anthea pursed her lips. Was Mrs. Ellerby going to ask her about Mr. Champion's health? Perhaps she wanted to know about the old man's will. Of course, she would say nothing.

"It's about the coronation," Mrs. Ellerby said.

Anthea stepped back in surprise. Why would Mrs. Ellerby think that she, Anthea, would know anything about the coronation?

"Do you think it's going to happen?" Mrs. Ellerby asked. "Has Mr. Champion said anything?"

Anthea shook her head. "Of course not. Mr. Champion knows a lot of things, but I don't think he has any special information about the coronation. It's not for another year."

"Yes," said Mrs. Ellerby, "but who will they crown?"

Anthea had always kept herself to herself, you're too rigid Anthea, and she had never been the recipient of everyday gossip. Of course, she read the gossip column in the newspaper and the colorful articles in her magazines, but no one had ever gossiped to her like this, not ever.

"I don't know what you mean."

"The Duke of Windsor," Mrs. Ellerby said with a sniff of dislike. "I've heard it said that he wants to be king."

"I've never heard that," Anthea declared. "He had his chance, Mrs. Ellerby, and he gave it up."

Mrs. Ellerby dropped her voice to a whisper. "Perhaps he wants a second chance."

"I don't think—"

"Mrs. Gibbons, who chars for the family at number twenty-seven, says she's seen him."

"Seen who?"

"The Duke of Windsor. Bold as brass on the Palace Pier."

"She's mistaken," Anthea said firmly. She tightened her hold on the cutting basket. "Where are the flowers you want me to cut?"

When Anthea walked out onto the terrace, she found Colonel Trewin waiting for her.

"Do you mind if I come with you, Miss Clark? I feel the need of fresh air."

Anthea felt the heat of a blush rising to her cheeks as the colonel placed a hand under her elbow to guide her toward the lawn.

Evening sunlight illuminated the walled garden. Daffodils, tulips, and grape hyacinths rioted in the flower beds; lilacs bloomed in purple and white, filling the air with their sweet scent, and flowering rhododendron bushes screened the view of neighboring houses. Anthea stood still for a moment and fought an unexpected guilt. Her house had a garden, not such a large one, but nonetheless a patch of earth to call her own. Why had she neglected it? Why had she turned her back on beauty?

She stepped down onto the lawn and turned to thank the colonel for accompanying her. She did not expect him to trail around the garden behind her. She was not some delicate maiden, and he was not a lovesick suitor. Perhaps he would sit on a bench in the sun.

"Miss Clark." The look on his face drove away her silly fantasies. When had she ever seen such sadness?

"Colonel, are you ill?"

He shook his head. "No, Miss Clark, I am not ill, but my mind is full of such possibilities; hope, despair, memories." His voice faltered. "Could we sit down?"

"Yes, of course."

Now it was her turn to guide him with a hand beneath his elbow. She found a bench that had been warmed by the sun, and stood back as he lowered himself shakily into a seated position.

"Could I fetch something for you, Colonel? A glass of water perhaps."

"No, no. A glass of water will make no difference. Please, Miss Clark, just sit here beside me and let me talk to you. I have to talk to someone. May I call you Anthea?"

Anthea blushed. Since the death of her mother, no one had called her Anthea, but she liked the idea. She had a feeling that the colonel was about to trust her with a long-held secret; of course he could call her by her given name.

"Yes, of course."

He reached out for her hand and squeezed it tentatively. How long since anyone had squeezed her hand? "Hugh," he said. "I am Hugh."

Anthea hesitated. "I'm afraid Mr. Champion would not like that."

"No," said Hugh, "I don't suppose he would. We shan't tell him. What he doesn't know won't hurt him. Please come and sit, Anthea."

Anthea blushed. "Thank you … Hugh."

It was a small bench, and when she sat, she could not avoid physical contact; her shoulder against his arm, her tweed skirt brushing his leg. She felt a sense of companionship that she had not felt in many years. She wanted him to look at her, but he kept his eyes focused on the sunlit garden. "It's young Eric," he said eventually. "He reminded me."

"Poor boy," said Anthea. "What will happen to him if …"

Her voice trailed away. Her companion was not listening. At that moment, Eric was not his chief concern; something else was gnawing at him and filling his eyes with a memory of a long-ago sadness.

He sighed and turned toward her. "I want to tell you about my son."

August 1906
Bodmin Moor, Cornwall
Hugh Trewin

Hugh heard his wife's voice rising in pitch. "Where's Jacob? Where is he? What have you done with him?"

He waited. Margaret's panic was not unusual. Jacob was a curious and energetic three-year-old adept at slipping away from his nanny and hiding in cupboards and under beds. Hugh was a sensible man; some would call him staid. It was Margaret's energy and love of drama that had attracted Hugh to her when they first met at a regimental ball. Now, eight years and two children later, Margaret's natural excitability had given way to a tendency toward hysterics. Jacob was naturally mischievous, and Margaret was unable to take his mischief in her stride.

He returned to his reading, a new volume of poetry from Rudyard Kipling, and waited for the tumult to die down. A few moments later, Margaret burst through the door of his study, dragging seven-year-old Enid, who had muddied her best shoes and ripped her white lawn dress.

Hugh turned his mind to his bank account. Enid would require a new dress and shoes. Margaret would have to take her to the dressmaker in Bodmin. This was not in his budget. What about Jacob? Was he equally muddy? He was out of petticoats and into boy's clothing, so perhaps he had not done as much expensive damage to himself as his sister had done to herself.

Margaret pushed Enid forward. "Tell your father. Go on, tell him."

"Tell me what?" Hugh asked, setting the book aside and looking at his daughter's sullen face.

Margaret gave her daughter no chance to answer. "She doesn't know where Jacob is."

"He's probably hiding under the sink, or behind the wardrobe," Hugh said. "You know how he is, Margaret."

Margaret's voice rose to a shriek. "He's not in the house." She gathered a handful of fabric on Enid's dress and shook her. "She took him out onto the moor."

Hugh's heart rose into his mouth. The moor lay all around them. Beneath the brief summer blossoming of purple heather and yellow gorse, the land was stony and treacherous; sudden mists, hidden sinkholes, and wandering animals were a constant danger. The children were forbidden to leave the granite-walled garden.

"He wanted to see the pony," Enid said. She looked at Hugh with wide cornflower-blue eyes and smiled. "I only wanted to show him the pony."

Margaret shook her again but Enid's smile remained in place. Margaret leaned down and was nose to nose with her daughter. "Where is he now? Why did you leave him?"

"He followed the pony," Enid said. "I came back to tell you so you would go and call him. He'll come if father calls him."

Hugh looked at his daughter, and she looked back with perfect equanimity. "Will you call him, father?"

"If what you tell me is true," Hugh asked, "and if you didn't go out onto the moor yourself, why are your boots so dirty? Why is your dress ripped?"

Enid shrugged her shoulders. "I went a little way, but the pony was running and Jacob wouldn't stop."

"He's always wanted a pony," Margaret wailed. "If only you'd bought him a pony, this would never have happened."

"I'm not sure that anything has happened," Hugh said with as much confidence as he could muster. "I'm not sure Enid is telling the truth. Are you telling the truth, Enid?"

"Of course I am. He followed one of the wild ponies out onto the moor, and I called and called for him. I looked for him everywhere, and when I couldn't find him, I came to tell you."

Hugh was well aware that his daughter's story was changing moment by moment. Obviously, she and her brother had been on the moor; she could not get so disheveled playing quietly in the garden. He glanced out of the study window. The sun was still shining, but clouds were gathering in the north. Rain and mist could descend at any moment. He had no time to ask questions.

"What are we going to do?" Margaret wailed.

"We're going to find him. I'll turn out a search party. You search the house."

"He's not in the house," Enid said.

Hugh ignored her. "Get cook and the kitchen maid, and search every cupboard and every room. Where's the nanny?"

"It's her day off," Margaret said. "I thought they'd be all right without her. I told them not to leave the garden." She choked on a sob. "This is my fault. I should have stayed with them. I had a headache and was lying down. It's my fault." Her voice rose to fever pitch. "What will I do if we don't find him?"

Hugh had no time for words of comfort. He was already making an inventory of the men he could call on to scour the moor. He would have to be quick. If a storm blew through, the boy wouldn't last the night.

Instead of starting her search of the house, Margaret followed him to the stable, where he was saddling his hunter. "I think Enid's lying. I think she's done something to him."

Hugh swung his leg over the saddle and leaned down to speak to his wife. "She's just a child."

"She hates him," Margaret whispered. "I should never have left them alone."

May 1952
Anthea Clark

The warmth of the sun did nothing to ward off the chill that ran through Anthea as she listened to Hugh's story. She tried to picture Enid as a child of seven. Had she been stick thin even then, or had she been a normal, healthy child with a sun-bronzed face from playing out of doors with her little brother? Was it guilt that had changed her into the pathetic, selfish creature that Anthea had met at The Laurels?

Although Hugh did not put the thought into words, she knew what he suspected. Enid Trewin had taken her little brother out onto Bodmin Moor and abandoned him. She did not need to see Hugh's face to know that the little boy had never been found. Every word of his story spoke of loss and regret.

"And no one saw anything?" Anthea asked, and then wanted to bite her tongue. What was she asking? Had anyone found his remains; little bones scattered on the moor?

"There were very few people around," Hugh replied. "Some gypsies were camping down near Launceston, a few people were passing by on walking holidays. We asked them all; we even searched the gypsy camp. Nothing."

Anthea groped for words. "Your wife?" she asked. What had happened to the wife who had been lying down with a headache while her precious children ran wild on the moor?

"Margaret was unable to recover from the guilt. When it became obvious that Jacob would not be found, she would not allow me to speak of it to Enid. One night, she called me to her room; she had kept herself from me ever since Jacob vanished ..."

Anthea struggled to accept the intimacy of Hugh's confession. She had kept herself from me; well, that could only mean one thing, and it was not something that should be mentioned by a man to an unmarried woman. He was still speaking. She recovered her composure and listened to what he had to say.

"She made me promise that I would never harm Enid and that I would never blame the child for what had happened. It was not an easy promise to make."

Anthea could see how hard this was for Hugh even now. How much harder it must have been when the loss of his son was new and raw, and Enid was there in front of him, telling her story of runaway ponies.

"We had the first snow of winter," Hugh said. "It was a true blizzard, impossible to see your hand in front of your face. That's when Margaret walked out of the house and onto the moor. We never found her." He raised his eyes heavenward. "I like to think she went looking for Jacob, and not that she just ... well, it's a crime, you know, to bring about your own death, not to mention a mortal sin."

So Enid had been responsible for two deaths, Anthea thought, and maybe more than two if the body in the mortuary was taken into consideration.

Hugh had fallen silent. Perhaps he was dwelling on his wife's suicide, maybe even her eternal damnation, as if anyone could believe such a thing. Well, they couldn't just sit here forever, and she had flowers to cut. Why had he mentioned his wife and his son? What had triggered his memory?

"Eric," said Hugh as if in answer to her question. "Of course, he's a boy of ten and my Jacob was only three, but the resemblance is startling. It brought back memories."

She knew that she should not say anything that would betray a client's confidence, but how could she justify remaining silent when the man beside her so desperately needed a glimmer of hope?

"I'm assuming that Mr. Whitby didn't tell you about Eric's mother," she said.

"Only that she's missing. It's a hell of a thing, his mother disappearing like that."

"Well," said Anthea, "I shouldn't tell you this, but I'm sure you would find out anyway. Eric's mother, Dorothy Findlay, claims that your grandson, Michael, is Eric's father. She claims to have met him when he was on leave during the war."

Hugh blew out his breath in a long sigh. "Are you suggesting that I'm Eric's great-grandfather?"

"I suppose I am."

Hugh rose from the bench. "Poor little chap. I must go to him and make sure he's all right."

"Don't say anything about—"

"No, of course not."

He leaned down, and before Anthea knew what was happening, he kissed her on the cheek.

When he had gone back into the house, she lifted her hand and felt the place where his moustache had brushed her cheek. Her face was warm. How many years had it been since she had blushed?

CHAPTER THIRTEEN

Anthea Clark

Mrs. Ellerby had outdone herself with a dinner that no doubt required a heavy investment in the black market. Anthea did not let the illegality bother her. She sat on one side of Hugh Trewin, and Eric, in a borrowed dressing gown, sat on the other side. She tried to resist the urge, but occasionally her hand strayed to her cheek. Had his moustache made a red mark? Of course not. It was her imagination.

Hugh rose at the end of the meal and dropped his napkin onto the table.

"Look here, Champion, I'm grateful for everything you've done already, but I need another favor. I need to borrow your motor so I can go and see that confounded daughter of mine. I have to get to the bottom of this." He glanced sideways at Eric, and Anthea hoped that no one else noticed. "All of this," he said. "I have to get to the bottom of all of it."

"Morton's gone home," Mr. Champion said. "You'll have to drive yourself. Can you find your own way? If not, perhaps Miss Clark could ..."

Anthea was blushing again as Hugh turned to her.

"What do you say?"

"Of course."

"Better take your dog with you," Penhelen said. "She won't like you leaving."

Anthea was glad of the dog's presence, not that a dog could be counted as a chaperone, but the dog's heavy breathing and wagging tail reduced the sense of intimacy.

Hugh handled the big Armstrong with care. She guessed that he was not accustomed to driving such a luxurious vehicle. She wondered what he drove in Cornwall. She wondered many things.

Hugh brought the car to a halt alongside the sagging front gate of The

Laurels. Lights could be glimpsed through the bushes that enshrouded the house; two upstairs, one in the hall, one in a front room.

"You wait here, Anthea," Hugh said.

"No. I'm coming with you."

"Things may get nasty," Hugh warned.

"But she's your daughter."

Hugh shook his head. "She's Michael's mother. She'll do anything to protect him."

Anthea thought of the large, threatening presence of Billy Cheviot. She hoped that he and the cook had been given the night off, although she had no idea what the likes of Billy Cheviot would do for entertainment in the genteel suburb of Hove.

"I just want to talk to the boy," Hugh said grimly. "I'm his grandfather."

Anthea was lost for a reply. Now that she knew about Hugh's missing son, she realized how much value he placed on Michael, his only heir, and how badly he wanted to be proud of him.

When Hugh turned toward her, his face illuminated in the glow of the dashboard lights, she knew that she was wrong. Hugh had already abandoned pride and hope of a happy outcome.

He spoke in a choked voice. "I want to know who they killed," he said, "and why."

The words were out of Anthea's mouth before she could hold them back. "You don't believe that Michael went to war?"

"No, I don't. I should have put two and two together a long time ago, but I wouldn't let myself do it. He moaned and complained and fought against the draft in every way he could, and then suddenly, out of the blue, he packed his kitbag and went off to Sandhurst, whistling and saluting. I should have known he was up to something.

He opened the door and heaved himself out of the car. "I'm going to get to the bottom of this. Wait there, please, Anthea."

Anthea did not wait. She fumbled with the door latch, realizing that usually Morton or Mr. Champion opened the door for her. She was quite certain that Hugh would have opened the door if he wanted her to go with him to the front door, but what Hugh wanted was not the only thought in her mind. She thought of the man she had met in Canterbury. He had been kind, polite, and respectful, everything that Michael Cheviot was not, and he had saved her life. She owed it to him to find out how he had come to be washed up on the beach at Brighton, without his hands, without a name, and without anyone to mourn him. Now she would be his mourner.

Daisy whined pleadingly from her position in the rear seat. Anthea leaned in and took hold of the dog's leash. The spaniel would not be much of a guard dog, but she could offer her as an excuse. She followed you. I didn't know what to do.

Light flooded from the front door. Someone must have heard the rumble of the Armstrong's big engine and the creak of the front gate.

Enid Cheviot's voice, tremulous with surprise, carried easily on the night air. "Daddy, what are you doing here? It's the middle of the night!"

Anthea, with Daisy straining at the leash, stepped up to the front door and stood beside Hugh. Daisy offered a low, suspicious growl as Billy Cheviot's voice rumbled from the hallway, where he loomed behind Enid.

"Yeah, what you doing here? And what's she doing with you?"

Hugh turned to look at Anthea. He did not seem surprised to see her beside him. "She," he said firmly, "is Miss Anthea Clark, and you will refer to her by name. I am here to see my grandson."

"Oh, you can't see Michael," Enid quavered. "He's not here."

"You surprise me," Hugh said. He pushed his way forward. "I understood that Michael's injuries were keeping him at home."

Enid stiffened as the unmistakable sound of piano music drifted toward them from the end of the long corridor. She turned her head. "He needs his music," she whispered.

Hugh's voice was a gruff bark. "Why?" he asked. "What in his life is so terrible that he can't see his grandfather and he has to waste his time playing the piano?"

"The war," Enid said weakly. "He had a terrible war. You should never have made him go."

"Good God, Enid, it wasn't up to me. Everyone had to go."

"Not Michael," she insisted. "He's all I have, and it's destroyed him. Shell shock—"

Hugh exploded in anger. "Shell shock be damned! He was never anywhere near the fighting, was he? Where did you hide him, Enid? What hole did he cower in while someone else fought on his behalf?"

The breathless silence that followed his outburst was broken only by the trilling of the distant piano. One part of Anthea's brain registered the piece as Debussy, Prélude à l'après-midi d'un faune, while another part of her brain recognized that Hugh Trewin had told his daughter a truth that they had both tried to deny. The Michael Cheviot who had covered himself with glory in Africa and Italy was not the same man who was now hiding behind a closed door.

Enid took a step back, obviously startled. Her gaze shifted to meet Billy Cheviot's small, malevolent eyes, and she gave a faint sigh. She recovered her composure and lifted a pale hand to her forehead, setting her chiffon sleeve fluttering. "I don't know what you mean."

Hugh caught the hand and held it, fixing her with his eyes. "Don't you?"

Billy made a threatening grunt, and Daisy lunged forward at the end of her leash, pulling Anthea from the doorstep into the house and leaving her standing next to Hugh.

Hugh released his daughter's hand. Enid fluttered away from him and flung her arms out to bar the hallway. Billy gave another grunt, and Daisy responded by dragging Anthea closer to the Londoner's immovable bulk.

Billy raised a threatening hand. Enid screamed; no, not Enid. Someone upstairs screamed. Billy turned and lunged past Anthea, knocking her aside as he pounded up the stairs. Daisy growled as he passed, and jerked her leash. Anthea, trying to restrain the dog, collided with a delicate hall table that held a bundle of mail and an assortment of china objets d'art. The sound of breaking china and splintering wood drowned the sound of Billy's heavy footsteps. A crashing of dissonant chords brought the piano recital to an end.

Enid was first to speak. "Now look what you've done," she said breathlessly, staring down at the objects scattered on the floor. She looked up at her father. "Why have you brought that woman here?"

Anthea choked back her instinctive apology and listened for another scream. She looked at Hugh. Had he heard what she had heard? His eyes were fixed on his daughter, and he seemed not to have noticed the scream or Billy's sudden exit.

She had to speak. She could not let the moment pass. "Who was that?" she asked. "Who screamed?"

"Who screamed?" Enid asked. She raised the back of her hand to her forehead and swayed slightly on her feet. "I screamed. What else do you expect me to do when you bring a vicious dog in here and allow it to run lose and destroy my precious mementos?"   Anthea leaned down to pick up a fragment of china. Precious mementos? They looked like cheap china souvenirs. She had not been raised with money, but she had been raised to recognize quality.

Enid grabbed the fragment from her hand and spoke to her father in a voice of scathing scorn. "Take her away, Daddy, and take that dog with you. I will not let you see Michael, not now, not ever. He's all I have."

Hugh's voice was soft, his tone flat and deadly. "You could have had a brother."

Anthea felt the air sparking between Hugh and his daughter. He had spoken words that could not be unspoken, and Anthea did not dare to move. Why now? What had happened to make this the night of all nights; the night that Hugh chose to confront his daughter about the loss of her brother? Was it the conversation in the garden? Had talking to her reawakened old wounds and old suspicions that could no longer be contained?

She wondered if she should go to him and offer him her support. Should she take his arm?

She heard a door opening at the end of the corridor, and Michael's voice, petulant and vicious, cut through the crackling air. "Mother, what is all this noise?"

She willed Hugh not to turn. Don't respond to the voice you have known from his childhood. Don't look for the little boy in the cowardly man. Don't give them another chance to hurt you.

"Who is that, Mother?"

Anthea knew that she could not have stopped Hugh from turning. It was Enid's words that stopped him.

"It's no one, Michael. No one at all."

Hugh drew in a sharp breath. He staggered away without looking at Michael, without looking at anyone, and stumbled out into the night.

Anthea followed him to the car. Hugh moved very quickly for an old man. He had already started the engine by the time she caught up with him. She pushed Daisy into the back seat and took her place in the front.

"No one," Hugh whispered. "She says I'm no one." He leaned forward, gripping the steering wheel with tense, arthritic knuckles. "I don't know where the hell to drive to."

"Just drive," Anthea said. "Just get away from here." Hugh made several attempts before he succeeded in slipping the car into first gear, and they proceeded around the corner in a series of kangaroo leaps. Anthea wondered if she should offer to drive. She had driven in the war; she had done many things in the war. She knew that she could do better than the colonel, who seemed unable to differentiate between the clutch and the brake.

He brought the car to a shuddering halt beneath the feeble glow of a streetlamp and leaned forward with his head on the steering wheel.

Anthea tried to reassure him with a hand on his arm. "You had to tell her."

His voice was muffled and he seemed unable to lift his head. "She already knew. They've been making a fool of me for years. Every time I asked about his experiences, every time I tried to talk to him as one soldier to another, they answered me with lies. They've been laughing at me behind my back."

"No, not laughing," Anthea said. "I think they were afraid. Every time you talked to him, it became obvious that he had no experiences to share with you. They knew you would realize it eventually."

"So where the hell did he spend the war?" Hugh asked.

"I don't know and I doubt he'll tell you."

Hugh lifted his head, although he still would not look at her. "It wasn't possible for a hale and hearty young man to be out and about in public without someone asking him why he wasn't in uniform."

"I imagine that the Cheviot family found a place for him," Anthea replied.

"Enid swore that she would have nothing to do with them. After Penhelen had Ronnie declared dead, and after she bought the house in Hove, she said she was finished with them."

"Obviously, that was not the case."

Hugh would not look at her. He stared out through the windshield. Their brief juddering journey had brought them within view of the ocean. The wind that had wafted a warm breeze to Mr. Champion's garden had grown in strength and was tussling with the waves, whipping them into white caps and sending them to crash and grind on the shingle beach.

Anthea moved in her seat and laid a comforting hand on Hugh's knee. The gesture felt as natural as breathing. He didn't seem to notice. His mind was somewhere else. He had spoken words that could not be retracted. He had dragged a dreadful truth from the deep cellar of his mind, and it would eat him alive if he didn't speak of it.

"Hugh?"

He placed his hand on the gear lever. "Where do you want to go?"

Anthea kept her hand on Hugh's knee. All of her life, she had suppressed her emotions, and she knew what that had done to her, to any chance of finding a new love. He had told her half of the story, but he was keeping something back. It was time for him to speak.

"What did Enid do to her brother?"

August 1906
Bodmin, Cornwall
Hugh Trewin

Hugh could sense the hostility as he entered the gypsy camp, but desperation replaced any natural wariness. He set no limit on the amount of gold he would give for information that would lead him to his son. If the gypsies wanted his horse, they could have it. If they wanted his gold watch, he would give it to them. No price was too high to pay for the clue that would lead him to Jacob.

Squire Moyle went ahead of him directly into the circle of painted wagons. Children, playing in the dirt with sticks and scraps, scattered at their approach. Young women drew scarves across their faces and stared at him with bold dark eyes. He caught the glint of gold in the rings that pierced their noses and ears, and the hint of seduction in the flash of their petticoats.

Roscoe, Hugh's horse, hesitated and tossed his head at the pungent smoke that drifted from a half dozen cook fires. Hugh urged him forward until he could speak to Moyle. "Where are the men?"

"Gone to the races," Moyle replied. "Old Tissie Lovell doesn't need men to protect her, not with the trio of daughters she has. Be careful, Trewin; they're the very devil with a knife."

"I just want her to—"

"I know what you want. I don't think it will help, but we'll do it," Moyle replied. "It's your gold."

He swung down from the saddle. A small boy, barefoot and naked apart from a short shirt, took the reins.

Moyle gestured to Hugh. "You can trust them. They can ride before they can walk."

Hugh slipped down from Roscoe's saddle, and another seminaked urchin came to take the reins. Roscoe rolled his eyes, looked to Hugh for reassurance, and then, inexplicably, nuzzled at the boy with soft lips.

"Told you," Moyle said. "It's like magic."

Moyle gestured to one of the painted wagons. Although all of the wagons were adorned with bright paintwork, this one stood out as being brighter than the others. Three women were seated on the painted steps that led up to the doorway, where a bead curtain screened the interior. As Hugh watched, he saw a dark, beringed hand twitch the curtain and felt himself come under the focus of a pair of dark eyes.

"My friend would like to speak to your mother," Moyle said to the three women.

They retreated behind their scarves and spoke to each other in a language Hugh had never heard.

"They're true Romanies," Moyle said softly. "None of your tinkers or travelers. These are the true thing. God only knows where they're from or what language they speak to each other, but they go to church."

Hugh knew that his surprise showed on his face. He had never seen a gypsy, tinker, or any other kind of traveler in church.

"Papists, of course," Moyle said. "Look out, here comes the mother."

The bead curtain rattled aside, and a small figure appeared on the top step. Unlike her daughters, Tissie Lovell was not veiled. Her long gray hair was uncovered and unrestrained by pins or ribbons. Her shoulders were covered by an embroidered and fringed scarf. When she lifted her skirt to descend the step, she revealed layers of colored petticoats. Although these details lodged themselves in Hugh's memory, he was not aware that he had taken note of them as he stared at her face. Tissie Lovell's skin had been darkened and wrinkled by years of exposure to the sun, and her lips were set in an uncompromising straight line. It was her eyes, wide, dark, and intense, that drew him forward.

"You've come for a reading." Her voice betrayed an accent that he could not place; not French, not German. In his youth, he had taken the grand tour required of all young gentlemen, Paris, Rome, Venice, Budapest, but nowhere had he heard Tissie's distinctive accent. Of course, he had never spoken to a gypsy, and he was not aware what country the Romany called home. Were they like the Jews, wandering the world with no country that they could claim, or was Cornwall now their home?

"I'm looking for my son," he said. "I will do anything."

She held out her hand. "Cross my palm with silver."

He reached into his pocket. Silver! She had not asked for gold.

It was as though she had read his mind. "The power is in the silver. Gold is for ornament and horses. For this, I need silver."

The hand that she held out was small, clawlike, and very dirty. He dropped a silver florin into her hand. He expected that the fingers would close greedily, but she allowed the coin to rest in her palm for a long, thoughtful moment before she dropped it into a velvet bag that hung at her waist.

She waved a dismissive hand at her daughters. "Let him come."

Hugh followed her into the dim interior of the caravan. He ducked his head and stood stoop-shouldered until Tissie ordered him to sit. He lowered himself onto a three-legged stool and brought his knees up to his chin. Tissie's caravan was hung with velvet drapes, a satin quilt covered the bed, a pot-bellied stove bright with new blacking stood in one corner, and the ceiling was painted vivid blue and ornamented with stars. Hugh felt as though he had no room to draw breath, and yet he must remain. She had his florin and surely she would tell him something.

She drew up another stool and sat beside him. She took his hand in her own. He felt her callouses, harder than his own. The hand was cold, but as she gripped him, she seemed to draw some of his anxious warmth into her own fingers.

"Your boy was lost. He wandered the moor."

His heart pounded as he pictured Jacob's small figure lost and alone among the heather. "Where is he now?"

"Ahhh ..." Her sighing breath seemed to fill the entire space.

This was a trick. She would ask for more money and he would give it to her.

She released his hand. "He has gone."

"What do you mean? Are you saying he's dead?"

She rose with a jingle of bracelets and a swish of petticoats. "He has gone too far for me to find him."

Hugh clasped at her bony brown arm. "Tell me if he's dead. I have to know."

She pulled her arm free and took a step backward, and he saw compassion on her face. "He is not dead."

"Where is he?"

117

"I have told you all that I know."

"You've told me nothing."

"I have told you that he is not dead, but you will not find him."

Hugh wondered how much of her knowledge his silver had purchased. Could she really read the future?

"I'll look for him," he said. "I will never stop looking."

"You have crossed my palm with silver," Tissie said, "and I have spoken the truth. You will not find him."

Hugh hesitated, torn between the pain he already felt and the pain that he would now invite. She was a fraud; she knew nothing and yet he had to ask.

"I have another question."

She lifted her head and fixed him with her dark eyes. A chill ran down his spine, and he felt the air around him change and become charged with some ancient, unknowable power.

"What? What do you wish to know?"

"Did he follow a wild pony?"

She shook her head. "No. There was no pony."

May 1952
Anthea Clark

Anthea had no words to say. She would not ask him if he had believed the gypsy, because she could not imagine the answer. If he believed the gypsy when she said the boy was gone but not dead, then he must believe her when she said there had been no pony. If there had been no pony, what had really happened on the moor? Why had Jacob run away?

She could hardly bear to think of the long, long years that Hugh had wrestled with the gypsy's words, before he set them aside and embraced the existence of Michael, his grandson. Now this. If Enid would lie for Michael, what other lies had she told?

"She was just an old gypsy woman," Hugh said. "Why should I believe her? How could she know?"

"She couldn't," Anthea replied.

"No, she couldn't. Enid was only a child. Margaret had gone, but I had promised her on the day that it happened that I would never blame Enid."

"So you never told your daughter about the gypsy?"

Hugh shrugged. "What would have been the point? I had no proof, just the word of Tissie Lovell, bought and paid for in silver."

Hugh pulled out a handkerchief and blew his nose. He took his time, folding the handkerchief and returning it to his pocket, before he turned to her. She saw the gleam of unshed tears in his tired eyes.

"You've brought me hope, Anthea. If Eric is Michael's son, I shall—"

"We have no proof," Anthea warned.

Hugh started the Armstrong's engine and set his hands on the wheel.

"What if Eric is not Michael's son?" he whispered. "What if …?"

She rested her hand on his knee and waited for him to say the words that would change his world forever.

Dorothy Findlay

"I don't have to keep you alive. Dead women don't scream."

Billy's hand was clamped over her mouth, and Dorothy could feel the stubble on his chin as he pressed his lips to her ear and hissed. "I'm not sure it's worth keeping you; you ain't that much to look at and you ain't no virgin."

"She looks much better since her bath," said the other man, who could not possibly be the Duke of Windsor. Why would the Duke be staying at The Laurels? Why would he even be in England instead of Paris, where he had a comfortable palace? Why would he now be assessing her appearance, fresh from a bath and wearing nothing but a loose shift?

She had not eaten since she was snatched in the middle of the night. That was not long ago; a night, a day, and now another night; not long enough to cause hallucinations.

"What do you have in mind for her?" the Duke asked. She decided to call him "the Duke" because she had no other name for him.

"Get her across to the Continent and sell her on to the Middle East," Billy said. "It's a good trade, so I've heard."

"So she'll cross when I cross?" the Duke asked.

Before Billy could answer, a woman's voice interrupted them.

"What about the boy?"

Dorothy twisted in Billy's grip and caught a glimpse of Michael's mother, the actress.

"What are you going to do about the boy?"

She was talking about Eric. Dorothy's heart pounded. He had done what she told him to do and hidden under the sink. Did they go back and find him?

"He ain't nothing without her," Billy said nonchalantly. "He'll be just some orphan kid. Without his mother, there's nothing to connect him to you. No one will know he's Michael's son."

Enid hissed her disapproval. "He is not Michael's son. She's invented this whole story. My son would have nothing to do with a creature like her."

"Oh, I don't know," Billy said. "Any port in a storm, if you know what I mean."

"No," said Enid, "I don't know what you mean. Tie her up again and keep her quiet. Any more noise from her and that will be the end of my patience."

"She'll be gone on the tide tomorrow," the Duke said softly, "and heaven help her."

Anthea Clark

Anthea examined her companion in the light of the streetlamp. His face was pale and his eyes were closed, but he was aware of her presence. She had not moved her hand from his knee, and he grasped it now as if he would never let it go.

What could he be thinking? In the course of one night, he had heard his daughter dismiss him as a nothing, a no one, someone to be ignored. At the same time, he had finally realized that Michael, his grandson, had not only taken the coward's way out of war but had also claimed for himself the honors that belonged to another man. She wondered if he had yet reached the next logical conclusion, that Enid and Michael were responsible for the nameless body in Brighton Mortuary.

Hugh tightened his grasp on her hand. She had no words of comfort to offer. How could she comfort a man who had finally acknowledged that almost half a century ago, his daughter had abandoned her baby brother to the wind and weather of Bodmin Moor?

Perhaps that was not what happened. Perhaps Enid had a different plan. She had been seven years old; not a baby, but a cunning little girl. The movie magazines had decried Enid Trewin's acting talent, but they had been mistaken. Enid could act. She had been acting on the day she said that her little brother had run away from her. She had still been acting on the day that Michael went off to join the army. She knew it was all a lie. She knew he would never be put in harm's way.

Hugh's hand twitched and moved. She sat quietly with no way to help him. He would have to fight this battle alone. He would have to put the pieces together just as she was putting them together, and then he would have to choose how to live, just as she had chosen.

March 1918
Horsham, Sussex

Anthea watched her father moving the hands of the big grandfather clock.

"Moving the clocks indeed," her mother grumbled. "It's playing God, if you ask me."

"No," said Father. "Adding another hour of daylight increases productivity and reduces fuel costs for industry. You should be used to it by now, Adele. It's been two years."

"I wonder if it will end when the war ends," Anthea said.

"I daresay that we'll find out soon," her father replied. "Now that the

Americans have finally joined in, we'll make short work of the Kaiser, and that young man of yours will be able to come home."

Anthea's mother fluttered her hands in exaggerated excitement. Adele Clark had attempted to teach her daughter her own feminine attributes; the fluttering of manicured hands, the dropped handkerchief, how to sit like a lady, how to walk without striding, how to ask only appropriate questions. The list was long, and Anthea had been able to master only a very few of the items. Nonetheless, Jack had proposed to her before he went off to war, and the possession of Jack's ring had been enough to keep her mother at bay.

Adele fluttered her hands again. "I forget to tell you, Anthea. You have a letter from France." She beamed at Anthea with eyes grown misty at the thought of Anthea's romance. An officer! A brave young man in uniform! Who could say what he would be when the war was over, but at this moment, he was Adele's hero and the key to Anthea's future happiness.

Anthea's heart skipped a beat. Not all letters were love letters. Some letters came edged in black, not from the loved one, but from an unknown officer who made a pretense of knowing and valuing the deceased.

Anthea's mother shook her head, her somewhat frivolous curls swaying with the movement. "It's from Jack himself. Maybe he's coming home. Perhaps he's been wounded." She raised a dismissive hand. "Nothing serious, just enough to have him sent home so we can all stop worrying."

Anthea considered whether or not she was worried, and concluded that she was not. She trusted that God had given her Jack and would not take him away again. Jack's proposal had been a surprise. She had accepted him, of course. He was a soldier leaving for war; she could hardly refuse him, although she knew very little about him. He was her father's curate, and he could have applied for a military chaplaincy, but he had chosen to accept a commission and fight on the front line. They had not discussed his decision; why should they? She hardly knew him. He was someone she encountered as she worked among the poor of her father's parish. His proposal, when he was already in uniform, had been a stammered, last-minute embarrassment to both of them, but she had accepted him; it was her duty to accept him.

She looked forward to his return and to hearing him put his love into words. They would have unchaperoned moments, stolen kisses, and shared dreams of a bright future. He would be given a parish, and there would be a marriage and everything that went with being husband and wife. She was somewhat hazy on the details, but she imagined she would do her duty and give birth to his children.

The letter was on the hall table. She took it to her room and read it by the spring sunlight that still streamed into the room courtesy of the authorities who had decreed the moving of the clocks.

He had met a Frenchwoman. The rest of the letter was a blur. Her tears surprised her as they fell on the paper. Why should she cry? He was not dead, he was simply no longer hers. As she wiped the back of her hand across her eyes, she felt a stone settle in her chest where her heart had once been. She went back downstairs to help her father with the clocks.

"Is everything all right, dear?"

"Yes, Mother."

"Good."

Two days later another letter arrived. This one was edged in black and had been written by Jack's captain, offering his condolences on her fiancé's death. Anthea saw no need to mention the fact that Jack was no longer her fiancé; no need to mention the Frenchwoman who would grieve in secret. She moved the pearl ring from her left hand to her right hand and was glad that her heart was already made of stone.

May 1952

The stone in her heart was gone now. She thought that it may have melted some time ago, but tonight she was certain.

Hugh released her hand and straightened himself in the seat.

"I'm so sorry, Anthea. I just needed a little time."

"I know."

"I should take you home."

"Yes, I think you should."

CHAPTER FOURTEEN

Toby Whitby

Early morning light flooded the office while Toby made the phone call he had tried to make the night before. He sat with his feet on the desk and the telephone receiver pressed to his ear to pick up the subtle nuances of Carol's voice. She had offered no explanation of why she had not answered the phone last night, and the lack of explanation rankled. Perhaps that was why this conversation was proving to be so difficult. It didn't matter how hard he listened, or how much he wished it was not the case, all he could hear in her voice was doubt.

"Rhodesia is so far away, Toby. What if we don't like it? What if Anita gets sick? It's Africa; there'll be all kinds of diseases."

He struggled to remain silent and not to respond with an impatient demand for her to make up her mind. He had loved Carol from the first moment he set eyes on her, but that first rush of love could only carry him so far. He had already risked his own life to save her and her daughter, and he had offered to be a father to her child; what more did she want?

He no longer knew what to say. His plan was logical and in Carol's own interest. If she went with him to Rhodesia, no one would know about her past. No one would know that Anita's father had been a German prisoner of war. She could be just another war widow with a new husband.

For the first time since he had met her in the village shop at Rose Hill, he admitted to himself that his ardor was beginning to flag. Carol had left Rose Hill in a hurry after Anita's parentage had been revealed, and had taken up a position in a post office on the Welsh coast. She said it was temporary, while she and Anita got used to each other, and while Toby made the arrangements for them to be married. While she hesitated and made excuses, time was passing, and the job offer from the Crown Court in Rhodesia would not remain open forever.

If only he could see her face to face, he was certain that he could put matters right between them. When he was in the hospital, recovering from the injuries he'd received while saving her life, she had accepted his engagement ring. Why was she hesitating now? Was it really because Rhodesia was so far away, or was it something else?

"What if we didn't go to Rhodesia?" he asked.

"But you want to go," Carol argued.

"Not if I have to go without you. We could go somewhere else."

"Where?"

"Anywhere. Canada, Australia, we could even stay here."

"Where everyone knows about Anita," Carol said softly.

He felt the first prickles of real annoyance. He was being as reasonable as it was possible for any man to be, but she wouldn't respond. No matter what he suggested, she couldn't summon any enthusiasm. Would she be like this after the marriage? No, surely not. She was Carol, his love-at-first-sight miracle. All he wanted was to make her happy.

"I'll come and see you," he offered. "We can talk about it face to face."

He tingled with the anticipation of having her in his arms. Surely that was all it would take. The physical attraction was strong. When they were together, he felt that nothing could come between them. It was only the distance that was making things difficult.

"When?" Carol asked.

"Tonight.'"

"But if you come tonight, you won't be back in time for work in the morning."

" I'll talk to Mr. Champion. I'm sure he'll give me the time off. I'll take the evening express. I should be in by midnight and with Anita asleep, we'll have the whole night to talk or ..."

His words hung suspended and unresolved and Carol remained silent while he felt a flush rising in his own cheeks. Why was he such a fool when it came to women? Why couldn't he be subtle? Why did he have to blurt it out just like that? His whole body yearned to move beyond kissing and holding but this wasn't something to be suggested over the telephone.

He floundered, trying to overcome his mistake. "Do you think your landlady can find a room for me?"

Carol's giggle brought on a renewal of confidence and a promise that belied her words. "My landlady is very proper. You would have to promise to stay out of my room."

"Of course."

"But I wouldn't have to promise to stay out of your room," she whispered.

He heard the outer door opening and hurriedly returned the receiver to its cradle. Everything would be fine. He had only imagined Carol's sharp tone. It was no more than a distortion from the long-distance line.

He glanced at his watch. Anthea Clark was running late, probably as a result of last night's dinner party at Mr. Champion's house.

He rose from his desk and walked out to greet her.

"Did you enjoy the dinner, Miss Clark?"

Anthea gave him a sharp look and her cheeks flushed red. "It was very pleasant. Mr. Penhelen is quite a talker when he has had a few glasses of wine. He seems to know everyone in society."

"He's the son of a baronet," Toby said.

Anthea nodded. "That explains it. He seems to be on good terms with the Duke of Windsor, although he still refers to him as the Prince of Wales, which I find rather odd. You would think a man like him, one who goes about in society, would be careful to use the Duke's new title. Once or twice he even referred to himself as a King's Counsel, although now we have a queen. Perhaps he is simply forgetful."

Toby frowned. Penhelen had not struck him as forgetful.

"You should have attended," Anthea scolded, "for the sake of your career."

Toby sighed. "I know, I know. I wanted to talk to Carol, but as it turned out, she wasn't answering the phone."

Anthea's look grew even sharper. "Indeed? And yet she was expecting your call?"

Toby waved away Anthea's dubious expression. "I talked to her this morning. I arranged to go up to Wales tomorrow morning. Do you think that will be all right with Mr. Champion?"

Anthea picked up a sheaf of papers from her desk. "We're very busy, Mr. Whitby, and if you want to get into Mr. Penhelen's good books …"

Toby shook his head. "I don't need to. Carol's coming with me to Rhodesia, and—" He stopped abruptly. He had not told anyone about Rhodesia. He planned to give his notice when the time came, but not now.

Anthea raised her eyebrows, not in surprise but in doubt. "Is she?"

Toby sighed. Obviously, Anthea knew about Rhodesia, and if Anthea knew, then no doubt Mr. Champion knew. He had no secrets.

Anthea glanced down at the papers in her hand. "Well, if you are planning to go to Wales tomorrow, we'd better get on with this today. These are the names of burn patients in private clinics around the county. I have only listed women's names, of course. Here you are. You can read them while I make tea. I think Mr. Champion will be late today; he ate far too much last night, and I know he smoked a cigar. It's not good for him. I understand that Mr. Penhelen will be going to London later today."

"What about Eric?"

"He's with his … He's with Colonel Trewin. They planned to take the dog for a walk."

Toby flicked through the papers. "So no word of his mother?"

"No."

"And did Colonel Trewin visit The Laurels?"

Anthea concentrated on filling the tea kettle. "Yes, he did. I went with him. It was not pleasant."

Toby stared down at the list of names. Annabelle DeVries at the Beeding Memorial Clinic, Lavinia Winthrop at St. Joseph's in Upper Steyning. Tissie Lovell at St. Elphege in Peacehaven.

Tissie! What kind of name was that?

He raised his voice to be sure she would hear. "Is Tissie a woman's name?"

The tea caddy fell from Anthea's hand, scattering tea leaves across the parquet flooring.

"Tissie," she said. "Tissie?"

"Yes, Tissie Lovell is a patient at St. Elphege private clinic. It's one of the names you gave me."

Anthea turned her back on the steaming kettle and took hold of Toby's arm. Her face was white and he thought she might faint. "Oh dear! Oh my goodness! How could I have forgotten? I didn't know if it was a man's name or a woman's name, but of course, it's a woman's name. Gypsies! It's a gypsy name. Oh, Toby, it's a gypsy name."

Toby! She almost never called him Toby. Whatever was troubling her, it was obviously something very serious.

Her hand clung to his arm but she was steady on her feet. This was not a fainting spell, this was overwhelming excitement.

"Oh my! Oh my!" She stared up at the ceiling for a moment and then back at Toby. "It's the same name and that means that … Oh dear. I can't tell him, not until we know. But why? How?"

The phone on Anthea's desk rang. She ignored it. She seemed to be lost in confusion.

Toby slipped past her and unplugged the tea kettle before he picked up the phone.

"Champion and Company. Toby Whitby speaking."

Slater's voice contained a hint of excitement. "Got some news for you, Whitby, about your client."

Toby knew that he had only one client, but that was not something that Slater needed to know. "Which client is that?" he asked.

Slater's voice went from excited to impatient. "Dorothy Findlay. Who the hell else would it be?"

Toby thought of Eric pining for his mother and felt ashamed of himself. This was no time for a game of one-upmanship with the detective.

"Have you found her?"

"Not yet, but she's been seen. Get yourself over here. Now!"

Anthea Clark

Toby's words came from far away and held no meaning. Inspector Slater had news about Dorothy. Toby had to go to the police station. He had to leave now. "No!" She heard her own voice, sharp and certain. "No, you can't go, not yet. You have to hear what I have to say."

"I'm sorry, Miss Clark, but I really have to go. Why don't you have a nice cup of tea and try to calm down? I'll nip over to the police station and see what Slater wants. Dorothy Findlay's our client. I have a duty to her."

Anthea was only dimly aware that she had renewed her clasp on Toby's arm. She knew that she needed to be calm, but her mind was racing. She pulled him toward her desk and stabbed a finger at the list of names.

"Tissie."

"What about her?"

Anthea stabbed her finger again. "Hugh told me ... Hugh said ... He said ..."

She felt her voice fading and knew she was making no sense. She couldn't even form a coherent sentence. She had forgotten that she was still clutching Toby's arm, but she felt him gently lift her hand as he guided her to a chair.

"All right, Miss Clark, take a deep breath and tell me what this name means to you."

She struggled for calm. She could not expect Toby to act without a clear explanation. She had to tell him why the name Tissie was so important. She put her thoughts in order.

"Sit down, Mr. Whitby, and let me explain. Hugh, that is to say, Colonel Trewin ... he asked me to call him Hugh ..."

Toby raised his eyebrows. "Is that so?"

Anthea ignored his apparent amusement. Now was not the time.

"A long time ago," she continued, "before the First World War, Hugh had two children. Enid and a little boy named Jacob. They lived on Bodmin Moor, and one day, Enid took her little brother out onto the moor and somehow managed to lose him."

She paused and looked at Toby. "Although it is hard for Hugh to admit, it is obvious that it was not accidental. Enid wanted to be rid of her brother."

She held up a finger to silence Toby's inevitable questions. "Just take my word for it, Mr. Whitby. Enid knew exactly what she was doing. She told her parents that Jacob had followed a wild pony out onto the moor and she had lost track of him. Hugh and his neighbors went out immediately to search, but they never found him. Everyone assumed that the little boy was dead, but they kept looking. They found gypsies camped nearby, and Hugh paid money to a gypsy fortune-teller to tell him whether Jacob had died. She told him the boy was still alive but that Hugh would never find him. The gypsy's name was Tissie Lovell."

Toby drew in a surprised breath but said nothing. Anthea looked down at the list of names.

"Someone is using that name again. Tissie Lovell is a patient in a private clinic. This is more than a coincidence."

She saw the look on Toby's face turn from puzzlement to understanding. He held up a finger to buy her silence while he went to make the tea.

The phone rang again. He ignored it. "It's probably Slater," he said, "making sure that I'm coming."

She didn't want him to leave but she had to say it. "Dorothy's our client. You should go."

He shook his head and spoke above the sound of the ringing phone. "No, I shouldn't. I don't care what Slater's found out; this is more important. What's going on here is more than just a missing woman, and a body on the beach. This goes deep and I think we're getting to the bottom of it."

The phone stopped ringing. Anthea looked at Toby. She saw what she had hoped to see. Behind the glasses, his eyes flashed with understanding. She knew her own mind was tied in emotional knots, but Toby was thinking clearly.

He brought her a cup of tea and perched himself on the corner of her desk.

"So, let's review what we know," he said. "I think we can now be certain that Hugh Trewin's son didn't die on the moor. The gypsies took him and sold him to someone who wanted a child. The boy, Jacob, was given a new name and a new family, but the gypsy's name lived on in family tradition. I assume that the man we found on the beach was one of Jacob's children, which makes him Michael Cheviot's cousin. If that is the case, then the resemblance is not surprising. As for the patient at St. Elphege, I would guess she is another member of Jacob's family; perhaps a sister to the deceased, which would make her Colonel Trewin's granddaughter."

Anthea had not thought that far ahead. "We don't know for certain."

Toby spooned sugar into Anthea's teacup. "I think we do. Really, Miss Clark, this is mostly good news for Colonel Trewin. His son did not die on the moor. He grew up and had children of his own. Hugh has grandchildren, and if one of them is Eric's father, then Hugh also has a great-grandchild."

Anthea sipped the tea, hot and strong, and felt her confusion receding.

Toby had taken her tangled thoughts and set them out in a straight line. Hugh's son, Jacob, had not died. He had been sold by the gypsies and raised by an adoptive family. His children, whether they knew it or not, were cousins to Michael Cheviot, and Hugh was their grandfather. Eric was his great-grandson. He had a whole new family. She touched her cheek as though it still held the mark of Hugh Trewin's kiss. She should tell Hugh what she had discovered. She looked up and saw Toby staring down at her.

"Feeling better?"

She let her hand slide away from her cheek. "Yes, much better. I'm sorry about the confusion. The last few days have been …"

Well, really, what could she say about the last few days and about the awakening of long-buried emotions and memories?

Toby jingled his car keys. "Shall we go?"

If she left with him, the office would be unattended. Clients would phone and she would not be there to answer. Mr. Champion would arrive and find the office door locked.

She shrugged. It didn't matter. An old and terrible deed was forcing its way into the light, and people were dying. Now that she knew the truth, perhaps she could stop the killing, and the woman in St. Elphege clinic was the key. She patted her hair. A long strand had escaped from its prison of hairpins. She brushed it aside and followed Toby out of the door.

Detective Inspector Percy Slater

The woman who had asked to see him was Enid Cheviot's neighbor. Her face was at war with itself, somewhere between smug satisfaction and shocked disdain. As she looked around the shabby interview room with narrowed, disapproving eyes, he thought that disdain had the upper hand.

He struggled to put aside his automatic resentment of the woman. He had nothing to go on except her name; Mrs. Lucinda Hogg-Prewett. The hyphen annoyed him. The ease with which she wore her tailored tweeds, the blue rinse on her tightly curled hair, and the large diamonds on her arthritic fingers all annoyed him. He noted the caution with which she lowered her ample backside onto the rickety old chair in the interview room. As he took his own seat opposite her, he saw her pale, disapproving eyes cataloging the scratches and burns on the table that stood between them.

"I always knew she would let the neighborhood down," Mrs. Hogg-Prewett declared, and smug satisfaction won out over disdain. "The general and I retired to Hove for peace and quiet and to be among our own kind of people. We had no idea that some flibbertigibbet film star would be living right next door with those awful Londoners she has working for her."

The pale eyes in her wrinkled and powdered face showed no embarrassment at her condemnation of Londoners. She may well have realized that Slater was a Londoner, but just as he refused to acknowledge his resentment of her station in life, she refused to acknowledge his humble origins. To her, he was a policeman, and she had a complaint to make.

Mrs. Hogg-Prewett glanced at her watch. "I told my story to your desk sergeant," she said. "I'm glad you are taking this seriously, but I don't know why I have to tell the story all over again. I have better things to do with my time."

"I'm sure you do," Slater replied, and he looked at his own watch. He had wanted Undercover Frankie to hear what Mrs. Hogg-Prewett had to say, but Frankie was now unavailable. After flaunting himself around the police station for days, he had apparently assumed a new disguise and disappeared from sight.

Whitby had been his second choice, but phone calls to Whitby's office produced no answer. He knew that should have puzzled him, but he had no time to be puzzled. Over the course of his career, he had learned to value the testimony of a nosy neighbor. Mrs. Hogg-Prewett was currently enjoying her role as bearer of suspicious news, but she could change her mind at any minute. She could decide that she needed to attend a hairdresser appointment, she could take offense at not being conducted to a more suitable office, or she could even demand to see the chief constable. Slater knew what kind of woman she was, and he knew he was on shaky ground with her. He had to push her now.

"Let's go over this again, Mrs. Prewett."

"Hogg-Prewett."

"Let's go over this again, Mrs. Hogg-Prewett."

Mrs. Hogg-Prewett leaned forward in her chair. "It's not that I pry. For heaven's sake, why would I want to know what those awful people are doing? What with the piano playing day and night and those awful Cockney people banging about in the kitchen and using the kind of language that—"

Slater interrupted the flow of speech. "I understand all that, but that's not what you told the desk sergeant."

"Of course not. I understand that we all have to put up with these petty annoyances now that we have a housing crisis. No, I don't complain; live and let live, that's what I say."

Slater doubted that the concept of "live and let live" was part of Mrs. Hogg-Prewett's personal code, but he let the statement slide.

"You told the desk sergeant about a woman," Slater prompted.

"I most certainly did. It started two nights ago. I didn't see her, but I certainly heard her. I think she was in the garden shed. I could hear muffled noises, and someone was banging on the walls, and then I heard that awful man that Mrs. Cheviot employs—"

"That would be Billy Cheviot."

"A relative? Oh really, I don't know what the world's coming to. Well, whoever he is, he certainly knows some colorful language. We are not used to people using that kind of language in Hove. I was going to complain to Mrs. Cheviot about the noise, but that awful man took care of it. He went out to the shed, and after that, everything was quiet for a while."

"Did you see him go out there?"

"I most certainly did. I can see into their garden from my bedroom window. The general and I both looked out of the window."

"But you didn't report it?"

"No, I didn't. The general told me that sometimes people like to … do … things. Pretend things. I really don't know what he meant, but he told me that a lady wouldn't need to know."

A faint flush made itself visible through the coating of powder on Mrs. Hogg-Prewett's cheeks, and she moved hastily to the next part of her story.

"The general went up to London yesterday morning for one of his regimental reunions, so I was alone all day. I saw a police car arrive at the house yesterday morning, and I thought perhaps someone else had complained, and that would be the end of it. However …"

At this point, Mrs. Hogg-Prewett paused for dramatic effect. Slater raised his eyebrows questioningly and she continued.

"However, after the police had driven away, I looked out of the window into the garden, and I saw the most extraordinary sight."

"Yes?"

"That man, Billy Cheviot, was dragging a woman around the back garden. I think she had been in the coal bunker. She was covered in soot and dirt. She looked at me and screamed."

"She screamed," Slater repeated between gritted teeth. "And what did you do?"

"I very nearly called the police to return," Mrs. Hogg-Prewett replied, "but I remembered what my husband said, that some people enjoy that kind of thing. I must say that I thought it very depraved. I suppose it doesn't shock you. You're probably accustomed to that sort of thing."

"No," Percy replied, "we are not."

He wanted to say more, but anything he said now would interrupt Mrs. Hogg-Prewett's flow of information, and he didn't think she had yet told him everything she knew.

"So," he said, "what has brought you here today? Have you seen the woman again?"

"Yes, I have. The general stayed at his club last night, so I was alone in the house. Of course, I was very curious about what was going on at The Laurels. Last night, someone visited in a limousine, and I heard a dog barking. I was hoping that they hadn't acquired the kind of dog that would bark all night, so I went up to the attic and opened the window so I could have a good look around."

"For a dog?"

"Yes, of course."

Slater imagined Mrs. Hogg-Prewett taking the absence of the general as a chance to fulfil her prurient curiosity about what was happening in the garden shed. The presence of a barking dog was the last thing on her mind.

"We had a moon last night," Mrs. Hogg-Prewett said, "and I could see quite clearly. The first thing I saw was a slight, silver-haired man just walking among the rosebushes. The garden is severely neglected; the roses haven't been pruned in years." She looked at Slater. "I digress."

Yes, you do, Slater thought.

Mrs. Hogg-Prewett continued without digression. "I was staring down at that man, and I was sure I had seen him before. I know this sounds absurd, Inspector, but I could swear that it was the Duke of Windsor. I don't know how that's possible, but I have met the Duke, that was when he was Prince of Wales, and I am sure this was the same man. Of course, that's not why I came here. It sounds foolish for me to say that the Duke of Windsor is not in Paris, but that he's living in the house next door. Who would ever believe such a story?"

Slater had his own personal answer that he kept to himself. Frankie! Frankie would believe such a story.

"The man, whoever he was, went inside the house, and then the big man, the one who is a relative of Mrs. Cheviot, came out. He was carrying a woman. Her hands were tied and she had a gag around her mouth. I must say, I really don't understand why anyone would want to do that, but that's what my husband tells me, and he has been all over the world."

She lowered her voice to a confidential whisper. "I have heard that the Duke of Windsor has some strange proclivities, and as for the woman he married, well ..."

Slater put an end to Mrs. Hogg-Prewett's musing on why the Duke of Windsor had married Mrs. Wallis Simpson.

"Tell me about the woman."

"She was clean; she must have had a bath. Blond hair. Quite young. She was wearing nothing but a cotton shift, very short, and I'm afraid she had no underwear. I'm glad that the general did not have to see what I saw. After the woman was locked away in the shed, Mrs. Cheviot came out, all chiffon scarves and fluttering hands. She's a ridiculous creature."

But dangerous, Slater thought. Being ridiculous doesn't stop her from being dangerous.

"I could hear every word she said," Mrs. Hogg-Prewett declared. "She asked how long she was expected to keep the woman, and the big man said it wouldn't be long. He said the boat would be in on the next high tide, and then she'd be on her way."

Slater probed for confirmation. "They said this woman would be taken on a boat at the next high tide?"

"No. I'm sorry, Inspector, I misspoke, not a boat. Now I come to think of it, she said it was a barge. The big man said that a barge was coming in. I can't imagine what he means by a barge, but that's what he said. Then he said that they could kill two birds with one stone. He said they'd get good money for the woman. I'm sure I don't know what that means; perhaps my husband would understand."

Perhaps he would, Slater thought.

"And," Mrs. Hogg-Prewett continued, "he said they could take the other one. When he said that, the other one, he jerked his head toward the rose garden. I was assuming he meant the man who looked so much like the Duke of Windsor."

Slater sighed. This was something that Frankie should be hearing. Frankie might not care about Dorothy Findlay, but he most definitely cared about a person who was either the Duke of Windsor or someone who looked remarkably like him.

Mrs. Hogg-Prewett furrowed her brow and assumed a look of honest concern. "I stayed awake all night, wondering what to do. I couldn't call the general in the middle of the night and ask his opinion, so I made up my own mind. It may be that this woman is some kind of paid ... some kind of ... you know ..."

Slater offered her the word she was looking for. "Prostitute."

"Yes, that's what I mean. But even if she is a ..."

"Prostitute."

"I'm sure she doesn't want to be put on a barge. It all sounds very suspicious, so I decided to come and tell you about it."

"You were quite right," Slater said.

A thin anticipatory smile curled the corners of Mrs. Hogg-Prewett's lips. "Would you like me to continue to watch from the attic?" she asked. "If I tell the general that I am doing it on behalf of the police, I am sure he will not object."

No, Slater thought. After tonight there will be no point in watching. Whatever's going down is going down at high tide tonight. He felt a grudging admiration for Frankie. It was exactly as the undercover agent had predicted; a flat-bottom barge running silently upriver on the flood tide and returning with the ebb. Where the hell was Frankie? This was not a job for a one-armed flatfoot.

"Well?" Mrs. Hogg-Prewett asked. "Should I continue to watch?"

Slater shook his head. He didn't want to think about what would happen if Billy Cheviot should happen to look up at the neighbor's window and spot Mrs. Hogg-Prewett watching his every move.

"I think that you should go up to London and join your husband," Slater said.

She stared at him. "At a regimental reunion?"

"Do some shopping," Slater snapped. "Treat yourself to tea at the Savoy. Don't go home."

She left the office, protesting that whereas she could certainly take tea at the Savoy on her own, she could not stay at her husband's club, where women were not allowed.

"Just don't go home," he repeated.

He wished he had someone to take with him. A minor crime wave had erupted in Brighton, and every available officer was fully occupied. Even Pierce, who could usually be relied on to give a hand, was out on a housebreaking call. He thought of taking Toby Whitby because Dorothy was his client, but Whitby had answered the phone once, promised to come, and then fallen silent.

Well, thanks to Mrs. Hogg-Prewett, he knew where Dorothy was, and that was where he had to go, even if he had to go alone.

The desk sergeant handed over the keys of the adapted Wolseley.

"You going on your own, Inspector? Are you sure you don't want to wait for a driver? Should be able to get someone by this afternoon."

"I don't need a driver," Slater snapped, "and I don't have time to waste waiting for one."

"And if anyone asks where you are?"

"I'm going to Hove to see Billy Cheviot."

The desk sergeant whistled through his teeth. "Billy Cheviot! Now that's a nasty piece of work."

Yes, it is, Slater thought. He saw, or imagined he saw, the desk sergeant's eyes scanning his body and taking in the empty sleeve.

Slater knew what the sergeant was thinking. How would a one-armed man take on someone like Billy? He needed an ace up his sleeve, or in his pocket.

"Sergeant."

"Yes, Inspector?"

"I'll need a firearm."

"Yes, Inspector. I'll sign out a Browning for you."

CHAPTER FIFTEEN

Toby Whitby

A statue of St. Elphege stood just outside the door of the clinic that bore his name. Although the saint himself, draped in stone robes, wore a mild expression, the shield carved into the doorway above his head displayed a grinning skull split by a buried axe. The legend informed the world that he was indeed St. Elphege, bishop and martyr.

Toby opened the door and ushered Anthea into a long hallway. The floor was polished marble, the walls were institutional green, and the smell was the ubiquitous odor of hospital food and hospital sanitation. Toby had little time to process the unhappy memories of his own hospital stay before a nun hove into sight like a ship in full sail. Her starched wimple caught the light from the high-set clerestory windows and billowed with each step. Keys jangled at her belt, and her shoes squeaked in protest as she came toward them, her angular face set in lines of disapproval.

"Visiting hours are not until this afternoon."

Toby fumbled in his pocket for a card. "Toby Whitby, solicitor, to see Miss Lovell."

The look she gave him was sharp and suspicious. "Miss Tissie Lovell?" she queried.

"Yes. Is there a problem?"

Her thin lips curled and her tone was cold. "A small matter of an unpaid bill and registration under a false name. I didn't expect you for another half an hour. I assume you have the ambulance outside and the money to pay for her stay here."

Anthea looked at Toby and then back at the nun. "Has she told you her true name?" she asked.

The nun shook her head and set the wimple quivering. "We found it for ourselves. The burns are painful, and she's been too sedated to say anything to help herself, but when her brother failed to return, we had to take matters into our own hands. We searched the pockets of her clothing—she had brought no other possessions with her—and we found Mrs. Enid Cheviot's name and address. Mrs. Cheviot confirmed that our patient's real name is Madeline and she is Mrs. Cheviot's daughter."

She leaned forward, the shadow of her wimple falling across her face so that Toby could only see her thin disapproving lips. "I don't know how young Madeline burned her feet, but her mother seemed relieved to know that she wasn't here for a confinement. I told her that we don't do that sort of thing here. Our order has a home for unwed mothers, but this is not it. She told me the girl had run away from home some time ago, and they'll be glad to have her back. As for the brother, well, he's gone. I doubt he was even her brother."

No, Toby thought, that is the one thing that isn't in doubt. The man who brought her here and registered her under a false name was her brother, and only death had prevented him from returning.

"As the girl is not pregnant," said the nun, "I don't know why you persist in using a false name, but that is none of my business. I assume the ambulance is outside."

"It's on its way," Toby said. "We'd like to go and see Madeline and make sure she's ready to be moved. Meantime, if you would please prepare an invoice and send it on, we will make sure you are paid."

The nun stared down at Toby's card. "Anyone can print a business card and pretend to be a solicitor. How do I know this is genuine?"

Toby drew himself up to his full height. The nun's wimple climbed to its own intimidating height, but he was taller and wider. "Are you suggesting that you would hold her as a guarantee for payment?" he asked. "Are you aware of the illegality of such action, Sister?"

He was tempted to dazzle the nun with a flurry of Latin phrases, but it occurred to him that the nun, who no doubt prayed in Latin, would fail to be dazzled. He settled for a firmly worded warning. "Habeas corpus, Sister."

Anthea clasped Toby's arm. "We should go and see the dear girl," she said. "Make sure she's ready to leave, and you, Sister, should wait for the ambulance. They may not know where to go."

"Down the corridor, second door on the right," the nun said. She strode away with the card still clutched in her hand.

"She's going to phone the office," Toby said under his breath.

"I don't think we should worry about that," Anthea replied. "As I am here with you, there will be no one to answer."

Toby had a sudden premonition of trouble ahead. "If she gets no answer from our office, what will she do next?"

"She might call the Cheviot house," Anthea muttered. She shook her head. "I don't think we should take any chances. We should call the police now. It's quite obvious that this is the woman from the burning car, and it's all tied together with Michael Cheviot's war service, and Hugh Trewin's missing son."

Toby thought of trying to explain the situation to Slater. The story had been almost fifty years in the making. Toby had made a leap of faith in untangling the threads, relying on intuition as much as logic. Slater would not be interested in Toby's intuition; he would want facts. What facts did Toby have? A little boy lost on the moor, a gypsy woman with an unusual name, an old man crying on Anthea's shoulder, a dead body, and a missing woman.

Slater might not dismiss him out of hand. Toby had seen the attraction between Slater and Dorothy, and he knew that this case was personal for him. If Toby could talk to him, he might listen, but all of that would take time.

"We don't have time," Toby replied. "If that nun calls the Cheviot house, it will only make things more difficult for us. Apparently, the ambulance is already on its way, and I don't think anything good is going to happen once it gets here. Let's go and take a look at this girl called Madeline and see what we can do to keep her alive."

She was asleep with her dark hair spread across a starched white pillowcase. Her hands rested on an equally starched sheet. Her long, elegant fingers reminded Toby of Michael Cheviot's fingers. He searched her sleeping face for additional similarities. She had the same pale complexion, but that could be the result of weeks of confinement in a hospital bed. He put her age as somewhere between twenty and thirty, certainly no older than that. He would know more when she was awake.

"Feet," Anthea whispered.

"What?"

Anthea pointed to the foot of the bed, where the sheet was lifted to cover a cage. "The burns are on her feet. They don't want the blankets to touch the dressings."

Toby sighed. Is this what Madeline had expected? What terrible bargain had she made where this was the price?

Anthea placed a hand lightly on Madeline's forehead. "Wake up."

The eyelids flickered but Madeline's eyes remained closed. Toby thought of Billy Cheviot, probably already on his way in the ambulance. Now was not the time to be gentle.

He shook Madeline's shoulder. "Wake up."

This time, her eyes opened and she stared up at Toby, awake but uncomprehending.

"We have to get out of here," Toby said. "Can you stand?"

He turned away from her and lifted the sheet. Her feet were bandaged. He wondered if he would have to carry her.

He left Anthea to talk to the girl while he opened the door and peered along the corridor. Was there another way out? Yes. Daylight streamed through an open door at the end of the hall. He glimpsed grass and trees.

He returned to the room. Madeline was sitting up now, her feet hanging over the side of the bed.

"She's drugged," Anthea said, "and I don't think she can walk."

Toby studied the girl for a moment. Her legs and arms were thin, and her body beneath the white hospital gown seemed to be little more than bones. He pulled the sheet from the bed and handed it to Anthea. "Wrap her in that."

"Turn your back," Anthea commanded.

Toby bit back and angry response. Did Anthea really think that he had any prurient interest in Madeline's bony body when he had Carol waiting for him just a train journey away? He busied himself opening locker doors and pulling out drawers. No clothes. Perhaps they had been too badly burned.

When he turned back, Madeline was lying immobile on the bed, wrapped so tightly that she could have been laid out for burial. There was an efficiency to the way she was wrapped that suggested Anthea had done this before; but perhaps not to a living person.

Madeline's eyes had closed again.

"She won't give you any trouble," Anthea said. "I don't know what they've given her, but it's something very strong." She shook her head. "Burns are painful," she said, "but I don't think she's feeling any pain right now."

Toby picked Madeline up and slung her over his shoulder. She offered no resistance. Anthea opened the door and looked out into the corridor.

"Anyone coming?" Toby asked.

"Not yet," Anthea replied.

Toby hesitated and wondered if it might be possible to use the front door. If he could slide out past the statue of St. Elphege unnoticed, he could put Madeline into his car. If he went the other way, his car would remain in the parking area where it could be seen by Billy Cheviot in the ambulance. Did Cheviot know that Toby drove a Morris?

The sound of women's voices came from the direction of the front door. Surely it was too soon for Billy to be here, but the sisters were in the front hall, talking to each other, and he couldn't just walk past them with Madeline over his shoulder.

Anthea tugged on his arm. "Give me the keys; I'll move the car."

"Can you drive?" He knew the question was ridiculous as soon as he had asked it. It deserved the contempt that Anthea gave to it.

"I was driving before you were even born, Mr. Whitby. Now give me the keys. I assume that you are going into the shrubbery that I see through that doorway."

"Yes, I—"

"Very well. Make your way to the roadside and I will find you. Now give me the keys and go."

Detective Inspector Percy Slater

Now what? An ambulance was parked in the driveway at The Laurels with its engine idling. Slater pulled past the house and brought the police car to a juddering halt several houses down from The Laurels, where it was hidden by the overgrown hedge of a derelict house. As he was climbing out of the driver's seat, he heard the rattle of wheels and turned to see a large brown horse pulling a milk cart and approaching from the opposite direction.

The driver brought the cart to a halt, jumped down from the seat, and went to the back of his cart to collect a tray of milk bottles.

Slater grimaced impatiently. The horse was in his way. If he had to turn the car and follow the ambulance, he would have to get the milkman to move his cart. He could see the man approaching in his white smock and striped apron, a tray of milk bottles rattling as he walked.

No! Something was not right. Slater had stopped outside a derelict house where bomb damage was still evident. The roof had caved in, the windows were boarded up. No one lived here. Why was the milkman delivering to a deserted house?

The milkman whistled through his teeth as he approached, and the whistle became words.

"Morning, Slater."

Slater stared at the milkman. His hair was tucked under a white cap, and his face was pale and freckled, with a small ginger moustache accenting a mouthful of snaggled teeth. Only the eyes were the same, dark and mocking.

Undercover Frankie reached out to stroke the horse's nose and adjust the bridle.

Slater finally found his voice. "What are you …?"

"What am I doing here?" Frankie asked. "I'm hunting some very big game."

"The Duke of Windsor?"

Frankie raised his eyebrows. "Maybe he is, maybe he isn't. Maybe what we have here is a double. I'm going to take a look."

"I'll come with you."

Frankie sighed. "What's the point in me dressing myself up like this and commandeering a milk cart if you're just going to drag your big copper's feet all over the crime scene? Leave it to me. I'll do a backdoor delivery. Two pints of gold top and a half dozen eggs all taken to the back door, and no questions asked."

"Why is the ambulance here?"

"I don't know. A couple of likely-looking lads dropped it off a few minutes ago. If you want to make yourself useful, you can wait here and follow the ambulance when it leaves. Maybe that's how they're moving the woman, or the Duke."

"Is he the Duke?"

"I don't know, but if you follow, you might find out. As for me, well …" He stroked the horse's nose, and the horse snorted its approval. "Larry here—and that's a really ridiculous name for a horse, by the way—is not much on galloping."

"Is he a police horse?"

Frankie shook his head. "No. He's the real thing. He knows this route, does it every day."

"But—"

Frankie snorted impatiently, and Larry joined in by tossing his head and jingling his bridle.

"If you want to find your lost woman, I suggest you find out where Billy is going in that ambulance. Seems to me that would be a good way to move an unconscious woman; better than the boot of a car. You should get a move on and get the car turned around."

"I don't need you to tell me how to do my job," Slater growled.

Frankie looked past Slater and shook his head. "I think you do. The ambulance is leaving and Billy's driving."

Slater pulled open the car door. "Get that damned horse out of my way."

Frankie's face was suddenly serious, all mockery set aside. "Be careful."

"You too."

"Yeah."

Frankie took hold of Larry's bridle and walked the horse forward. Slater started his engine as the cart rumbled by with the milk bottles rattling cheerfully. He pulled forward, struggling as always with the gearshift, and wrestled the big Wolseley into a three-point turn.

He saw the ambulance turning left onto the main road. He would have to hang back and keep his distance. The Wolseley was a conspicuous vehicle with its police badge and bell, and Billy was not one to ignore a police car.

He nosed the car out onto the main highway, where he had a clear view of the sparsely traveled road across the Downs. He caught a glimpse of the ambulance speeding eastward. Storm clouds had gathered above the hills, and the white of ambulance shone against the looming purple sky. Good. He would be easy to follow. He spared a thought for Larry the horse waiting patiently beneath a threatening sky. What if Dorothy was not in the ambulance? What if she was still at the house? Would Frankie take action? Mrs. Hogg-Prewett said that Billy had talked about a barge leaving at high tide. Frankie had already suggested that the barge would leave from Shoreham, but the ambulance was heading in the opposite direction. Had he made the wrong choice in following Billy?

He shook his head. He was committed now. He would have to trust Frankie to take care of whatever he was able to find at The Laurels. Frankie had two arms.

He settled back and tried to concentrate on driving smoothly and carefully, keeping his distance and not drawing attention. The problem was not in the car, it was in his brain. For the first thirty years of his life, he had possessed two arms, and this new reality in which one arm no longer existed was something his mind had not yet come to accept. His brain still wanted him to use the right arm that he had left behind in France.

He forced himself to relive the moment when it had all begun.

June 6, 1944
Gold Beach, Normandy, France
Sergeant Percy Slater, 4th County of London Yeomanry

Slater felt a sudden change in the motion of the vessel. They were no longer tossing helplessly in the waves; they were moving toward the shore. He checked on his lieutenant. For the past few hours, Parrish had been fighting seasickness, retching until nothing but bile dribbled from his slack mouth, but through it all, he remained determinedly alert and focused.

Although the deck of the landing craft was awash with vomit, Slater was immune to seasickness. Even as a kid, working the sailing barges with his father, he'd been able to keep down his breakfast whatever the weather.

Lieutenant Parrish staggered to his feet. He, too, had felt the change in motion. Their eyes met and Parrish looked down. Slater shook his head. No point in being ashamed of seasickness. It could happen to anyone. In fact, it was happening to almost everyone. It wasn't the seasickness that mattered, it was the ability to get up and move despite the seasickness.

Parrish waved a hand. "Carry on, Sarge. Get them ready."

They didn't need to be told. The men who had been sprawled on the deck were alert now; twelve months of training kicking in automatically as they lined up shoulder to shoulder. All around them, large ships and small craft were in motion. Adrenaline surged through Slater's veins. He'd shared his lieutenant's resentment at being held back for so long and left to toss and vomit eight miles from shore, but it was over now.

Slater took his place beside the lieutenant at the bow of the landing craft. No one spoke. It was too late for words. He felt himself driven blindly forward,

141

the destination hidden from view by the raised metal landing ramp.

The warning klaxon surprised him; he had thought it would take longer to reach the beach, but this was it; they had arrived as close to land as the craft's commander was willing to go. The metal plates, just inches from Slater's face, groaned and separated, and the whole nightmare vista opened before him.

He had no time to take in the entire scene as the landing craft was lifted by a wave, just time for an impression of smoke, flames, and a beach littered with wreckage. They sank into a trough between the waves, and when they rose again, they were much closer to the beach; barbed wire, anti-tank traps, abandoned vehicles stranded in the surf, and black shapes, some moving, some lying horribly still.

He felt rather than heard the sudden intake of breath from the lieutenant. "Steady, sir," he said, without turning to look at him.

"I'm steady, Sarge, but it looks like we've drifted off target. We'll be swimming."

The landing craft nosed into the surf, and the landing ramp dropped. As far as Slater could see to his right and his left, wave after wave of infantrymen were struggling in the waves, weighted down by their heavy packs and weakened by their hours of seasickness. The landing craft had missed the target and the tide. The water was rough and deep. Soldiers who had trained for a year or more were drowning before they could get ashore, and those who made it through the surf were coming under mortar fire from German gun emplacements that should have been taken out.

Slater lunged forward, holding his weapon above his head until he found a firm footing. He broke through the surf and ran up onto the beach, feeling the press of his comrades behind him. He kept his eyes on his lieutenant, dismayed to see that Parrish was standing still, surveying the beach. He needed the lieutenant alive; Parrish was the only one who knew the plan, if there was still a plan.

At last the lieutenant dropped to his knees in the shelter of a burned-out tank and unfolded a map. Slater fell to the ground beside him.

"Orders, sir?"

"Right," said Parrish, his eyes on the map. "We're not where we're supposed to be." He stabbed a finger at the map. "Le Hamel, that's our target. We'll have a long walk; better get going. First, we need to find a way off this beach. Get the men up and moving."

Slater looked around. Most of his men had already taken cover, bellies down in the sand, using whatever protection they could find; vehicles, tank traps, the dark shapes of the dead. Their eyes were fixed on him. He would have to be first on his feet. He stood. Parrish rose beside him and took two steps.

Slater would never know for certain what exploded. It was probably a mine—the beach was seeded with mines—or it could have been a shell from the German gun emplacement. It didn't matter. The explosion took Parrish's legs out from under him and flung Slater aside, landing him heavily on his right arm.

May 1952

The first drops of rain spattered the windshield. Slater fumbled for the wiper controls and dragged his mind away from the beaches of Normandy. The explosion had been the end of Lieutenant Parrish's war, but it should not have been the end of Slater's. It should not have cost him his arm.

The ambulance was turning from the main road. A sharp gust of wind brought the rumble of thunder and a sudden downpour of rain. The ambulance disappeared behind a curtain of water. Lightning crackled, and he caught a glimpse of the white ambulance against the sudden dark. He put his foot down on the accelerator. He was not going to lose him, not now.

He didn't know what happened next or why it happened. One moment he was closing the gap between himself and the ambulance, and the next moment brought a crash of metal. The Wolseley juddered to a halt as Slater jammed his foot on the brake. He had hit something, or something had hit him.

He considered backing up and going around the new obstruction, but common sense took control of him. The Wolseley was a heavy vehicle, but the car in front him, the car he had collided with, was something small and crumpled. Another flash of lightning showed him a cloud of steam rising from the other car's damaged radiator.

He peered through the rain. The ambulance was nowhere in sight, but the driver of the other car was climbing out on shaking legs.

He put his hand to his mouth as he saw the angular figure in the tweed skirt. Anthea Clark! What the hell was she doing here?

Dorothy Findlay

Streaks of daylight crept begrudgingly into the shed, making their way through a cracked and dusty window and revealing that the scythe had been removed from the wheelbarrow and hung high up on the wall. No sharp objects were anywhere within her reach.   She supposed that she should be grateful that she had not been put back in the coal bunker. At least she was clean, and she had been given a blanket to sit on, but she was in no mood to count her blessings. She needed to find a way out. If only she could get the gag out of her mouth, she could scream and hope that the woman next door would hear her. She had pegged the neighbor as a nosy woman whose curiosity was already aroused by what she'd seen. If Dorothy knew anything about nosy neighbors, she knew that the woman would be lurking by the window, watching and listening.

She couldn't get her hands or feet free, but surely she could loosen the gag and spit it out. The fabric felt like silk, probably one of Enid Cheviot's silk scarves. She couldn't work it loose with her teeth, but if she could find something to use as an anchor, she could surely loosen the knot and slide the scarf out of her mouth.

She shuffled across the rough floorboards on her backside, picking up splinters on the way. She could see a nail protruding from one of the floorboards. She crouched on the floor and lowered her head until she could slide the fabric of the scarf over the nailhead. She started to move her head, working the scarf, waiting for the knot to become loose. All she needed was a fraction of an inch; just enough that she could work herself free; just enough that she could open her mouth and scream.

Thunder rumbled outside. It was going to rain before long. She wondered if the woman next door would be able to hear her above the sound of the rain. She pulled harder on the gag. The thunder was still some distance away, and it had not drowned out the sounds of the garden; birds singing, a lawnmower somewhere in the distance, the rattle of milk bottles, and a cheerful whistle.

A milkman! He was delivering to the back door. She worked frantically at the gag. Milkmen were trained to spot anything unusual on their rounds. If someone had not taken in their milk or put out their empties, it could trigger a visit from the police to check on a lonely shut-in. Milkmen would watch for an unlocked back door and signs of someone trying to break into a house. Milkmen were the eyes of the neighborhood. A milkman would respond to screams from the shed.

The rusty old nail dug into her cheek as she worked. She ignored the blood that trickled into her mouth, and pulled harder against the nail. She felt the moment when the knot began to slide. She worked with her tongue and her teeth, and at last she spat the sodden, bloodstained fabric out of her mouth. She drew in a deep breath and began to scream.

The thunder was closer now, and she heard the first heavy drops of rain on the roof, but she could still hear the milkman rattling his bottles and whistling. He seemed to be coming closer. She screamed again. The door crashed open, and the shed was flooded with rain-soaked daylight. The milkman stood on the threshold. His white coat was just a blur, but his face was in sharp focus, dark eyes, a ginger moustache, and an expression completely lacking in surprise. Surely he should be surprised. Surely he hadn't expected to find a half-naked woman in Enid Cheviot's garden shed.

"Dorothy!" It was not a question. He knew her name.

"Get me out of here."

He took a step forward. His eyes were fixed on her and he was smiling reassuringly; he didn't see the shadow that loomed behind him.

The crack of the gunshot blended with the crackle of lightning striking somewhere close by. She thought for an instant that she had only imagined the shot, but then she saw the milkman's startled expression, saw his hands fly up in the air, and saw his knees collapse. Her scream died in her throat as she recognized the face of the man who loomed behind him; the face of a man she had met many years ago in Canterbury.

Shock seemed to have destroyed her hearing. The man she had claimed as Eric's father was opening and closing his mouth, but his words meant nothing. She took a deep breath and tried to steady her nerves. Was the milkman in fact dead? If she ran to him now and tried to stem the trickle of blood from the corner of his mouth, could she somehow save him?

A woman's voice, shrill and petulant, replaced the echoing remnants of thunder and gunshot. "Don't let him bleed in here."

Enid Cheviot flung herself down beside the bleeding milkman and used one of her many scarves to staunch the flow of blood while she looked up at her son.

"Really, Michael, did you have to do it here? Now we'll have to move him. No one must know it happened here."

"Oh really, Mother, give the police some credit," Michael said. "Milk cart outside, broken bottles on the doorstep. Even they can put two and two together."

"Not if we put him back on his cart," Enid argued. "I know a thing or two about horses, and I promise you that if we can get that horse moving, he'll just plod on around his route. It will be hours before he turns up at the dairy, and we'll be long gone."

"And what about her?"

Dorothy met Michael's contemptuous gaze as he jerked his thumb at her. She realized that there would be no point in screaming. If she opened her mouth now, she'd probably be treated the same way as her would-be rescuer, and she couldn't allow that to happen. She had to stay alive for Eric's sake. Her captors had kept her alive so far, so if she didn't scream, and didn't make trouble, perhaps she wouldn't die. If they'd wanted to kill her, it would have happened already, so they had some other plan for her.

Michael placed a rough hand under her chin and stared into her eyes. "Do you know me?"

She looked into his angry eyes. She thought of the man in Canterbury. "No," she said, "I don't know you."

"So why did you tell your lawyer that I was the father of your misbegotten child?"

"I thought that you were …"

"Were what?"

"Someone I met in Canterbury. He looked like you."

Michael took a step back and allowed his eyes to sweep the length of Dorothy's body in its skimpy shift. He shook his head contemptuously. "As if I would ..."

As if I would ... Dorothy thought in agreement. She looked at his petulant mouth, his dark eyes that held no hint of kindness, and the hunched, weak set of his shoulders. This was not the man and she was glad. There was a physical resemblance. The man who had fathered Eric had the same dark eyes, but they had been kind eyes. He had the same chin, the same mouth, but the mouth had grinned at her, the eyes had winked, and the voice had lacked the sullen servitude that Michael showed to his mother, who was even now issuing commands.

"Pick him up, Michael, and drag him out to the cart. There's no one around on the street. No one will see you."

"I'll wait for Uncle Billy to come back."

"He's not coming back. He's gone out to the St. Elphege clinic to collect the girl that you failed to kill, but I fear that he'll be too late. We're leaving, Michael. It's time to get out of England."

Dorothy followed Michael's glance down to his right hand and, for the first time, realized that he was still holding a pistol, presumably the one he had used on the milkman. He raised the pistol.

"You expect me to take care of her as well?" he asked.

Enid lifted her hand in a fluttering but decisive gesture of dismissal. "For some reason, your Uncle Billy wants to keep her."

"What will he do with her?"

"He says he can get a good price for her on the Continent."

Michael subjected Dorothy to another one of his scathing examinations. "Really?"

Dorothy tugged uncomfortably at the hem of her short cotton shift while her heart turned somersaults. This wasn't the first mention of taking her to the Continent and getting a good price. She wished that she didn't know what Enid Cheviot was talking about, but she did know. She read the newspapers. She had heard the rumors. Women, preferably blond-haired women, could be sold overseas. She didn't know who did the buying, and she couldn't imagine who would want to buy her, but apparently, her kidnappers knew what to do with her.

She looked at the pistol in Michael's hand. She saw his fingers twitching. He wanted to kill her. She had upset him with her lawsuit. She was sure now that he wasn't Eric's father, but he had been up to something; something that made him so guilty that he was willing to kill an innocent milkman to keep it quiet.

They didn't have Eric, she was confident of that much. If they had Eric, Michael would be taunting her now with that fact. No, she had to cling to the hope that Eric had managed to reach Inspector Slater, or failing that, Toby Whitby. One or the other of them would surely be looking for her even now. All she had to do was stay alive and somehow avoid being shipped across the Channel.

Michael handed the pistol to his mother. "Do you know how to use this?"

She arched her penciled eyebrows. "Don't be silly; of course I do. House parties, my dear. Before you were even born, I was out with the guns at some of the best houses in the county. Even with the Prince of Wales."

"What about him, Mother? What shall we do with him?"

"He'll have to go across on the barge. Arrangements have been made."

Dorothy made room in her panicked mind for the possibility that the man she had seen in the garden, the man who had protested against her treatment, was not an imposter. Could he really be the man who was once the Prince of Wales? If so, would he feel obligated to help her? Would noblesse oblige?

Michael slipped his arms under the milkman's prone body while Enid leveled the pistol at Dorothy. Despite Enid's bone-thin frailty, her arms was steady.

Michael's face was a study in disgust as he dragged the corpse backward from the shed. "Don't tell me we're expected to cross the Channel on a barge."

"Of course not, dear. We'll put this creature on board ourselves, and then we'll drive to Dover and cross on the ferry." "And then?"

"Oh, America, I think. We'll stay until things have calmed down a little. Everything will change, you know, after the coronation."

Michael's voice was a little breathless; apparently, the milkman was not easy to move. "If there is a coronation," he panted.

"There'll be one, dear," Enid said.

She looked at Dorothy and shook her head in disgust. "How could anyone think that you would be attracted to this creature?"

CHAPTER SIXTEEN

Toby Whitby

Anthea should be here by now. Toby positioned himself at the edge of the shrubbery so he could see the road that ran past the back of the convent. He waited while the sky turned an ominous purple, and thunder rumbled all around. The unconscious woman groaned and made small movements. When the first heavy raindrops spattered the ground, he retreated into the bushes. He set his burden down on the ground and pushed and pulled it into the sparse cover of a yew tree. The ground here was dry, and the drenching rain could not penetrate the branches of the old tree.

He peered out through the curtain of rain. Where was Anthea? What was taking her so long?

"What? Who?"

He turned back to see that Madeline was thrashing on the ground like a butterfly trying to escape its chrysalis. He crawled back to her and set a hand on her shoulder.

"Get off me."

"I'm here to help you."

The girl made an attempt to stand. He pressed her down. "Don't, you'll hurt yourself."

She fought against him, pulled herself free of his grasp, and set her feet on the ground. Her attempt to stand brought a scream of pain. He lunged at her and pulled her to the ground and clamped his hand over her mouth.

She stared at him with wide, pain-filled eyes.

"I'm not going to hurt you."

Her eyes told him that she did not believe him. He felt her teeth against his hand and clamped down tighter.

"I'm not going to hurt you. I'll take my hand away if you promise not

148

to scream."

The look she gave him convinced him that screaming was still an option. He kept his hand in place.

"Your brother told the nuns that your name is Tissie Lovell; do you know why he did that?"

She glared and Toby rethought his position. That should not have been his first question. In fact, it was foolish to ask questions of someone who would only scream in alarm if he removed his hand. He had to talk to her and tell her what he knew before he had any chance of having her answer a question.

Well, he didn't know everything, but he knew enough. "My name is Toby Whitby and I am a solicitor."

She rolled her eyes. No, that wasn't the place to start.

"You wanted to help your brother," he said. "Your brother took the place of someone else and fought in the war under a false name."

She grunted and made another attempt to bite his hand.

"Don't," he said. "Don't do that, or I won't tell you what I know, and don't try to get up. Your feet are badly burned. I'll try to get you some help as soon as I can, but not until you talk to me."

She groaned. He let a moment of silence pass with no sound but the rain lashing the trees just beyond their shelter.

"I don't know why your brother did what he did, but I think it was because he wanted to fight. He wanted to do the right thing but he had flat feet. Someone approached him and offered him a chance to take the place of a man who didn't want to fight." Her eyes were round now, not glaring, not panicked, just interested. He was on the right track.

"He took the place of Lieutenant Michael Cheviot in the Royal East Kent," Toby said. "He fought well. You should be proud of him."

Another grunt.

"And then the war was over and he wanted his life back."

She made muffled sounds. He loosened his hold on her mouth.

Her voice was hesitant. "He wanted his son," she whispered. "He wanted to claim his son."

"Dorothy Findlay's son?"

"Is that her name?"

"Yes. Her name is Dorothy and the boy's name is Eric. Your brother met Dorothy in Canterbury in 1942. He told her he was Michael Cheviot."

Madeline made a sudden lunging attempt to stand and cried out in pain.

"Don't do that, Madeline," Toby said.

"How do you know my name? Max said he used a different name. How do you know all this? We've never told anyone. Did Max tell you?"

"Max?"

"My brother."

Toby winced. The dead man had a name. Max. When was he going to tell her that Max was dead? When was he going to tell her that Dorothy was missing? Start somewhere else. Start somewhere that wouldn't be so painful.

"How did your brother and Michael Cheviot find each other? Do you know why they look so alike?"

Madeline nodded. "Apparently, Max and I are related to Michael. We didn't know anything about it until Michael's mother turned up on Max's doorstep. Our father always told us that he was an orphan, and he didn't know where he came from."

"Your father wasn't an orphan," Toby said grimly. "He had a family; a mother, a father, and a sister. I think you've already met the sister."

"No, I haven't. No … wait a minute. Do you …? Do you mean Michael's mother?"

"Yes, I do."

"She's my father's sister?"

"Yes."

"She didn't say that," Madeline said. "She just said we were related. Is she really my aunt?"

"I'm afraid so," Toby said. "Didn't you wonder how she found you? Your father didn't know she existed, but somehow she knew where to find your brother."

"I don't understand."

Toby waved a dismissive hand. It was too soon to tell her what had happened on the moor. He had no proof, only a suspicion that was slowly turning to a certainty.

"Max didn't ask any questions," Madeline said. "He was just so glad to have a second chance. He had already been turned down for military service, and then this woman came to him. She never said she was our aunt, just that she was a distant relative. Her name's Enid. I think she's someone famous."

"Only in her own mind." Toby was surprised at how much pleasure he found in dismissing Enid's half-hearted movie career.

"She said that my brother and her son looked so alike that she wanted Max to take the army physical instead of Michael, and she would give him money, a lot of money. She said that was all he had to do. She knew Max would fail because of his flat feet, so if he reported in and gave his name as Michael Cheviot, it would look like Michael had failed the physical, and so Michael wouldn't have to fight. Max was angry. He said he'd give anything to fight, and he wouldn't do anything to help Michael to get out of his duty. He called Michael a coward."

Madeline drew a deep breath. She seemed relieved to be telling her story at last. "After Max said no, that should have been the end of it, but it wasn't, because then Max had an idea of his own."

Toby nodded. "I think I know the rest. Your brother struck a deal with Michael and his mother. Instead of taking a physical he knew that he would fail, Max persuaded Michael to take the physical, and Michael, of course, passed. Then Max and Michael swapped places. Your brother had a chance to fight, and Michael had a chance to hide."

Madeline nodded. "That's exactly what happened. It seemed like a good idea at the time, but after Max got home, it was all so complicated. It wasn't just that Michael was taking credit for all the things that Max had done. Max didn't care about that, but he cared about this woman he'd met in Canterbury while he was pretending to be Michael. Now he wanted to find her again. He said he couldn't stop thinking about her."

"But if he found her, he would have to tell her what he'd done," Toby muttered.

"He didn't care. I tried to talk him out of it, but he found out that she was in Brighton," Madeline said, "and that she had a child. He saw the boy from a distance, and he was certain it was his child, and after that, there was nothing I could to do stop him. He insisted that he was going to tell her who he was.

"He went to see Michael just to tell him what he planned to do, but Michael's mother wouldn't let him near her son. She has him tied to her apron strings, and she's the one who decides everything. She told Max that she'd harm the woman and the child if Max tried to see them and tell them who he was. She has this man, a thug who—"

"I know who he is."

Madeline sat up straight and began to unwind the sheet that encased her. "I have to find Max."

Toby put out a hand. "Don't do that. You only have a hospital gown. You'll get cold."

Madeline lifted the edge of the sheet and looked down at herself. "Did you do this?"

Toby felt himself blushing; a ridiculous reaction given the circumstances. "No. Miss Clark, our secretary, wrapped it around you."

"Where is she?"

"I wish I knew. She should be here by now. The nuns looked in your clothing and found Enid Cheviot's address. They phoned her to come and get you. She's on her way now."

"No! Why?"

"Because your brother has not been paying the bill. They haven't seen him for several days."

Madeline frowned. "Where is he? Max wouldn't leave me like that. I did this for him and he felt terrible about it."

Toby heard a hint of dread in her voice, but he wasn't ready to answer her question. What would she do if he told her about Max? He couldn't risk her grief; not until he had more information.

"Why did he register you as Tissie Lovell? It's a strange name."

Madeline looked at him distractedly. "It's a family name. Apparently, we have gypsy blood, and Tissie Lovell is some old relative. My father met her when he was a little boy. I suppose my grandparents know who she is."

"Are your grandparents alive?"

"My father's mother, the one who adopted him, is alive."

"And she told him about this name?"

Madeline was annoyed. "I don't know. What does it matter?"

"It all matters," Toby said, thinking of the light that was being shone on a long-ago crime. He thought back over Madeline's words. Madeline's grandmother was still alive. The woman to whom the gypsies had given, or more likely sold, a stolen child was still alive to tell the tale. He wondered if Enid was aware that there was someone who could still point a finger to her guilt.

The old crime and the new crime were coming together, and no one who knew the story would be safe.

He spoke as calmly as he could. "I have to see if our ride is here. I think the rain is coming to an end, and we should be able to move."

He was certain that the end of the rain would signal the beginning of a search. Billy had surely arrived with the ambulance by now. He didn't know where Anthea was, or if she had moved his car. He could only hope.

He ducked out from under the cover of the yew tree and looked down at the road. The rain abruptly turned from a downpour to a few drops, the thunder rolled away beyond the hills, and in the silence that followed, he heard voices from the convent.

He pulled Madeline deeper into the shadow of the old yew tree, but he knew she could not stay hidden for very long. He crawled to the edge of the shrubbery, where the grounds of the convent met the road. He wondered if Anthea had lost her way, or perhaps she had been stopped by the nuns before she could leave the clinic. No, Anthea would have been more than a match for a dozen nuns. He could only assume that Billy Cheviot had arrived with the ambulance and discovered Anthea trying to drive away in the Morris. The sight of Toby's Morris would tell him that Toby knew everything, or almost everything, and Anthea would not be safe.

Anthea Clark

Anthea fretted against the absurd male pride that made Inspector Slater insist upon driving the police car. She had abandoned the Morris at the side of the road. She was uncertain as to the extent of the damage, but the cloud of steam rising from under the bonnet told her that Toby's car was not going anywhere anytime soon.

Gears crashed and whined as Slater fumbled with the adapted controls of the Wolseley. Anthea pursed her lips and resisted the urge to speak. She concentrated on watching the bushes at the side of the road.

"If he comes out of the shrubbery, he'll be somewhere along here," she said. "He's expecting the Morris, so I'm not sure if he'll show himself to a police car."

"Why don't you get out and walk?" Slater said through gritted teeth.

"I beg your pardon!"

Slater jerked his head to indicate the left-hand side of the road. "The clinic's up there. If the shrubbery is at the back of the clinic, we should be alongside it at any minute now. So, if you get out and walk, he'll see you. I'll wait here round the bend while you walk up the road and see if you can find him."

He was right of course. Anthea nodded her approval. Slater brought the car to a stuttering halt, and Anthea climbed out onto the rain-soaked road. Although she was wearing her usual sensible shoes, her feet were soaked by the time she had walked around the curve in the road. She could see where the overgrown rhododendrons of the shrubbery had spread all the way to the road. She walked slowly, peering in through the deep green undergrowth and calling softly.

"Mr. Whitby. Toby. Are you in there?"

She heard a sudden gasp, and someone bit back a plaintive mew of pain.

"Mr. Whitby, it's me. You can come out now."

The bushes shook, showering her with water, and Toby was beside her, carrying Madeline over his shoulder.

"Where have you been?"

Before Anthea could answer, which would mean admitting to damaging Toby's precious motorcar, she heard voices close by. The searchers were in the shrubbery. She tugged at Toby's sleeve.

"Hurry up. There's a police car …"

"Why?"

"It doesn't matter. Just hurry."

She held the branches aside as Toby pushed through to the road.

"Where's my car."

"Not now," Anthea said. "Inspector Slater's waiting just round the corner. Hurry up."

Slater saw them coming and climbed out of the driver's seat. As he beckoned to Toby, his intention was obvious. Toby would drive. Anthea knew that this was not the moment to protest, but she promised herself that the day would come when she would show them, all of them, what she was capable of doing.

For the time being, she played the traditional role in the back seat, with an arm around Madeline's shoulders and a soothing voice to tell her that she was safe now.

Safe? Yes, Madeline was safe, but what of Dorothy?

She leaned forward to listen to Toby as he pieced the story together for Slater's benefit. Now she had a name for the man she had met in Canterbury. He was Madeline's brother, Max. She listened to Slater's questions and took note of Toby's answers. Slater was thinking only of Dorothy. That was natural, of course. Dorothy could still be saved, but Max was beyond saving. Max was in the mortuary, and someone would have to tell Madeline.

Her thoughts turned to Hugh Trewin and what all of this would mean to him. He was a strong man, a soldier, a stoic who had accepted the loss of his son and the suicide of his wife, and somehow continued his life. Madeline's story would open old wounds, but perhaps there would also be healing. There could be no doubt now that seven-year-old Enid had taken her little brother out onto the moor and given him to Tissie Lovell's gypsy band. Given or sold? What did it matter? Young as she was, Enid had made a plan to rid herself of her brother.

The good news for Hugh was the fact that his son had not died. He had been given a home and another family. He was Madeline's father, and he was still alive. After all these years, Hugh would see his son again.

Hugh had grandchildren, not just Michael, but also Madeline, who was here and safe. He would never have the chance to meet Max, but Max had left a legacy. Max was the father of Dorothy's child. Eric was Hugh's great-grandson.

Slater swiveled in his seat and looked at Madeline. "Should we take you to a hospital?"

"I want to see Max," Madeline said. "Where's Max?"

Anthea felt Slater's eyes on her. Did he expect her to do this? Would she have to be the bearer of bad news? She sighed. Yes, she would do it. She was a clergyman's daughter. She had grown up in a house where people came bearing black-banded envelopes and looking for comfort.

She would do it, but not yet; certainly not in the back seat of a police car. Hugh Trewin was at Mr. Champion's house. They would go there, and somehow the story would be told.

In the meantime, she had questions, and talking would take Madeline's mind off the pain of her burns.

April 1952
Brighton, Sussex
Madeline Randolph

The afternoon sun was bright on Max's face, but his eyes were dark with worry, and the smile he had inherited from their father lacked conviction.

"You don't have to do it if you don't want to ..."

Madeline waved away her brother's words. "I'm doing it, Max."

The spring breeze blowing across the hillside ruffled Max's hair, and he pushed it back impatiently. "It's a lot to ask of you, and if—"

"It's okay. Really, it's okay. It's what sisters are for." She filled her voice with a conviction that she did not actually feel. Of course, she would prefer not to put herself in, or anywhere near, a burning car, but this was what was needed.

"I wish there was some other way," Max said. "In fact, I wish I'd never got involved in the first place."

"Well, you did," Madeline replied, "and now we have to put it right."

"When they came to me about faking the physical, all I could think of was the chance to be in uniform," Max confessed.

Madeline smiled. She knew this already. Max had told her all about it when it happened. In 1941, with conscription a reality, a woman had approached Max and showed him a picture of her son. The resemblance between Max and Michael was almost uncanny, and the woman's request was simple. She already knew that Max had flat feet. All Max had to do was present himself as Michael Cheviot and fail the physical on Michael's behalf. She had offered money, but Max had not measured the agreement in pounds and shillings. His price was honor and a chance to wear his country's uniform.

Max had taken Michael Cheviot's place in the regiment and covered Michael's name with glory. When the war ended, he had returned home and reclaimed his old name and his old reputation as someone who had been unfit to fight. No one except Max and Madeline would ever know what Max had done, but it didn't matter to Max. He said he didn't need the glory for himself, and Madeline believed him. When he mentioned Michael's family, he always did so with a grimace. He had not liked them. He thought the mother was neurotic and the son was a coward. He was glad he wouldn't have to see them again.

It had taken ten years for Max to tell his sister about the woman in Canterbury. She had sensed his restlessness but she didn't know the cause, not until he came to ask for her help. He wasn't proud of himself for what he had done; picking up a lonely woman in a restaurant, spending the night with her in a hotel, and giving her a false name. He had lied about who he was, but the woman had told no lies. She was Dorothy Findlay, a trainee welder. Dorothy Findlay. Such an ordinary name, and by all accounts, an ordinary woman, pleasant, pretty, and kind to a lonely soldier.

"She has a son," Max had said. "He's ten years old. He's mine."

"Is that what she told you?" Madeline asked.

"I haven't spoken to her. I watched him from a distance. I'm absolutely sure he's my son."

"Well," Madeline said, "if he's your son, I'm his aunt. So I want to meet him. When can I meet him?"

"Not yet," Max said. "I can't speak to Dorothy yet. I have to get clear with the Cheviots. I have to admit to Dorothy that I was only pretending to be an officer in the Royal East Kent. If she doesn't like what I tell her, and if anything leads back to Michael Cheviot, he's going to be branded a deserter. They shoot deserters, don't they?"

Madeline sat in the passenger seat of the small car, picking nervously at her fingers. Today they were going to perform their final act for the Cheviot family, and after that, Max would be free to see his son. Today Max and Michael would both lose their fingerprints, rendering the War Office's intake records useless. No prints. No proof. No desertion.

Max and Madeline sat side by side, looking out from the crest of the Downs to the distant blue of the ocean. The Cheviot family had provided the car, a bright green prewar Austin.

"It's stolen, isn't it?" Madeline asked.

Max nodded. "I suppose so. That way it won't be traced back to us, or back to the Cheviots. Anyway, it will be burned, so no fingerprints or anything like that."

"About the burning ..." Madeline said.

Max's eyes filled with concern. "You don't have to do it. I'll find another way."

"No, I'll do it. I want you to be able to meet your son, and I want the Cheviots out of our lives. This just seems so extreme."

Max shook his head. "I know. It's not fair that you have to be involved, but I can't ask anyone else. No one knows except you, and Dad, and I can't ask Dad."

"Couldn't Michael just burn his prints off with acid or something like that?"

"I can do that," Max said, "because no one cares about me. Max Randolph doesn't have medals, or a regimental record, or a mother who is a film star. I can get rid of my prints, but Michael needs to lose his in a way that's completely above suspicion. He wants to be the hero he never was. He has a photographer standing by. No one can connect him to you, because you've never met him. You'll just be a woman in a car that caught fire. He'll rescue you, so to speak, and burn his fingertips."

"Burns are really painful," Madeline said.

Max laughed. "That's his problem. I took a couple of bullets on his behalf, and they were also really painful. I'm not worried if it hurts him. I'm only worried you'll get hurt, but I promise I'll have you out of the car before anything happens. I parked my motorcycle down beside the road. We'll be away in no time at all. Michael will be a hero with no fingerprints that can be checked by the War Office, and I'll be free to go and see Dorothy and tell her who I am, and then you'll be able to meet your nephew."

May 1952
Anthea Clark

Anthea looked at the pale-faced girl leaning wearily against the back of the seat. Madeline glanced down at her bandaged feet.

"I think I was supposed to die," she said softly.

Anthea could not summon even a small gasp of surprise. Madeline was only telling her what she already knew. The Cheviots wanted no witnesses. A failed rescue attempt would be just as effective in removing Michael's fingerprints as a successful one. If Madeline died in the fire, that would be one more witness out of the way.

"I think they planned to kill Max as well," Madeline said. She turned an anguished face to Anthea. "Do you know where he is?"

Toby spoke from the driver's seat without turning his head. "What happened next?"

Anthea felt a surge of relief. She would have to tell the girl about her brother, but not yet; not just yet.

"Max parked the car and got out," Madeline said, "and I stayed in the passenger seat. I made sure the door was unlocked, and I kept my hand on the door latch. Michael and this other man arrived in a big blue car. The other man was huge."

"Billy Cheviot," Slater grunted, and Anthea realized that the police inspector was also listening carefully to the conversation.

"I saw Michael quite clearly," Madeline said, "and he does look exactly like Max, only thinner and paler. He's like Max but with all the good things removed, if you know what I mean."

When no one replied, Anthea realized that was because neither Slater nor Toby had seen Max alive. The only thing they knew of Max Randolph was a bloated, drowned corpse.

Of course, Anthea had seen Max alive; just once. She patted Madeline's hand. "I know what you mean, dear."

"Was there a photographer?" Slater asked.

"No. They didn't bring anyone else. The big man had a camera, just a Brownie, I think. Nothing fancy."

"Wouldn't need to be," Slater muttered.

157

"Better all round if the pictures are out of focus," Toby agreed.

Anthea tried to imagine how Madeline must have felt, sitting alone in a stolen car and waiting with her hand on the door handle for someone to start a fire.

Slater turned in his seat. "Who started the fire?"

"The big man, Billy."

"How?"

Anthea saw the pain on Madeline's face and jabbed a finger at Slater's shoulder. "Does it matter how? Why ask her to remember?"

"Because we have arson inspectors," Slater replied, "and if I told them how the fire started ..."

"The car's gone," Madeline said. "It's totally burned. Nothing left."

She turned and buried her head in Anthea's shoulder, and her voice was muffled for a moment. When she lifted her head, her voice trembled. "He set something down next to the driver's door, but it didn't burn very much at first. I think it was a fire starter, like the one you use on campfires. It was just a slow burn, but the driver's door was getting hot. I saw Michael dancing around, not wanting to put his fingers near the flames. Billy told him to get on with it, so Michael just sort of jabbed at the door, and then he started screaming about how much it hurt. He was shouting and asking if Billy had got the pictures he wanted. No one was looking at me, so I thought I'd try to get out, but Billy shouted that I had to stay because he needed pictures of me escaping."

Madeline choked back a tear, and the tremble left her voice. Now she was angry. "The big man told Michael to stand still so he could get a picture, but Michael was making a horrible fuss about his fingers, screaming and dancing around. He wouldn't stand still, so the big man pushed him out of the way. After that, he came round to the front of the car and leaned down. I don't know what he did, but suddenly I saw flames leaping up all around me. They were coming from under the car, from the ground under the car. I could hear Max shouting at me from the side of the road to get out of the car. I wanted to, but Billy had his camera out and he said I had to wait. And then ..."

Madeline sat forward in her seat, her eyes and face reliving the horror. "The whole car was on fire," she whimpered. "There was a sheet of flames, and I could see Billy beyond the flames. He had his camera out and was taking pictures. He didn't do anything to help me; he just took pictures. The flames had come up from underneath, and the floor was on fire. I couldn't think. I knew I had to get out, but all I could think of was the pain. I've never felt pain like that before. I thought I was going to die, and then Max came out of nowhere and pulled me out."

"Hush now," Anthea said. "You don't have to say any more."

"Yes, she does," Slater barked, turning in his seat. "What happened next?"

"Max carried me. I don't think that Billy or Michael knew that he'd taken me. Michael was screaming about his fingers hurting, but I knew I couldn't scream. I don't know how I knew, but I knew that they were going to kill me and kill Max if they caught up with us, so I had to keep quiet."

"So Max took you on his motorcycle?" Slater asked.

"Yes."

"But how did—?"

Anthea jabbed again as hard as she could. "That's enough. Don't you dare ask her another question."

She could tell from the expression on Slater's face that he was not going to be silent, and she could not stop him from asking questions. She saw the flicker of determination in his eyes. He was going to tell Madeline that her brother was dead, and he was not going to do it kindly or gently.

She sighed. Perhaps he was right. In the end, there was no kind or gentle way of telling Madeline that the Cheviots had provided their own solution to the problem of fingerprints. Michael's prints were scarred and unrecognizable, and Max's prints were gone along with his hands.

Anthea took one of Madeline's hands into her own grasp. "Madeline, dear, I'm afraid I have to tell you—"

She didn't know what words she had planned to use, but it no longer mattered. The radio suddenly crackled into life. Toby jerked the wheel in surprise, and Anthea found herself flung sideways on the wide back seat. As she scrabbled to right herself, she managed to tread on one of Madeline's bandaged feet. Madeline screamed.

The radio static became words. Anthea hushed Madeline and tried to listen to make sense of the words. Something about a horse. Slater leaned forward angrily and switched off the radio.

"Are you allowed to do that?" Toby asked.

"It's just babble," Slater grunted. "Nothing to do with us."

CHAPTER SEVENTEEN

Detective Inspector Percy Slater

"We should call an ambulance," Slater said as he watched Toby carrying Madeline into Edwin Champion's house.

Anthea shook her head. "No, not yet. We have to tell her about her brother."

Slater wiped his hand across his forehead as he thought of all the things that Madeline Randolph would have to be told. Her brother was dead but he had left a son. Edith Cheviot was her aunt, who had sold her own brother to the gypsies on Bodmin Moor. Hugh Trewin was her grandfather.

Robert Penhelen passed him in the doorway with an anxious expression on his face. He looked at Slater and shook his head. "Terrible business," he muttered. "What are you going to do about it?"

"I don't know."

Penhelen raised his elegant gray eyebrows. "You don't know?"

"Someone has to tell her about her brother."

"And many other things," Penhelen added.

"Well," Slater said, "you and the colonel go a long way back, don't you? Perhaps you should tell him what we know. He'll take it better coming from you. I'm just a policeman."

Penhelen sighed. "I would like to, of course. I would like to stay, but I have business to attend to in London. I'm sorry. I have to leave this in your hands. Perhaps Miss Clark can help you. She seems to be a very competent woman."

"But—"

Penhelen shook his head. "I have a taxi waiting. I have to go."

Slater studied Penhelen's elegant figure as he walked out to the road, where a black taxi had pulled up to the curb. He wondered what business could possibly be more important than supporting his old friend at such a time, but Penhelen was an aristocrat, and aristocrats made their own rules.

He walked slowly and thoughtfully into the drawing room and saw that Anthea had already taken charge. She had brought Daisy into the room, and the old dog rested her head on Hugh's knees while Hugh's eyes leaked the tears he had been holding back for a lifetime. She gently but firmly encouraged Eric to sit beside his aunt Madeline and to hold her hand while she came to terms with the loss of her brother.

At last she looked at Slater. "I am confident that Inspector Slater is going to find Eric's mother," she said.

All eyes turned to Slater, and he summoned up a look of confidence. Dorothy had not been in the ambulance, so she must still be at The Laurels, unless Frankie had already found her, but there had been nothing on the radio, not that he had been listening to the radio.

He should call in and see if anyone had heard from the undercover agent. He wondered if Frankie had let anyone in on his plan to disguise himself as a milkman, or had he worked alone?

He crossed the hall to Mr. Champion's study and put in a call to the station.

"Hold for the chief constable."

The chief constable? Why? Slater straightened his spine and waited. He did not have long to wait.

"Slater, where the hell are you?"

"I ... uh ... I'm pursuing a lead on the identity of the body in the mortuary."

"Has your radio ceased to function?"

"No, sir, not that I know of."

"Not that you know of! What does that mean?"

"Well, I was tied up with the pursuit ..."

"Pursuit of what?"

"Billy Cheviot, sir, in an ambulance."

"I gave no orders."

"No, sir, but—"

The chief constable seemed to be speaking through gritted teeth. "Your orders were to work with the Met."

"Yes, sir, but—"

"You were to work with a partner."

"No, sir. I don't have a partner."

"No, you don't."

Slater was silent. The chief constable's words made no sense. Partner?

Did he mean Frankie? Frankie had not wanted a partner. Had Frankie lodged a complaint against him?

"Sir, I don't understand."

"Horses!" said the chief constable. "Clever animals. Always know the way home."

Sick despair formed a lump in the pit of Slater's stomach. A horse had found its own way home. He could only think of one reason why this would be important. He remembered Frankie's snaggle-toothed grin as he praised Larry, the milkman's brown horse. Knows the route. Does it every day. Something had happened to Frankie, and Larry the horse had made his own way home along his accustomed route.

The chief constable's voice was cold. "If we'd got to your partner sooner, he might still be alive. If you'd called in; if you'd answered your radio ... A whole lot of ifs, Slater."

"Sir ..."

"I don't care where you are or what you're doing. Get in here now. Now!"

Toby Whitby

Toby caught Slater as he opened the front door.

"Are you leaving?"

"What the hell do you think?" the policeman snapped. The blood had drained from his face, and his mouth was set in a tight line.

"I could drive you," Toby offered.

"I don't need you to drive me," Slater snapped. "Get off my back. I can drive myself."

Toby stepped back.

"If you say so."

Slater glared. "What is that supposed to mean?"

"Nothing." Toby shrugged. "Go ahead. Drive yourself."

He watched the detective climb awkwardly into the big Wolseley and set off in a series of kangaroo leaps. He wondered what he should do next. The man in the mortuary, Max Randolph, was Eric's father. Dorothy had no claim on Michael Cheviot. Her lawsuit was null and void. Dorothy was no longer his client, but he couldn't just walk away. Someone had to find her.

Edwin Champion, unsteady on his feet and leaning on a cane, dangled a set of car keys in front of Toby's eyes.

"Go to the office, Whitby."

"There's nothing for me to do there, sir. We no longer have a case."

"Forget the case," Champion snapped. "Dorothy Findlay may not be our client but she's still our responsibility. I want you to be where Slater can find you, because he's going to need you. He won't come here—he's too proud for that—and you can't go to him, but he'll need you. Mark my words, Whitby, he's going to need you. Take the Armstrong and go to the office."

Toby parked the Armstrong on the street outside the office and unlocked the door. The air inside was still. Anthea's typewriter was shrouded in its utilitarian gray cover, and Mr. Champion's door was closed. He sat down at his own desk and stared at his empty in tray and equally empty out tray. He watched as the sun marked its slow passage across the sky in a pattern of shifting shadows on the surface of the desk. The office grew warm and stuffy. He settled back in his chair and studied the dust motes he had created as they rose up for a brief sunlit dance. He closed his eyes.

The phone rang. He opened his eyes. The shadows had shifted; the sunbeams came through the window at a long low angle. How long had he slept?

Carol! He sat up straight. He had told her he would catch the evening train. He should be on his way to Wales by now. How had he managed to forget something so important? If he answered the phone she would know that he was not on the train. He hesitated with his hand hovering above the instrument and waited for it to ring again while he wondered what excuse he could give for not being with her. He could hardly tell her tell her about the case and betray client confidentiality.

He was still without an excuse when the phone rang for a second time. Reluctantly he lifted the receiver. "Champion and Company. Toby Whitby speaking." "Whitby, I'm up the road in the Dog and Duck; get yourself over here."

"Slater?"

"Yeah, that's right. Get moving, we don't have much time."

"Time for what?"

"Time to get your client back."

"Dorothy Findlay?"

"Do you have another one?"

We don't even have that one, Toby thought, but he swallowed his anger at the taunt, pushed his problems with Carol to the back of his mind, and hurried out of the office. The Armstrong was still at the curb, but he decided to leave it where it was. It was not the kind of car that should be left outside a pub like the Dog and Duck, and it was only a short walk.

The Dog and Duck was in a narrow building wedged between two rows of terraced cottages. It was a pub for working men. When Toby pushed the door open, he was greeted by a wave of smoke from pipe tobacco and cheap cigarettes. The oak-planked floor was sticky beneath his feet. The bar was crowded with men in shirtsleeves and braces, all of whom had turned their backs on the sunny evening and the fresh sea breeze to lean their weary elbows on the old bar and bewail the fate of the working man.

He spotted Slater at a table set in a corner by the empty fireplace. Despite the press of men at the bar, the Inspector sat in solitary state. Toby made his way through the crowd and saw the way that men looked at him with hooded eyes as they watched his progress toward the man they knew to be a policeman. Toby wished he'd removed his jacket and tie before he entered. Even Slater had removed his tie.

Slater pushed a pint glass at him. "I took you for a pale ale man," he said.

Although the comment sounded like an insult, Toby took the beer and drank greedily. He was halfway down the glass before he set it down and wiped his mouth with the back of his hand.

"Well?"

Slater leaned forward and Toby noticed for the first time that Slater had two empty glasses in front of him. The beer seemed to have mellowed him. He spoke almost pleadingly. "I need your help."

"Really?"

"Yeah."

"Why?"

Slater fixed him with dark, serious eyes. "Don't mess with me, Whitby. This is important."

"You said you could find my client?"

"I have a lead." Slater gestured to his empty sleeve. "I can't do this alone. I need you to drive again. In fact, I don't even have a vehicle. What's happened to your Morris?"

Toby was taken aback. He'd spent an entire afternoon sitting helplessly at his desk when he should have been making arrangements to have the Morris towed to a garage. Now he was angry at the world in general, with himself, with Anthea for crashing into Slater, with Slater for crashing into Anthea. He didn't know the truth of what had happened or who had been at fault, but he nursed his anger, knowing that, more than anything else, he was angry that he had forgotten Carol. Angry and puzzled. How had he managed to forget her so entirely?

He pushed the problem aside as something to think about later tonight when he would make an apologetic phone call to explain why he was not on the train. He turned his attention back to Slater.

"You want to know what happened to my Morris?" he asked. "Why don't you tell me? You were there."

"She came out of nowhere," Slater replied. "Women drivers, that's all I can say about that. So, do you have your car? Is it drivable?"

Toby shrugged. "I don't know about my Morris, but I have something else."

"What?"

"I have Mr. Champion's Armstrong."

"We'll take that."

"Where?"

"Shoreham Harbour." Slater was on his feet. "Come on, let's get going."

Toby hesitated, staring down at his half-empty glass. Why was Slater here? Why were they meeting at an out-of-the-way pub and not at the police station? Why didn't Slater have a police car and a driver?

He picked up the glass and took a slow, measured sip.

"Now!" Slater hissed. "We have to go now."

Toby took another sip, presenting a calm exterior while his mind was working. There was something about Slater. Something he had noticed and dismissed. Now he reconsidered.

"Where's your tie?"

Slater glared at him. "What are you talking about?"

"If you're on duty, where's your tie? Aren't you supposed to wear a tie?"

Slater's face grew red with impatience and something else. Guilt?

"I don't give a damn about my tie."

"But I do," Toby said. He could see that his question, innocuous as it seemed, had hit a nerve. He set his glass down on the table and gestured Slater back to his seat.

"I'm going nowhere," Toby said, "and that means I'm not driving you anywhere, until you tell me what's going on."

Slater flung himself into a chair and glowered as Toby leaned forward.

"Look, Slater," Toby said, "I know you don't like me, and I can't say I like you, but you want me to help you, so the very least you can do is be honest with me. You don't have your tie, you don't have a police car, and you've had a couple of pints of beer, which you would never do if you were on duty. Therefore, I'm going to assume that you're off duty. "He hesitated, searching Slater's red, impatient face. "You're not just off duty, are you? You're off the case. This trip to Shoreham, this is all you, isn't it? What are you getting us into?"

Slater's face crumpled. His tone was arrogant and pleading at the same time. "Are you going to help me or not?"

"Are you telling me the truth about Dorothy? Are we going to find my client?"

Slater nodded. "Yeah, we'll find her if you stop poncing around in here and start driving."

Toby stood up and drained his glass. The beer and the movement sent a rush of blood to his brain. He felt a surge of adrenaline. Whatever was about to happen in Shoreham was infinitely more exciting than snoozing at his desk and worrying about Carol. His day had been spent in helpless frustration over crimes already committed and lies that had festered for half a century. Here was his chance to move out of the shadow of the past and reach into the future to make sure that no one else would die to cover up the crimes of Enid Cheviot and her son.

Detective Inspector Percy Slater

Edwin Champion's limousine purred softly as Toby drove it out of the town and up onto the Downs. The long summer twilight was drawing to a close, and the sun dragged a blanket of darkness behind it as it sank below the horizon. They left the lights of Brighton behind, and night closed in around them as they crossed the dark hills. Slater felt cocooned and protected in the orange glow from the instrument panel of the Armstrong, as though he could escape the repercussions to come. He slipped his hand into the pocket of his raincoat and felt the reassuring bulk of the Browning 9 mm. He should have returned it, but no one had asked for it. Perhaps no one except the desk sergeant knew he had it. He was on suspension, no longer on official police business. If he used the pistol, would it be murder?

Toby's driving was slow and steady, even a little cautious. Slater's first thought was that Toby was afraid he might damage his employer's luxury vehicle, but then he saw the way that Toby leaned forward against the steering wheel and peered through the windshield. He fought against frustration and despair. Recruiting Toby had been his only option, but even if they combined their strengths, they were hardly a formidable fighting force; Toby with his bad eyesight and Slater with his missing arm.

To Slater's surprise, Toby stopped the car at the crest of the Downs, where a fine day would usually present a view of the ocean. Nighttime had brought an onshore breeze and scudding clouds sending dappled moonlight across the line where the sea melted into the horizon. The lights of Shoreham were not yet in view. Time was wasting.

"Why have you stopped?"

Toby set the hand brake. The ratcheting sound was decisive and left no room for argument. Toby was in control.

"Okay, Slater, tell me why."

"Why what?"

The dashboard lights created an orange glow on Toby's spectacles and highlighted his impatient expression.

"Do you really want to do that?" Toby asked.

"Do what?"

"Answer a question with a question. We can stay here all night, or you can give me a straight answer. What's happened? Why are you off duty? Have you been fired?"

"No, not fired. Not yet."

"Then what?"

"I failed to report an interview with a witness who gave vital information on a highly sensitive case. I took a vehicle equipped with a radio, but I did not report my position or answer radio requests in a timely manner."

He would not look at Toby. He didn't want to see his own disappointment reflected in the lawyer's face.

"He wasn't my partner," Slater muttered. "Partners consult. Partners don't go off on their own."

Toby said nothing, and Slater struggled to find the words for his own justification. His partnership with Frankie had not even begun. Frankie had said nothing to him about commandeering a milkman's horse and wandering the streets of Hove. Frankie was the one who had told him to go after Billy Cheviot in the ambulance.

He could still see the anger in the chief constable's face, the contempt of his fellow officers, the accusing eyes as he walked through the squad room. He could argue that Frankie was not his partner, but he could not argue the facts. He had failed to report his position, failed to report the collision with the Morris, failed to listen to his radio.

Toby waited, silent and patient. Slater knew they would get no nearer to Shoreham until he admitted the truth. "I failed to support my partner and now he's dead."

Toby drew in a sharp breath. "I assume you had a good reason," he said.

Slater nodded. "Dorothy."

"You did all of that for Dorothy?"

"I couldn't let Billy Cheviot have her."

"Hmm ..."

"That's all you're going to say?" Slater snapped.

"What is it with you and Billy Cheviot?" Toby asked.

"I don't have time to tell you."

"Make time. If we're going into whatever this is together, I need to know everything."

Slater shifted his right shoulder and the vestigial stump of his arm. "He gave me this."

"I thought you were wounded."

"Oh yes, I was wounded. D-Day, Gold Beach. I was with the Fourth County of London Yeomanry. My lieutenant stepped on a mine. It blew him halfway to hell. He didn't have a chance, but I wasn't too bad. I walked out of there under my own steam. It should not have cost me an arm."

"So why did it?"

Eileen Enwright Hodgetts

June 6, 1944
Normandy, France
Sergeant Percy Slater

Slater's arm was broken, but shock held the pain at bay. A bone splinter showed white beneath the tatters of his sleeve, and blood oozed from the wound. He assessed the blood flow and saw it as minor. He was in no danger of bleeding to death. Lieutenant Parrish was a few feet away, lying on his back. A pool of blood had taken the place of his legs. Slater crawled across to him and willed himself to find relief in what he saw. The lieutenant would never know. He would not awake to find himself without legs. He would not suffer the pain of a shattered body. His eyes had already glazed over, and he stared sightlessly at the smoke-filled sky. For him, the battle was over.

Slater staggered to his feet. He still had his legs, and he could issue the orders that should have come from Parrish. The pain in his arm was something to be ignored until his men were off the beach.

Hours passed, night came, and at long last they were beyond the killing zone, and he could surrender to his injuries.

His journey to healing took him to a field station, where his arm was splinted. He passed a day and a night. The morphine wore off, and the sounds of battle were sharp and clear; planes passing overhead, explosions, gunfire, vehicles roaring up from the beach, and the constant flow of the wounded and broken. He had trained for this. He should be out there. He reassured himself that he would be back one day soon; back in time for Berlin. It was a broken arm. Broken bones would mend.

Morning came, and with it the doctors and nurses with stretcher bearers and orderlies to take the wounded to a hospital ship.

He struggled to sit up as the doctor made his way among the wounded, checking, assessing who should go first.

"I'm all right, Doc."

"Of course you are. Relax, Sergeant, we'll give you something for the pain and get you moved onto the ship. It's a bad break but you'll mend."

A nurse. A kind face. Morphine and a gentle drifting away to a place where nothing mattered. The drifting stopped at the sudden shock of recognition. He knew the face that hovered above the bed. With recognition came a presentiment of something bad about to happen.

He should have known that Billy Cheviot would find a comfortable berth for himself. Medical Corps; stretcher bearer, well out of the line of fire.

He heard Cheviot's sharp intake of breath. He fought against the morphine as Cheviot leaned close to whisper. "I know you. Slater, right? I didn't expect to

168

find a policeman here; thought you'd be back in London, locking up people who are just trying to make a living."

He couldn't respond or even move. The morphine dragged him into a distant dream. He felt a rough hand at his neck, a tug at his dog tags.

"Yeah, it's you. Hurt your arm, have you? Let's have a look."

The pain shocked him back into reality. He felt the twisting and splintering. His arm was wet with blood, not a trickle, but a flow.

"Oh, look at that," Billy said. "That's an artery, ain't it? You just might bleed to death."

Billy's face was very close now, his expression malevolent. A rough hand poked and peeled at the field dressing.

"That's bone, ain't it?" Billy asked. "Let's see what we can do with that."

The morphine's gentle distance was gone now, and the pain was real and present. Slater screamed a curse as Billy manipulated the bone.

He heard another voice. A woman, a nurse. "What's going on? What's the matter?"

Billy was gone, vanishing as though he had been no more than a bad dream. Nothing now but the horror-struck face of a nurse followed by the calm face of a doctor, hands prodding at his arm; the prick of a needle.

Time slid by while his mind seemed to be separated from his body. He heard snatches of words. "Severed artery ... This is a nasty one ... The arm will have to go."

When he came to full consciousness, he was tucked in between stiff white sheets. A doctor with a set expression on his face moved from bed to bed, explaining that he had done his best. This one had lost a leg; this one had lost two legs. By the time he came to Slater's bed, Slater already knew what he had lost. Only one arm. When he managed to get out of bed and stand, he saw the envy in the eyes of men who would never stand again.   He kept his anger to himself and allowed it to burrow into him, where it had spent the past ten years growing roots and sending forth sprouts of resentment.

May 1952

Slater had said more than he intended to say. He should have told Toby to mind his own business. He didn't need Toby's sympathy.

He said it aloud. "I don't need your sympathy."

"I'm not offering it," Toby said calmly. "I'm just assessing what we're up against. A one-armed man and a half-blind lawyer—"

"You're not half-blind."

"I'm fine until someone knocks my glasses off, and then I'm half-blind. I would think you could have found a better partner in crime."

"No. You're all I have."

"Okay. Given your interpersonal skills that doesn't surprise me," Toby said. He lightened the sting of his remark with an ingenuous smile. "So, next question. Why Shoreham? What are we going to do in Shoreham?"

"We're going to see if Dorothy is on board an old Belgian sailing barge that slips in and out of the harbor on the river tide, bringing in black market goods. I have reason to believe that he's also transporting people."

"You sure?"

"I got a tip from an undercover agent from the Met in London."

It hurt him to speak casually of Frankie, but he couldn't face any more of Toby's questions. Frankie was dead, but his information still mattered.

"How do they know about Dorothy?" Toby asked.

"It's not about Dorothy. It's about the Cheviots. Enid Cheviot's mixed up in something that's a lot bigger than just the abduction of one woman. The agent I spoke of is part of a task force charged with looking into Soviet interference with the coronation. They think that Enid Cheviot is involved."

He looked at Toby's incredulous face and shook his head. "I didn't believe it at first, but I changed my mind this morning."

"Why?"

"Because of what Mrs. Hogg-Prewett had to say for herself. She turned up in my office this morning and told me that the Duke of Windsor is hiding out in the house next door. The house next door happens to be The Laurels, where she believes perverted sex acts are taking place on account of the woman who screams in the night."

Toby's mouth now hung open in surprise. Slater imagined that the lawyer was groping for words. He didn't give him time to speak.

"When I got the tip, I went there. Mrs. Hogg-Prewett's testimony would be enough for a search warrant, but I didn't intend to wait, so I went on my own. Undercover was already there."

He spared a thought for Larry the horse. How long had he waited for his driver to return before he decided to make his way back to the stable? Had he stopped at all the usual stops, or had he quickened his pace as the storm broke? Had he been able to smell the blood of the dead man propped up in the driver's seat?

"I saw Billy leaving in the ambulance," he said. "I tried to follow him, but your secretary ran into me with your car, and you know the rest of the story."

"Do I?"

"You know as much as I do," Slater said. "I lost track of Billy but I found Madeline Randolph, and I know the identity of the body in the mortuary; not that it makes any difference at this point. The thing is, I still believe that Billy Cheviot plans on transporting Dorothy to the Middle East and selling her off. Given everything that's happened today, I think he'll go tonight."

"What about your undercover officer? What does he say?"

"He's not saying anything," Slater said.

At least Toby had the decency not to ask. He slipped the car into gear and they continued their journey in silence.

CHAPTER EIGHTEEN

Toby Whitby

The approach to the harbor was unguarded. Toby had to remind himself that an unguarded harbor was normal. The war had been over for six years, but some things still felt wrong. Mainland Europe was so close, less than a hundred miles across the English Channel, and he could not rid himself of the idea that an enemy lurked there, beyond the horizon. Hitler no longer lay in wait, but what about the Soviets? When would they come, or had they already come?

The harbor arm lay in semidarkness, with only a few antiquated streetlights casting their reflections on the dark water. Toby angled the Armstrong's headlights toward the harbor wall, and the high beams revealed a half a dozen pleasure craft and a couple of small freighters lying alongside the wall.

"Should we find the harbormaster?" Toby asked.

"I doubt the harbormaster will be here," Slater grunted, "but there'll be a night watchman. Pull in at the end of the dock and turn those damned lights off. We don't want to let the whole world know we're here."

Toby stopped the car and extinguished his headlights. A moment later he saw the dark shape of a man walking toward them along the harbor arm.

Slater, making awkward use of his left hand, opened the car door and stepped out to meet the watchman. Toby heard the whispered conversation.

"Police."

"In a limousine? You're pulling my leg."

"Do you want to see my warrant card?"

"I do. Can't be too careful."

"Right."

A pause followed while Slater undertook another awkward shuffling with his left hand, and the watchman ostentatiously produced a flashlight to shine on Slater's warrant card. Toby was surprised that Slater still had the card. Shouldn't he have turned it in?

After a thorough examination of the card, the watchman turned his light on Toby.

"None of that," Slater said impatiently. "We don't have time for that. Have you seen any movement on any of these vessels? Anyone going on board or leaving?"

"No ..." The watchman drew the word out and ended it in a thoughtful sigh. "Those two freighters haven't moved in weeks. Waiting for fuel." He laughed mirthlessly. "They'll have a long wait. Our bunkers are empty. The Belgian barge is the only one moving these days. Comes and goes on the tide, don't even need a motor."

Slater's voice was sharp. "Is he here now?"

The watchman sucked air in through his teeth. "I couldn't say. He just comes and goes, and it's all a nudge and a wink, if you know what I mean."

"No," Slater snapped. "I don't know what you mean. Tell me about the Belgian."

The watchman offered up another sigh before he spoke in tones of strained patience. "I don't know as how he's actually Belgian, because I've never spoken to him, so I can't swear to what he is, but he flies a Belgian flag. The barge is a Dutch rig, but it's a long way from Holland to here, so I reckon he comes over from Belgium or France."

"And where is he now?"

"I only just came on watch. I don't know."

Slater seemed to strain for patience. "But if he is here, where would he be?"

"He'd be upriver, unloading his stuff. I don't know why you want to mess with him. It's just food and we're glad to have it. Our local bobbies leave him alone."

"I'm not a local bobby."

"Well, perhaps you should talk to our locals before you go sticking your nose in," the watchman remarked truculently. "It's not like he's hurting anyone. My wife says that his sausages are—"

"I don't give a damn about his sausages," Slater snapped.   The discussion of sausages jolted Toby's memory. He leaned out of the window and hissed at Slater. "I think I know what he's talking about. There's a man who sells black market sausages in Brighton. I'm thinking he brings them in from the Continent and runs them up the river here. They're probably horsemeat."

"I don't care if they're elephant meat," Slater snapped. "I just want to know if the Belgian and his damned barge are up the river now, or if they're waiting for the tide."

The night watchman lifted the flashlight and shone it full in Slater's face. "What you going to do to him?"

Slater batted the light away. "Does your harbormaster know you've been allowing a foreign vessel to come and go without inspection?"

"We all like our sausages," the watchman replied.

"You won't be getting sausages in prison," Slater threatened. "You'll all be in prison if I have my way; you, the harbormaster, and anyone else who is supposed to be guarding this harbor. Are you really telling me that this foreign vessel—"

"Belgian. He's only Belgian. It's not like he's Russian or anything."

"It's a foreign vessel, and it comes in and out of here without you even seeing it."

The watchman's voice took on a wheedling, ingratiating tone. "We see him. It's not like we don't see him. You've got it all wrong, Officer."

Slater's voice was harsh with impatience. "I don't think so. According to what you just told me, he slips in an out of here on the tide, and you don't see him."

"We see him; we just don't say nothing. You know, we just wave, friendly like."

"Friendly like," Slater repeated. "So he doesn't tie up in the harbor? He doesn't go through customs?"

"No."

"So where do you see him?"

Now the watchman was anxious to please. "It's the current. When he's going out on the ebb tide, the current brings him right along here, no more than a couple of feet from the harbor arm. We take a good look, you know, see if he's …"

The watchman's voice faded into silence under Slater's unwavering glare.

"See if he's what?" Slater asked.

"Carrying anything."

"He wouldn't be carrying anything on his way out, would he?" Slater hissed.

The watchman remained silent. Slater stared out at the dark water of the harbor. He uttered a long, drawn-out sigh, as if releasing his frustrations. "So, if he's here now, where is he? How do I find him? I'm not waiting out here all night so I can wave goodbye when he leaves. Where does he unload?"

"Drive about a mile up the road," the watchman muttered, "and turn left at the farm with the big white barn. Follow the farm lane and you'll come to the old wharf. That's where he unloads."

While Slater walked back and opened the passenger door, Toby leaned out of the window and spoke to the rapidly retreating watchman.

"What's the tide now?"

The watchman had already extinguished his light, and his voice came from the darkness. "It's already turned. If he's up there, he'll be getting ready to leave, if he hasn't left already."

Lucinda Hogg-Prewett

Lucinda perched on the edge of a satin-upholstered armchair. The Ladies Lounge at the Boulevardier Club in Knightsbridge was a small room tucked away in a corner and begrudgingly provided with furniture that would have been more appropriate for a boudoir. Lucinda, taking in the generally raffish air of her husband's club, thought that perhaps the only ladies to be entertained in this room were those who were normally entertained in the boudoir. She thought that the use of the word lady was somewhat of a stretch for the kind of woman who would meet a man at the Boulevardier Club. Nonetheless, she was here with her social antennae quivering because her husband had not seen fit to return her telephone messages.

A waiter, young and sly, entered with two glasses on a tray; whisky and soda for Lester, and a dry sherry for Lucinda. Lester dismissed the waiter.

"Make sure we're not disturbed."

"General?"

Lucinda could hear the question in the waiter's voice. Really, what reason could he have to sound so suspicious and so inappropriately amused? Surely Lester was not in the habit of ...

Lucinda turned her mind to the task at hand and continued her story. "The police inspector told me that I would not be safe at home. He told me that I should come up to London at once."

"Did he tell you to speak to me?"

"No, not exactly, and I did tell him that I could not possibly disturb you at your club." She took a judicious sip of her sherry, wishing for something a little stronger, and looked around the room. "I was not aware that your club had a Ladies Lounge." She hoped that Lester would take note of the emphasis she had placed on the word Ladies.

Lester swilled the ice cubes in his glass. Ice cubes! He never asked for ice cubes at home. "So," he said, "you've been looking out the window again. I told you not to. It's not something you have to understand, and—"

Lucinda interrupted him before he could tell her once again that she did not understand the proclivities of certain men. "She's being taken away, tonight," she said, "and they talked about selling her. I'm sorry, Lester, but I don't care who she is or how low her morals are, that does not sound right. I cannot condone the selling of women, not after the things we saw in India."

"Tonight?" Lester asked.

"Yes, dear, tonight. The big man, the one who is unfortunately related to Mrs. Cheviot, said that they would put her on a barge and she would leave at high tide, along with the other man."

"Other man?"

"You know who I mean; the one who looks like the Duke of Windsor."

"And you told all of this to the police?"

"I certainly did. I was unable to speak to the chief constable, but I spoke to an inspector who was very appreciative. He told me he would look into it immediately."

Lester mumbled something under his breath. Stupid woman? No, he would never call her a stupid woman; she must have misheard.

He set his glass down with such force that the small spindle-legged table he had chosen rocked precariously. "I will have someone phone the Savoy and reserve a room for you," he said. "The doorman will call you a taxi."

"Are you coming with me?" Lucinda asked.

"No. I have urgent business elsewhere tonight. You should go now."

"But—"

Lester pressed a five-pound note into her hand. "It will be safe for you to return home in the morning," he said. "Make sure you take a seat in the ladies-only carriage."

Lucinda stared down at the five-pound note and back at her husband.

"You seem to know a lot about this, Lester."

He bristled his eyebrows at her and made the harrumphing, blustering sound that usually presaged a lie. "No, of course not. It's nothing to do with me. Off you go."

While she waited for the doorman to call a taxi, she looked back into the foyer of the club and saw Lester enter a phone booth. He looked up, saw her watching, and waved her away.

Toby Whitby

Toby leaned forward against the steering wheel, searching through the near darkness for any sign of a white barn.

"There," Slater said, pointing to something that was no more than a pale smudge within the greater darkness.

Toby angled the Armstrong until the headlights picked up the skeletal remains of a shed. It was not by any stretch of the imagination a barn, but its few remaining boards bore the memory of whitewash, and it was the only building that even vaguely fitted the night watchman's description.

"He didn't want us to find this," Slater muttered.

"He doesn't want his supply of sausages interrupted," Toby replied.

"Yeah, well, we'll see about that," Slater growled. He gestured for Toby to move ahead. "Down there. I can see a gap in the hedge. Probably the lane he was talking about."

Toby moved tentatively forward until his lights picked up a lane and a small hand-lettered sign. Millers Wharf.

Slater growled again as Toby made the turn. "Turn off your damned headlights. You want the whole world to know we're coming?"

Toby had glimpsed the road before he turned off his lights. It was little more than a cart track, rutted and edged with hedges. The big limousine scraped noisily against the bushes on either side, and he drove more by sound than by sight, wondering what Mr. Champion would say about the condition of his car when this was all over.

Creeping along with only an occasional glimmer of moonlight to show him the way brought a painful reminder of the wartime blackout. Now Toby wondered how he had managed to find his way around for those six long years of darkness.

Slater, with his head out of the window, grunted for Toby to stop and pull over. Toby adjusted his glasses and saw the distant gleam of starlight reflected in rippling black river water. Ahead of them lay the dark bulk of a wharf, and alongside the wharf, two thick masts were silhouetted against the sky.

"Wait here," Slater said. He climbed from the passenger seat and closed the door quietly behind him.

Toby ignored him. He didn't say what he wanted to say. How are you going to get on board one-handed? What if you run into trouble? He didn't need to say it. He simply opened his door, closed it quietly behind him, and followed Slater down the chalky path to the wharf.

Slater turned and hissed at him. "You just going to leave the car for anyone to find?"

So much for gratitude, Toby thought as he trudged back to the car. He didn't have to be out here in the middle of the night on Slater's unofficial investigation. He could be at home in bed, or he could be in the pub, or he could even go to Mr. Champion's house and ingratiate himself with Robert Penhelen.

He climbed back into the car. For a moment, he considered turning it around and driving away, but he couldn't do it. He considered the frustration caused by his own poor eyesight against the frustration Slater experienced as he navigated life with only one arm. Toby's eyesight could be fixed with a pair of eyeglasses, but Slater's problem could not be fixed. The situation had to be endured, and Slater was still unable to endure it with any kind of grace.

He started the car and backed it up the path until he could pull off the track and onto the edge of a ploughed field and the partial concealment of a sparse hedge. The car wasn't well concealed, but it was the best he could do without leaving Slater alone for any length of time.

When he returned, Slater was still standing on the dock, examining the boat.

"You took your own sweet time," Slater grunted.

Toby chose to ignore the remark. Slater was worried. He imagined how he would feel if Carol had disappeared; murdered or sold to slavers. He would move heaven and earth to find her, and he would allow no one to stand in his way. That was all Slater wanted; he wanted Dorothy back and he needed Toby's help to do it. If that made him impatient, so be it.

The dock creaked and groaned as the dark bulk of the barge fought against its mooring ropes.

"Tide's turned," Slater said. "Wonder what they're waiting for."

Toby studied the barge. A clumsy cabin rose from the deck like an unfortunate afterthought. A short mast in the stern and a taller mast in the center of the boat swayed with the movement of waves. The barge's canvas sails, wrapped loosely around the boom, were pale in the starlight. He leaned forward to look down at the hull and the row of tiny portholes just above the waterline. No lights, and no hint of movement.

"I don't think anyone's here," Toby said.

Slater produced a flashlight from the pocket of his raincoat and shone its faint beam across the deck. He switched the light off and returned it to his pocket. "Stay here. I'm going to look."

"Should I come with you?"

"Do you know anything about sailing barges?"

"No."

"Then leave it to me," Slater said. His face was almost invisible, but his voice was confident and soft with memory. "I'm Gravesend born and bred. My dad was on the barges going down from Gravesend and up to Ipswich. Coal, grain, you name it. I went with him when I was a lad. I know my way around an old boat like this."

Maybe you do, Toby thought, but it's not the same when you only have one arm. He bit his tongue. He would not speak the words. Slater never needed to be reminded of his handicap. He lived and breathed the struggle and the resentment.

He saw Slater move and stretch out his arm. He caught hold of one of the stays that held the mast upright, swung himself gracefully aboard, and landed silently on the deck. He looked up at Toby. "Wait there. Warn me if anyone comes."

Toby watched Slater moving stealthily across the deck, a dark, silent shape, barely visible in the starlight. The cabin door creaked as Slater opened it. Toby winced and looked around in alarm, but nothing stirred on the boat or on the dock. Slater's shadowy shape vanished from sight. He had gone below.

Toby took a step forward and rested his hand on one of the stays. The wire sang in his grasp as the old boat danced in the tidal current. He looked down at the waterline, where the portholes showed him the faint glow of Slater's flashlight as he moved through whatever space lay beneath the deck. Cabins maybe, or just a vast empty hold where the Belgian stored his black market goods.

He considered climbing aboard to help Slater with his search. The barge was bigger than he had expected, long and wide and smelling of creosote and the residue of sausage spices.

His stomach rumbled, enslaved by the aroma of food. He considered the many sausages he'd known before the war. Pork, beef, chipolatas, saveloys, Cumberland, Gloucester, even black pudding. How many years since he'd had a decent sausage? The sound of an approaching vehicle dragged his mind back from the safe place where it had chosen to hide and catalog sausages. He turned in time to see headlights lighting a path along the rutted road and picking out the spring greenery of the hedges. He thought of the Armstrong, barely concealed at the edge of the path. Where was Slater? Had he heard the approaching vehicle?

He took one last look down at the portholes. No light shone from them. Either Slater had turned off his light, or he was somewhere else on the barge. Toby had no time to find out. The headlights of the approaching vehicle illuminated the wharf, and he flung himself into the meagre concealment of a pile of crab pots. He crouched as low as he could and peered through a narrow gap that gave him a view of the wharf and the stern of the barge.

The old timber of the wharf groaned as a heavy black car drove onto the planking and came to a halt with its headlights illuminating the deck of the barge. Slater had not reappeared. Where was he?

The driver killed the engine. A man climbed from the front passenger seat and opened the rear door. Three other men emerged into the light.

Toby took careful note of them as they passed in front of the lights. One of them, a tall man in a knitted cap, stood at the edge of the wharf and looked down at the water. He spoke with a sing-song accent, not German, something softer. "Hurry. It's late. We will miss the tide."

"Yeah, well, whose fault is that?"

Toby recognized the voice and the shape of the man who had come to stand beside the complaining foreigner. Billy Cheviot. So Slater's hunch had been right. Billy Cheviot was up to his neck in this smuggling operation, and if Dorothy was still alive, and if Cheviot intended to sell her into slavery in the Middle East, then this is how he would get her out of the country. It was all supposition, of course; if this and if that, and nothing certain in any of it. More than likely, Dorothy was already dead and lying at the bottom of the Channel.

"You had to sell all your sausages, didn't you?" Cheviot said. "I told you we'd make it up to you."

The foreigner shook his head. "I don't like this. The tide has already turned."

Cheviot slapped the sailor on the back. "Don't be such a nancy. Just get a move on."

The sailor grunted and called out in his own language. A ragged boy darted forward and set to work loosening the lines that held the barge against the dock. They were leaving.

Toby stared. What was he supposed to do? The car's headlights bathed the wharf in light. If he crept from his hiding place, he would be seen immediately, and what if Slater was no longer on the barge? What if he'd managed to slip over the side into the river?

Toby thought his best plan would be to wait for the barge to leave and then see if Slater was somewhere along the bank, or in the river. He could retrieve the car and use the headlights to search, and if he didn't find Slater, he would drive to the nearest police call box and report in with everything he knew. He knew that Slater was currently suspended and persona non grata, but surely the police would still come.

The driver had returned to his seat, and only one person remained; a slightly built man in a suit and tie. He was fine featured and silver haired. He stood with his hands in his pockets, watching the activity with a worried frown creasing his face.

His voice was cultured, and he affected a slight drawl as though asking questions was somehow beneath him; a task that nonetheless had to be done. "Are you sure about this?" he asked. "If it's too late for the tide, we can leave tomorrow."

"We leave now," Cheviot said bluntly. "Get on board."

Toby blinked and tried to focus. He dared not move his hand to adjust his glasses, so perhaps he was mistaken. The man in the suit could not possibly be the Duke of Windsor. Cheviot was an ignorant piece of work, but even he wouldn't speak that way to the former king. But if this man wasn't the Duke of Windsor, who was he, and why was he here?

Toby closed his eyes for a moment. Sometimes resting helped them to swim back into focus. Slater was here unofficially, but before his warrant was revoked, he'd received a tip. Someone higher up the command chain was suspicious about this smuggling operation, and not because of sausages, and not because of the disappearance of a local woman. Dorothy had never been the target of the Met's investigation, but could this silver-haired man be the target?

No, Toby thought, this could not be the Duke. His Highness had been allowed to return for his brother's funeral in February, and then he'd been sent back to France to live out his exile and stay out of the way of the new queen. To be here was an act of ... what? Treason? Sedition?

He opened his eyes again but he found no improvement. The silver-haired man still looked like the Duke of Windsor, and Toby still didn't see how that was possible.

The driver of the car started his engine, swung the vehicle in a tight circle, and bumped away along the rutted lane. Toby struggled to see in the sudden darkness. The yellow glow of a lantern illuminated the cockpit and lit the way for Billy Cheviot to step on board. The man in the suit followed without difficulty. The sailor in the knitted cap took up his station with his hands on the old barge's massive tiller. The boy untied the last of the mooring lines and flung them and himself aboard.

The dock creaked and swayed as the barge freed itself and was taken up by the tidal current.

Where was Slater? Surely he knew by now whether Dorothy had been brought on board.

The sound of voices calling out instructions carried across the water for a few moments. Toby traced the path of the barge by watching the yellow light of the oil lamp and saw it pick up speed as it swung out into the center of the river.

The rumble of the car engine died away, and all he could hear was the water lapping against the dock, and the distant hoot of an owl.

He crept out from his hiding place and stretched his arms and legs. He called out for Slater and listened for an answer. Nothing. Slater was still on the barge, and the light of the barge was receding rapidly. Toby turned and ran up the lane toward the car. There would be no time to call the police. He would have to do this himself.

Dorothy Findlay
She awoke to darkness. Her hands and feet were tied, but this time, she had not been gagged. What did that mean? Did it mean that she was in a place where no one would hear her screams?

She'd been drugged. She could think of no other explanation for the hours that she had obviously missed. She remembered the milkman and the blood that trickled from the corner of his mouth. She remembered Michael's words of contempt and his warning that Billy Cheviot wanted to keep her to sell. That was why she wasn't dead.

She struggled against the ropes that held her. So Billy intended to sell her in some foreign slave market; well, that was better than being dead. Where would she be taken? India? China? Somewhere in Arabia? It didn't matter. Eric needed her, and while she had life in her body, she would not stop trying to escape.

What was this place? She strained her eyes to see through the darkness, but she could not find even a glimmer of light. She sniffed the air and identified the odor of decaying seaweed, like a beach at low tide. Her next breath brought another odor, faint but familiar. What was it? She fought against the last lingering remnants of the drug. She had to concentrate. She had to know where she was. She sniffed the air again and recognized the odor. Sausages! She could smell sausages, and not just any sausages; she could smell the distinctive spices of the sausages she had bought on the black market for Eric's breakfast. She caught her breath at the thought of Eric and tamped down the desire to weep. If she was sold into some foreign harem, it would be years before she would see him again, but she would see him. She would.

Detective Inspector Percy Slater

He was at the top of the steps, his head level with the deck, when he heard the voices. Hs risked a glance at the dock. Toby was nowhere in sight, but he could see four figures silhouetted in the headlights of the vehicle that had just arrived.

Men. They were all men. He recognized the bulk of Billy Cheviot's broad shoulders before he heard his voice. The other men were unfamiliar. One was no more than a boy, one was a tall foreigner in a knit cap, and one was slightly built and silver haired. He held his breath and waited for them to return to the car and fetch their prisoner. He imagined that she would be tied, maybe gagged, but he was confident that she would be with them.

Billy Cheviot stepped aboard. That was wrong. If not Billy, then who would bring Dorothy aboard? The silver-haired man and the man in the knit cap swung themselves onto the deck. The boy scrabbled among the ropes that held the barge to the dock. The car door slammed.

No, the car was leaving; driving back along the lane. Where was Dorothy?

Slater raised himself onto the top step of the companionway. He had to get off the barge. Dorothy wasn't here and the barge was leaving, heading for France, or Belgium or some other place where he did not want to be. He could see the barge skipper in the stern of the boat with his hand on the massive tiller. Billy and the other man stood beside him. The car headlights faded in the distance, and Slater searched the dock for any sign of Toby. The boy untied the last of the mooring lines and jumped lightly aboard.

Slater made a decision. Somehow or another, he had to get off this boat. Maybe he'd be seen as he dashed across the deck, but what did that matter? The gap between the dock and the boat was widening. He would have to do it now, and if he missed the dock, he'd have to hope that Toby would emerge from wherever he was hiding to pull him out of the water.

He would need to be quick; lever himself out onto the deck and go.

He leaned his weight onto his left arm and raised himself on his toes. At the last moment, he hesitated. He thought he heard something from below in the hold, a plaintive mewing sound. A kitten? A woman? Dorothy? No, it was just his imagination; his own wishful thinking. She was not here and he had to go.

He reached out with his right arm, the arm that no longer existed, and the world fell away from him as he tumbled backward into the hold.

He was winded, but nothing was really hurt except his pride. He had managed to keep his mouth shut as he fell, not that anyone would have heard him if he had cursed the missing arm the way he had cursed in the field hospital. The barge was alive with sounds far louder than any sounds Slater could make and far louder than the plaintive mewing he had imagined.

The old boat was moving. Her timbers creaked and groaned, and her wires sang as they slapped against the masts. He sat upright and found the floor steady beneath him. The barge was running on the tide like the barges of his childhood. The skipper had not raised the sails or started the motor or lit the navigation lights. He knew his business. He knew how to ghost on the current that would carry him out of the harbor. The waves would come later.

Slater crouched in the darkness of the hold, breathing in the aroma and feeling the movement. The barges of his boyhood had not carried such exotic odors. He remembered the sweet summer smell of grain competing with the acrid tang of tar. It was all a long time ago. He had once been a nimble deckhand with two arms, but how would he fare with only one arm once the barge was out of the harbor and riding on the wind and tide.

He thought back to D-Day, the last time he had been on a boat, if a landing craft could even be called a boat. The memory gave him confidence. Despite the horror of the Channel crossing and the hours spent rolling and tossing off the French coast, he had not suffered seasickness. If he had not vomited in the stench and terror of the landing craft, he was not going to vomit now. Whatever happened next, he would not be curled up in a ball and wishing for the boat to sink, and he still had the Browning in his pocket as an equalizer.

Well, he was here now, and he was going to be here for a while. He had plenty of time to sit in the dark and regret his own foolishness. Dorothy's disappearance had somehow robbed him of common sense. He shouldn't be here. He shouldn't be on suspension. He should be back at HQ, trying to get himself reinstated; trying to do the work that Frankie could no longer do.

He felt disappointment and regret settle like a cold stone in his stomach. He had risked everything for the idea that Dorothy was still alive. Mrs. Hogg-Prewett had reported seeing a woman at the Cheviots' house, and maybe that woman had been Dorothy. Maybe Billy had intended to keep her alive and transport her for sale on the Continent, but the discovery of Madeline Randolph had changed everything.

Slater could only guess at the panic at The Laurels when Enid Cheviot discovered that Madeline was alive and talking. The story of Michael's wartime cowardice would soon be public knowledge and so would the story of Enid's abandonment of her baby brother. He imagined that Enid and her son would waste no time in booking passage to America or Australia or somewhere they could hide their faces and change their names. Obviously, Billy Cheviot had already made his decision. He was making his escape, and he wasn't going to be slowed down by dragging Dorothy along with him. The icy stone in Slater's stomach grew larger as his certainty increased. Dorothy was dead. Billy would not have left her alive.

He felt the weight of the Browning in his pocket. He could end this now. Billy had no idea that Slater was on board. All the advantage would be on Slater's side. A single bullet would even the score. It would be murder, but who would complain? The barge captain and his apprentice were smugglers; they would say nothing. The silver-haired man, whoever he was, was leaving the country under a veil of darkness. He would say nothing. Billy Cheviot would disappear, and no one would dare to ask what happened to him.

Slater started to climb. He reached the top step and poked his head out to look around. The barge was moving easily with the current, and he could see the harbor lights ahead. The barge was wrapped in darkness, apart from the flickering light of an oil lamp in the stern. He could make out the outline of the skipper, with his hand on the tiller, and the crew and passengers gathered around him.

Not yet. They were too close to land, and Billy's body would wash ashore. He would have to wait until they were well out to sea. He would need to get Billy on his own. He had no wish to harm anyone else. He slipped his hand into his pocket and felt the cool metal of the pistol. This would be the equalizer. This was payback for his missing arm. This was revenge for Dorothy.

Revenge? No! This was murder. He snatched his hand away from the pistol as though it had suddenly become red hot. What was he doing? Was he really going to commit murder? He shook his head and gathered his scattered thoughts. There was a way to do this that didn't involve breaking every oath he had made as an officer of the law.

If he could alert Interpol, Billy could be picked up as soon as the barge approached the French coast. The silver-haired man, whoever he was, could be questioned. If he was truly the Duke of Windsor, he would be returned to his home in Paris. If he was an imposter, people very high up in the chain of command would want to know why.

Slater stared ahead at the harbor lights. Somehow he would have to get off the barge before it hit open water, which meant he would have to get off now. He levered himself out of the hold and slithered into the darkness of the foredeck. The night watchman had said that the barge would come in close to the harbor arm. He would have to pick his moment.

CHAPTER NINETEEN

Toby Whitby

The night watchman came out of the shadows to meet him.

"He ain't here. I told you he's up the river."

"He's coming," Toby said. "You told the inspector that the current brings him close to the harbor wall. Show me where."

The night watchman's voice was a whine of protest. "What do you think I can do? I can't stop him."

"I'm not asking you to stop him," Toby said. "Just show me where he comes up against the harbor wall."

A pale half-moon had emerged from the clouds, and its light revealed the resentment on the night watchman's face.

"I don't know what you mean."

"Yes, you do," Toby said. "Show me the place where he usually throws you a packet of sausages on his way in."

"He don't."

"Of course he does. It's the price of your silence; you and the harbormaster, and the dockers. He keeps you supplied and you keep quiet."

"I don't see what it has to do with you," the night watchman complained. "What's any of this got to do with the Brighton police?"

So, Toby thought, he believes I'm a police officer. Well, that will make everything a bit easier, not that any of it is going to be easy. He would have to push.

"I could arrest you right now for failure to assist the police."

The night watchman shrugged. "All right, all right. I'll show you. Park that blooming great car and follow me. Don't know what things are coming to when the police are driving around in a limousine."

Toby parked the Armstrong. The orange glow of the dashboard lights gave him just enough illumination to pull out a pen and a business card. He wrote a number on the back of the card, tucked it into his pocket, and then sat for a moment with the car keys in his hand. Finally he decided not to surrender them to the night watchman and give him an opportunity to take the car home to impress his friend. He left the keys on the seat. If things went wrong, he would be back to collect them. If things went right …? He didn't want to think too hard about that.

He followed the night watchman along the harbor arm, stumbling in the darkness that lay between the intermittent pools of light. His guide stopped halfway along the harbor arm, where a rusted iron ladder led down into the water.

Toby stood for a moment, listening to the slap of waves against the harbor wall.

The night watchman's irritated voice brought him back from the edge of terror. "This is it."

"How close does he come?"

The night watchman sniffed, looked up at the sky and down at the water. "Tide's running out fast. He'll come close."

"When?"

The night watchman sniffed again, and his voice carried contempt. "Any minute now. I can see his lights on the river."

"What? Where?"

Toby turned to look back along the river, where he saw the faint glow of an orange light. He looked back down at the water. It was worth a try. He thought of removing his shoes. If he had to swim, they would weigh him down, but if he didn't end up in the drink, he would need them. He left them on. What about his glasses? The barge was big. Even his weak eyes would be able to see it. He took his glasses off, and as he had done when he was a boy, he tucked them in his undershirt, next to his skin.

"What you doing?"

"I'm going to board her."

The night watchman's voice held a reluctant note of respect. "You're mad."

"Maybe I am."

"Why?"

Toby wondered what he could say that would make the surly night watchman take him seriously; make him do what needed to be done. No use in mentioning that Slater was on board. He knew what the man thought of the police, but what did he think of the Queen?

"The Queen's enemies are on board."

"What?"

"You heard me. Enemies of the Queen; people who are trying to stop the coronation."

"No. Pull the other one; it's got bells on."

"I mean it. Russians."

"He ain't Russian."

"He's carrying Russians. Look, you fought in the war, didn't you?"

"Yes, but ..."

"This is another war and you're still needed. You have a duty."

"Yes, but ..."

Toby could hear the change of tone. His dramatic appeal was having its effect.

"I'm not asking you to do anything dangerous ..."

He hesitated. No, that wasn't the right thing to say. He had to make this bigger.

"Why do you think we have that car? That's not your average police car, is it?"

"Well, no ..."

"We're a special unit."

The night watchman made the leap. "A unit to keep the Queen safe?"

"Yes."

The pause seemed to stretch into eternity before the night watchman straightened his shoulders and his spine.

"All right then, what do you want me to do?"

Toby handed him the card. "After I get on board, if I get on board, you call that number and tell that person who answers what you've seen tonight. Tell him Toby gave you the number."

"Is this the number for MI5?"

The orange light was approaching rapidly. Toby had no time to create another deception. He told the night watchman what he obviously wanted to hear.

"Of course. Someone who sounds like an old man will answer the phone. Tell him what you saw. That's all you have to do."

"I could call him over."

"Call who over? What do you mean?"

The night watchman's voice dripped with cunning. "I could call the barge skipper over and warn him someone's looking for him. I wouldn't say nothing about you, but it would bring him closer. Wouldn't slow him down, not when the current's running, but it would give you a chance." He drew in a deep breath. "Are you really going to do it?"

"I'm going to try," Toby said. "Can I trust you to make that phone call?"

"Yes, of course ... sir."

Toby grinned. Now he was "sir". It was amazing what could be done by invoking the Queen's name.

He sat down on the cement and lowered his feet over the edge until he felt the first rung of the ladder. The first few rungs were smooth and slippery beneath his hands. As he went lower and the waves slapped against his legs, he felt barnacles beneath his fingers. He flattened himself against the ladder as he heard the night watchman calling out across the water.

The skipper answered. The barge loomed out of the darkness. She was moving fast, the bow coming straight at him. If he didn't move soon, he would be pinned against the ladder. He climbed one step higher. He clung to the ladder with one hand as he leaned out. The bowsprit slid past, and then the bulk of the barge was beneath him, scraping its way along the cement wall as the skipper exchanged words with the night watchman.

This was it. This was the one chance he would have. Toby released his hold of the ladder and leaped out toward the darkness below. His feet touched the deck and he staggered forward to catch his balance. He collided with an obstruction that sent him sprawling across the deck.

A voice hissed at him from the darkness. "Whitby?"

"Slater?"

"What are you playing at?"

Toby sat up. Slater was a dark shape rising from the deck beside him, looming and angry.

"I came to give you a hand," Toby whispered.

"Give me a hand?" Slater growled. "You want to give me a hand?"

"Sorry," Toby muttered. "An unfortunate turn of phrase. When I realized that you were still on here, I thought I should come and help you. You didn't get off, and—"

Slater's interruption was an angry hiss. "I was about to get off. I was going for the ladder until you landed on me."

Toby looked behind him. Without his glasses, the world was fuzzy and the harbor lights no more than a misty glow, but even he could see that they were receding rapidly. "Too late now."

Slater offered his opinion in an angry whisper. "You're a bloody idiot, Whitby."

Toby had an overwhelming urge to throw a punch. He clenched his fist and resisted the temptation as he staggered to his feet and found his balance on the moving foredeck.

"I take it she's not on board."

Slater responded in a cold imitation of Toby's accent. "I take it she's not on board? No, she's not on board, but I am, thanks to you."

Toby clenched his fist tightly, with his fingernails digging into his hand. Slater wanted to get off. He could arrange that. It wouldn't be difficult. He imagined heaving the surly policeman over the deck railing.

He unclenched his fist. He would do it. He would grab his raincoat and ...

A shouted instruction penetrated the red haze of his anger.

Somewhere in the stern of the barge, the skipper was issuing instructions.

"They're raising the sails," Slater said.

"How? Where?"

"Right here. If we don't move, we'll be over the side. Come on."

"If we go back there, they'll see us."

"Yeah," said Slater. "I know."

"So what do we do?"

Slater moved forward. Was he going to jump? Was that his solution? If so, it wasn't much of a solution.

"Here," Slater hissed. "Get over here and lift this hatch."

Toby moved forward. The barge was now beyond the protection of the harbor wall, out in the open water and pitching uneasily in the waves. Toby staggered, dropped to his knees, and crawled.

Slater had his hand on a square hatch cover and was trying to lift. Toby, all thoughts of jumping overboard forgotten, joined him, and between them they lifted the hatch.

"What is this?" Toby asked.

"Anchor locker," Whitby replied. "No one will find us down there."

Toby peered into the dark space. "It's a long way down."

"Just bloody go," Slater said, "before the sail knocks you overboard."

Toby turned to see that the mass of canvas that had been draped over the deck was changing shape, shaking free of its folds and rising slowly.

"Go," Slater said.

Toby dropped down into the dark.

Anthea Clark

Anthea was the only person awake. Eric was curled up on the sofa, using Daisy as a headrest. Madeline, refusing to return to hospital, had succumbed to pain medication and allowed herself to be tucked into a bed upstairs. Mr. Champion was in his study. When she peeked in, she saw him slumped in his chair, eyes closed, breathing shallow, uncomfortable breaths. He was not well. She feared what this added strain would do to him. She wished that Mr. Penhelen would return so that he could be consulted on the legal aspects of Madeline Randolph's case, but she had to assume that he had spent the night in London.

Hugh sat bolt upright in a wing chair, his alert posture seeming to deny the fact that he was not only asleep, but he was actually snoring. Anthea felt a slight catch in her throat as she looked at him. She had not expected romance of any kind to enter her life, but here it was in the form of an old Cornishman who wooed her gently with the courtesies of a bygone age.

She walked to the window and looked out into the back garden. Dawn light was creeping across the flower beds. An early bird, a speckled thrush, stalked the lawn with its head cocked to one side, listening for the sound of breakfast worms moving beneath the surface. It was all so peaceful; so normal; so very English.

She turned from the window and looked at the telephone, willing it to ring.

She could not imagine how Toby had been so foolish. What had possessed him to impersonate an MI5 agent and get on board the smuggler's barge? It made no sense.

The chief constable had been less than helpful when Mr. Champion phoned him to tell him of the message from the night watchman at Shoreham Harbour. He had suggested that Toby could be assisting Inspector Slater, that the French police would be alerted and ready to board the barge when it came into port, and that they should stop worrying, because everything was under control. As for the possibility that Billy Cheviot was also on board the barge, well, the French police would arrest him.

What about Enid Cheviot and her son?

It seemed that they had left England. Where and when, he could not say. The message was received and understood, and no further action was necessary. That barge crossed the Channel safely several times a week; there was no reason to think that this voyage would be any different.

Anthea remained lost in her own thoughts until the jangling phone brought the drawing room to sudden life. Hugh, cut off in midsnore, closed his mouth with a snap and stared at the phone with fierce attention. Anthea glanced through the study door and saw Mr. Champion making an attempt to pull himself together. Well, he was in no fit state to answer the phone. She would do it for him.

She lifted the receiver. "The Champion residence."

"Miss Clark?"

"Yes."

"Robert Penhelen here. I'm still in London, but I've heard a disturbing rumor."

Anthea knew how to be discreet, and now was the time to do just that. "What have you heard?"

"Your young associate, Whitby."

"Yes?"

"I heard that he may be in trouble. "

Anthea considered her answer carefully. Penhelen had already left for London when the phone call came from the night watchman. He couldn't know what was happening unless someone had phoned him.

"Where did you hear this?" she asked.

Penhelen's voice was firm and brooked no nonsense. "Miss Clark, please do not play games with me. I have it on good authority that Toby Whitby and Inspector Slater have somehow managed to get themselves on board a barge that is now crossing the Channel and carrying Billy Cheviot and ... someone ... else."

Good authority, Anthea thought. What good authority would that be? Who had told Penhelen, and who was the someone else?

A cold but firm hand closed over her fingers, and she saw that Mr. Champion was attempting to wrest the receiver from her grasp.

"I'll take care of this, Miss Clark."

She reluctantly ceded control of the receiver and retreated into her own thoughts. Someone had interrupted Robert Penhelen's business in London to tell him about Toby Whitby's predicament. Why? The Brighton police said that they had everything under control. Who had spoken to Penhelen?

CHAPTER TWENTY

Detective Inspector Percy Slater

The weight of bitterness and frustration that he had carried for so long lifted in the moment he saw her. The flashlight trapped Dorothy in its beam, eyes blinking and hair disheveled, but even more lovely than he remembered.

She was tied hand and foot, and had been dumped on top of a coiled anchor rope. At first glance all he saw was her face and her bruises, and then he saw that she was almost naked.

He turned the beam of light away from her and shucked off his raincoat.

"Take this."

"Inspector Slater?"

"Call me Percy."

He draped the coat around her and turned the flashlight on again so that he could untie her hands and feet.

The cramped anchor locker gave him very little room to move, and he bit back a curse as he stumbled over Toby. No need for cursing. He had done what he set out to do. He had found Dorothy.

"Where are we?" she asked.

"Crossing the Channel."

"They were going to sell me."

"I won't let them," he promised.

He felt Toby moving beside him. "What are you doing?"

"Putting on my glasses."

Toby's hand dipped inside his shirt, and in a moment, his spectacles were on his nose and a smile was on his face as he looked at Dorothy.

"Miss Findlay, I am happy to tell you that your son is safe. He's a very bright boy."

She seemed ready to hug Toby, but Slater held her back.

"We'll do that later. We should be able to find a way out of here."

Toby looked up at the hatch.

Slater shook his head, remembering what it was like to be on board a barge with the sails set and waves breaking across the bow. "You won't last five minutes up there."

"Why?"

Slater ignored the question. Now was not the time to share his memories of boyhood voyages along the east coast of England. He swung the flashlight along the walls of their prison until he found what he was looking for, a narrow doorway that would lead into the hold.

As the light picked out the opening, Toby lurched toward the door, the motion of the barge making him clumsy and setting him off-balance.

Slater shook his head. "Not yet."

"Why?"

"If you go out there, you'll be in the hold, and anyone who comes below will see you. We'll have to stay hidden here for as long as we can. I'm going to turn off the flashlight to preserve the battery. Sit down and hold on, she'll start heeling into the waves any minute now."

He turned off the light and sank down onto the coiled ropes. He felt someone beside him and warm breath on his cheek.

"Thank you, Percy."

"Don't thank me yet. We're not safe yet."

Damn, why did he say that? Couldn't he have said something comforting? Should he put his arm around her for reassurance? It would be a natural gesture, wouldn't it?

The problem solved itself. The barge heeled abruptly and Dorothy was thrown against him. He extended his arm and held her close. She didn't speak, but she made no attempt to pull away.

Toby Whitby

Even in the dark, Toby knew what was happening. He had always thought that his poor eyesight had resulted in improved hearing. Of course, he wasn't actually blind, but nonetheless, he had always felt a need to listen as well as look. Now he listened to the sound of two people breathing and concluded that they were sitting very close together.

He sat quietly in the malodorous darkness and tried not to worry.

He listened to the sounds of Dorothy and Slater breathing side by side and realized that they were sleeping. He imagined Dorothy with her head against Slater's chest, his arm around her to keep her steady. He sighed and thought of Carol. He had to force an answer from her. Any answer? Yes, he would accept any answer. The idea of marriage was slowly losing its charm. If she didn't want him; if she didn't feel about him the way he felt about her ... How did he feel about her? His mind wandered to a government bungalow somewhere in Africa; a big dog for company, colorful local markets, red earth, and grass huts. He tried to paint Carol and Anita into his picture. He saw Anita sick with malaria and Carol wandering unhappily through the market, searching for familiar foods.

The French coast was hours away. The image of the market faded, and the big dog ran beyond the horizon. He dozed.

He was startled awake by a hailstorm of noise. His hiding place echoed with thuds and bangs from the deck above his head. Slater jerked awake with a snort that could have been a snore cut off in midbreath.

Dorothy's voice was unafraid and still clogged with sleep. "What is it?"

"He's stopped," Slater said.

"Can he do that?" Toby asked. "Can a sailing boat just stop? It's not like he can turn off the engine or put on the brakes."

"He's brought her into the wind," Slater snapped.

His tone did not invite questions, but apparently, Dorothy was not sensitive to Slater's tones, and she whispered a question.

"What do you mean?"

"Well ..." Slater said, his irritation apparently forgotten. "He's stopped our forward progress by pointing her bow directly into the wind and letting the sails flap. All that thudding and banging is ropes and tackle beating on the deck. Can you feel the change of motion under us?"

Toby was silent for a moment, feeling the barge rocking in the waves without the smooth motion that had carried them through the night.

"Why would he do that?" Dorothy asked.

"I don't know," Slater replied. He switched on his flashlight and looked at his watch. "Six o'clock. It's daylight up there."

"Do you think we've arrived?" Dorothy asked.

"I doubt it," Slater replied. He sounded worried.

"Maybe we're approaching a harbor," Dorothy said hopefully.

"No, we're not." Slater's voice was flat, without emotion, but without doubt. "We're still at sea. You can tell from the motion of the waves. Deep water."

Toby was becoming aware of another noise that had added itself to the cacophony from the deck boards; a low rumble. A powerful engine, far more powerful than anything carried on the barge, was somewhere close.

Slater cocked his head to one side. "A rendezvous," he muttered.

"In the middle of the Channel?" Toby asked.

Slater looked at his watch again. "Apparently so. If we're meeting up with someone out here, it's because we're in international waters. The British navy has no control here." He looked up at the deck boards above his head. "I don't like the feel of this."

Toby could hear voices. Someone was shouting orders. A thud echoed through the hull, and the barge rocked violently.

Slater drew in a sharp breath. "Collision."

Another thud, a sharp crack, and Dorothy cried out in alarm. "Water! I'm getting wet."

Toby looked up at a chink of daylight showing through separated deck boards, and a steady trickle of water.

Slater's voice was calm but authoritative. "Time to move. Open that door Whitby and get us out of here before we drown."

"It's just a trickle," Dorothy said. "Do we have to move? What about the people out there? I don't ... I don't ... I ..."

"I'm not going to let anyone harm you," Slater said in a choked voice. "Whatever is going on out there, no one is going to harm you, but that water is more than a trickle."

As if in response to Slater's claim, the trickle of water above their heads turned to a steady flow, and the chink of daylight grew wider.

"She's taken a hit on the bow," Slater said. "Get on with it, Whitby."

Toby struggled with the door and got nowhere until he stepped back and gave it a solid kick. He scrambled out into the hold. As he turned to help Dorothy, he realized that he was standing in water. We're sinking, he thought. No need to say anything; Slater will already know.

The voices were louder now, and the rumbling engine shook the floor beneath their feet.

"We have to go up," Slater said. "You go first, Whitby; stick your head out and take a look around."

Toby made his way through the ankle-deep water to the ladder and went up, hand over hand. When he raised his head above deck level, everything became suddenly and frighteningly clear.

The sun was well above the horizon in a clear blue sky that reflected its color onto the waves that broke across the bow of the barge. The thuds and cracks on the deck were easily explained. The sails were flapping wildly as the barge wallowed in the breaking waves. Ropes and fittings beat a tattoo on the foredeck, pounding on the hatch cover that had been above their heads. The angry bellowing voice came from the barge skipper, who stood anxiously in the cockpit, waving his arms and shouting. Above it all loomed the high superstructure of a deep-sea trawler, its idling engine sending vibrations through the barge's ancient hull planks.

As Toby watched, the gap between the trawler and the barge grew wider, and he saw that the trawler had lowered a boat. Was this a rescue attempt? Was the barge sinking? If that was the case, someone would surely go below to find Dorothy; or perhaps not. Revealing her presence would be admitting to a crime. If these were British trawlermen, they would not stand idly by and allow Billy Cheviot to keep his captive. Even if they were French, or Belgian, or any other nationality, they would ask questions.

So, Toby thought, Billy would say nothing and let Dorothy go down with the ship. It was quite possible that the skipper had no idea that Dorothy was on board. He certainly didn't know that he had two additional stowaways. Toby would have to make his presence known.

He climbed to the next step on the ladder. He would have to clamber out of the hold and confront the skipper, which meant confronting Billy Cheviot. He would wait until the fishermen in the rescue boat were standing by and able to see what was happening. Deep-sea fishermen were a tough breed, and they would surely do something if they saw him being murdered. Murdered? Yes, Billy Cheviot had proved himself capable of murder.

Toby studied the trawler, with its rusted gray hull and once white superstructure. Something was wrong. Where were the nets? In place of the mast and booms that should have held nets, this trawler's topside bristled with antennae and dishes. Toby's eyes flicked to the writing on the hull. Cyrillic lettering. This was no deep-sea trawler; this was a Soviet spy ship.

The presence of Soviet ships off the coast of Britain was no secret. Just a few weeks earlier, Mr. Champion had shown Toby a letter printed in The Times. The writer had railed against Britain's inability to prevent Soviet surveillance ships, thinly disguised as trawlers, from lurking off the coast, watching the movement of British submarines, and listening in on radio chatter. Mr. Champion had been taken with a coughing fit as he tried to read the letter aloud. By the time he had been restored with a glass of water and a judicious pat on the back, he had only been able to gasp out a few sentences. "Nothing can be done," he had croaked. "International waters are open to everyone. It's a disgrace, Whitby. I never thought the day would come when Britannia was unable to rule the waves. I don't know what the world is coming to."

Toby's memory of his employer's anger was interrupted by renewed shouting from the cockpit. He swiveled his head and saw the silver-haired man, the one who so closely resembled the Duke of Windsor, climbing over the side of the barge with Billy following close behind.

Was this it? Was the skipper abandoning his leaking barge without any attempt to save her?

"Whitby!" Slater's voice came from far below. "What's going on?"

"I don't know. I think they're abandoning ship."

"I'm coming up."

Toby turned to look down into the hold. He could see the top of Slater's head. He was already halfway up the ladder. Dorothy was below him with her feet on the bottom rung. Daylight, seeping in from above, reflected on water sloshing from side to side in the hold.

Toby climbed out of the hold and stood upright. No one was looking in his direction, and now he could see what was really happening. It was not as he had thought.

The silver-haired man was already in the Soviet rowboat, which was manned by half a dozen men in uniforms that marked them as Soviet sailors. Four men were on the oars, and two stood in the bow of their boat to fend off Billy's attempt to board.

Billy's voice, aggrieved and afraid, rose above the rumble of the spy ship's engines and the shouting of the barge captain.

"Hey, I'm coming with you. You ain't gonna leave me here. You promised."

The silver-haired man shook his head. "I promised you nothing."

"You promised Enid."

"You are not Enid."

"But you've gone and sunk our ship."

The silver-haired man gave a shrug that was eloquent in its lack of concern. The sailors dug deeply with their oars, and the boat moved away, leaving Billy dangling precariously from the hull of the barge.

The barge skipper let loose a string of words that were obviously curses. The apprentice skipped nimbly across the deck, dodging flailing ropes, and pulled Billy back on board. He received a clip round the ear for his trouble. Toby wished with all his heart that the boy had allowed Billy to fall. He thought that he could deal with the barge skipper; the man was a black marketeer but not a hardened criminal; Billy was another story altogether.

Anthea Clark

She had to do something. It was not in her nature to sit idly by when action was needed. Perhaps she should go to the kitchen and help Mrs. Ellerby, who was now faced with unexpected breakfast guests. She crossed the hall and glanced into Mr. Champion's office. He was no longer in his chair. She assumed he had gone upstairs to his bedroom and would be occupied in restoring himself to his usual fastidious appearance.

She passed the dining room and looked out at the walled garden. She saw that Hugh and Eric were deep in conversation and taking no notice of the fact that Daisy was happily digging a hole in the peony bed.

Well, the destruction of the flower bed was not her problem. Really, none of it was her problem. Her mind skipped back across a span of fifty years, and she saw her mother's face and heard her mother's warning. You have to resist the temptation to interfere, dear. No one likes a busybody.

Her mother was mistaken. She had spent the last two days interfering and with excellent results. Madeline had been found and rescued. The body in the mortuary had been identified. Inspector Slater was on the trail of Dorothy Findlay. Hugh had discovered a grandchild and a great-grandchild. And Toby was ... well, she was not quite sure where Toby was, but he was not in Wales visiting his fiancée, and even that was a problem she could solve.

She went back into Mr. Champion's study and stood for a moment looking at the telephone. Toby had said that Carol was working at the post office in a Welsh village, Blen ...? No, it was a Welsh village, so probably not Blen, maybe Blyn, yes, Blyn. She smiled in silent triumph as the name surfaced in her memory. Blynaffon. Carol was working at the Blynaffon Post Office.

She obtained the number from directory assistance and placed her call. A voice, distinctly Welsh, answered and informed her that Carol could not take calls unless they were of an urgent nature.

"This is urgent," Anthea insisted. "This is very urgent."

She heard Carol's voice, ragged with anxiety. "What's the matter? What's happened? Is it Anita?"

"No, not Anita. This is Miss Clark from Champion and Company. I'm calling about Toby, Mr. Whitby, your fiancé."

"Oh."

Anthea could not interpret the flatness of Carol's tone. Was she simply relieved that nothing had happened to Anita? Was she angry? Was she curious?

"It's about your fiancé," Anthea repeated.

"Has something happened to him?" Carol asked. "He was supposed to come up on the train last night, but he's not here." Anthea frowned, trying to find the same anxiety in Carol's voice that she had heard when Carol asked about Anita. The concern was not there. Of course, Anthea had never been a mother, so she could not judge a mother's feelings, but she had been a fiancée once long ago.

"He's been involved in something," Anthea said, "a murder investigation, and he's—"

"He's not my fiancé," Carol said. "I haven't agreed to—"

"I'm not sure that he's safe," Anthea interrupted. "He's on a boat, and—"

"I don't want to go to Rhodesia."

Anthea's frown deepened. The conversation was taking a very strange turn, and she wished she could see the other woman's face. She remembered her appearance, of course. Carol had red hair that curled around a freckled face and an upturned nose. She was small but curvaceous, and when she smiled, she brightened the room. Toby had fallen in love at first sight, and finding out that Carol had given birth to a child fathered by a

German prisoner of war had not dampened his ardor. Even the discovery that Carol had given the child to another woman to take to America under a false name had not discouraged him.

Anthea was now trying very hard to like the woman who had stolen Toby's heart, but she was finding it a struggle.

"You don't understand," Anthea said. "I'm trying to tell you that he wanted to catch the train, but this murder investigation ..."

"It will always be something," Carol said. "I will always be in second place. His work comes first."

"That's not fair," Anthea protested. "He didn't have a choice. I'm sure he would have phoned you if he could, but we haven't heard a word from him. For all I know, he's been kidnapped or drowned."

She heard the breath catch in Carol's throat.

"If you could try to understand," Anthea pleaded.

"I don't want to understand," Carol said. "I'm sorry, Miss Clark, but I can't do this. It's enough for me to worry about Anita; I can't worry about Toby all the time."

All the time, Anthea thought. Surely that's an exaggeration. Toby's job was not inherently dangerous, although Toby had a tendency to throw himself into his work.

Carol was still speaking. "What would I do in Africa?" she asked. "I would worry all the time. He could get eaten by a lion or killed by bandits, and what about Anita?"

"Does Anita worry about him?" Anthea asked.

"No, of course not," Carol snapped. "I would never tell her anything like this ... this ... well, whatever he's involved in this time. It's hopeless, Miss Clark. I can't do it. I refuse to put myself and Anita through all that worry. I'm not going to Africa with him."

"I'm sure he would be willing to stay here with you," Anthea said.

Carol's voice carried a hint of sadness. "Yes, Miss Clark, I'm sure he would, but I'm not going to allow that to happen. He needs to follow his dreams and go to Africa, where he can be everything he wants to be. He was kept out of active service in the war, and he'll never get over the way that made him feel unless he does something now; something to prove he's more than a pen pusher in a legal office."

Anthea's half-hearted protest died unspoken as Carol continued to speak.

"He's surrounded by men who fought in uniform, and he flinches every time someone asks him what he did in the war; I've seen him do it. He needs to get away from here and I need to stay. I want to stay."

Anthea found her voice at last. "But he loves you."

"He doesn't even know me," Carol said.

"He knows what you did," Anthea snapped, "and he still wants to marry you."

In the silence that followed, Anthea knew she had said too much. She had no right to interfere in Toby's love life. She had wanted to put things right, and now she had made them worse.

"I can't marry him," Carol said.

There it was; plain and simple. Carol would not marry him.

Carol's voice was conciliatory. "I'm sorry, Miss Clark. I had no business saying these things to you. I have to say them to Toby in person."

"If you get a chance," Anthea snapped. "I phoned you to tell you that—"

"That he's in trouble. Yes, I heard what you said. A murder investigation, wasn't it?"

"Yes, he's—"

"No, don't tell me anything else. I don't want to know. Tell him to phone me when he can."

"And if he can't? If something ...?"

"Then you phone me."

Anthea stifled an angry retort that dealt with the temperature in the underworld, and the length of time that would pass before Anthea would be willing to speak to Carol again.

She imagined Carol growing old alone, tight lipped and unwilling to pay the price of loving. She knew what such a woman would look like; she had only to look at herself in the mirror.

She replaced the receiver and ended the conversation without saying goodbye. She wondered if she would have the chance to tell Toby what Carol had said, and concluded that it would be wiser to keep silent and let Toby find out for himself. He would soon arrive in France, where Interpol could take charge of the Cheviot clan. She would hear something soon.

She crossed her fingers. Her father would have prayed, of course, but Anthea settled for crossing her fingers and wishing.

CHAPTER TWENTY ONE

Toby Whitby

The silver-haired man sat in the bow, and the Soviet sailors rowed with practiced efficiency, crossing the gap between the barge and the trawler-that-was-not-a-trawler. The barge, with its sails flapping, seemed to be drifting away on the wind and current, and the ribbon of open water between the two vessels widened rapidly.

Billy Cheviot was back on the barge deck. His posture, hunched and threatening, struck Toby as absurd. The Soviet sailors had rejected him, and now he was on the barge with no hope of escape. For all his threats, he was just another passenger on a sinking ship. The only skill that mattered now was the ability to swim.

The old boat was down by the bow, the sails still flapping while waves broke across the foredeck. The Soviet vessel lowered ropes and ladders. The small boat and its passengers were taken on board, and the fake trawler pulled away, its engines thrumming and picking up speed.

As Toby watched it depart, he thought he heard another sound, another engine battering the air at a higher pitch. He searched the waves and saw nothing. He looked up at the dawn-washed sky and saw a small plane passing high overhead; some wealthy person on a private flight to the Continent. The plane circled above them.

Slater's voice was commanding and urgent. "Wave!"

Toby turned his head and saw Slater holding on to Dorothy, who wavered unsteadily in his grasp. No sea legs. Slater was steady, his childhood experience helping him to stand, but he needed his arm to keep Dorothy upright.

"Wave," Slater yelled again.

Toby waved with both arms. From the corner of his eye, he saw the skipper also waving and the apprentice jumping up and down. He watched anxiously for the plane to waggle its wings, the universal sign that he had seen a vessel in trouble or, most recently, a downed plane or a pilot in a life raft. The plane described a lazy circle in the sky and flew on, shadowing the path of the trawler that was now moving away at speed. Coincidence? Perhaps not.

For the time it had taken the plane to fly away, Toby had forgotten Billy. Now he saw that Billy was on the roof of the ramshackle cabin, kneeling and concentrating on untying ropes. What was he doing?

The skipper shouted in fractured English. "Hey, you! Yes, I help."

His long legs carried him up from the cockpit, and he scrambled onto the cabin roof.

"Life raft," Slater said. "He has a life raft. Go help him, Whitby."

A small, unsteady voice drew Toby's attention. "Who you? Why you on my boat?"

Toby turned to see the apprentice standing with feet braced in the cockpit. He was grasping a battered bolt-action rifle, which he aimed unsteadily at Toby, targeting first his head and then his chest.

Of course, the boy had no idea the barge had been carrying stowaways. He must see them as enemies. Toby raised his hands. "Friend."

"No friend. Who you?"

Another voice interrupted. "Anton."

The boy looked up at the sound of the skipper's voice, and the gun barrel wavered as he turned his attention to the cabin roof. Toby slithered out of the line of fire. From the corner of his eye, he saw Slater pushing Dorothy back toward the ladder into the hold, urging her away from the boy and the gun.

"Anton," the skipper called. "Nee! Stoppen."

"Papa!"

So, the boy, Anton, was the skipper's son.

"We moeten nu gaan. Help mij!"

The boy dropped the weapon and scuttled across the cockpit toward the cabin roof. Toby reached for the rifle. Now he had something to use against Billy if the man came against him.

He watched the three figures on the cabin roof as they untied the life raft. It was small and battered, seemingly made of cork floats and scrap wood. Maybe it would hold one man, maybe two, the skipper and his son. It would not hold all of them.

He could see that Billy had already made an assessment and was taking matters into his own hands. Billy reached down and shoved Anton. The boy fell into the cockpit, landing with a splash and a thump in the water that was rising slowly through the floorboards. He lay with one leg crumbled beneath him.

Now Billy and the skipper were grappling hand to hand on the cabin roof. The skipper was tall and rangy, strong from years of working the barge, but he was no match for Billy, who went for the groin and the eyes in a rapid sequence of kicks and punches that left the skipper on his knees, gasping in pain and wiping his eyes.

Toby headed for the cabin roof. He had no time to remove his glasses. He would have to risk losing them. He tossed the rifle to Slater.

"Take him down if you can."

He didn't hear Slater's reply. A thought zipped through his brain. Could a one-armed man fire a rifle? He couldn't take time to think about it; he was already on the roof, dodging past the gasping skipper and hurling himself at Billy's knees.

Billy staggered but stayed upright. He shoved Toby away. The life raft was free from its ropes and slid back and forth on the roof as the barge settled sluggishly into the water, barely rising on the waves but rolling fiercely from side to side. The skipper staggered to his feet, and Billy aimed another vicious kick that sent the Belgian to follow his son into the cockpit.

Toby stayed on his knees and flung his body forward, wrapping his arms around Billy's ankles. There was nothing glorious about this fight, nothing of the movie heroics of blows traded and men standing tall. This fight was a degrading scuffle with Billy kicking and cursing and Toby hanging onto Billy's ankles and struggling for a better grip. He needed help. He needed the skipper to recover and come back with his long arms, or he needed Slater to take control of the rifle.

Billy managed to free one foot and aimed a kick at Toby's head. Toby felt a sharp pain on the bridge of his nose as his glasses shattered. It didn't matter; this fight was about feeling, not seeing. Billy freed his other foot. He loomed above Toby, close enough that Toby could still see what he was doing. Billy hefted the life raft into an upright position and hurled it over the side.

Toby reached out blindly. He was not going to let this man get into that life raft. He thought of the boy Anton, with all his life in front of him; of Dorothy, who had a child waiting for her. They should be saved, not Billy Cheviot, who had never done a decent thing in his life.

He grabbed at Billy's knees, holding him back, stopping him from leaping into the ocean. Billy's momentum carried them both forward. Toby wouldn't let go. They were going to fall together. It didn't matter. If they fell together, they would drown together; less people on the life raft, better hope of rescue.

Billy dragged himself to the edge of the roof, cursing and trying to kick himself free. He landed another blow against the side of Toby's head. Against his will, Toby's fingers released their grip. He could do no more. He could not stop Billy from following the raft into the water, where the current would carry him away with the light raft moving faster than the wallowing, sinking barge.

Crack! A gunshot, but not a rifle shot. Billy's shape wavered above him. Another gunshot and Toby heard a sudden explosive release of breath and saw Billy fling his arms in the air. Toby watched him stagger away and fall. He crawled forward, looking through the warped prism of shattered lenses at Billy's body spread-eagled on the foredeck of the barge, with blood coating his body as he was flailed by thrashing ropes. So far as he could tell, Billy was beyond caring.

Who had shot him? No time to worry about that now. The life raft was in the water, bobbing in the waves alongside the hull. Soon it would be beyond reach. Toby kicked off his shoes and his jacket. He took a last look at the life raft, fixing its position in his mind, and dove into the water.

Detective Inspector Percy Slater

Dorothy still held the Browning. Slater had forgotten it was in the pocket of his raincoat; the coat he had given to Dorothy. She had handled it like an expert while he had fumbled with the rifle, trying to find a way to work the bolt and aim the weapon one-handed. She had saved Toby, probably saved them all. He felt nothing but admiration. She had done what he couldn't, but it wasn't a blow to his pride. What did it matter who did the saving, so long as they were saved?

If they were saved. There were still a great many bumps on their road to salvation. Toby had succeeded in swimming out to the raft and getting on board. The skipper had somehow brought the wallowing barge under control. The boy Anton, with his leg badly broken, was handling the tiller. The skipper had hauled in on the sails and given the wallowing barge direction toward the life raft, and now he was heaving a line in Toby's direction.

"Can we sail it to shore?" Dorothy asked.

Percy could not resist a smile at the uncertainty, maybe even timidity, in her voice. He was not fooled. This woman was the woman who had taken down Billy Cheviot, something he could not do. She had no need of timidity.

He answered her question with a shake of his head. "No, we can't stay afloat much longer. We'll have to salvage what we can and rely on the life raft and life jackets. We're just trying to get close enough to throw Whitby a rope; not that he'll be able to see it. He's broken his damned glasses again."

So, Toby's disability was as real as his own. He'd had little sympathy for Toby when he had compared his poor eyesight to Slater's loss of his arm, but Toby had not been wrong. Toby's eyes were a very real problem, and they would have to be very close to him before he would be able to see the rope snaking across the water to him.

"Are we close to the coast?" Dorothy asked.

Slater scanned the horizon in all directions. He thought he saw something behind them, a faint interruption in the line where the sky met the sea. Behind them? If the compass was correct, and surely it was, Ostend, on the Belgian coast, should be ahead of them, not behind them. The Channel was just over a hundred miles wide at this point. They should not be able to see the English coast behind them.

He assumed that the rendezvous with the Soviet trawler had put them far from the barge's normal course, so where on earth were they, and how would they ever be found?

He deflected Dorothy's question with one of his own. "Where did you learn to fire a Browning?"

"We didn't have enough men to guard the factory," Dorothy said, "and the women didn't feel safe. We guarded ourselves."

She nodded her head toward the rifle that Slater held clumsily at his side. "I was going to fire that, but I felt in the pocket of your coat and found the Browning."

"You'd better give it to me," Slater said.

She gave him an inquiring look. "Why?"

"It's a police weapon. You shouldn't have it. If Billy Cheviot washes up somewhere with one of my bullets in him, it's better that I say that I did it." He handed her the rifle. "How about we swap?"

She grinned and took the rifle from him before she passed the Browning to him, butt first. He looked down at the weapon nestled in his hand. It was signed out in his name. He was no longer an active-duty police officer; no longer entitled to have that weapon in his possession, and if Billy washed ashore ...

A triumphant shout interrupted his train of thought. Toby had finally managed to catch the rope and was working hand over hand to pull the raft closer to the wallowing barge.

The skipper pointed to a locker in the cockpit and looked at Slater. "Zwemvest."

"Zwemvest," Slater repeated. His mind was on the desk sergeant who had signed out the Browning. He'd be for the high jump if Slater couldn't get the weapon back to him, but on the other hand, how would he account for the fact that it had been fired?

"Life jacket," Dorothy said. "He's talking about life jackets. Hurry up."

As if to remind him of the need for speed, a cresting wave broke over the cockpit, sending a gush of water over Anton where he sat grasping the tiller. His face was pale and his leg was bent at an impossible angle.

Slater dove for the locker and found a tangled mess of old cork life jackets. Dorothy was beside him in a moment, her hands working to untangle the straps.

"Aren't these supposed to be ready to use?" she asked.

"I suppose he was relying on the life raft," Slater said. "He wasn't expecting passengers."

Another wave broke across the side of the barge. Now the water was up to their knees, and this time, it was not draining away.

"Couple more like that," Slater said, "and she'll be gone."

Dorothy released one life jacket, brown, mildewed, and frayed, from the tangle of webbing straps. She brought it to Anton and helped him into it.

She held up another one. "Now you."

Slater held out his hand; his only hand. "I'll do it."

She shook her head. "Let me."

Another wave broke across the cockpit, dousing the skipper, who had relieved his son at the tiller. Slater struggled into a life vest, and Dorothy settled the cork panels across his back and chest.

"I swear Noah had these on the ark," she muttered. "Is this all he has?"

"We go," the skipper called, raising his hand from the tiller and diving forward to put his arms around his son. He stretched out a hand toward the bundle of life jackets. "Give me."

Dorothy struggled with the straps. "You should look after your equipment," she declared angrily.

He looked her without comprehension. The barge wallowed in the trough of a wave, and a deluge of water rolled toward them from the bow.

Dorothy threw the whole bundle of life jackets to the skipper and wrapped her arms around Slater. Slater dragged in a deep breath as they went into the water together.

The water was cold but not deadly, not yet, but it would be soon if they couldn't get up on the raft.

He managed to keep his mind clear as he went down, swallowing mouthfuls of seawater. The life jacket dragged him back to the surface and held him suspended with his nose just above water. Why was he so low? Dorothy. She was still holding him with her arms around his neck and her legs wrapped around his waist from behind. In any other circumstances, he would have welcomed this.

"I'll swim for us," she shouted in his ear, suddenly releasing her grasp. He bobbed to the surface now, his head and shoulders above water. She had hooked an arm through the straps and was swimming, towing him. Towing him where?

"Here, over here."

Toby was clinging to the raft. It was small, too small for all of them. The skipper, holding the bundle of life jackets with one hand, was attempting to heave his son out of the water and onto the raft. The boy cried out in pain. Slater thought it was only a matter of time until the boy would pass out. He knew the pain of broken limbs and bone grinding on bone.

Dorothy was thrashing her arms and legs, but she didn't seem to be bringing them any closer to the life raft. It was drifting on the surface while he and Dorothy wallowed in the wave troughs. And the barge? Gone. A wave lifted him to its crest. As he watched, something broke the surface, and then something else, more objects. The barge, diving down to the bottom, was being scraped clean of everything that was not tied down. Planks, hatch covers, so many things; things that could float.

Toby Whitby

The water was cold, not the kind of cold that would kill with a sudden shock, but a cold that would slowly creep into the bones, sap the will and numb the brain.

The boy Anton was finally on the raft, held in place by his father, who was still in the water. Toby had done what he could to make the father climb on board and had met with a firm refusal. The father was obviously afraid that his added weight would tip the raft, so now Toby clung to one side, and the skipper to the other side, and the raft had just enough buoyancy to carry the boy and rise and fall with the waves.

Toby still wore his broken glasses, and he saw the world in shattered images, a kaleidoscope of sky and clouds, and an occasional unfocused glimpse of Dorothy and Slater side by side, clinging to something long and narrow that had broken loose of the sunken barge; a piece of the hull, a part of the rigging?

He realized that his squinting and frowning as he attempted to identify the flotsam was just a desperate attempt to distract himself from the hopelessness of their position. He had sent a message by way of the night watchman at Shoreham Harbour, but it had not been a cry for help. It had not said anything about sinking and drowning somewhere far away from the shipping lanes.

Even if the message had been delivered, and he was not at all sure that would happen, it only said that he and Slater were on the barge. Perhaps Interpol had officers waiting in Ostend, but what good would that do? The barge would not arrive in Ostend. It would not arrive anywhere ever again.

He clung with cold fingers as a wave lifted him for a moment before it slapped him in the face and filled his mouth with the bitter taste of salt water. He heard the boy on the raft cry out as another wave washed across the raft. Either the raft was sinking or the waves were building. Another one like that, and the raft would tip over. The boy had done nothing. He deserved a chance to live. The raft would float better without Toby hanging on to the side.

He thought about Carol as he released his hold. She wouldn't have to make a decision now. She wouldn't have to choose to go with him to Rhodesia, because he wouldn't be going to Rhodesia. He wouldn't be going anywhere except here. The next wave slapped him in the face, but even with fractured lenses, he saw the raft, relieved of Toby's weight, lift as the wave passed beneath it without swamping. For the moment, the boy was out of the water.

Toby spread his arms and closed his eyes, tired of squinting. He let himself drift.

"Oi!"

The voice was close. He felt himself caught and dragged by the straps of his life vest.

"Where do you think you're going, mate?"

His eyes slammed open at the sound of Slater's unmistakable London voice. Couldn't the man leave him alone to die in peace?

Someone was in the water beside him. Not Slater; Slater was clinging to a long wooden plank. Dorothy was doing the dragging. She held the plank with one hand and pulled Toby with the other.   "Hold on here," she said, lifting his unwilling arm and draping it across the floating plank.

"Can't give up yet," Dorothy said.

"I wasn't giving up," Toby lied. "My weight was pulling the boy down. I thought …"

"He couldn't be bothered to say what he thought. He didn't have to justify his behavior. He knew what his motives had been.

"I saw what you did," Slater grunted. "Won't make no difference in the long run, but well done, mate."

Toby sighed. Now that it was too late to make any difference, he'd finally won Slater's approval.

A wave, fiercer than those that had gone before, slapped him in the face, and a piece of glass broke loose from his shattered lenses. He reached up impatiently and pulled the glasses away, committing them to the waves. He wouldn't need to see what happened next.

Another wave broke across him. His added weight was too much for the floating wood. He would have to let go. He wanted to say something; some words of reassurance to Dorothy to let her know that her son would be cared for. Did he have time to tell her everything that had happened? He would have to make time.

"Dorothy, about your boy. He's going to be—"

The boy on the raft's voice, shrill with excitement, interrupted him. Was the raft tipping? Had Toby's gesture been meaningless?

"Ik kan een boot zien."

Beside him Dorothy heaved herself upward, pressing the plank down until Toby lost his fingerhold, and Slater offered a couple of soldierly oaths.

"It's a boat," Dorothy shouted. "The kid saw a boat."

"How do you know?" Toby spluttered, spitting seawater from his mouth.

Dorothy's voice rose to a shriek that matched the joy in the boy's voice. "Because I can see it. It's a lifeboat."

CHAPTER TWENTY TWO

Detective Inspector Percy Slater

Slater was surprised to find that Anthea Clark was not at her post. As usual, a hand-knitted cardigan was draped across her office chair, but her typewriter was covered and her desk was clear of papers. The door to Edwin Champion's office was closed; no doubt the elderly man was still at home, recovering from the many shocks of the past few days.

Toby called to him from his cubbyhole beside the front door.

"In here. I have something to show you."

Slater scowled. "This had better be important. I had plans for today."

Toby pushed back a lock of hair that had fallen across his face and surveyed him through thick lenses. "Still no tie?"

Slater shook his head. "Still suspended," he confirmed. "The best I can hope for is a demotion."

Toby smiled, a reaction that Slater considered inappropriate in the circumstances. He was about to be demoted from inspector down to sergeant, or even constable, and Toby seemed to find that a source of enjoyment.

"I think I can help with that," Toby said.

"You've already helped," Slater grunted. "Any more help from you and I'll be out of the force altogether."

"They should give you a medal," Toby said.

"I acted without orders and destroyed government property," Slater replied.

"What government property?"

"The Browning. I … er … failed to return it. I reported it lost during the shipwreck. If Billy Cheviot's body ever surfaces with my bullet in him,

I'll have some explaining to do, but I think we're safe in saying he's full fathom five."

"You didn't shoot him," Toby said.

Slater's heart skipped a beat. "If you ever say that it was Dorothy, I'll—"

"No, of course not. I won't say anything." Toby grinned. "How is it going with her?"

"None of your business. I don't ask you about your love life."

Toby sighed. "There's nothing to say about it. I don't think it exists."

"Sorry to hear that. So, what do you want? Why did you phone me?"

"Well," Toby replied, "I've had three days to dry out and think about this, and I've come up with something interesting. I want your opinion, and if I'm right in what I'm thinking, we'll have to do something."

Slater was tempted to walk away. If he left now, he could be at Dorothy's flat in less than five minutes. He could take her to lunch; perhaps he could take Eric fishing. If he had to be suspended, at least he could do something pleasant with his time.

Toby turned to his desk and opened a dusty old atlas. "I want you to look at this."

"It's prewar," Slater sniffed.

"I know. I couldn't get an up-to-date map, but it doesn't matter. The shape of the coast hasn't changed. The towns are still where they always were. Come and look."

Slater joined him and looked down at the map. The atlas was open to a map of the south coast of England, showing the coastal towns. A swathe of blue represented the English Channel, and the coastlines of France and Belgium were indicated at the top of the page.

"Well?" Slater asked.

Toby stabbed his finger at the map. "This is Shoreham. This is where we started our crossing. The barge always travels from Shoreham to Ostend." He traced a line across the light-blue space marking the English Channel. "Shoreham to Ostend is about a hundred miles, and he does it at least once a week."

Slater stared down at the map. He could see that something had excited Toby, but he could see nothing new or interesting in the route that Toby had traced.

"We didn't take that route," Toby said.

Slater shook his head. "No, we didn't, but what's so surprising about that? Obviously, the skipper knew about the Soviet trawler, and he knew where to meet it. He's in custody, with some serious questions to answer, but he's a foreign national, so I'm not sure he can be charged with anything other than smuggling, especially if I don't tell anyone about Billy Cheviot."

Toby stabbed at the map again, ignoring Slater's comments about the barge skipper. "This is Selsey. We were picked up by the Selsey lifeboat. Selsey is eighty miles down the coast from Shoreham, and we weren't very far offshore, barely into international waters."

"Good thing too," Slater said. "If we'd been any farther out, they would never have reached us in time."

Toby stood back and looked Slater in the eye. "That's the question, isn't it? How did they find us? How did they know where we were?"

Slater scowled. Why was Toby wasting his time with these questions? He thought about Anthea Clark's empty desk and Mr. Champion's shuttered office. Perhaps Toby had nothing better to do with his time, or perhaps the sinking of the barge and the time spent in cold water had affected his memory. The army had a word for it. Shell shock. Could a civilian suffer from shell shock? Toby hadn't been in combat; perhaps this was all too much for him.

He took a deep breath and spoke as patiently as he could. "Robert Penhelen saw us. He took an early morning plane ride and he spotted us. He's the one who radioed the lifeboat station at Selsey. Instead of huddling in here over that map, you should be shaking him by the hand."

"Should I?" Toby asked.

"Yes."

Toby looked down at the map again, saying nothing, just staring.

"Come on," Slater said. "Spit it out. What's got you so worried?"

Toby's finger retraced the route from Shoreham to Ostend. "This is the route the barge takes every time. How did Penhelen know to call the Selsey lifeboat? It's nowhere near our route."

"But we weren't on the normal route," Slater said. "The Soviet trawler …" He ran out of words to say because suddenly he could see where Toby was leading him. So much ocean, and yet Penhelen had flown directly overhead.

"When we were in the water," Toby asked, "when the barge was sinking, did you see a plane fly over?"

"No."

"If Penhelen had seen us, wouldn't he have come down low and waggled his wings to let us know we'd been seen?"

Yes, Slater thought, that is what he would have done. That was the protocol.

"I saw a plane," Toby said, "before we sank. It flew over when we made the rendezvous with the Soviet trawler. It was high up, but it circled, and then it followed the path of the trawler, and then all hell broke loose on the barge, and I didn't have time to think what it meant."

"Are you saying that was Penhelen's plane?"

"I am, and I am also saying that he wasn't looking for us. He was making sure that our mysterious passenger made it safely onto the Soviet ship."

Toby ran his hand across the map again. "There's the route Shoreham to Ostend, and there's where we were, miles off course. We'd been sailing all night westward along the English coast, close to the shore. Penhelen didn't just happen to see us, he was already out there looking for the Soviet trawler, and when he found it, he followed it. So how did he know we were sinking?"

Slater's mind was racing. How did Penhelen know? No one else knew, and Penhelen had not seen it happen; he had already left.

"Someone told him," Toby said. "Someone with a conscience told him that the trawler had rammed the barge, probably on purpose, and the barge was sinking."

Slater considered the possibilities. It had to be a radio transmission. He thought about the silver-haired man who had been transferred to the trawler. Did he have a guilty conscience? Had he insisted on Penhelen calling out the lifeboat? Was he someone Penhelen would obey without question? He rubbed his hand across his chin and scowled at Toby as he recognized that he would not be seeing Dorothy today, and he would not be taking Eric fishing. Suddenly he was a policeman again, an officer of the law, his suspension forgotten.

"Are you willing to stand by what you're saying?" he asked.

Toby nodded. "I'm saying that Robert Penhelen QC knew that the Duke of Windsor was being transferred onto a Soviet spy ship, and he had flown out to see the transfer take place."

"Have you told anyone else?"

"No. I don't even know who to tell. I assume you told your superiors about the trawler."

"Yeah, I told them."

"And the Duke of Windsor?"

Slater recalled his uncomfortable interview with the chief constable. "I could only say that I saw someone who looked like the Duke of Windsor. I couldn't be sure."

"Penhelen knows if he's an imposter or the real thing," Toby prompted.

Slater felt a surge of excitement. "Is Penhelen still here?"

"Oh yes, he's here. I'm sure he thinks he got away with it. He cleared his conscience by calling out the lifeboat, but he thinks we're too stupid to put two and two together."

Slater looked at Toby with grudging respect. Toby was many things, but he was not stupid, and surely Penhelen knew that. Slater looked down at the map and the wide blue expanse of the English Channel. "If Penhelen hadn't called out the lifeboat, we would have drowned. He knew that he was risking discovery, and maybe that will count in his favor. That's not up to me to say. I'll have to call my superiors."

He lifted the telephone receiver on Toby's desk. "You don't happen to know where Penhelen is at this moment, do you?"

Slater heard footsteps shuffling across the office. He paused with the telephone in his hand and saw Edwin Champion framed in the doorway.

"I am old," Mr. Champion said, "and quite infirm, but my hearing is excellent. I am in complete agreement with Mr. Whitby's supposition, and I can tell you exactly where Robert Penhelen is."

Toby Whitby

Morton, the chauffeur, seemed delighted to have the chance to put the Armstrong through its paces. The big limousine made short work of the road across the Downs, and soon Toby was looking down at the graceful white terminal building of the Shoreham Aerodrome. Penhelen's De Havilland was already standing on the grass taxiway, just a short distance from the runway.

"Can you go any faster?" Toby asked.

Morton turned his head slightly and grinned at Toby's challenge. He put his foot down and the engine roared. Toby spared a thought for his employer's many weaknesses, but Mr. Champion seemed to be enjoying the ride, hanging on to a strap in the back seat and almost chortling with excitement.

The Armstrong's brakes actually screeched as Morton pulled up outside the terminal building. Toby had the door open and was almost out of the vehicle before Slater caught hold of him.

"We have to wait."

"Wait for what?"

"Backup. They're on their way."

Toby shrugged himself free of Slater's arm, knowing that he was taking advantage of Slater's disability. Now was not the time for polite pretense. Slater could not hold him. Penhelen was already walking out onto the taxiway. The Armstrong's dramatic approach had caught his attention. He turned his head to look behind him, obviously puzzled but not yet alarmed.

"I have no authority," Slater warned.

"Citizen's arrest," Toby said. "Basic common law, you can't stop me."

Penhelen stood still for a moment and watched the short scuffle between Toby and Slater, and then he quickened his pace. He knows, Toby thought. Penhelen knows that I've worked it out.

In the back seat of the car, Edwin Champion raised his voice in a wheezing command. "Don't let him take off."

Penhelen began to run, and Toby raced after him with his dress shoes slipping on the grass. He had come dressed for a day at the office, not a sprint across wet, rough-cut grass. When he saw Penhelen open the door of the cockpit, he forced his legs to move faster. Penhelen was already inside with his hands on the controls when Toby hurtled across the last few yards and grabbed for whatever he could reach on the aircraft. His hands closed around a spar beneath the wing, and he pulled himself upward. The engine was already running, with the propeller whirring and throwing up a cloud of dust and grass clippings.

Toby pulled himself up and wrenched open the cabin door. The plane lurched forward and began to jounce erratically across the grass toward the runway.

Toby clung to the doorframe, and his feet scrabbled for purchase on the single step.

Penhelen turned his head. "I did you a favor," he shouted.

"Traitor!" The word was out of Toby's mouth before he had time to think, and it gave him the impetus he needed to haul the top half of his body in through the doorway. The door, swinging open, crashed against his back.

Penhelen was concentrating on the controls, and was no longer looking at Toby as he spoke. "I sent help."

Toby struggled to draw breath as his legs dangled from the doorway. The doorframe cut into his chest, and the door swung wildly, slamming his back over and over again.

He wouldn't be able to hold on for long, but he could hold on long enough to ask a question.

"Who is he?" Toby gasped. "Is he an imposter?"

"I'm no traitor," Penhelen said grimly. "We can't have a weak woman on the throne. She's just a girl. We need a man."

"No," Toby shouted. "We have laws."

Penhelen shook his head. "I saved you once, Whitby; don't kill yourself over this. History will be on our side. Just let go before you kill yourself."

"No," Toby shouted. The door slammed hard against his back, and the plane bounced upward. It seemed to hang in the air for a moment; more than a bounce, the beginning of a lift. It slammed down again, wrenching one of Toby's hands free of its grasp on the frame.

They lifted again, and Toby knew he couldn't stop Penhelen from taking off; perhaps he had already taken off. Toby's legs thrashed at the air. How far was he above the ground? What would happen if he let go?

The plane slammed down again. Toby grabbed at the spar that held the wing, and looked down between his legs. They had already left the grass taxiway, and the paved runway was rushing below him at speed. If he let go now, he was in for a hard landing, and he still didn't have his answer.

"Was it him?" he shouted. "Was it really the Duke?"

Penhelen didn't answer. He was leaning forward, concentrating on something ahead of him. The plane bounced again, tried to lift, and failed. Toby wondered if it was his weight hanging from the side that was preventing takeoff. If so, he would have to hang on, although that was rapidly becoming impossible.

He heard Penhelen cursing and saw him struggling with the controls. The plane slewed from side to side, slowing its frantic pace and swinging Toby in a pendulum arc until he could hold on no longer.

He tumbled onto the runway, rolling and gasping but, apparently, not yet dead. Cheating death twice in one week had to mean something.

He lay for a moment taking inventory of his injuries. Nothing was broken. He sat up and stared up into the sky. Penhelen had succeeded in throwing him off, so surely he was up and away now. Where would he go? Probably to Paris to join the Duke, or maybe to Moscow to plot the overthrow of the government.   Penhelen was wrong, of course. His thinking was medieval. Elizabeth was queen; that was the law.

He blinked. Of course, he'd lost his glasses again. No point in searching the sky for Penhelen when he could only see a few hundred feet down the runway. He squinted, not at the sky, but at the runway ahead of him. His eyes were not fooling him. Penhelen's plane was right there, at a standstill. Why? He could have taken off. Toby was in no position to stop him.

He staggered to his feet and saw the reason why Penhelen was still on the ground. Edwin Champion's limousine was blocking the runway. A figure came toward him, fuzzy at first but soon devolving into the familiar shape of his employer, slightly stooped but sprightly with excitement.

"Very dramatic, Whitby, but not really necessary. Inspector Slater suggested we block the runway, and that did the trick. I must say that I thought you were going to hurt yourself."

"I did hurt myself," Toby muttered.

"Ah well," his employer said, "you're young. You'll mend."

Toby limped back toward the Armstrong, and Slater came into focus, dragging Penhelen from the cockpit with the assistance of Morton. With the plane engine silenced, Toby could hear the clanging of police alarm bells approaching across the Downs.   He moved away. Slater needed this moment. Perhaps Penhelen's capture would go some way to ending Slater's suspension, maybe even preventing a demotion.

He reviewed the terse responses he'd received from Penhelen. He'd admitted he was involved, and he thought a strong man should be on the throne. Toby sniffed. It was several centuries since an actual battle had been fought over the right to ascend to the throne of Britain. The country didn't need a soldier with a sword; it needed peace, stability, the rule of law, and a spectacular coronation to keep the people's minds of their problems. It needed a new Queen Elizabeth.

And what of the man who had transferred to a Soviet ship? Was he a look-alike sent to Britain to cause unrest, or was he the Duke himself, making secret plans to steal the throne he had once rejected?

Toby walked with his head down, retracing his route along the runway in the hope that he would find his glasses. He had now lost two pairs in one week, and he had no more spares. He sensed someone walking beside him and looked up. Sturdy, sensible shoes, a tweed skirt, a cardigan. What was Anthea doing here?

She held out a hand. "I found your glasses."

"Thank you."

"I thought you needed to take a good look at the people I brought with me."

Toby frowned as he automatically polished the lenses on his handkerchief.

"You should look now," Anthea urged. "Hugh ... the colonel ... my ... er ..."

"Your what?" Toby asked.

"Never you mind what," Anthea scolded. "Put your glasses on and see who has come all the way from Wales."

Toby's heart pounded. He wasn't sure he wanted to wear his glasses. If he didn't see who had come, he couldn't be disappointed. No, that was ridiculous. He settled his spectacles on his nose.

Miss Clark was still speaking. "I told her that love is too rare and too precious to waste. She's not afraid of Africa, Toby, she's afraid that she's not good enough for you."

Toby looked up and saw a group of figures standing outside the terminal building. A tall, gray-headed man with a military moustache, a black-and-white dog, a red-headed woman, and a child with strawberry-blond curls.

Anthea looked at him with a sparkle in her pale eyes. "I must say that you put on a very dramatic display."

"It wasn't a display, it was ..."

Anthea smiled. "It was just what she needed. Now she knows that you don't have to go to Africa to get yourself killed; you can do it here, twice in one week. I think you made your point."

"Anthea, I ... You've ... well done."

"I've done what was necessary," Anthea replied.

Toby looked at the colonel standing patiently while Daisy strained at her leash.

"What about you?" Toby asked.

Anthea's cheeks flushed a pale, youthful pink. "None of your business, Mr. Whitby."

Toby looked at her with a fondness he had never expected to feel. "If you need someone to give you away …"

Now she was really blushing. She waved a flustered hand. "Go away. Go and claim your family."

"Will they let me?" Toby asked.

His answer came without words as Carol grasped her daughter's hand and ran to meet him.

THE END

If you would like to know more about Toby's war years, you can receive a free copy of **Alibi** an introductory novella set during the early years of World War Two. To receive your free e-book novella visit www.eileenenwrighthodgetts.com and sign up for Eileen's newsletter.

We hope you enjoyed **Imposter.** This is the second novel in the Toby Whitby Mystery series. **Air Raid,** the first story in the series is available in e-book format, paperback, and audio. Details are available at www.eileenenwrighthodgetts.com or purchase through Amazon.

Made in the USA
Middletown, DE
13 June 2021